Under Fire

Lambeth
Libraries

Under Fire

by Henri Barbusse

Wilder Publications, LLC.
PO Box 3005
Radford VA 24143-3005

ISBN 10: 1-61720-093-X
ISBN 13: 978-1-61720-093-9

Table of Contents:

The Vision

MONT BLANC, the Dent du Midi, and the Aiguille Verte look across at the bloodless faces that show above the blankets along the gallery of the sanatorium. This roofed-in gallery of rustic wood-work on the first floor of the palatial hospital is isolated in Space and overlooks the world. The blankets of fine wool—red, green, brown, or white—from which those wasted cheeks and shining eyes protrude are quite still. No sound comes from the long couches except when some one coughs, or that of the pages of a book turned over at long and regular intervals, or the undertone of question and quiet answer between neighbors, or now and again the crescendo disturbance of a daring crow, escaped to the balcony from those flocks that seem threaded across the immense transparency like chaplets of black pearls.

Silence is obligatory. Besides, the rich and high-placed who have come here from all the ends of the earth, smitten by the same evil, have lost the habit of talking. They have withdrawn into themselves, to think of their life and of their death.

A servant appears in the balcony, dressed in white and walking softly. She brings newspapers and hands them about.

"It's decided," says the first to unfold his paper. "War is declared."

Expected as the news is, its effect is almost dazing, for this audience feels that its portent is without measure or limit. These men of culture and intelligence, detached from the affairs of the world and almost from the world itself, whose faculties are deepened by suffering and meditation, as far remote from their fellow men as if they were already of the Future—these men look deeply into the distance, towards the unknowable land of the living and the insane.

"Austria's act is a crime," says the Austrian.

"France must win," says the Englishman.

"I hope Germany will be beaten," says the German.

They settle down again under the blankets and on the pillows, looking to heaven and the high peaks. But in spite of that vast purity, the silence is filled with the dire disclosure of a moment before.

War!

Some of the invalids break the silence, and say the word again under their breath, reflecting that this is the greatest happening of the age, and perhaps of all ages. Even on the lucid landscape at which they gaze the news casts something like a vague and somber mirage.

The tranquil expanses of the valley, adorned with soft and smooth pastures and hamlets rosy as the rose, with the sable shadow-stains of the majestic mountains and the black lace and white of pines and eternal snow, become alive with the movements of men, whose multitudes swarm in distinct masses. Attacks develop, wave by wave, across the fields and then stand still. Houses are eviscerated like human beings and towns like houses. Villages appear in crumpled whiteness as though fallen from heaven to earth. The very shape of the plain is changed by the frightful heaps of wounded and slain.

Each country whose frontiers are consumed by carnage is seen tearing from its heart ever more warriors of full blood and force. One's eyes follow the flow of these living tributaries to the River of Death. To north and south and west ajar there are battles on every side. Turn where you will, there is war in every corner of that vastness.

One of the pale-faced clairvoyants lifts himself on his elbow, reckons and numbers the fighters present and to come—thirty millions of soldiers. Another stammers, his eyes full of slaughter, "Two armies at death-grips—that is one great army committing suicide."

"It should not have been," says the deep and hollow voice of the first in the line. But another says, "It is the French Revolution beginning again." "Let thrones beware!" says another's undertone.

The third adds, "Perhaps it is the last war of all." A silence follows, then some heads are shaken in dissent whose faces have been blanched anew by the stale tragedy of sleepless night—"Stop war? Stop war? Impossible! There is no cure for the world's disease."

Some one coughs, and then the Vision is swallowed up in the huge sunlit peace of the lush meadows. In the rich colors of the glowing kine, the black forests, the green fields and the blue distance, dies the reflection of the fire where the old world burns and breaks. Infinite silence engulfs the uproar of hate and pain from the dark swarmings of mankind. They who have spoken retire one by one within themselves, absorbed once more in their own mysterious malady.

But when evening is ready to descend within the valley, a storm breaks over the mass of Mont Blanc. One may not go forth in such peril, for the last waves of the storm-wind roll even to the great veranda, to that harbor where they have taken refuge; and these victims of a great internal wound encompass with their gaze the elemental convulsion.

They watch how the explosions of thunder on the mountain upheave the level clouds like a stormy sea, how each one hurls a shaft of fire and a column of cloud together into the twilight; and they turn their wan and sunken faces to follow the flight of the eagles that wheel in the sky and look from their supreme height down through the wreathing mists, down to earth.

"Put an end to war?" say the watchers.—"Forbid the Storm!"

Cleansed from the passions of party and faction, liberated from prejudice and infatuation and the tyranny of tradition, these watchers on the threshold of another world are vaguely conscious of the simplicity of the present and the yawning possibilities of the future.

The man at the end of the rank cries, "I can see crawling things down there"—"Yes, as though they were alive"—"Some sort of plant, perhaps"—"Some kind of men"—

And there amid the baleful glimmers of the storm, below the dark disorder of the clouds that extend and unfurl over the earth like evil spirits, they seem to see a great livid plain unrolled, which to their seeing is made of mud and water, while figures appear and fast fix themselves to the surface of it, all blinded and borne down with filth, like the dreadful castaways of shipwreck. And it seems to them that these are soldiers.

The streaming plain, seamed and seared with long parallel canals and scooped into water-holes, is an immensity, and these castaways who strive to exhume themselves from it are legion. But the thirty million slaves, hurled upon one another in the mud of war by guilt and error, uplift their human faces and reveal at last a bourgeoning Will. The future is in the hands of these slaves, and it is clearly certain that the alliance to be cemented some day by those whose number and whose misery alike are infinite will transform the old world.

In the Earth

THE great pale sky is alive with thunderclaps. Each detonation reveals together a shaft of red falling fire in what is left of the night, and a column of smoke in what has dawned of the day. Up there—so high and so far that they are heard unseen—a flight of dreadful birds goes circling up with strong and palpitating cries to look down upon the earth.

The earth! It is a vast and water-logged desert that begins to take shape under the long-drawn desolation of daybreak. There are pools and gullies where the bitter breath of earliest morning nips the water and sets it a-shiver; tracks traced by the troops and the convoys of the night in these barren fields, the lines of ruts that glisten in the weak light like steel rails, mud-masses with broken stakes protruding from them, ruined trestles, and bushes of wire in tangled coils. With its slime-beds and puddles, the plain might be an endless gray sheet that floats on the sea and has here and there gone under. Though no rain is falling, all is drenched, oozing, washed out and drowned, and even the wan light seems to flow.

Now you can make out a network of long ditches where the lave of the night still lingers. It is the trench. It is carpeted at bottom with a layer of slime that liberates the foot at each step with a sticky sound; and by each dug-out it smells of the night's excretions. The holes themselves, as you stoop to peer in, are foul of breath.

I see shadows coming from these sidelong pits and moving about, huge and misshapen lumps, bear-like, that flounder and growl. They are "us." We are muffled like Eskimos. Fleeces and blankets and sacking wrap us up, weigh us down, magnify us strangely. Some stretch themselves, yawning profoundly. Faces appear, ruddy or leaden, dirt-disfigured, pierced by the little lamps of dull and heavy-lidded eyes, matted with uncut beards and foul with forgotten hair.

Crack! Crack! Boom!—rifle fire and cannonade. Above us and all around, it crackles and rolls, in long gusts or separate explosions. The flaming and melancholy storm never, never ends. For more than fifteen months, for five hundred days in this part of the world where we are, the rifles and the big guns have gone on from morning to night and from night to morning. We are buried deep in an everlasting battlefield; but like the ticking of the clocks at home in the days gone by—in the now almost legendary Past—you only hear the noise when you listen.

A babyish face with puffy eyelids, and cheek-bones as lurid as if lozenge-shaped bits of crimson paper had been stuck on, comes out of the ground, opens one eye, then the other. It is Paradis. The skin of his fat cheeks is scored with the marks of the folds in the tent-cloth that has served him for night-cap. The glance of his little eye wanders all round me; he sees me, nods, and says—"Another night gone, old chap."

"Yes, sonny; how many more like it still?"

He raises his two plump arms skywards. He has managed to scrape out by the steps of the dug-out and is beside me. After stumbling over the dim obstacle of a man who sits in the shadows, fervently scratches himself and sighs hoarsely, Paradis makes off—lamely splashing like a penguin through the flooded picture.

One by one the men appear from the depths. In the corners, heavy shadows are seen forming—human clouds that move and break up. One by one they become recognizable. There is one who comes out hooded with his blanket—a savage, you would say, or rather, the tent of a savage, which walks and sways from side to side. Near by, and heavily framed in knitted wool, a square face is disclosed, yellow-brown as though iodized, and patterned with blackish patches, the nose broken, the eyes of Chinese restriction and red-circled, a little coarse and moist mustache like a greasing-brush.

"There's Volpatte. How goes it, Firmin?"

"It goes, it goes, and it comes," says Volpatte. His heavy and drawling voice is aggravated by hoarseness. He coughs—"My number's up, this time. Say, did you hear it last night, the attack? My boy, talk about a bombardment—something very choice in the way of mixtures!" He sniffles and passes his sleeve under his concave nose. His hand gropes within his greatcoat and his jacket till it finds the skin, and scratches. "I've killed thirty of them in the candle," he growls; "in the big dug-out by the tunnel, mon vieux, there are some like crumbs of metal bread. You can see them running about in the straw like I'm telling you."

"Who's been attacking? The Boches?"

"The Boches and us too—out Vimy way—a counterattack—didn't you hear it?"

"No," the big Lamuse, the ox-man, replies on my account; "I was snoring; but I was on fatigue all night the night before."

"I heard it," declares the little Breton, Biquet; "I slept badly, or rather, didn't sleep. I've got a doss-house all to myself. Look, see, there it is—the damned thing." He points to a trough on the ground level, where on a meager mattress of muck, there is just body-room for one. "Talk about home in a nutshell!" he declares, wagging the rough and rock-hard little head that looks as if it had never been finished. "I hardly snoozed. I'd just got off, but was woke up by the relief of the 129th that went by—not by the noise, but the smell. Ah, all those chaps with their feet on the level with my nose! It woke me up, it gave me nose-ache so."

I knew it. I have often been wakened in the trench myself by the trail of heavy smell in the wake of marching men.

"It was all right, at least, if it killed the vermin," said Tirette.

"On the contrary, it excites them," says Lamuse; "the worse you smell, the more you have of 'em."

"And it's lucky," Biquet went on, "that their stink woke me up. As I was telling that great tub just now, I got my peepers open just in time to seize the tent-cloth that shut my hole up—one of those muck-heaps was going to pinch it off me."

"Dirty devils, the 129th." The human form from which the words came could now be distinguished down below at our feet, where the morning had not yet reached it. Grasping his abundant clothing by handsful, he squatted and wriggled. It was Papa Blaire. His little eyes blinked among the dust that luxuriated on his face. Above the gap of his toothless mouth, his mustache made a heavy sallow lump. His hands were horribly black, the top of them shaggy with dirt, the palms plastered in gray relief. Himself, shriveled and dirtbedight, exhaled the scent of an ancient stewpan. Though busily scratching, he chatted with big Barque, who leaned towards him from a little way off.

"I wasn't as mucky as this when I was a civvy," he said.

"Well, my poor friend, it's a dirty change for the worse," said Barque.

"Lucky for you," says Tirette, going one better; "when it comes to kids, you'll present madame with some little niggers!"

Blaire took offense, and gathering gloom wrinkled his brow. "What have you got to give me lip about, you? What next? It's war-time. As for you, bean-face, you think perhaps the war hasn't changed your phizog and your manners? Look at yourself, monkey-snout, buttock-skin! A man must be a beast to talk as you do." He passed his hand over the dark deposit on his face, which the rains of those days had proved finally indelible, and added, "Besides, if I am as I am, it's my own choosing. To begin with, I have no teeth. The major said to me a long time ago, 'You haven't a single tooth. It's not enough. At your next rest,' he says, 'take a turn round to the estomalogical ambulance.'"

"The tomatological ambulance," corrected Barque.

"Stomatological," Bertrand amended.

"You have all the making of an army cook—you ought to have been one," said Barque.

"My idea, too," retorted Blaire innocently. Some one laughed. The black man got up at the insult. "You give me belly-ache," he said with scorn. "I'm off to the latrines."

When his doubly dark silhouette had vanished, the others scrutinized once more the great truth that down here in the earth the cooks are the dirtiest of men.

"If you see a chap with his skin and toggery so smeared and stained that you wouldn't touch him with a barge-pole, you can say to yourself, 'Probably he's a cook.' And the dirtier he is, the more likely to be a cook."

"It's true, and true again," said Marthereau.

"Tiens, there's Tirloir! Hey, Tirloir!"

He comes up busily, peering this way and that, on an eager scent. His insignificant head, pale as chlorine, hops centrally about in the cushioning collar of a greatcoat that is much too heavy and big for him. His chin is pointed, and his upper teeth protrude. A wrinkle round his mouth is so deep with dirt that it looks like a muzzle. As usual, he is angry, and as usual, he rages aloud.

"Some one cut my pouch in two last night!"

"It was the relief of the 129th. Where had you put it?"

He indicates a bayonet stuck in the wall of the trench close to the mouth of a funk-hole—"There, hanging on the toothpick there."

"Ass!" comes the chorus. "Within reach of passing soldiers! Not dotty, are you?"

"It's hard lines all the same," wails Tirloir. Then suddenly a fit of rage seizes him, his face crumples, his little fists clench in fury, he tightens them like knots in string and waves them about. "Alors quoi? Ah, if I had hold of the mongrel that did it! Talk about breaking his jaw—I'd stave in his bread-pan, I'd—there was a whole Camembert in there, I'll go and look for it." He massages his stomach with the little sharp taps of a guitar player, and plunges into the gray of the morning, grinning yet dignified, with his awkward outlines of an invalid in a dressing-gown. We hear him grumbling until he disappears.

"Strange man, that," says Pepin; the others chuckle. "He's daft and crazy," declares Marthereau, who is in the habit of fortifying the expression of his thought by using two synonyms at once.

"Tiens, old man," says Tulacque, as he comes up. "Look at this."

Tulacque is magnificent. He is wearing a lemon-yellow coat made out of an oilskin sleeping-sack. He has arranged a hole in the middle to get his head through, and compelled his shoulder-straps and belt to go over it. He is tall and bony. He holds his face in advance as he walks, a forceful face, with eyes that squint. He has something in his hand. "I found this while digging last night at the end of the new gallery to change the rotten gratings. It took my fancy off-hand, that knick-knack. It's an old pattern of hatchet."

It was indeed an old pattern, a sharpened flint hafted with an old brown bone—quite a prehistoric tool in appearance.

"Very handy," said Tulacque, fingering it. "Yes, not badly thought out. Better balanced than the regulation ax. That'll be useful to me, you'll see." As he brandishes that ax of Post-Tertiary Man, he would himself pass for an ape-man, decked out with rags and lurking in the bowels of the earth.

One by one we gathered, we of Bertrand's squad and the half-section, at an elbow of the trench. Just here it is a little wider than in the straight part where when you meet another and have to pass you must throw yourself against the side, rub your back in the earth and your stomach against the stomach of the other.

Our company occupies, in reserve, a second line parallel. No night watchman works here. At night we are ready for making earthworks in front, but as long as the day lasts we have nothing to do. Huddled up together and linked arm in arm, it only remains to await the evening as best we can.

Daylight has at last crept into the interminable crevices that furrow this part of the earth, and now it finds the threshold of our holes. It is the melancholy light of the North Country, of a restricted and muddy sky, a sky which itself, one would say, is heavy with the smoke and smell of factories. In this leaden light, the uncouth array of these dwellers in the depths reveals the stark reality of the huge and hopeless misery that brought it into being. But that is like the rattle of rifles and the verberation of artillery. The drama in which we are actors has lasted much too long for us to be surprised any more, either at the stubbornness we have evolved or the garb we have devised against the rain that comes from above, against the mud that comes from beneath, and against the cold—that sort of infinity that is everywhere. The skins of animals, bundles of blankets, Balaklava helmets, woolen caps, furs, bulging mufflers (sometimes worn turban-wise), paddings and quiltings, knittings and double-knittings, coverings and roofings and cowls, tarred or oiled or rubbered, black or all the colors (once upon a time) of the rainbow—all these things mask and magnify the men, and wipe out their uniforms almost as effectively as their skins. One has fastened on his back a square of linoleum, with a big draught-board pattern in white and red, that he found in the middle of the dining-room of some temporary refuge. That is Pepin. We know him afar off by his harlequin placard sooner even than by his pale Apache face. Here is Barque's bulging chest-protector, carven from an eiderdown quilt, formerly pink, but now fantastically bleached and mottled by dust and rain. There, Lamuse the Huge rises like a ruined tower to which tattered posters still cling. A cuirass of moleskin, with the fur inside, adorns little Eudore with the burnished back of a beetle; while the golden corselet of Tulacque the Big Chief surpasses all.

The "tin hat" gives a certain sameness to the highest points of the beings that are there, but even then the divers ways of wearing it—on the regulation cap like Biquet, over a Balaklava like Cadilhac, or on a cotton cap like Barque—produce a complicated diversity of appearance.

And our legs! I went down just now, bent double, into our dug-out, the little low cave that smells musty and damp, where one stumbles over empty jam-pots and dirty rags, where two long lumps lay asleep, while in the corner a kneeling shape rummaged a pouch by candle-light. As I climbed out, the rectangle of entry afforded me a revelation of our legs. Flat on the ground, vertically in the air, or aslant; spread about, doubled up, or mixed together; blocking the fairway and cursed by passers-by, they present a collection of many colors and many shapes—gaiters, leggings black or yellow, long or short, in leather, in tawny cloth, in any sort of waterproof stuff; puttees in dark blue, light blue, black, sage green, khaki, and beige. Alone of all his kind, Volpatte has retained the modest gaiters of mobilization. Mesnil Andre has displayed for a fortnight a pair of thick woolen stockings, ribbed and green; and Tirette has always been known by his gray cloth puttees with white stripes, commandeered from a pair of civilian trousers that was hanging goodness knows where at the beginning of the war. As for Marthereau's puttees, they are not both of the same hue, for he failed to find two fag-ends of greatcoat equally worn and equally dirty, to be cut up into strips.

There are legs wrapped up in rags, too, and even in newspapers, which are kept in place with spirals of thread or—much more practical—telephone wire. Pepin fascinated his friends and the passers-by with a pair of fawn gaiters, borrowed from a corpse. Barque, who poses as a resourceful man, full of ideas—and Heaven knows what a bore it makes of him at times!—has white calves, for he wrapped surgical bandages round his leg-cloths to preserve them, a snowy souvenir at his latter end of the cotton cap at the other, which protrudes below his helmet and is left behind in its turn by a saucy red tassel. Poterloo has been walking about for a month in the boots of a German soldier, nearly new, and with horseshoes on the heels. Caron entrusted them to Poterloo when he was sent back on account of his arm. Caron had taken them himself from a Bavarian machine-gunner, knocked out near the Pylones road. I can hear Caron telling about it yet—

"Old man, he was there, his buttocks in a hole, doubled up, gaping at the sky with his legs in the air, and his pumps offered themselves to me with an air that meant they were worth my while. 'A tight fit,' says I. But you talk about a job to bring those beetle-crushers of his away! I worked on top of him, tugging, twisting and shaking, for half an hour and no lie about it. With his feet gone quite stiff, the patient didn't help me a bit. Then at last the legs of it—they'd been pulled about so—came unstuck at the knees, and his breeks tore away, and all the lot came, flop! There was me, all of a sudden, with a full boot in each fist. The legs and feet had to be emptied out."

"You're going it a bit strong!"

"Ask Euterpe the cyclist if it isn't true. I tell you he did it along of me, too. We shoved our arms inside the boots and pulled out of 'em some bones and bits of sock and bits of feet. But look if they weren't worth while!"

So, until Caron returns, Poterloo continues on his behalf the wearing of the Bavarian machine-gunner's boots.

Thus do they exercise their wits, according to their intelligence, their vivacity, their resources, and their boldness, in the struggle with the terrible discomfort. Each one seems to make the revealing declaration, "This is all that I knew, all I was able, all that I dared to do in the great misery which has befallen me."

Mesnil Joseph drowses; Blaire yawns; Marthereau smokes, "eyes front." Lamuse scratches himself like a gorilla, and Eudore like a marmoset. Volpatte coughs, and says, "I'm kicking the bucket." Mesnil Andre has got out his mirror and comb and is tending his fine chestnut beard as though it were a rare plant. The monotonous calm is disturbed here and there by the outbreaks of ferocious resentment provoked by the presence of parasites—endemic, chronic, and contagious.

Barque, who is an observant man, sends an itinerant glance around, takes his pipe from his mouth, spits, winks, and says—"I say, we don't resemble each other much."

"Why should we?" says Lamuse. "It would be a miracle if we did."

Our ages? We are of all ages. Ours is a regiment in reserve which successive reinforcements have renewed partly with fighting units and partly with Territorials. In our half-section there are reservists of the Territorial Army, new recruits, and demi-poils. Fouillade is forty; Blaire might be the father of Biquet, who is a gosling of Class 1913. The corporal calls Marthereau "Grandpa" or "Old Rubbish-heap," according as in jest or in earnest. Mesnil Joseph would be at the barracks if there were no war. It is a comical effect when we are in charge of Sergeant Vigile, a nice little boy, with a dab on his lip by way of mustache. When we were in quarters the other day, he played at skipping-rope with the kiddies. In our ill-assorted flock, in this family without kindred, this home without a hearth at which we gather, there are three generations side by side, living, waiting, standing still, like unfinished statues, like posts.

Our races? We are of all races; we come from everywhere. I look at the two men beside me. Poterloo, the miner from the Calonne pit, is pink; his eyebrows are the color of straw, his eyes flax-blue. His great golden head involved a long search in the stores to find the vast steel-blue tureen that bonnets him. Fouillade, the boatman from Cette, rolls his wicked eyes in the long, lean face of a musketeer, with sunken cheeks and his skin the color of a violin. In good sooth, my two neighbors are as unlike as day and night.

Cocon, no less, a slight and desiccated person in spectacles, whose tint tells of corrosion in the chemical vapors of great towns, contrasts with Biquet, a Breton in the rough, whose skin is gray and his jaw like a paving-stone; and Mesnil Andre, the comfortable chemist from a country town in Normandy, who has such a handsome and silky beard and who talks so much and so well—he has little in common with Lamuse, the fat peasant of Poitou, whose cheeks and neck are like underdone beef. The suburban accent of Barque, whose long legs have scoured the streets of Paris in all directions, alternates with the semi-Belgian cadence of those Northerners who came from the 8th Territorial; with the sonorous speech, rolling on the syllables as if over cobblestone, that the 144th pours out upon us; with the dialect blown from those ant-like clusters that the Auvergnats so obstinately form among the rest. I remember the first words of that wag, Tirette, when he arrived—"I, mes enfants, I am from Clichy-la-Garenne! Can any one beat that?"—and the first grievance that Paradis brought to me, "They don't give a damn for me, because I'm from Morvan!"

Our callings? A little of all—in the lump. In those departed days when we had a social status, before we came to immure our destiny in the molehills that we must always build up again as fast as rain and scrap-iron beat them down, what were we? Sons of the soil and artisans mostly. Lamuse was a farm-servant, Paradis a carter. Cadilhac, whose helmet rides loosely on his pointed head, though it is a juvenile size—like a dome on a steeple, says Tirette—owns land. Papa Blaire was a small farmer in La Brie. Barque, porter and messenger, performed acrobatic tricks with his carrier-tricycle among the trains and taxis of Paris, with solemn abuse (so they say) for the pedestrians, fleeing like bewildered hens across the big streets and squares. Corporal Bertrand, who keeps himself always a little aloof, correct, erect, and silent, with a strong and handsome face and forthright gaze, was foreman in a case-factory. Tirloir daubed carts with paint—and without grumbling, they say. Tulacque was barman at the Throne Tavern in the suburbs; and Eudore of the pale and pleasant face kept a roadside cafe not very far from the front lines. It has been ill-used by the shells—naturally, for we all know that Eudore has no luck. Mesnil Andre, who still retains a trace of well-kept distinction, sold bicarbonate and infallible remedies at his pharmacy in a Grande Place. His brother Joseph was selling papers and illustrated story-books in a station on the State Railways at the same time that, in far-off Lyons, Cocon, the man of spectacles and statistics, dressed in a black smock, busied himself behind the counters of an ironmongery, his hands glittering with plumbago; while the lamps of Becuwe Adolphe and Poterloo, risen with the dawn, trailed about the coalpits of the North like weakling Will-o'-th'-wisps.

And there are others amongst us whose occupations one can never recall, whom one confuses with one another; and the rural nondescripts who peddled ten trades at once in their packs, without counting the dubious Pepin, who can have had none at all. (While at the depot after sick leave, three months ago, they say, he got married—to secure the separation allowance.)

The liberal professions are not represented among those around me. Some teachers are subalterns in the company or Red Cross men. In the regiment a Marist Brother is sergeant in the Service de Sante; a professional tenor is cyclist dispatch-rider to the Major; a "gentleman of independent means" is mess corporal to the C.H.R. But here there is nothing of all that. We are fighting men, we others, and we include hardly any intellectuals, or men of the arts or of wealth, who during this war will have risked their faces only at the loopholes, unless in passing by, or under gold-laced caps.

Yes, we are truly and deeply different from each other. But we are alike all the same. In spite of this diversity of age, of country, of education, of position, of everything possible, in spite of the former gulfs that kept us apart, we are in the main alike. Under the same uncouth outlines we conceal and reveal the same ways and habits, the same simple nature of men who have reverted to the state primeval.

The same language, compounded of dialect and the slang of workshop and barracks, seasoned with the latest inventions, blends us in the sauce of speech with the massed multitudes of men who (for seasons now) have emptied France and crowded together in the North-East.

Here, too, linked by a fate from which there is no escape, swept willy-nilly by the vast adventure into one rank, we have no choice but to go as the weeks and months go—alike. The terrible narrowness of the common life binds us close, adapts us, merges us one in the other. It is a sort of fatal contagion. Nor need you, to see how alike we soldiers are, be afar off—at that distance, say, when we are only specks of the dust-clouds that roll across the plain.

We are waiting. Weary of sitting, we get up, our joints creaking like warping wood or old hinges. Damp rusts men as it rusts rifles; more slowly, but deeper. And we begin again, but not in the same way, to wait. In a state of war, one is always waiting. We have become waiting-machines. For the moment it is food we are waiting for. Then it will be the post. But each in its turn. When we have done with dinner we will think about the letters. After that, we shall set ourselves to wait for something else.

Hunger and thirst are urgent instincts which formidably excite the temper of my companions. As the meal gets later they become grumblesome and angry. Their need of food and drink snarls from their lips—"That's eight o'clock. Now, why the hell doesn't it come?"

"Just so, and me that's been pining since noon yesterday," sulks Lamuse, whose eyes are moist with longing, while his cheeks seem to carry great daubs of wine-colored grease-paint.

Discontent grows more acute every minute.

"I'll bet Plumet has poured down his own gullet my wine ration that he's supposed to have, and others with it, and he's lying drunk over there somewhere."

"It's sure and certain"—Marthereau seconds the proposition.

"Ah, the rotters, the vermin, these fatigue men!" Tirloir bellows. "An abominable race—all of 'em—mucky-nosed idlers! They roll over each other all day long at the rear, and they'll be damned before they'll be in time. Ah, if I were boss, they should damn quick take our places in the trenches, and they'd have to work for a change. To begin with, I should say, 'Every man in the section will carry grease and soup in turns.' Those who were willing, of course—"

"I'm confident," cries Cocon, "it's that Pepere that's keeping the others back. He does it on purpose, firstly, and then, too, he can't finish plucking himself in the morning, poor lad. He wants ten hours for his flea-hunt, he's so finicking; and if he can't get 'em, monsieur has the pip all day."

"Be damned to him," growls Lamuse. "I'd shift him out of bed if only I was there! I'd wake him up with boot-toe, I'd—"

"I was reckoning, the other day," Cocon went on; "it took him seven hours forty-seven minutes to come from thirty-one dug-out. It should take him five good hours, but no longer."

Cocon is the Man of Figures. He has a deep affection, amounting to rapacity, for accuracy in recorded computation. On any subject at all, he goes burrowing after statistics, gathers them with the industry of an insect, and serves them up on any one who will listen. Just now, while he wields his figures like weapons, the sharp ridges and angles and triangles that make up the paltry face where perch the double discs of his glasses, are contracted with vexation. He climbs to the firing-step (made in the days when this was the first line), and raises his head angrily over the parapet. The light touch of a little shaft of cold sunlight that lingers on the land sets a-glitter both his glasses and the diamond that hangs from his nose.

"And that Pepere, too, talk about a drinking-cup with the bottom out! You'd never believe the weight of stuff he can let drop on a single journey."

With his pipe in the corner, Papa Blaire fumes in two senses. You can see his heavy mustache trembling. It is like a comb made of bone, whitish and drooping.

"Do you want to know what I think? These dinner men, they're the dirtiest dogs of all. It's 'Blast this' and 'Blast that'—John Blast and Co., I call 'em."

"They have all the elements of a dunghill about them," says Eudore, with a sigh of conviction. He is prone on the ground, with his mouth half-open and the air of a martyr. With one fading eye he follows the movements of Pepin, who prowls to and fro like a hyaena.

Their spiteful exasperation with the loiterers mounts higher and higher. Tirloir the Grumbler takes the lead and expands. This is where he comes in. With his little pointed gesticulations he goads and spurs the anger all around him.

"Ah, the devils, what? The sort of meat they threw at us yesterday! Talk about whetstones! Beef from an ox, that? Beef from a bicycle, yes rather! I said to the boys, 'Look here, you chaps, don't you chew it too quick, or you'll break your front teeth on the nails!'"

Tirloir's harangue—he was manager of a traveling cinema, it seems—would have made us laugh at other times, but in the present temper it is only echoed by a circulating growl.

"Another time, so that you won't grumble about the toughness, they send you something soft and flabby that passes for meat, something with the look and the taste of a sponge—or a poultice. When you chew that, it's the same as a cup of water, no more and no less."

"Tout ca," says Lamuse, "has no substance; it gets no grip on your guts. You think you're full, but at the bottom of your tank you're empty. So, bit by bit, you turn your eyes up, poisoned for want of sustenance."

"The next time," Biquet exclaims in desperation, "I shall ask to see the old man, and I shall say, 'Mon capitaine'—"

"And I," says Barque, "shall make myself look sick, and I shall say, 'Monsieur le major'—"

"And get nix or the kick-out—they're all alike—all in a band to take it out of the poor private."

"I tell you, they'd like to get the very skin off us!"

"And the brandy, too! We have a right to get it brought to the trenches—as long as it's been decided somewhere—I don't know when or where, but I know it—and in the three days that we've been here, there's three days that the brandy's been dealt out to us on the end of a fork!"

"Ah, malheur!"

"There's the grub!" announces a poilu who was on the look-out at the corner.

"Time, too!"

And the storm of revilings ceases as if by magic. Wrath is changed into sudden contentment.

Three breathless fatigue men, their faces streaming with tears of sweat, put down on the ground some large tins, a paraffin can, two canvas buckets, and a file of loaves, skewered on a stick. Leaning against the wall of the trench, they mop their faces with their handkerchiefs or sleeves. And I see Cocon go up to Pepere with a smile, and forgetful of the abuse he had been heaping on the other's reputation, he stretches out a cordial hand towards one of the cans in the collection that swells the circumference of Pepere, after the manner of a life-belt.

"What is there to eat?"

"It's there," is the evasive reply of the second fatigue man, whom experience has taught that a proclamation of the menu always evokes the bitterness of disillusion. So they set themselves to panting abuse of the length and the difficulties of the trip they have just accomplished: "Some crowds about, everywhere! It's a tough job to get along—got to disguise yourself as a cigarette paper, sometimes."—" And there are people who say they're shirkers in the kitchens!" As for him, he would a hundred thousand times rather be with the company in the trenches, to mount guard and dig, than earn his keep by such a job, twice a day during the night!

Paradis, having lifted the lids of the jars, surveys the recipients and announces, "Kidney beans in oil, bully, pudding, and coffee—that's all."

"Nom de Dieu!" bawls Tulacque. "And wine?" He summons the crowd: "Come and look here, all of you! That—that's the limit! We're done out of our wine!"

Athirst and grimacing, they hurry up; and from the profoundest depths of their being wells up the chorus of despair and disappointment, "Oh, Hell!"

"Then what's that in there?" says the fatigue man, still ruddily sweating, and using his foot to point at a bucket.

"Yes," says Paradis, "my mistake, there is some."

The fatigue man shrugs his shoulders, and hurls at Paradis a look of unspeakable scorn—" Now you're beginning! Get your gig-lamps on, if your sight's bad." He adds, "One cup each—rather less perhaps—some chucklehead bumped against me, coming through the Boyau du Bois, and a drop got spilled." "Ah!" he hastens to add, raising his voice, "if I hadn't been loaded up, talk about the boot-toe he'd have got in the rump! But he hopped it on his top gear, the brute!"

In spite of this confident assurance, the fatigue man makes off himself, curses overtaking him as he goes, maledictions charged with offensive reflections on his honesty and temperance, imprecations inspired by this revelation of a ration reduced.

All the same, they throw themselves on the food, and eat it standing, squatting, kneeling, sitting on tins, or on haversacks pulled out of the holes where they sleep—or even prone, their backs on the ground, disturbed by passers-by, cursed at and cursing. Apart from these fleeting insults and jests, they say nothing, the primary and universal interest being but to swallow, with their mouths and the circumference thereof as greasy as a rifle-breech. Contentment is theirs.

At the earliest cessation of their jaw-bones' activity, they serve up the most ribald of raillery. They knock each other about, and clamor in riotous rivalry to have their say. One sees even Farfadet smiling, the frail municipal clerk who in the early days kept himself so decent and clean amongst us all that he was taken for a foreigner or a convalescent. One sees the tomato-like mouth of Lamuse dilate and divide, and his delight ooze out in tears. Poterloo's face, like a pink peony, opens out wider and wider. Papa Blaire's wrinkles flicker with frivolity as he stands up, pokes his head forward, and gesticulates with the abbreviated body that serves as a handle for his huge drooping mustache. Even the corrugations of Cocon's poor little face are lighted up.

Becuwe goes in search of firewood to warm the coffee. While we wait for our drink, we roll cigarettes and fill pipes. Pouches are pulled out. Some of us have shop-acquired pouches in leather or rubber, but they are a minority. Biquet extracts his tobacco from a sock, of which the mouth is drawn tight with string. Most of the others use the bags for anti-gas pads, made of some waterproof material which is an excellent preservative of shag, be it coarse or fine; and there are those who simply fumble for it in the bottom of their greatcoat pockets.

The smokers spit in a circle, just at the mouth of the dug-out which most of the half-section inhabit, and flood with tobacco-stained saliva the place where they put their hands and feet when they flatten themselves to get in or out.

But who notices such a detail?

Now, a propos of a letter to Marthereau from his wife, they discuss produce.

"La mere Marthereau has written," he says. "That fat pig we've got at home, a fine specimen, guess how much she's worth now?"

But the subject of domestic economy degenerates suddenly into a fierce altercation between Pepin and Tulacque. Words of quite unmistakable significance are exchanged. Then—"I don't care a what you say or what you don't say! Shut it up!"—"I shall shut it when I want, midden!"—"A seven-pound thump would shut it up quick enough!"—"Who from? Who'll give it me?"—"Come and find out!"

They grind their teeth and approach each other in a foaming rage. Tulacque grasps his prehistoric ax, and his squinting eyes are flashing. The other is pale and his eyes have a greenish glint; you can see in his blackguard face that his thoughts are with his knife.

But between the two, as they grip each other in looks and mangle in words, Lamuse intervenes with his huge pacific head, like a baby's, and his face of sanguinary hue: "Allons, allons! You're not going to cut yourselves up! Can't be allowed!"

The others also interpose, and the antagonists are separated, but they continue to hurl murderous looks at each other across the barrier of their comrades. Pepin mutters a residue of slander in tones that quiver with malice—

"The hooligan, the ruffian, the blackguard! But wait a bit! I'll see him later about this!"

On the other side, Tulacque confides in the poilu who is beside him: "That crab-louse! Non, but you know what he is! You know—there's no more to be said. Here, we've got to rub along with a lot of people that we don't know from Adam. We know 'em and yet we don't know 'em; but that man, if he thinks he can mess me about, he'll find himself up the wrong street! You wait a bit. I'll smash him up one of these days, you'll see!"

Meanwhile the general conversation is resumed, drowning the last twin echoes of the quarrel.

"It's every day alike, alors!" says Paradis to me; "yesterday it was Plaisance who wanted to let Fumex have it heavy on the jaw, about God knows what—a matter of opium pills, I think. First it's one and then it's another that talks of doing some one in. Are we getting to be a lot of wild animals because we look like 'em?"

"Mustn't take them too seriously, these men," Lamuse declares; "they're only kids."

"True enough, seeing that they're men."

The day matures. A little more light has trickled through the mists that enclose the earth. But the sky has remained overcast, and now it dissolves in rain; With a slowness which itself disheartens, the wind brings back its great wet void upon us. The rain-haze makes everything clammy and dull—even the Turkey red of Lamuse's cheeks, and even the orange armor that caparisons Tulacque. The water penetrates to the deep joy with which dinner endowed us, and puts it out. Space itself shrinks; and the sky, which is a field of melancholy, comes closely down upon the earth, which is a field of death.

We are still there, implanted and idle. It will be hard to-day to reach the end of it, to get rid of the afternoon. We shiver in discomfort, and keep shifting our positions, like cattle enclosed.

Cocon is explaining to his neighbor the arrangement and intricacy of our trenches. He has seen a military map and made some calculations. In the sector occupied by our regiment there are fifteen lines of French trenches. Some are abandoned, invaded by grass, and half leveled; the others solidly upkept and bristling with men. These parallels are joined up by innumerable galleries which hook and crook themselves like ancient streets. The system is much more dense than we believe who live inside it. On the twenty-five kilometers' width that form the army front, one must count on a thousand kilometers of hollowed lines—trenches and saps of all sorts. And the French Army consists of ten such armies. There are then, on the French side, about 10,000 kilometers of trenches, and as much again on the German side. And the French front is only about one-eighth of the whole war-front of the world.

Thus speaks Cocon, and he ends by saying to his neighbor, "In all that lot, you see what we are, us chaps?"

Poor Barque's head droops. His face, bloodless as a slum child's, is underlined by a red goatee that punctuates his hair like an apostrophe: "Yes, it's true, when you come to think of it. What's a soldier, or even several soldiers?—Nothing, and less than nothing, in the whole crowd; and so we see ourselves lost, drowned, like the few drops of blood that we are among all this flood of men and things."

Barque sighs and is silent, and the end of his discourse gives a chance of hearing to a bit of jingling narrative, told in an undertone: "He was coming along with two horses—Fs-s-s—a shell; and he's only one horse left."

"You get fed up with it," says Volpatte.

"But you stick it," growls Barque.

"You've got to," says Paradis.

"Why?" asks Marthereau, without conviction.

"No need for a reason, as long as we've got to."

"There is no reason," Lamuse avers.

"Yes, there is," says Cocon. "It's—or rather, there are several."

"Shut it up! Much better to have no reason, as long as we've got to stick it."

"All the same," comes the hollow voice of Blaire, who lets no chance slip of airing his pet phrase—"All the same, they'd like to steal the very skin off us!"

"At the beginning of it," says Tirette, "I used to think about a heap of things. I considered and calculated. Now, I don't think any more."

"Nor me either."

"Nor me."

"I've never tried to."

"You're not such a fool as you look, flea-face," says the shrill and jeering voice of Mesnil Andre. Obscurely flattered, the other develops his theme—

"To begin with, you can't know anything about anything."

Says Corporal Bertrand, "There's only one thing you need know, and it's this; that the Boches are here in front of us, deep dug in, and we've got to see that they don't get through, and we've got to put 'em out, one day or another—as soon as possible."

"Oui, oui, they've got to leg it, and no mistake about it. What else is there? Not worth while to worry your head thinking about anything else. But it's a long job."

An explosion of profane assent comes from Fouillade, and he adds, "That's what it is!"

"I've given up grousing," says Barque. "At the beginning of it, I played hell with everybody—with the people at the rear, with the civilians, with the natives, with the shirkers. Yes, I played hell; but that was at the beginning of the war—I was young. Now, I take things better."

"There's only one way of taking 'em—as they come!"

"Of course! Otherwise, you'd go crazy. We're dotty enough already, eh, Firmin?"

Volpatte assents with a nod of profound conviction. He spits, and then contemplates his missile with a fixed and unseeing eye.

"You were saying?" insists Barque.

"Here, you haven't got to look too far in front. You must live from day to day and from hour to hour, as well as you can."

"Certain sure, monkey-face. We've got to do what they tell us to do, until they tell us to go away."

"That's all," yawns Mesnil Joseph.

Silence follows the recorded opinions that proceed from these dried and tanned faces, inlaid with dust. This, evidently, is the credo of the men who, a year and a half ago, left all the corners of the land to mass themselves on the frontier: Give up trying to understand, and give up trying to be yourself. Hope that you will not die, and fight for life as well as you can.

"Do what you've got to do, oui, but get out of your own messes yourself," says Barque, as he slowly stirs the mud to and fro.

"No choice"—Tulacque backs him up. "If you don't get out of 'em yourself, no one'll do it for you."

"He's not yet quite extinct, the man that bothers about the other fellow."

"Every man for himself, in war!"

"That's so, that's so."

Silence. Then from the depth of their destitution, these men summon sweet souvenirs—"All that," Barque goes on, "isn't worth much, compared with the good times we had at Soissons."

"Ah, the Devil!"

A gleam of Paradise lost lights up their eyes and seems even to redden their cold faces.

"Talk about a festival!" sighs Tirloir, as he leaves off scratching himself, and looks pensively far away over Trenchland.

"Ah, nom de Dieu! All that town, nearly abandoned, that used to be ours! The houses and the beds—"

"And the cupboards!"

"And the cellars!"

Lamuse's eyes are wet, his face like a nosegay, his heart full.

"Were you there long?" asks Cadilhac, who came here later, with the drafts from Auvergne.

"Several months."

The conversation had almost died out, but it flames up again fiercely at this vision of the days of plenty.

"We used to see," said Paradis dreamily, "the poilus pouring along and behind the houses on the way back to camp with fowls hung round their middles, and a rabbit under each arm, borrowed from some good fellow or woman that they hadn't seen and won't ever see again."

We reflect on the far-off flavor of chicken and rabbit. "There were things that we paid for, too. The spondu-licks just danced about. We held all the aces in those days."

"A hundred thousand francs went rolling round the shops."

"Millions, oui. All the day, just a squandering that you've no idea of, a sort of devil's delight."

"Believe me or not," said Blaire to Cadilhac, "but in the middle of it all, what we had the least of was fires, just like here and everywhere else you go. You had to chase it and find it and stick to it. Ah, mon vieux, how we did run after the kindlings!"

"Well, we were in the camp of the C.H.R. The cook there was the great Martin Cesar. He was the man for finding wood!"

"Ah, oui, oui! He was the ace of trumps! He got what he wanted without twisting himself."

"Always some fire in his kitchen, young fellow. You saw cooks chasing and gabbling about the streets in all directions, blubbering because they had no coal or wood. But he'd got a fire. When he hadn't any, he said, 'Don't worry, I'll see you through.' And he wasn't long about it, either."

"He went a bit too far, even. The first time I saw him in his kitchen, you'd never guess what he'd got the stew going with! With a violin that he'd found in the house!"

"Rotten, all the same," says Mesnil Andre. "One knows well enough that a violin isn't worth much when it comes to utility, but all the same—"

"Other times, he used billiard cues. Zizi just succeeded in pinching one for a cane, but the rest—into the fire! Then the arm-chairs in the drawing-room went by degrees—mahogany, they were. He did 'em in and cut them up by night, case some N.C.O. had something to say about it."

"He knew his way about," said Pepin. "As for us, we got busy with an old suite of furniture that lasted us a fortnight."

"And what for should we be without? You've got to make dinner, and there's no wood or coal. After the grub's served out, there you are with your jaws empty, with a pile of meat in front of you, and in the middle of a lot of pals that chaff and bullyrag you!"

"It's the War Office's doing, it isn't ours."

"Hadn't the officers a lot to say about the pinching?"

"They damn well did it themselves, I give you my word! Desmaisons, do you remember Lieutenant Virvin's trick, breaking down a cellar door with an ax? And when a poilu saw him at it, he gave him the door for firewood, so that he wouldn't spread it about."

"And poor old Saladin, the transport officer. He was found coming out of a basement in the dusk with two bottles of white wine in each arm, the sport, like a nurse with two pairs of twins. When he was spotted, they made him go back down to the wine-cellar, and serve out bottles for everybody. But Corporal Bertrand, who is a man of scruples, wouldn't have any. Ah, you remember that, do you, sausage-foot!"

"Where's that cook now that always found wood?" asks Cadilhac.

"He's dead. A bomb fell in his stove. He didn't get it, but he's dead all the same—died of shock when he saw his macaroni with its legs in the air.

Heart seizure, so the doc' said. His heart was weak—he was only strong on wood. They gave him a proper funeral—made him a coffin out of the bedroom floor, and got the picture nails out of the walls to fasten 'em together, and used bricks to drive 'em in. While they were carrying him off, I thought to myself, 'Good thing for him he's dead. If he saw that, he'd never be able to forgive himself for not having thought of the bedroom floor for his fire.'—Ah, what the devil are you doing, son of a pig?"

Volpatte offers philosophy on the rude intrusion of a passing fatigue party: "The private gets along on the back of his pals. When you spin your yarns in front of a fatigue gang, or when you take the best bit or the best place, it's the others that suffer."

"I've often," says Lamuse, "put up dodges so as not to go into the trenches, and it's come off no end of times. I own up to that. But when my pals are in danger, I'm not a dodger any more. I forget discipline and everything else. I see men, and I go. But otherwise, my boy, I look after my little self."

Lamuse's claims are not idle words. He is an admitted expert at loafing, but all the same he has brought wounded in under fire and saved their lives. Without any brag, he relates the deed—

"We were all lying on the grass, and having a hot time. Crack, crack! Whizz, whizz! When I saw them downed, I got up, though they yelled at me, 'Get down!' Couldn't leave 'em like that. Nothing to make a song about, seeing I couldn't do anything else."

Nearly all the boys of the squad have some high deed of arms to their credit, and the Croix de Guerre has been successively set upon their breasts.

"I haven't saved any Frenchmen," says Biquet, "but I've given some Boches the bitter pill." In the May attacks, he ran off in advance and was seen to disappear in the distance, but came back with four fine fellows in helmets.

"I, too," says Tulacque, "I've killed some." Two months ago, with quaint vanity, he laid out nine in a straight row, in front of the taken trench. "But," he adds, "it's always the Boche officer that I'm after."

"Ah, the beasts!" The curse comes from several men at once and from the bottom of their hearts.

"Ah, mon vieux," says Tirloir, "we talk about the dirty Boche race; but as for the common soldier, I don't know if it's true or whether we're codded about that as well, and if at bottom they're not men pretty much like us."

"Probably they're men like us," says Eudore.

"Perhaps!" cries Cocon, "and perhaps not."

"Anyway," Tirloir goes on, "we've not got a dead set on the men, but on the German officers; non, non, non, they're not men, they're monsters. I tell you, they're really a specially filthy sort o' vermin. One might say that they're the microbes of the war. You ought to see them close to—the infernal great stiff-backs, thin as nails, though they've got calf-heads."

"And snouts like snakes."

Tirloir continues: "I saw one once, a prisoner, as I came back from liaison. The beastly bastard! A Prussian colonel, that wore a prince's crown, so they told me, and a gold coat-of-arms. He was mad because we took leave to graze against him when they were bringing him back along the communication trench, and he looked down on everybody—like that. I said to myself, 'Wait a bit, old cock, I'll make you rattle directly!' I took my time and squared up behind him, and kicked into his tailpiece with all my might. I tell you, he fell down half-strangled."

"Strangled?"

"Yes, with rage, when it dawned on him that the rump of an officer and nobleman had been bust in by the hobnailed socks of a poor private! He went off chattering like a woman and wriggling like an epileptic—"

"I'm not spiteful myself," says Blaire, "I've got kiddies. And it worries me, too, at home, when I've got to kill a pig that I know—but those, I shall run 'em through—Bing!—full in the linen-cupboard."

"I, too."

"Not to mention," says Pepin, "that they've got silver hats, and pistols that you can get four quid for whenever you like, and field-glasses that simply haven't got a price. Ah, bad luck, what a lot of chances I let slip in the early part of the campaign! I was too much of a beginner then, and it serves me right. But don't worry, I shall get a silver hat. Mark my words, I swear I'll have one. I must have not only the skin of one of Wilhelm's red-tabs, but his togs as well. Don't fret yourself; I'll fasten on to that before the war ends."

"You think it'll have an end, then?" asks some one.

"Don't worry!" replies the other.

Meanwhile, a hubbub has arisen to the right of us, and suddenly a moving and buzzing group appears, in which dark and bright forms mingle.

"What's all that?"

Biquet has ventured on a reconnaissance, and returns contemptuously pointing with his thumb towards the motley mass: "Eh, boys! Come and have a squint at them! Some people!"

"Some people?"

"Oui, some gentlemen, look you. Civvies, with Staff officers."

"Civilians! Let's hope they'll stick it!"

It is the sacramental saying and evokes laughter, although we have heard it a hundred times, and although the soldier has rightly or wrongly perverted the original meaning and regards it as an ironical reflection on his life of privations and peril.

Two Somebodies come up; two Somebodies with overcoats and canes. Another is dressed in a sporting suit, adorned with a plush hat and binoculars. Pale blue tunics, with shining belts of fawn color or patent leather, follow and steer the civilians.

With an arm where a brassard glitters in gold-edged silk and golden ornament, a captain indicates the firing-step in front of an old emplacement and invites the visitors to get up and try it. The gentleman in the touring suit clambers up with the aid of his umbrella.

Says Barque, "You've seen the station-master at the Gare du Nord, all in his Sunday best, and opening the door of a first-class compartment for a rich sportsman on the first day of the shooting? With his 'Montez, monsieur le Propritaire!'—you know, when the toffs are all togged up in brand-new outfits and leathers and ironmongery, and showing off with all their paraphernalia for killing poor little animals!"

Three or four poilus who were quite without their accouterments have disappeared underground. The others sit as though paralyzed. Even the pipes go out, and nothing is heard but the babble of talk exchanged by the officers and their guests.

"Trench tourists," says Barque in an undertone, and then louder—"
This way, mesdames et messieurs"—in the manner of the moment.

"Chuck it!" whispers Farfadet, fearing that Barque's malicious tongue
will draw the attention of the potent personages.

Some heads in the group are now turned our way. One gentleman who
detaches himself and comes up wears a soft hat and a loose tie. He has a
white billy-goat beard, and might be an artiste. Another follows him,
wearing a black overcoat, a black bowler hat, a black beard, a white tie
and an eyeglass.

"Ah, ah! There are some poilus," says the first gentleman. "These are
real poilus, indeed."

He comes up to our party a little timidly, as though in the Zoological
Gardens, and offers his hand to the one who is nearest to him—not
without awkwardness, as one offers a piece of bread to the elephant.

"He, he! They are drinking coffee," he remarks.

"They call it 'the juice,'" corrects the magpie-man.

"Is it good, my friends?" The soldier, abashed in his turn by this alien
and unusual visitation, grunts, giggles, and reddens, and the gentleman
says, "He, he!" Then, with a slight motion of the head, he withdraws
backwards.

The assemblage, with its neutral shades of civilian cloth and its
sprinkling of bright military hues—like geraniums and hortensias in the
dark soil of a flowerbed—oscillates, then passes, and moves off the
opposite way it came. One of the officers was heard to say, "We have yet
much to see, messieurs les journalistes."

When the radiant spectacle has faded away, we look at each other.
Those who had fled into the funk-holes now gradually and head first
disinter themselves. The group recovers itself and shrugs its shoulders.

"They're journalists," says Tirette.

"Journalists?"

"Why, yes, the individuals that lay the newspapers. You don't seem to
catch on, fathead. Newspapers must have chaps to write 'em."

"Then it's those that stuff up our craniums?" says Marthereau.

Barque assumes a shrill treble, and pretending that he has a newspaper
in front of his nose, recites—"'The Crown Prince is mad, after having
been killed at the beginning of the campaign, and meanwhile he has all the

diseases you can name. William will die this evening, and again
to-morrow. The Germans have no more munitions and are chewing wood.
They cannot hold out, according to the most authoritative calculations,
beyond the end of the week. We can have them when we like, with their
rifles slung. If one can wait a few days longer, there will be no desire to
forsake the life of the trenches. One is so comfortable there, with water
and gas laid on, and shower-baths at every step. The only drawback is that
it is rather too hot in winter. As for the Austrians, they gave in a long time
since and are only pretending.' For fifteen months now it's been like that,
and you can hear the editor saying to his scribes, 'Now, boys, get into it!
Find some way of brushing that up again for me in five secs, and make it
spin out all over those four damned white sheets that we've got to
mucky.'"

"Ah, yes!" says Fouillade.

"Look here, corporal; you're making fun of it—isn't it true what I
said?"

"There's a little truth in it, but you're too slashing on the poor boys, and
you'd be the first to make a song about it if you had to go without papers.
Oui, when the paper-man's going by, why do you all shout, 'Here, here'?"

"And what good can you get out of them all?" cries Papa Blaire. "Read
'em by the tubful if you like, but do the same as me—don't believe 'em!"

"Oui, oui, that's enough about them. Turn the page over, donkey-nose."

The conversation is breaking up; interest in it follows suit and is
scattered. Four poilus join in a game of manille, that will last until night
blacks out the cards. Volpatte is trying to catch a leaf of cigarette paper
that has escaped his fingers and goes hopping and dodging in the wind
along the wall of the trench like a fragile butterfly.

Cocon and Tirette are recalling their memories of barrack-life. The
impressions left upon their minds by those years of military training are
ineffaceable. Into that fund of abundant souvenirs, of abiding color and
instant service, they have been wont to dip for their subjects of
conversation for ten, fifteen, or twenty years. So that they still frequent it,
even after a year and a half of actual war in all its forms.

I can hear some of the talk and guess the rest of it. For it is everlastingly
the same sort of tale that they get out of their military past;—the narrator
once shut up a bad-tempered N.C.O. with words of extreme

appropriateness and daring. He wasn't afraid, he spoke out loud and strong! Some scraps of it reach my ears—

"Alors, d'you think I flinched when Nenoeil said that to me? Not a bit, my boy. All the pals kept their jaws shut but me; I spoke up, 'Mon adjudant,' I says, 'it's possible, but—'" A sentence follows that I cannot secure—"Oh, tu sais, just like that, I said it. He didn't get shirty; 'Good, that's good,' he says as he hops it, and afterwards he was as good as all that, with me."

"Just like me, with Dodore, 'jutant of the 13th, when I was on leave—a mongrel. Now he's at the Pantheon, as caretaker. He'd got it in for me, so—"

So each unpacks his own little load of historical anecdote. They are all alike, and not one of them but says, "As for me, I am not like the others."

The post-orderly! He is a tall and broad man with fat calves; comfortable looking, and as neat and tidy as a policeman. He is in a bad temper. There are new orders, and now he has to go every day as far as Battalion Headquarters. He abuses the order as if it had been directed exclusively against himself; and he continues to complain even while he calls up the corporals for the post and maintains his customary chat en passant with this man and that. And in spite of his spleen he does not keep to himself all the information with which he comes provided. While removing the string from the letter-packets he dispenses his verbal news, and announces first, that according to rumor, there is a very explicit ban on the wearing of hoods.

"Hear that?" says Tirette to Tirloir. "Got to chuck your fine hood away!"

"Not likely! I'm not on. That's nothing to do with me," replies the hooded one, whose pride no less than his comfort is at stake.

"Order of the General Commanding the Army."

"Then let the General give an order that it's not to rain any more. I want to know nothing about it."

The majority of Orders, even when less peculiar than this one, are always received in this way—and then carried out.

"There's a reported order as well," says the man of letters, "that beards have got to be trimmed and hair got to be clipped close."

"Talk on, my lad," says Barque, on whose head the threatened order directly falls; "you didn't see me! You can draw the curtains!"

"I'm telling you. Do it or don't do it—doesn't matter a damn to me."

Besides what is real and written, there is bigger news, but still more dubious and imaginative—the division is going to be relieved, and sent either to rest—real rest, for six weeks—or to Morocco, or perhaps to Egypt.

Divers exclamations. They listen, and let themselves be tempted by the fascination of the new, the wonderful.

But some one questions the post-orderly: "Who told you that?"

"The adjutant commanding the Territorial detachment that fatigues for the H.Q. of the A.C."

"For the what?"

"For Headquarters of the Army Corps, and he's not the only one that says it. There's—you know him—I've forgotten his name—he's like Galle, but he isn't Galle—there's some one in his family who is Some One. Anyway, he knows all about it."

"Then what?" With hungry eyes they form a circle around the story-teller.

"Egypt, you say, we shall go to? Don't know it. I know there were Pharaohs there at the time when I was a kid and went to school, but since—"

"To Egypt!" The idea finds unconscious anchorage in their minds.

"Ah, non," says Blaire, "for I get sea-sick. Still, it doesn't last, sea-sickness. Oui, but what would my good lady say?"

"What about it? She'll get used to it. You see niggers, and streets full of big birds, like we see sparrows here."

"But haven't we to go to Alsace?"

"Yes," says the post-orderly, "there are some who think so at the Pay-office."

"That'd do me well enough."

But common sense and acquired experience regain the upper hand and put the visions to flight. We have been told so often that we were going a long way off, so often have we believed it, so often been undeceived! So, as if at a moment arranged, we wake up.

"It's all my eye—they've done it on us too often. Wait before believing—and don't count a crumb's worth on it."

We reoccupy our corner. Here and there a man bears in his hand the light momentous burden of a letter.

"Ah," says Tirloir, "I must be writing. Can't go eight days without writing."

"Me too," says Eudore, "I must write to my p'tit' femme."

"Is she all right, Mariette?"

"Oui, oui, don't fret about Mariette."

A few have already settled themselves for correspondence. Barque is standing up. He stoops over a sheet of paper flattened on a note-book upon a jutting crag in the trench wall. Apparently in the grip of an inspiration, he writes on and on, with his eyes in bondage and the concentrated expression of a horseman at full gallop.

When once Lamuse—who lacks imagination—has sat down, placed his little writing-block on the padded summit of his knees, and moistened his copying-ink pencil, he passes the time in reading again the last letters received, in wondering what he can say that he has not already said, and in fostering a grim determination to say something else.

A sentimental gentleness seems to have overspread little Eudore, who is curled up in a sort of niche in the ground. He is lost in meditation, pencil in hand, eyes on paper. Dreaming, he looks and stares and sees. It is another sky that lends him light, another to which his vision reaches. He has gone home.

In this time of letter-writing, the men reveal the most and the best that they ever were. Several others surrender to the past, and its first expression is to talk once more of fleshly comforts.

Through their outer crust of coarseness and concealment, other hearts venture upon murmured memories, and the rekindling of bygone brightness: the summer morning, when the green freshness of the garden steals in upon the purity of the country bedroom; or when the wind in the wheat of the level lands sets it slowly stirring or deeply waving, and shakes the square of oats hard by into quick little feminine tremors; or the winter evening, with women and their gentleness around the shaded luster of the lamp.

But Papa Blaire resumes work upon the ring he has begun. He has threaded the still formless disc of aluminium over a bit of rounded wood, and rubs it with the file. As he applies himself to the job, two wrinkles of mighty meditation deepen upon his forehead. Anon he stops, straightens himself, and looks tenderly at the trifle, as though she also were looking at it.

"You know," he said to me once, speaking of another ring, "it's not a question of doing it well or not well. The point is that I've done it for my wife, d'you see? When I had nothing to do but scratch myself, I used to have a look at this photo"—he showed me a photograph of a big, chubby-faced woman—"and then it was quite easy to set about this damned ring. You might say that we've made it together, see? The proof of that is that it was company for me, and that I said Adieu to it when I sent it off to Mother Blaire."

He is making another just now, and this one will have copper in it, too. He works eagerly. His heart would fain express itself to the best advantage in this the sort of penmanship upon which he is so tenaciously bent.

As they stoop reverently, in their naked earth-holes, over the slender rudimentary trinkets—so tiny that the great hide-bound hands hold them with difficulty or let them fall—these men seem still more wild, more primitive, and more human, than at all other times.

You are set thinking of the first inventor, the father of all craftsmen, who sought to invest enduring materials with the shapes of what he saw and the spirit of what he felt.

"People coming along," announces Biquet the mobile, who acts as hall-porter to our section of the trench—"buckets of 'em." Immediately an adjutant appears, with straps round his belly and his chin, and brandishing his sword-scabbard.

"Out of the way, you! Out of the way, I tell you! You loafers there, out of it! Let me see you quit, hey!" We make way indolently. Those at the sides push back into the earth by slow degrees.

It is a company of Territorials, deputed to our sector for the fortification of the second line and the upkeep of its communication trenches. They come into view—miserable bundles of implements, and dragging their feet.

We watch them, one by one, as they come up, pass, and disappear. They are stunted and elderly, with dusty faces, or big and broken-winded, tightly enfolded in greatcoats stained and over-worn, that yawn at the toothless gaps where the buttons are missing.

Tirette and Barque, the twin wags, leaning close together against the wall, stare at them, at first in silence. Then they begin to smile.

"March past of the Broom Brigade," says Tirette.

"We'll have a bit of fun for three minutes," announces Barque.

Some of the old toilers are comical. This one whom the file brings up has bottle-shaped shoulders. Although extremely narrow-chested and spindle-shanked, he is big-bellied. He is too much for Barque. "Hullo, Sir Canteen!" he says.

When a more outrageously patched-up greatcoat appears than all the others can show, Tirette questions the veteran recruit. "Hey, Father Samples! Hey, you there!" he insists.

The other turns and looks at him, open-mouthed.

"Say there, papa, if you will be so kind as to give me the address of your tailor in London!"

A chuckle comes from the antiquated and wrinkle-scrawled face, and then the poilu, checked for an instant by Barque's command, is jostled by the following flood and swept away.

When some less striking figures have gone past, a new victim is provided for the jokers. On his red and wrinkled neck luxuriates some dirty sheep's-wool. With knees bent, his body forward, his back bowed, this Territorial's carriage is the worst.

"Tiens!" bawls Tirette, with pointed finger, "the famous concertina-man! It would cost you something to see him at the fair—here, he's free gratis!"

The victim stammers responsive insults amid the scattered laughter that arises.

No more than that laughter is required to excite the two comrades. It is the ambition to have their jests voted funny by their easy audience that stimulates them to mock the peculiarities of their old comrades-in-arms, of those who toil night and day on the brink of the great war to make ready and make good the fields of battle.

And even the other watchers join in. Miserable themselves, they scoff at the still more miserable.

"Look at that one! And that, look!"

"Non, but take me a snapshot of that little rump-end! Hey, earth-worm!"

"And that one that has no ending! Talk about a sky-scratcher! Tiens, la, he takes the biscuit. Yes, you take it, old chap!"

This man goes with little steps, and holds his pickax up in front like a candle; his face is withered, and his body borne down by the blows of lumbago.

"Like a penny, gran'pa?" Barque asks him, as he passes within reach of a tap on the shoulder.

The broken-down poilu replies with a great oath of annoyance, and provokes the harsh rejoinder of Barque: "Come now, you might be polite, filthy-face, old muck-mill!"

Turning right round in fury, the old one defies his tormentor.

"Hullo!" cries Barque, laughing, "He's showing fight; the ruin! He's warlike, look you, and he might be mischievous if only he were sixty years younger!"

"And if he wasn't alone," wantonly adds Pepin, whose eye is in quest of other targets among the flow of new arrivals.

The hollow chest of the last straggler appears, and then his distorted back disappears.

The march past of the worn-out and trench-foul veterans comes to an end among the ironical and almost malevolent faces of these sinister troglodytes, whom their caverns of mud but half reveal.

Meanwhile, the hours slip away, and evening begins to veil the sky and darken the things of earth. It comes to blend itself at once with the blind fate and the ignorant dark minds of the multitude there enshrouded.

Through the twilight comes the rolling hum of tramping men, and another throng rubs its way through.

"Africans!"

They march past with faces red-brown, yellow or chestnut, their beards scanty and fine or thick and frizzled, their greatcoats yellowish-green, and their muddy helmets sporting the crescent in place of our grenade. Their eyes are like balls of ivory or onyx, that shine from faces like new pennies, flattened or angular. Now and again comes swaying along above the line the coal-black mask of a Senegalese sharpshooter. Behind the company goes a red flag with a green hand in the center.

We watch them in silence. These are asked no questions. They command respect, and even a little fear.

All the same, these Africans seem jolly and in high spirits. They are going, of course, to the first line. That is their place, and their passing is the sign of an imminent attack. They are made for the offensive.

"Those and the 75 gun we can take our hats off to. They're everywhere sent ahead at big moments, the Moroccan Division."

"They can't quite fit in with us. They go too fast—and there's no way of stopping them."

Some of these diabolical images in yellow wood or bronze or ebony are serious of mien, uneasy, and taciturn. Their faces have the disquieting and secret look of the snare suddenly discovered. The others laugh with a laugh that jangles like fantastic foreign instruments of music, a laugh that bares the teeth.

We talk over the characteristics of these Africans; their ferocity in attack, their devouring passion to be in with the bayonet, their predilection for "no quarter." We recall those tales that they themselves willingly tell, all in much the same words and with the same gestures. They raise their arms over their heads—"Kam'rad, Kam'rad!" "Non, pas Kam'rad!" And in pantomime they drive a bayonet forward, at belly-height, drawing it back then with the help of a foot.

One of the sharpshooters overhears our talk as he passes. He looks upon us, laughs abundantly in his helmeted turban, and repeats our words with significant shakes of his head: "Pas Kam'rad, non pas Kam'rad, never! Cut head off!"

"No doubt they're a different race from us, with their tent-cloth skin," Barque confesses, though he does not know himself what "cold feet" are. "It worries them to rest, you know; they only live for the minute when the officer puts his watch back in his pocket and says, 'Off you go!'"

"In fact, they're real soldiers."

"We are not soldiers," says big Lamuse, "we're men." Though the evening has grown darker now, that plain true saying sheds something like a glimmering light on the men who are waiting here, waiting since the morning, waiting since months ago.

They are men, good fellows of all kinds, rudely torn away from the joy of life. Like any other men whom you take in the mass, they are ignorant and of narrow outlook, full of a sound common sense—which some-times gets off the rails—disposed to be led and to do as they are bid, enduring under hardships, long-suffering.

They are simple men further simplified, in whom the merely primitive instincts have been accentuated by the force of circumstances—the instinct of self-preservation, the hard-gripped hope of living through, the joy of food, of drink, and of sleep. And at intervals they are cries and dark shudders of humanity that issue from the silence and the shadows of their great human hearts.

When we can no longer see clearly, we hear down there the murmur of a command, which comes nearer and rings loud—"Second half-section! Muster!" We fall in; it is the call.

"Gee up!" says the corporal. We are set in motion. In front of the tool-depot there is a halt and trampling. To each is given a spade or pickax. An N.C.O. presents the handles in the gloom: "You, a spade; there, hop it! You a spade, too; you a pick. Allons, hurry up and get off."

We leave by the communication trench at right angles to our own, and straight ahead towards the changeful frontier, now alive and terrible.

Up in the somber sky, the strong staccato panting of an invisible aeroplane circles in wide descending coils and fills infinity. In front, to right and left, everywhere, thunderclaps roll with great glimpses of short-lived light in the dark-blue sky.

The Return

RELUCTANTLY the ashen dawn is bleaching the still dark and formless landscape. Between the declining road on the right that falls into the gloom, and the black cloud of the Alleux Wood—where we hear the convoy teams assembling and getting under way—a field extends. We have reached it, we of the 6th Battalion, at the end of the night. We have piled arms, and now, in the center of this circle of uncertain light, our feet in the mist and mud, we stand in dark clusters (that yet are hardly blue), or as solitary phantoms; and the heads of all are turned towards the road that comes from "down there." We are waiting for the rest of the regiment, the 5th Battalion, who were in the first line and left the trenches after us.

Noises; "There they are!" A long and shapeless mass appears in the west and comes down out of the night upon the dawning road.

At last! It is ended, the accursed shift that began at six o'clock yesterday evening and has lasted all night, and now the last man has stepped from the last communication trench.

This time it has been an awful sojourn in the trenches. The 18th company was foremost and has been cut up, eighteen killed and fifty wounded—one in three less in four days. And this without attack—by bombardment alone.

This is known to us, and as the mutilated battalion approaches down there, and we join them in trampling the muddy field and exchanging nods of recognition, we cry, "What about the 18th?" We are thinking as we put the question, "If it goes on like this, what is to become of all of us? What will become of me?"

The 17th, the 19th, and the 20th arrive in turn and pile arms. "There's the 18th!" It arrives after all the others; having held the first trench, it has been last relieved.

The light is a little cleaner, and the world is paling. We can make out, as he comes down the road, the company's captain, ahead of his men and alone. He helps himself along with a stick, and walks with difficulty, by reason of his old wound of the Marne battle that rheumatism is troubling; and there are other pangs, too. He lowers his hooded head, and might be attending a funeral. We can see that in his mind he is indeed following the dead, and his thoughts are with them.

Here is the company, debouching in dire disorder, and our hearts are heavy. It is obviously shorter than the other three, in the march past of the battalion.

I reach the road, and confront the descending mass of the 18th. The uniforms of these survivors are all earth-yellowed alike, so that they appear to be clad in khaki. The cloth is stiff with the ochreous mud that has dried underneath. The skirts of their greatcoats are like lumps of wood, jumping about on the yellow crust that reaches to their knees. Their faces are drawn and blackened; dust and dirt have wrinkled them anew; their eyes are big and fevered. And from these soldiers whom the depths of horror have given back there rises a deafening din. They talk all at once, and loudly; they gesticulate, they laugh and sing. You would think, to see them, that it was a holiday crowd pouring over the road!

These are the second section and its big sub-lieutenant, whose greatcoat is tightened and strapped around a body as stiff as a rolled umbrella. I elbow my way along the marching crowd as far as Marchal's squad, the most sorely tried of all. Out of eleven comrades that they were, and had been without a break for a year and a half, there were three men only with Corporal Marchal.

He sees me—with a glad exclamation and a broad smile. He lets go his rifle-sling and offers me his hands, from one of which hangs his trench stick—"Eh, vieux frere, still going strong? What's become of you lately?"

I turn my head away and say, almost under my breath, "So, old chap, it's happened badly."

His smile dies at once, and he is serious: "Eh, oui, old man; it can't be helped; it was awful this time. Barbier is killed."

"They told us—Barbier!"

"Saturday night it was, at eleven o'clock. He had the top of his back taken away by a shell," says Marchal, "cut off like a razor. Besse got a bit of shell that went clean through his belly and stomach. Barthlemy and Baubex got it in the head and neck. We passed the night skedaddling up and down the trench at full speed, to dodge the showers. And little Godefroy—did you know him?—middle of his body blown away. He was emptied of blood on the spot in an instant, like a bucket kicked over. Little as he was, it was remarkable how much blood he had, it made a stream at least fifty meters long. Gougnard got his legs cut up by one explosion. They picked him up not quite dead. That was at the listening post. I was there on duty with them. But when that shell fell I had gone into the trench to ask the time. I found my rifle, that I'd left in my place, bent double, as if some one had folded it in his hands, the barrel like a corkscrew, and half of the stock in sawdust. The smell of fresh blood was enough to bring your heart up."

"And Mondain—him, too?"

"Mondain—that was the day after, yesterday in fact, in a dug-out that a shell smashed in. He was lying down, and his chest was crushed. Have they told you about Franco, who was alongside Mondain? The fall of earth broke his spine. He spoke again after they'd got him out and set him down. He said, with his head falling to one side, 'I'm dying,' and he was gone. Vigile was with them, too; his body wasn't touched, but they found him with his head completely flattened out, flat as a pancake, and huge-as big as that. To see it spread out on the ground, black and distorted, it made you think of his shadow—the shadow one gets on the ground sometimes when one walks with a lantern at night."

"Vigile—only Class 1913—a child! And Mondain and Franco—such good sorts, in spite of their stripes. We're so many old special pals the less, mon vieux Marchal."

"Yes," says Marchal. But he is swallowed up in a crowd of his friends, who worry and catechise him. He bandies jests with them, and answers their raillery, and all hustle each other, and laugh.

I look from face to face. They are merry, and in spite of the contractions of weariness, and the earth-stains, they look triumphant.

What does it mean? If wine had been possible during their stay in the first line, I should have said, "All these men are drunk."

I single out one of the survivors, who hums as he goes, and steps in time with it flippantly, as hussars of the stage do. It is Vanderborn, the drummer.

"Hullo, Vanderborn, you look pleased with yourself!" Vanderborn, who is sedate in the ordinary, cries, "It's not me yet, you see! Here I am!" With a mad gesticulation he serves me a thump on the shoulder. I understand.

If these men are happy in spite of all, as they come out of hell, it is because they are coming out of it. They are returning, they are spared. Once again the Death that was there has passed them over. Each company in its turn goes to the front once in six weeks. Six weeks! In both great and minor matters, fighting soldiers manifest the philosophy of the child. They never look afar, either ahead or around. Their thought strays hardly farther than from day to day. To-day, every one of those men is confident that he will live yet a little while.

And that is why, in spite of the weariness that weighs them down and the new slaughter with which they are still bespattered, though each has seen his brothers torn away from his side, in spite of all and in spite of themselves, they are celebrating the Feast of the Survivors. The boundless glory in which they rejoice is this—they still stand straight.

Volpatte and Fouillade

AS we reached quarters again, some one cried: "But where's Volpatte?"—"And Fouillade, where's he?"

They had been requisitioned and taken off to the front line by the 5th Battalion. No doubt we should find them somewhere in quarters. No success. Two men of the squad lost!

"That's what comes of lending men," said the sergeant with a great oath. The captain, when apprised of the loss, also cursed and swore and said, "I must have those men. Let them be found at once. Allez!"

Farfadet and I are summoned by Corporal Bertrand from the barn where at full length we have already immobilized ourselves, and are growing torpid: "You must go and look for Volpatte and Fouillade."

Quickly we got up, and set off with a shiver of uneasiness. Our two comrades have been taken by the 5th and carried off to that infernal shift. Who knows where they are and what they may be by now!

We climb up the hill again. Again we begin, but in the opposite direction, the journey done since the dawn and the night. Though we are without our heavy stuff, and only carry rifles and accouterments, we feel idle, sleepy, and stiff; and the country is sad, and the sky all wisped with mist. Farfadet is soon panting. He talked a little at first, till fatigue enforced silence on him. He is brave enough, but frail, and during all his prewar life, shut up in the Town Hall office where he scribbled since the days of his "first sacrament" between a stove and some ageing cardboard files, he hardly learned the use of his legs.

Just as we emerge from the wood, slipping and floundering, to penetrate the region of communication trenches, two faint shadows are outlined in front. Two soldiers are coming up. We can see the protuberance of their burdens and the sharp lines of their rifles. The swaying double shape becomes distinct—"It's them!"

One of the shadows has a great white head, all swathed—"One of them's wounded! It's Volpatte!"

We run up to the specters, our feet making the sounds of sinking in sponge and of sticky withdrawal, and our shaken cartridges rattle in their pouches. They stand still and wait for us. When we are close up, "It's about time!" cries Volpatte.

"You're wounded, old chap?"—"What?" he says; the manifold bandages all round his head make him deaf, and we must shout to get through them. So we go close and shout. Then he replies, "That's nothing; we're coming from the hole where the 5th Battalion put us on Thursday."

"You've stayed there—ever since?" yells Farfadet, whose shrill and almost feminine voice goes easily through the quilting that protects Volpatte's ears.

"Of course we stayed there, you blithering idiot!" says Fouillade. "You don't suppose we'd got wings to fly away with, and still less that we should have legged it without orders?"

Both of them let themselves drop to a sitting position on the ground. Volpatte's head—enveloped in rags with a big knot on the top and the same dark yellowish stains as his face—looks like a bundle of dirty linen.

"They forgot you, then, poor devils?"

"Rather!" cries Fouillade, "I should say they did. Four days and four nights in a shell-hole, with bullets raining down, a hole that stunk like a cesspool."

"That's right," says Volpatte. "It wasn't an ordinary listening-post hole, where one comes and goes regularly. It was just a shell-hole, like any other old shell-hole, neither more nor less. They said to us on Thursday, 'Station yourselves in there and keep on firing,' they said. Next day, a liaison chap of the 5th Battalion came and showed his neb: 'What the hell are you doing there?'—'Why, we're firing. They told us to fire, so we're firing,' I says. 'If they told us to do it, there must be some reason at the back of it. We're wanting for them to tell us to do something else.' The chap made tracks. He looked a bit uneasy, and suffering from the effects of being bombed. 'It's 22,' he says."

"To us two," says Fouillade, "there was a loaf of bread and a bucket of wine that the 18th gave us when they planted us there, and a whole case of cartridges, my boy. We fired off the cartridges and drank the booze, but we had sense to keep a few cartridges and a hunch of bread, though
we didn't keep any wine."

"That's where we went wrong," says Volpatte, "seeing that it was a thirsty job. Say, boys, you haven't got any gargle?"

"I've still nearly half a pint of wine," replies Farfadet. "Give it to him," says Fouillade, pointing to Volpatte, "seeing that he's been losing blood. I'm only thirsty."

Volpatte was shivering, and his little strapped-up eyes burned with fever in the enormous dump of rags set upon his shoulders. "That's good," he says, drinking.

"Ah! And then, too," he added, emptying—as politeness requires—the drop of wine that remained at the bottom of Farfadet's cup, "we got two Boches. They were crawling about outside, and fell into our holes, as blindly as moles into a spring snare, those chaps did. We tied 'em up. And see us then—after firing for thirty-six hours, we'd no more ammunition. So we filled our magazines with the last, and waited, in front of the parcels of Boche. The liaison chap forgot to tell his people that we were there. You, the 6th, forgot to ask for us; the 18th forgot us, too; and as we weren't in a listening-post where you're relieved as regular as if at H.Q., I could almost see us staying there till the regiment came back. In the long run, it was the loafers of the 204th, come to skulk about looking for fuses, that mentioned us. So then we got the order to fall back—immediately, they said. That 'immediately' was a good joke, and we got into harness at once. We untied the legs of the Boches, led them off and handed them over to the 204th, and here we are."

"We even fished out, in passing, a sergeant who was piled up in a hole and didn't dare come out, seeing he was shell-shocked. We slanged him, and that set him up a bit, and he thanked us. Sergeant Sacerdote he called himself."

"But your wound, old chap?"

"It's my ears. Two shells, a little one and a big one, my lad—went off while you're saying it. My head came between the two bursts, as you might say, but only just; a very close shave, and my lugs got it."

"You should have seen him," says Fouillade, "it was disgusting, those two ears hanging down. We had two packets of bandages, and the stretcher-men fired us one in. That makes three packets he's got rolled round his nut."

"Give us your traps, we're going back."

Farfadet and I divide Volpatte's equipment between us. Fouillade, sullen with thirst and racked by stiff joints, growls, and insists obstinately on keeping his weapons and bundles.

We stroll back, finding diversion—as always—in walking without ranks. It is so uncommon that one finds it surprising and profitable. So it is a breach of liberty which soon enlivens all four of us. We are in the country as though for the pleasure of it.

"We are pedestrians!" says Volpatte proudly. When we reach the turning at the top of the hill, he relapses upon rosy visions: "Old man, it's a good wound, after all. I shall be sent back, no mistake about it."

His eyes wink and sparkle in the huge white clump that dithers on his shoulders—a clump reddish on each side, where the ears were.

From the depth where the village lies we hear ten o'clock strike. "To hell with the time," says Volpatte "it doesn't matter to me any more what time it is."

He becomes loquacious. It is a low fever that inspires his dissertation, and condenses it to the slow swing of our walk, in which his step is already jaunty.

"They'll stick a red label on my greatcoat, you'll see, and take me to the rear. I shall be bossed this time by a very polite sort of chap, who'll say to me, 'That's one side, now turn the other way—so, my poor fellow.' Then the ambulance, and then the sick-train, with the pretty little ways of the Red Cross ladies all the way along, like they did to Crapelet Jules, then the base hospital. Beds with white sheets, a stove that snores in the middle of us all, people with the special job of looking after you, and that you watch doing it, regulation slippers—sloppy and comfortable—and a chamber-cupboard. Furniture! And it's in those big hospitals that you're all right for grub! I shall have good feeds, and baths. I shall take all I can get hold of. And there'll be presents—that you can enjoy without having to fight the others for them and get yourself into a bloody mess. I shall have my two hands on the counterpane, and they'll do damn well nothing, like things to look at—like toys, what? And under the sheets my legs'll be white-hot all the way through, and my trotters'll be expanding like bunches of violets."

Volpatte pauses, fumbles about, and pulls out of his pocket, along with his famous pair of Soissons scissors, something that he shows to me: "Tiens, have you seen this?"

It is a photograph of his wife and two children. He has already shown it to me many a time. I look at it and express appreciation.

"I shall go on sick-leave," says Volpatte, "and while my ears are sticking themselves on again, the wife and the little ones will look at me, and I shall look at them. And while they're growing again like lettuces, my friends, the war, it'll make progress—the Russians—one doesn't know, what?" He is thinking aloud, lulling himself with happy anticipations, already alone with his private festival in the midst of us.

"Robber!" Feuillade shouts at him. "You've too much luck, by God!"

How could we not envy him? He would be going away for one, two, or three months; and all that time, instead of our wretched privations, he would be transformed into a man of means!

"At the beginning," says Farfadet, "it sounded comic when I heard them wish for a 'good wound.' But all the same, and whatever can be said about it, I understand now that it's the only thing a poor soldier can hope for if he isn't daft."

We were drawing near to the village and passing round the wood. At its corner, the sudden shape of a woman arose against the sportive sunbeams that outlined her with light. Alertly erect she stood, before the faintly violet background of the wood's marge and the crosshatched trees. She was slender, her head all afire with fair hair, and in her pale face we could see the night-dark caverns of great eyes. The resplendent being gazed fixedly upon us, trembling, then plunged abruptly into the undergrowth and disappeared like a torch.

The apparition and its flight so impressed Volpatte that he lost the thread of his discourse.

"She's something like, that woman there!"

"No," said Fouillade, who had misunderstood, "she's called Eudoxie. I knew her because I've seen her before. A refugee. I don't know where she comes from, but she's at Gamblin, in a family there."

"She's thin and beautiful," Volpatte certified; "one would like to make her a little present—she's good enough to eat—tender as a chicken. And look at the eyes she's got!"

"She's queer," says Fouillade. "You don't know when you've got her. You see her here, there, with her fair hair on top, then—off! Nobody about. And you know, she doesn't know what danger is; marching about, sometimes, almost in the front line, and she's been seen knocking about in No Man's Land. She's queer."

"Look! There she is again. The spook! She's keeping an eye on us. What's she after?"

The shadow-figure, traced in lines of light, this time adorned the other end of the spinney's edge.

"To hell with women," Volpatte declared, whom the idea of his deliverance has completely recaptured.

"There's one in the squad, anyway, that wants her pretty badly. See—when you speak of the wolf—"

"You see its tail—"

"Not yet, but almost—look!" From some bushes on our right we saw the red snout of Lamuse appear peeping, like a wild boar's.

He was on the woman's trail. He had seen the alluring vision, dropped to the crouch of a setting dog, and made his spring. But in that spring he fell upon us.

Recognizing Volpatte and Fouillade, big Lamuse gave shouts of delight. At once he had no other thought than to get possession of the bags, rifles, and haversacks—"Give me all of it—I'm resting—come on, give it up."

He must carry everything. Farfadet and I willingly gave up Volpatte's equipment; and Fouillade, now at the end of his strength, agreed to surrender his pouches and his rifle.

Lamuse became a moving heap. Under the huge burden he disappeared, bent double, and made progress only with shortened steps.

But we felt that he was still under the sway of a certain project, and his glances went sideways. He was seeking the woman after whom he had hurled himself. Every time he halted, the better to trim some detail of the load, or puffingly to mop the greasy flow of perspiration, he furtively surveyed all the corners of the horizon and scrutinized the edges of the wood. He did not see her again.

I did see her again, and got a distinct impression this time that it was one of us she was after. She half arose on our left from the green shadows of the undergrowth. Steadying herself with one hand on a branch, she leaned forward and revealed the night-dark eyes and pale face, which showed—so brightly lighted was one whole side of it—like a crescent moon.

I saw that she was smiling. And following the course of the look that smiled, I saw Farfadet a little way behind us, and he was smiling too. Then she slipped away into the dark foliage, carrying the twin smile with her.

Thus was the understanding revealed to me between this lissom and dainty gypsy, who was like no one at all, and Farfadet, conspicuous among us all—slender, pliant and sensitive as lilac. Evidently—!

Lamuse saw nothing, blinded and borne down as he was by the load he had taken from Farfadet and me, occupied in the poise of them, and in finding where his laden and leaden feet might tread.

But he looks unhappy; he groans. A weighty and mournful obsession is stifling him. In his harsh breathing it seems to me that I can hear his heart beating and muttering. Looking at Volpatte, hooded in bandages, and then at the strong man, muscular and full-blooded, with that profound and eternal yearning whose sharpness he alone can gauge, I say to myself that the worst wounded man is not he whom we think.

We go down at last to the village. "Let's have a drink," says Fouillade. "I'm going to be sent back," says Volpatte. Lamuse puffs and groans.

Our comrades shout and come running, and we gather in the little square where the church stands with its twin towers—so thoroughly mutilated by a shell that one can no longer look it in the face.

Sanctuary

THE dim road which rises through the middle of the night-bound wood is so strangely full of obstructing shadows that the deep darkness of the forest itself might by some magic have overflowed upon it. It is the regiment on the march, in quest of a new home.

The weighty ranks of the shadows, burdened both high and broad, hustle each other blindly. Each wave, pushed by the following, stumbles upon the one in front, while alongside and detached are the evolutions of those less bulky ghosts, the N.C.O.'s. A clamor of confusion, compound of exclamations, of scraps of chat, of words of command, of spasms of coughing and of song, goes up from the dense mob enclosed between the banks. To the vocal commotion is added the tramping of feet, the jingling of bayonets in their scabbards, of cans and drinking-cups, the rumbling and hammering of the sixty vehicles of the two convoys—fighting and regimental—that follow the two battalions. And such a thing is it that trudges and spreads itself over the climbing road that, in spite of the unbounded dome of night, one welters in the odor of a den of lions.

In the ranks one sees nothing. Sometimes, when one can lift his nose up, by grace of an eddy in the tide, one cannot help seeing the whiteness of a mess-tin, the blue steel of a helmet, the black steel of a rifle. Anon, by the dazzling jet of sparks that flies from a pocket flint-and-steel, or the red flame that expands upon the lilliputian stem of a match, one can see beyond the vivid near relief of hands and faces to the silhouetted and disordered groups of helmeted shoulders, swaying like surges that would storm the sable stronghold of the night. Then, all goes out, and while each tramping soldier's legs swing to and fro, his eye is fixed inflexibly upon the conjectural situation of the back that dwells in front of him.

After several halts, when we have allowed ourselves to collapse on our haversacks at the foot of the stacked rifles—stacks that form on the call of the whistle with feverish haste and exasperating delay, through our blindness in that atmosphere of ink-dawn reveals itself, extends, and acquires the domain of Space. The walls of the Shadow crumble in vague ruin. Once more we pass under the grand panorama of the day's unfolding upon the ever-wandering horde that we are.

We emerge at last from this night of marching, across concentric circles as it seems, of darkness less dark, then of half-shadow, then of gloomy light. Legs have a wooden stiffness, backs are benumbed, shoulders bruised. Faces are still so gray or so black, one would say they had but half rid themselves of the night. Now, indeed, one never throws it off altogether.

It is into new quarters that the great company is going—this time to rest. What will the place be like that we have to live in for eight days? It is called, they say—but nobody is certain of anything—Gauchin-l'Abbe. We have heard wonders about it—"It appears to be just it."

In the ranks of the companies whose forms and features one begins to make out in the birth of morning, and to distinguish the lowered heads and yawning mouths, some voices are heard in still higher praise. "There never were such quarters. The Brigade's there, and the court-martial. You can get anything in the shops."—"If the Brigade's there, we're all right."—

"Think we can find a table for the squad?"—"Everything you want, I tell you."

A pessimist prophet shakes his head: "What these quarters'll be like where we ye never been, I don't know," he says. "What I do know is that it'll be like the others."

But we don't believe him, and emerging from the fevered turmoil of the night, it seems to all that it is a sort of Promised Land we are approaching by degrees the light brings us out of the east and the icy air towards the unknown village.

At the foot of a bill in the half-light, we reach some houses, still slumbering and wrapped in heavy grayness.

"There it is!"

Poof! We've done twenty-eight kilometers in the night. But what of that? There is no halt. We go past the houses, and they sink back again into their vague vapors and their mysterious shroud.

"Seems we've got to march a long time yet. It's always there, there, there!"

We march like machines, our limbs invaded by a sort of petrified torpor; our joints cry aloud, and force us to make echo.

Day comes slowly, for a blanket of mist covers the earth. It is so cold that the men dare not sit down during the halts, though overborne by weariness, and they pace to and fro in the damp obscurity like ghosts. The besom of a biting wintry wind whips our skin, sweeps away and scatters our words and our sighs.

At last the sun pierces the reek that spreads over us and soaks what it touches, and something like a fairy glade opens out in the midst of this gloom terrestrial. The regiment stretches itself and wakes up in truth, with slow-lifted faces to the gilded silver of the earliest rays. Quickly, then, the sun grows fiery, and now it is too hot. In the ranks we pant and sweat, and our grumbling is louder even than just now, when our teeth were chattering and the fog wet-sponged our hands and faces.

It is a chalk country through which we are passing on this torrid forenoon—"They mend this road with lime, the dirty devils!" The road has become blinding—a long-drawn cloud of dessicated chalk and dust that rises high above our columns and powders us as we go. Faces turn red, and shine as though varnished; some of the full-blooded ones might be plastered with vaseline. Cheeks and foreheads are coated with a rusty paste which agglutinates and cracks. Feet lose their dubious likeness to feet and might have paddled in a mason's mortar-trough. Haversacks and rifles are powdered in white, and our legion leaves to left and right a long milky track on the bordering grass. And to crown all—"To the right! A convoy!"

We bear to the right, hurriedly, and not without bumpings. The convoy of lorries, a long chain of foursquare and huge projectiles, rolling up with diabolical din, hurls itself along the road. Curse it! One after another, they gather up the thick carpet of white powder that upholsters the ground and send it broadcast over our shoulders! Now we are garbed in a stuff of light gray and our faces are pallid masks, thickest on the eyebrows and mustaches, on beards, and the cracks of wrinkles. Though still ourselves, we look like strange old men.

"When we're old buffers, we shall be as ugly as this," says Tirette.

"Tu craches blanc," declares Biquet.

When a halt puts us out of action, you might take us for rows of plaster statues, with some dirty indications of humanity showing through.

We move again, silent and chagrined. Every step becomes hard to complete. Our faces assume congealed and fixed grimaces under the wan leprosy of dust. The unending effort contracts us and quite fills us with dismal weariness and disgust.

We espy at last the long-sought oasis. Beyond a hill, on a still higher one, some slated roofs peep from clusters of foliage as brightly green as a salad. The village is there, and our looks embrace it, but we are not there yet. For a long time it seems to recede as fast as the regiment crawls towards it.

At long last, on the stroke of noon, we reach the quarters that had begun to appear a pretense and a legend. In regular step and with rifles on shoulders, the regiment floods the street of Gauchin-l'Abbe right to its edges. Most of the villages of the Pas du Calais are composed of a single street, but such a street! It is often several kilometers long. In this one, the street divides in front of the mairie and forms two others, so that the hamlet becomes a big Y, brokenly bordered by low-built dwellings.

The cyclists, the officers, the orderlies, break away from the long moving mass. Then, as they come up, a few of the men at a time are swallowed up by the barns, the still available houses being reserved for officers and departments. Our half-company is led at first to the end of the village, and then—by some misunderstanding among the quartermasters—back to the other end, the one by which we entered. This oscillation takes up time, and the squad, dragged thus from north to south and from south to north, heavily fatigued and irritated by wasted walking, evinces feverish impatience. For it is supremely important to be installed and set free as early as possible if we are to carry out the plan we have cherished so long—to find a native with some little place to let, and a table where the squad can have its meals. We have talked a good deal about this idea and its delightful advantages. We have taken counsel, subscribed to a common fund, and decided that this time we will take the header into the additional outlay.

But will it be possible? Very many places are already snapped up. We are not the only ones to bring our dream of comfort here, and it will be a race for that table. Three companies are coming in after ours, but four were here before us, and there are the officers, the cooks of the hospital staff for the Section, and the clerks, the drivers, the orderlies and others, official cooks of the sergeants' mess, and I don't know how many more. All these men are more influential than the soldiers of the line, they have more mobility and more money, and can bring off their schemes beforehand. Already, while we march four abreast towards the barn assigned to the squad, we see some of these jokers across the conquered thresholds, domestically busy.

Tirette imitates the sounds of lowing and bleating—"There's our cattle-shed." A fairly big barn. The chopped straw smells of night-soil, and our feet stir up clouds of dust. But it is almost enclosed. We choose our places and cast off our equipment.

Those who dreamed yet once again of a special sort of Paradise sing low—yet once again. "Look now, it seems as ugly as the other places."—"It's something like the same."—"Naturally."

But there is no time to waste in talking. The thing is to get clear and be after the others with all strength and speed. We hurry out. In spite of broken backs and aching feet, we set ourselves savagely to this last effort on which the comfort of a week depends.

The squad divides into two patrols and sets off at the double, one to left and one to right along the street, which is already obstructed by busy questing poilus; and all the groups see and watch each other—and hurry. In places there are collisions, jostlings, and abuse.

"Let's begin down there at once, or our goose'll be cooked!" I have an impression of a kind of fierce battle between all the soldiers, in the streets of the village they have just occupied. "For us," says Marthereau, "war is always struggling and fighting—always, always."

We knock at door after door, we show ourselves timidly, we offer ourselves like undesirable goods. A voice arises among us, "You haven't a bit of a corner, madame, for some soldiers? We would pay."

"No—you see, I've got officers—under-officers, that is—you see, it's the mess for the band, and the secretaries, and the gentlemen of the ambulance—"

Vexation after vexation. We close again, one after the other, all the doors we had half-opened, and look at each other, on the wrong side of the threshold, with dwindling hope in our eyes.

"Bon Dieu! You'll see that we shan't find anything," growls Barque. "Damn those chaps that got on the midden before us!"

The human flood reaches high-water mark everywhere. The three streets are all growing dark as each overflows into another. Some natives cross our path, old men or ill-shapen, contorted in their walk, stunted in the face; and even young people, too, over whom hovers the mystery of secret disorders or political connections. As for the petticoats, there are old women and many young ones—fat, with well-padded cheeks, and equal to geese in their whiteness.

Suddenly, in an alley between two houses, I have a fleeting vision of a woman who crossed the shadowy gap—Eudoxie! Eudoxie, the fairy woman whom Lamuse hunted like a satyr, away back in the country, that morning we brought back Volpatte wounded, and Fouillade, the woman I saw leaning from the spinney's edge and bound to Farfadet in a mutual smile. It is she whom I just glimpsed like a gleam of sunshine in that alley. But the gleam was eclipsed by the tail of a wall, and the place thereof relapsed upon gloom. She here, already! Then she has followed our long and painful trek! She is attracted—?

And she looks like one allured, too. Brief glimpse though it was of her face and its crown of fair hair, plainly I saw that she was serious, thoughtful, absentminded.

Lamuse, following close on my heels, saw nothing, and I do not tell him. He will discover quite soon enough the bright presence of that lovely flame where he would fain cast himself bodily, though it evades him like a Will-o'-th'-wisp. For the moment, besides, we are on business bent. The coveted corner must be won. We resume the hunt with the energy of despair. Barque leads us on; he has taken the matter to heart. He is trembling—you can see it in his dusty scalp. He guides us, nose to the wind. He suggests that we make an attempt on that yellow door over there. Forward!

Near the yellow door, we encounter a shape down-bent. Blaire, his foot on a milestone, is reducing the bulk of his boot with his knife, and plaster-like debris is falling fast. He might be engaged in sculpture.

"You never had your feet so white before," jeers Barque. "Rotting apart," says Blaire, "you don't know where it is, that special van?" He goes on to explain: "I've got to look up the dentist-van, so they can grapple with my ivories, and strip off the old grinders that's left. Oui, seems it's stationed here, the chop-caravan."

He folds up his knife, pockets it, and goes off alongside the wall, possessed by the thought of his jaw-bones' new lease of life.

Once more we put up our beggars' petition: "Good-day, madame; you haven't got a little corner where we could feed? We would pay, of course, we would pay—"

Through the glass of the low window we see lifted the face of an old man—like a fish in a bowl, it looks—a face curiously flat, and lined with parallel wrinkles, like a page of old manuscript.

"You've the little shed there."

"There's no room in the shed, and when the washing's done there—"

Barque seizes the chance. "It'll do very likely. May we see it?"

"We do the washing there," mutters the woman, continuing to wield her broom.

"You know," says Barque, with a smile and an engaging air, "we're not like those disagreeable people who get drunk and make themselves a nuisance. May we have a look?"

The woman has let her broom rest. She is thin and inconspicuous. Her jacket hangs from her shoulders as from a valise. Her face is like cardboard, stiff and without expression. She looks at us and hesitates, then grudgingly leads the way into a very dark little place, made of beaten earth and piled with dirty linen.

"It's splendid," cries Lamuse, in all honesty.

"Isn't she a darling, the little kiddie!" says Barque, as he pats the round cheek, like painted india-rubber, of a little girl who is staring at us with her dirty little nose uplifted in the gloom. "Is she yours, madame?"

"And that one, too?" risks Marthereau, as he espies an over-ripe infant on whose bladder-like cheeks are shining deposits of jam, for the ensnaring of the dust in the air. He offers a half-hearted caress in the direction of the moist and bedaubed countenance. The woman does not deign an answer.

So there we are, trifling and grinning, like beggars whose plea still hangs fire.

Lamuse whispers to me, in a torment of fear and cupidity, "Let's hope she'll catch on, the filthy old slut. It's grand here, and, you know, everything else is pinched!"

"There's no table," the woman says at last.

"Don't worry about the table," Barque exclaims. "Tenez! there, put away in that corner, the old door; that would make us a table."

"You're not going to trail me about and upset all my work!" replies the cardboard woman suspiciously, and with obvious regret that she had not chased us away immediately.

"Don't worry, I tell you. Look, I'll show you. Hey, Lamuse, old cock, give me a hand."

Under the displeased glances of the virago we place the old door on a couple of barrels.

"With a bit of a rub-down," says I, "that will be perfect."

"Eh, oui, maman, a flick with a brush'll do us instead of tablecloth."

The woman hardly knows what to say; she watches us spitefully: "There's only two stools, and how many are there of you?"

"About a dozen."

"A dozen. Jesus Maria!"

"What does it matter? That'll be all right, seeing there's a plank here—and that's a bench ready-made, eh, Lamuse?"

"Course," says Lamuse.

"I want that plank," says the woman. "Some soldiers that were here before you have tried already to take it away."

"But us, we're not thieves," suggests Lamuse gently, so as not to irritate the creature that has our comfort at her disposal.

"I don't say you are, but soldiers, vous savez, they smash everything up. Oh, the misery of this war!"

"Well then, how much'll it be, to hire the table, and to heat up a thing or two on the stove?"

"It'll be twenty sous a day," announces the hostess with restraint, as though we were wringing that amount from her.

"It's dear," says Lamuse.

"It's what the others gave me that were here, and they were very kind, too, those gentlemen, and it was worth my while to cook for them. I know it's not difficult for soldiers. If you think it's too much, it's no job to find other customers for this room and this table and the stove, and who wouldn't be in twelves. They're coming along all the time, and they'd pay still more, if I wanted. A dozen!—"

Lamuse hastens to add, "I said 'It's dear,' but still, it'll do, eh, you others?" On this downright question we record our votes.

"We could do well with a drop to drink," says Lamuse. "Do you sell wine?"

"No," said the woman, but added, shaking with anger, "You see, the military authority forces them that's got wine to sell it at fifteen sous! Fifteen sous! The misery of this cursed war! One loses at it, at fifteen sous, monsieur. So I don't sell any wine. I've got plenty for ourselves. I don't say but sometimes, and just to oblige, I don't allow some to people that one knows, people that knows what things are, but of course, messieurs, not at fifteen sous."

Lamuse is one of those people "that knows what things are." He grabs at his water-bottle, which is hanging as usual on his hip. "Give me a liter of it. That'll be what?"

"That'll be twenty-two sous, same as it cost me. But you know it's just to oblige you, because you're soldiers."

Barque, losing patience, mutters an aside. The woman throws him a surly glance, and makes as if to hand Lamuse's bottle back to him. But Lamuse, launched upon the hope of drinking wine at last, so that his cheeks redden as if the draught already pervaded them with its grateful hue, hastens to intervene—

"Don't be afraid—it's between ourselves, la mere, we won't give you away."

She raves on, rigid and bitter, against the limited price on wine; and, overcome by his lusty thirst, Lamuse extends the humiliation and surrender of conscience so far as to say, "No help for it, madame! It's a military order, so it's no use trying to understand it."

She leads us into the store-room. Three fat barrels occupy it in impressive rotundity. "Is this your little private store?"

"She knows her way about, the old lady," growls Barque.

The shrew turns on her heel, truculent: "Would you have me ruin myself by this miserable war? I've about enough of losing money all ways at once."

"How?" insists Barque.

"I can see you're not going to risk your money!"

"That's right—we only risk our skins."

We intervene, disturbed by the tone of menace for our present concern that the conversation has assumed. But the door of the wine-cellar is shaken, and a man's voice comes through. "Hey, Palmyra!" it calls.

The woman hobbles away, discreetly leaving the door open. "That's all right—we've taken root!" Lamuse says.

"What dirty devils these, people are!" murmurs Barque, who finds his reception hard to stomach.

"It's shameful and sickening," says Marthereau.

"One would think it was the first time you'd had any of it!"

"And you, old gabbler," chides Barque, "that says prettily to the wine-robber, 'Can't be helped, it's a military order'! Gad, old man, you're not short of cheek!"

"What else could I do or say? We should have had to go into mourning for our table and our wine. She could make us pay forty sous for the wine, and we should have had it all the same, shouldn't we? Very well, then, got to think ourselves jolly lucky. I'll admit I'd no confidence, and I was afraid it was no go."

"I know; it's the same tale everywhere and always, but all the same—"

"Damn the thieving natives, ah, oui! Some of 'em must be making fortunes. Everybody can't go and get killed."

"Ah, the gallant people of the East!"

"Yes, and the gallant people of the North!"

"Who welcome us with open arms!"

"With open hands, yes—"

"I tell you," Marthereau says again, "it's a shame and it's sickening."

"Shut it up—there's the she-beast coming back." We took a turn round to quarters to announce our success, and then went shopping. When we returned to our new dining-room, we were hustled by the preparations for lunch. Barque had been to the rations distribution, and had managed, thanks to personal relations with the cook (who was a conscientious objector to fractional divisions), to secure the potatoes and meat that formed the rations for all the fifteen men of the squad. He had bought some lard—a little lump for fourteen sous—and some one was frying. He had also acquired some green peas in tins, four tins. Mesnil Andre's tin of veal in jelly would be a hors-d'oeuvre.

"And not a dirty thing in all the lot!" said Lamuse, enchanted.

We inspected the kitchen. Barque was moving cheerfully about the iron Dutch oven whose hot and steaming bulk furnished all one side of the room.

"I've added a stewpan on the quiet for the soup," he whispered to me. Lifting the lid of the stove—"Fire isn't too hot. It's half an hour since I chucked the meat in, and the water's clean yet."

A minute later we heard some one arguing with the hostess. This extra stove was the matter in dispute. There was no more room left for her on her stove. They had told her they would only need a casserole, and she had believed them. If she had known they were going to make trouble she would not have let the room to them. Barque, the good fellow, replied jokingly, and succeeded in soothing the monster.

One by one the others arrived. They winked and rubbed their hands together, full of toothsome anticipation, like the guests at a wedding-breakfast. As they break away from the dazzling light outside and penetrate this cube of darkness, they are blinded, and stand like bewildered owls for several minutes.

"It's not too brilliant in here," says Mesnil Joseph. "Come, old chap, what do you want?" The others exclaim in chorus, "We're damned well off here." And I can see heads nodding assent in the cavern's twilight.

An incident: Farfadet having by accident rubbed against the damp and dirty wall, his shoulder has brought away from it a smudge so big and black that it can be seen even here. Farfadet, so careful of his appearance, growls, and in avoiding a second contact with the wall, knocks the table so that his spoon drops to the ground. Stooping, he fumbles among the loose earth, where dust and spiders' webs for years have silently fallen. When he recovers his spoon it is almost black, and webby threads hang from it. Evidently it is disastrous to let anything fall on the ground. One must live here with great care.

Lamuse brings down his fat hand, like a pork-pie, between two of the places at table. "Allons, a table!" We fall to. The meal is abundant and of excellent quality. The sound of conversation mingles with those of emptying bottles and filling jaws. While we taste the joy of eating at a table, a glimmer of light trickles through a vent-hole, and wraps in dusty dawn a piece of the atmosphere and a patch of the table, while its reflex lights up a plate, a cap's peak, an eye. Secretly I take stock of this gloomy little celebration that overflows with gayety. Biquet is telling about his suppliant sorrows in quest of a washerwoman who would agree to do him the good turn of washing some linen, but "it was too damned dear." Tulacque describes the queue outside the grocer's. One might not go in; customers were herded outside, like sheep. "And although you were outside, if you weren't satisfied, and groused too much, they chased you off."

Any news yet? It is said that severe penalties have been imposed on those who plunder the population, and there is already a list of convictions. Volpatte has been sent down. Men of Class '93 are going to be sent to the rear, and Pepere is one of them.

When Barque brings in the harvest of the fry-pan, he announces that our hostess has soldiers at her table—ambulance men of the machine-guns. "They thought they were the best off, but it's us that's that," says Fouillade with decision, lolling grandly in the darkness of the narrow and tainted hole where we are just as confusedly heaped together as in a dug-out. But who would think of making the comparison?

"Vous savez pas," says Pepin, "the chaps of the 9th, they're in clover! An old woman has taken them in for nothing, because of her old man that's been dead fifty years and was a rifleman once on a time. Seems she's even given them a rabbit for nix, and they're just worrying it jugged."

"There's good sorts everywhere. But the boys of the 9th had famous luck to fall into the only shop of good sorts in the whole village."

Palmyra comes with the coffee, which she supplies. She thaws a little, listens to us, and even asks questions in a supercilious way: "Why do you call the adjutant 'le juteux'?"

Barque replies sententiously, "'Twas ever thus."

When she has disappeared, we criticize our coffee. "Talk about clear! You can see the sugar ambling round the bottom of the glass."—"She charges six sous for it."—"It's filtered water."

The door half opens, and admits a streak of light. The face of a little boy is defined in it. We entice him in like a kitten and give him a bit of chocolate.

Then, "My name's Charlie," chirps the child. "Our house, that's close by. We've got soldiers, too. We always had them, we had. We sell them everything they want. Only, voila, sometimes they get drunk."

"Tell me, little one, come here a bit," says Cocon, taking the boy between his knees. "Listen now. Your papa, he says, doesn't he, 'Let's hope the war goes on,' eh?"

"Of course," says the child, tossing his head, "because we're getting rich. He says, by the end of May, we shall have got fifty thousand francs."

"Fifty thousand francs! Impossible!"

"Yes, yes!" the child insists, stamping, "he said it to mamma. Papa wished it could be always like that. Mamma, sometimes, she isn't sure, because my brother Adolphe is at the front. But we're going to get him sent to the rear, and then the war can go on."

These confidences are disturbed by sharp cries, coming from the rooms of our hosts. Biquet the mobile goes to inquire. "It's nothing," says he, coming back; "it's the good man slanging the woman because she doesn't know how to do things, he says, because she's made the mustard in a tumbler, and he never heard of such a thing, he says."

We get up, and leave the strong odor of pipes, wine, and stale coffee in our cave. As soon as we have crossed the threshold, a heaviness of heat puffs in our faces, fortified by the mustiness of frying that dwells in the kitchen and emerges every time the door is opened. We pass through legions of flies which, massed on the walls in black hordes, fly abroad in buzzing swarms as we pass: "It's beginning again like last year! Flies outside, lice inside.—"

"And microbes still farther inside!"

In a corner of this dirty little house and its litter of old rubbish, its dusty debris of last year and the relics of so many summers gone by, among the furniture and household gear, something is moving. It is an old simpleton with a long bald neck, pink and rough, making you think of a fowl's neck which has prematurely molted through disease. His profile is that of a hen, too—no chin and a long nose. A gray overlay of beard felts his receded cheek, and you see his heavy eyelids, rounded and horny, move up and down like shutters on the dull beads of his eyes.

Barque has already noticed him: "Watch him—he's a treasure-seeker. He says there's one somewhere in this hovel that he's stepfather to. You'll see him directly go on all-fours and push his old phizog in every corner there is. Tiens, watch him."

With the aid of his stick, the old man proceeded to take methodical soundings. He tapped along the foot of the walls and on the floor-tiles.. He was hustled by the coming and going of the occupants of the house, by callers, and by the swing of Palmyra's broom; but she let him alone and said nothing, thinking to herself, no doubt, that the exploitation of the national calamity is a more profitable treasure than problematical caskets.

Two gossips are standing in a recess and exchanging confidences in low voices, hard by an old map of Russia that is peopled with flies. "Oui, but it's with the Picon bitters that you've got to be careful. If you haven't got a light touch, you can't get your sixteen glasses out of a bottle, and so you lose too much profit. I don't say but what one's all right in one's purse, even so, but one doesn't make enough. To guard against that, the retailers ought to agree among themselves, but the understanding's so difficult to bring off, even when it's in the general interest."

Outside there is torrid sunshine, riddled with flies. The little beasts, quite scarce but a few days ago, multiply everywhere the murmur of their minute and innumerable engines. I go out in the company of Lamuse; we are going for a saunter. One can be at peace today—it is complete rest, by reason of the overnight march. We might sleep, but it suits us much better to use the rest for an extensive promenade. To-morrow, the exercise and fatigues will get us again. There are some, less lucky than we, who are already caught in the cogwheels of fatigue. To Lamuse, who invites him to come and stroll with us, Corvisart replies, screwing up the little round nose that is laid flatly on his oblong face like a cork, "Can't—I'm on manure!" He points to the shovel and broom by whose help he is performing his task of scavenger and night-soil man.

We walk languidly. The afternoon lies heavy on the drowsy land and on stomachs richly provided and embellished with food. The remarks we exchange are infrequent.

Over there, we hear noises. Barque has fallen a victim to a menagerie of housewives; and the scene is pointed by a pale little girl, her hair tied behind in a pencil of tow and her mouth embroidered with fever spots, and by women who are busy with some unsavory job of washing in the meager shade before their doors.

Six men go by, led by a quartermaster corporal. They carry heaps of new greatcoats and bundles of boots. Lamuse regards his bloated and horny feet—"I must have some new sheds, and no mistake; a bit more and you'll see my splay-feet through these ones. Can't go marching on the skin of my tongs, eh?"

An aeroplane booms overhead. We follow its evolutions with our faces skyward, our necks twisted, our eyes watering at the piercing brightness of the sky.

Lamuse declares to me, when we have brought our gaze back to earth, "Those machines'll never become practical, never."

"How can you say that? Look at the progress they've made already, and the speed of it."

"Yes, but they'll stop there. They'll never do any better, never."

This time I do not challenge the dull and obstinate denial that ignorance opposes to the promise of progress, and I let my big comrade alone in his stubborn belief that the wonderful effort of science and industry has been suddenly cut short.

Having thus begun to reveal to me his inmost thoughts, Lamuse continues. Coming nearer and lowering his head, he says to me, "You know she's here—Eudoxie?"

"Ah!" said I.

"Yes, old chap. You never notice anything, you don't, but I noticed," and Lamuse smiles at me indulgently. "Now, do you catch on? If she's come here, it's because we interest her, eh? She's followed us for one of us, and don't you forget it."

He gets going again. "My boy, d'you want to know what I say? She's come after me."

"Are you sure of it, old chap?"

"Yes," says the ox-man, in a hollow voice. "First, I want her. Then, twice, old man, I've found her exactly in my path, in mine, d'you understand? You may tell me that she ran away; that's because she's timid, that, yes—"

He stopped dead in the middle of the street and looked straight at me. The heavy face, greasily moist on the cheeks and nose, was serious. His rotund fist went up to the dark yellow mustache, so carefully pointed, and smoothed it tenderly. Then he continued to lay bare his heart to me "I want her; but, you know, I shall marry her all right, I shall. She's called Eudoxie Dumail. At first, I wasn't thinking of marrying her. But since I've got to know her family name, it seems to me that it's different, and I should get on all right. Ah, nom de Dieu! She's so pretty, that woman! And it's not only that she's pretty—ah!"

The huge child was overflowing with sentiment and emotion, and trying to make them speak to me. "Ah, my boy, there are times when I've just got to hold myself back with a hook," came the strained and gloomy tones, while the blood flushed to the fleshy parts of his cheeks and neck. "She's so beautiful, she's—and me I'm—she's so unlike—you'll have noticed it, surely, you that notices—she's a country girl, oui; eh bien, she's got a God knows what that's better than a Parisienne, even a toffed-up and stylish Parisienne, pas? She—as for me, I—"

He puckered his red eyebrows. He would have liked to tell me all the splendor of his thoughts, but he knew not the art of expressing himself, so he was silent. He remained alone in his voiceless emotion, as always alone.

We went forward side by side between the rows of houses. In front of the doors, drays laden with casks were drawn up. The front windows blossomed with many-hued heaps of jam-pots, stacks of tinder pipe-lighters—everything that the soldier is compelled to buy. Nearly all the natives had gone into grocery. Business had been getting out of gear locally for a long time, but now it was booming. Every one, smitten with the fever of sum-totals and dazzled by the multiplication table, plunged into trade.

Bells tolled, and the procession of a military funeral came out. A forage wagon, driven by a transport man, carried a coffin wrapped in a flag. Following, were a detachment of men, an adjutant, a padre, and a civilian.

"The poor little funeral with its tail lopped off!" said Lamuse. "Ah, those that are dead are very happy. But only sometimes, not always—voila!"

We have passed the last of the houses. In the country, beyond the end of the street, the fighting convoy and the regimental convoy have settled themselves, the traveling kitchens and jingling carts that follow them with odds and ends of equipment, the Red Cross wagons, the motor lorries, the forage carts, the baggage-master's gig. The tents of drivers and conductors swarm around the vehicles. On the open spaces horses lift their metallic eyes to the sky's emptiness, with their feet on barren earth. Four poilus are setting up a table. The open-air smithy is smoking. This heterogeneous and swarming city, planted in ruined fields whose straight or winding ruts are stiffening in the heat, is already broadly valanced with rubbish and dung.

On the edge of the camp a big, white-painted van stands out from the others in its tidy cleanliness. Had it been in the middle of a fair, one would have said it was the stylish show where one pays more than at the others.

This is the celebrated "stomatological" van that Blaire was asking about. In point of fact, Blaire is there in front, looking at it. For some long time, no doubt, he has been going round it and gazing. Field-hospital orderly Sambremeuse, of the Division, returning from errands, is climbing the portable stair of painted wood which leads to the van door. In his arms he carries a bulky box of biscuits, a loaf of fancy bread, and a bottle of champagne. Blaire questions him—"Tell me, Sir Rump, this horse-box—is it the dentist's?"

"It's written up there," replies Sambremeuse—a little corpulent man, clean, close-shaven, and his chin starch-white. "If you can't see it, you don't want the dentist to look after your grinders, you want the vet to clean your eyesight."

Blaire comes nearer and scrutinizes the establishment. "It's a queer shop," he says. He goes nearer yet, draws back, hesitates to risk his gums in that carriage. At last he decides, puts a foot on the stair, and disappears inside the caravan.

We continue our walk, and turn into a footpath where are high, dusty bushes and the noises are subdued. The sunshine blazes everywhere; it heats and roasts the hollow of the way, spreading blinding and burning whiteness in patches, and shimmers in the sky of faultless blue.

At the first turning, almost before we had heard the light grating of a footstep, we are face to face with Eudoxie!

Lamuse utters a deep exclamation. Perhaps he fancies once more that she is looking for him, and believes that she is the gift of his destiny. He goes up to her—all the bulk of him.

She looks at him and stops, framed by the hawthorn. Her strangely slight and pale face is apprehensive, the lids tremble on her magnificent

eyes. She is bareheaded, and in the hollowed neck of her linen corsage
there is the dawning of her flesh. So near, she is truly enticing in the
sunshine, this woman crowned with gold, and one's glance is impelled and
astonished by the moon-like purity of her skin. Her eyes sparkle; her teeth,
too, glisten white in the living wound of her half-open mouth, red as her
heart.

"Tell me—I am going to tell you," pants Lamuse. "I like you so
much—" He outstretches his arm towards the motionless, beloved
wayfarer.

She starts, and replies to him, "Leave me alone—you disgust me!"

The man's hand is thrown over one of her little ones. She tries to draw
it back, and shakes it to free herself. Her intensely fair hair falls loose,
flaming. He draws her to him. His head bends towards her, and his lips are
ready. His desire—the wish of all his strength and all his life—is to caress
her. He would die that he might touch her with his lips. But she struggles,
and utters a choking cry. She is trembling, and her beautiful face is
disfigured with abhorrence.

I go up and put my hand on my friend's shoulder, but my intervention is
not needed. Lamuse recoils and growls, vanquished.

"Are you taken that way often?" cries Eudoxie.

"No!" groans the miserable man, baffled, overwhelmed, bewildered.

"Don't do it again, vous savez!" she says, and goes off panting, and he
does not even watch her go. He stands with his arms hanging, gazing at
the place whence she has gone, tormented to the quick, torn from his
dreams of her, and nothing left him to desire.

I lead him away and he comes in dumb agitation, sniffling and out of
breath, as though he had run a long way. The mass of his big head is bent.
In the pitiless light of eternal spring, he is like the poor Cyclops who
roamed the shores of ancient Sicily in the beginnings of time—like a huge
toy, a thing of derision, that a child's shining strength could subdue.

The itinerant wine-seller, whose barrow is hunchbacked with a barrel,
has sold several liters to the men on guard duty. He disappears round the
bend in the road, with his face flat and yellow as a Camembert, his scanty,
thin hair frayed into dusty flakes, and so emaciated himself that one could
fancy his feet were fastened to his trunk by strings through his flopping
trousers.

And among the idle poilus of the guard-room at the end of the place,
under the wing of the shaking and rattling signboard which serves as

advertisement of the village, a conversation is set up on the subject of this wandering buffoon.

"He has a dirty neb," says Bigornot; "and I'll tell you what I think—they've no business to let civvies mess about at the front with their pretty ringlets, and especially individuals that you don't know where they come from."

"You're quite crushing, you portable louse," replies Cornet.

"Never mind, shoe-sole face," Bigornot insists; "we trust 'em too much. I know what I'm saying when I open it."

"You don't," says Canard. "Pepere's going to the rear."

"The women here," murmurs La Mollette, "they're ugly; they're a lot of frights."

The other men on guard, their concentrated gaze roaming in space, watch two enemy aeroplanes and the intricate skeins they are spinning. Around the stiff mechanical birds up there that appear now black like crows and now white like gulls, according to the play of the light, clouds of bursting shrapnel stipple the azure, and seem like a long flight of snowflakes in the sunshine.

As we are going back, two strollers come up—Carassus and Cheyssier. They announce that mess-man Pepere is going to the rear, to be sent to a Territorial regiment, having come under the operation of the Dalbiez Act.

"That's a hint for Blaire," says Carassus, who has a funny big nose in the middle of his face that suits him ill.

In the village groups of poilus go by, or in twos, joined by the crossing bonds of converse. We see the solitary ones unite in couples, separate, then come together again with a new inspiration of talk, drawn to each other as if magnetized.

In the middle of an excited crowd white papers are waving. It is the newspaper hawker, who is selling for two sous papers which should be one sou. Fouillade is standing in the middle of the road, thin as the legs of a hare. At the corner of a house Paradis shows to the sun face pink as ham.

Biquet joins us again, in undress, with a jacket and cap of the police. He is licking his chops: "I met some pals and we've had a drink. You see, to-morrow one starts scratching again, and cleaning his old rags and his catapult. But my greatcoat!—going to be some job to filter that! It isn't a greatcoat any longer—it's armor-plate."

Montreuil, a clerk at the office, appears and hails Biquet: "Hey, riff-raff! A letter! Been chasing you an hour. You're never to be found, rotter!"

"Can't be both here and there, looney. Give us a squint." He examines the letter, balances it in his hand, and announces as he tears the envelope, "It's from the old woman."

We slacken our pace. As he reads, he follows the lines with his finger, wagging his head with an air of conviction, and his lips moving like a woman's in prayer.

The throng increases the nearer we draw to the middle of the village. We salute the commandant and the black-skirted padre who walks by the other's side like his nurse. We are questioned by Pigeon, Guenon, young Escutenaire, and Chasseur Clodore. Lamuse appears blind and deaf, and concerned only to walk.

Bizouarne, Chanrion, and Roquette arrive excitedly to announce big news—"D'you know, Pepere's going to the rear."

"Funny," says Biquet, raising his nose from his letter, "how people kid themselves. The old woman's bothered about me!" He shows me a passage in the maternal epistle: "'When you get my letter,'" he spells out, "'no doubt you will be in the cold and mud, deprived of everything, mon pauvre Eugene'" He laughs: "It's ten days since she put that down for me, and she's clean off it. We're not cold, 'cos it's been fine since this morning; and we're not miserable, because we've got a room that's good enough. We've had hard times, but we're all right now."

As we reach the kennel in which we are lodgers, we are thinking that sentence over. Its touching simplicity affects me, shows me a soul—a host of souls. Because the sun has shown himself, because we have felt a gleam and a similitude of comfort, suffering exists no longer, either of the past or the terrible future. "We're all right now." There is no more to say.

Biquet establishes himself at the table, like a gentleman, to write a reply. Carefully he lays abroad his pen ink, and paper, and examines each, then smilingly traces the strictly regular lines of his big handwriting across the meager page.

"You'd laugh," he says, "if you knew what I've written to the old woman." He reads his letter again, fondles it, and smiles to himself.

Habits

WE are enthroned in the back yard. The big hen, white as a cream cheese, is brooding in the depths of a basket near the coop whose imprisoned occupant is rummaging about. But the black hen is free to travel. She erects and withdraws her elastic neck in jerks, and advances with a large and affected gait. One can just see her profile and its twinkling spangle, and her talk appears to proceed from a metal spring. She marches, glistening black and glossy like the love-locks of a gypsy; and as she marches, she unfolds here and there upon the ground a faint trail of chickens.

These trifling little yellow balls, kept always by a whispering instinct on the ebb-tide to safety, hurry along under the maternal march in short, sharp jerks, pecking as they go. Now the train comes to a full stop, for two of the chickens are thoughtful and immobile, careless of the parental clucking.

"A bad sign," says Paradis; "the hen that reflects is ill." And Paradis uncrosses and recrosses his legs. Beside him on the bench, Blaire extends his own, lets loose a great yawn that he maintains in placid duration, and sets himself again to observe, for of all of us he most delights in watching fowls during the brief life when they are in such a hurry to eat.

And we watch them in unison, not forgetting the shabby old cock, worn threadbare. Where his feathers have fallen appears the naked india-rubber leg, lurid as a grilled cutlet. He approaches the white sitter, which first turns her head away in tart denial, with several "No's" in a muffled rattle, and then watches him with the little blue enamel dials of her eyes.

"We're all right," says Barque.

"Watch the little ducks," says Blaire, "going along the communication trench."

We watch a single file of all-golden ducklings go past—still almost eggs on feet—their big heads pulling their little lame bodies along by the string of their necks, and that quickly. From his corner, the big dog follows them also with his deeply dark eye, on which the slanting sun has shaped a fine tawny ring.

Beyond this rustic yard and over the scalloping of the low wall, the orchard reveals itself, where a green carpet, moist and thick, covers the rich soil and is topped by a screen of foliage with a garniture of blossom, some white as statuary, others pied and glossy as knots in neckties. Beyond again is the meadow, where the shadowed poplars throw shafts of dark or golden green. Still farther again is a square patch of upstanding hops, followed by a patch of cabbages, sitting on the ground and dressed in line. In the sunshine of air and of earth we hear the bees, as they work and make music (in deference to the poets), and the cricket which, in defiance of the fable, sings with no humility and fills Space by himself.

Over yonder, there falls eddying from a poplar's peak a magpie—half white, half black, like a shred of partly-burned paper.

The soldiers outstretch themselves luxuriously on the stone bench, their eyes half closed, and bask in the sunshine that warms the basin of the big yard till it is like a bath.

"That's seventeen days we've been here! After thinking we were going away day after day!"

"One never knows," said Paradis, wagging his head and smacking his lips.

Through the yard gate that opens on to the road we see a group of poilus strolling, nose in air, devouring the sunshine; and then, all alone, Tellurure. In the middle of the street he oscillates the prosperous abdomen of which he is proprietor, and rocking on legs arched like basket-handles, he expectorates in wide abundance all around him.

"We thought, too, that we should be as badly off here as in the other quarters. But this time it's real rest, both in the time it lasts and the kind it is."

"You're not given too many exercises and fatigues."

"And between whiles you come in here to loll about."

The old man huddled up at the end of the seat—no other than the treasure-seeking grandfather whom we saw the day of our arrival—came nearer and lifted his finger. "When I was a young man, I was thought a lot of by women," he asserted, shaking his head. "I have led young ladies astray!"

"Ah!" said we, heedless, our attention taken away from his senile prattle by the timely noise of a cart that was passing, laden and laboring.

"Nowadays," the old man went on, "I only think about money."

"Ah, oui, the treasure you're looking for, papa."

"That's it," said the old rustic, though he felt the skepticism around him. He tapped his cranium with his forefinger, which he then extended towards the house. "Take that insect there," he said, indicating a little beast that ran along the plaster. "What does it say? It says, 'I am the spider that spins the Virgin's thread.'" And the archaic simpleton added, "One must never judge what people do, for one can never tell what may happen."

"That's true," replied Paradis politely. "He's funny," said Mesnil Andre, between his teeth, while he sought the mirror in his pocket to look at the facial benefit of fine weather. "He's crazy," murmured Barque in his ecstasy.

"I leave you," said the old man, yielding in annoyance.

He got up to go and look for his treasure again, entered the house that supported our backs, and left the door open, where beside the huge fireplace in the room we saw a little girl, so seriously playing with a doll that Blaire fell considering, and said, "She's right."

The games of children are a momentous preoccupation. Only the grown-ups play.

After we have watched the animals and the strollers go by, we watch the time go by, we watch everything.

We are seeing the life of things, we are present with Nature, blended with climates, mingled even with the sky, colored by the seasons. We have attached ourselves to this corner of the land where chance has held us back from our endless wanderings in longer and deeper peace than elsewhere; and this closer intercourse makes us sensible of all its traits and habits. September—the morrow of August and eve of October, most affecting of months—is already sprinkling the fine days with subtle warnings. Already one knows the meaning of the dead leaves that flit about the flat stones like a flock of sparrows.

In truth we have got used to each other's company, we and this place. So often transplanted, we are taking root here, and we no longer actually think of going away, even when we talk about it.

"The 11th Division jolly well stayed a month and a half resting," says Blaire.

"And the 375th, too, nine weeks!" replies Barque, in a tone of challenge.

"I think we shall stay here at least as long—at least, I say."

"We could finish the war here all right."

Barque is affected by the words, nor very far from believing them. "After all, it will finish some day, what!"

"After all!" repeat the others.

"To be sure, one never knows," says Paradis. He says this weakly, without deep conviction. It is, however, a saying which leaves no room for reply. We say it over again, softly, lulling ourselves with it as with an old song.

Farfadet rejoined us a moment ago. He took his place near us, but a little withdrawn all the same, and sits on an overturned tub, his chin on his fists.

This man is more solidly happy than we are. We know it well, and he knows it well. Lifting his head he has looked in turn, with the same distant gaze, at the back of the old man who went to seek his treasure, and at the group that talks of going away no more. There shines over our sensitive and sentimental comrade a sort of personal glamour, which makes of him a being apart, which gilds him and isolates him from us, in spite of himself, as though an officer's tabs had fallen on him from the sky.

His idyll with Eudoxie has continued here. We have had the proofs; and once, indeed, he spoke of it. She is not very far away, and they are very near to each other. Did I not see her the other evening, passing along the wall of the parsonage, her hair but half quenched by a mantilla, as she went obviously to a rendezvous? Did I not see that she began to hurry and to lean forward, already smiling? Although there is no more between them yet than promises and assurances, she is his, and he is the man who will hold her in his arms.

Then, too, he is going to leave us, called to the rear, to Brigade H.Q., where they want a weakling who can work a typewriter. It is official; it is in writing; he is saved. That gloomy future at which we others dare not look is definite and bright for him.

He looks at an open window and the dark gap behind it of some room or other over there, a shadowy room that bemuses him. His life is twofold in hope; he is happy, for the imminent happiness that does not yet exist is the only real happiness down here.

So a scanty spirit of envy grows around him. "One never knows," murmurs Paradis again, but with no more confidence than when before, in the straitened scene of our life to-day, he uttered those immeasurable words.

Entraining

THE next day, Barque began to address us, and said: "I'll just explain to you what it is. There are some i—"

A ferocious whistle cut his explanation off short, on the syllable. We were in a railway station, on a platform. A night alarm had torn us from our sleep in the village and we had marched here. The rest was over; our sector was being changed; they were throwing us somewhere else. We had disappeared from Gauchin under cover of darkness without seeing either the place or the people, without bidding them good-by even in a look, without bringing away a last impression.

A locomotive was shunting, near enough to elbow us, and screaming full-lunged. I saw Barque's mouth, stoppered by the clamor of our huge neighbor, pronounce an oath, and I saw the other faces grimacing in deafened impotence, faces helmeted and chin-strapped, for we were sentries in the station.

"After you!" yelled Barque furiously, addressing the white-plumed whistle. But the terrible mechanism continued more imperiously than ever to drive his words back in his throat. When it ceased, and only its echo rang in our ears, the thread of the discourse was broken for ever, and Barque contented himself with the brief conclusion, "Oui."

Then we looked around us. We were lost in a sort of town. Interminable strings of trucks, trains of forty to sixty carriages, were taking shape like rows of dark-fronted houses, low built, all alike, and divided by alleys. Before us, alongside the collection of moving houses, was the main line, the limitless street where the white rails disappeared at both ends, swallowed up in distance. Sections of trains and complete trains were staggering in great horizontal columns, leaving their places, then taking them again. On every side one heard the regular hammering on the armored ground, piercing whistles, the ringing of warning bells, the solid metallic crash of the colossal cubes telescoping their steel stumps, with the counter-blows of chains and the rattle of the long carcases' vertebrae. On the ground floor of the building that arises in the middle of the station like a town ball, the hurried bell of telegraph and telephone was at work, punctuated by vocal noises. All about on the dusty ground were the goods sheds, the low stores through whose doors one could dimly see the stacked interiors—the pointsmen's cabins, the bristling switches, the hydrants, the latticed iron posts whose wires ruled the sky like music-paper; here and there the signals, and rising naked over this flat and gloomy city, two steam cranes, like steeples.

Farther away, on waste ground and vacant sites in the environs of the labyrinth of platforms and buildings, military carts and lorries were standing idle, and rows of horses, drawn out farther than one could see.

"Talk about the job this is going to be!"—"A whole army corps beginning to entrain this evening!"—"Tiens, they're coming now!"

A cloud which overspread a noisy vibration of wheels and the rumble of horses' hoofs was coming near and getting bigger in the approach to the station formed by converging buildings.

"There are already some guns on board." On some flat trucks down there, between two long pyramidal dumps of chests, we saw indeed the outline of wheels, and some slender muzzles. Ammunition wagons, guns and wheels were streaked and blotched with yellow, brown, and green.

"They're camoufles. Down there, there are even horses painted. Look! spot that one, there, with the big feet as if he had trousers on. Well, he was white, and they've slapped some paint on to change his color."

The horse in question was standing apart from the others, which seemed to mistrust it, and displayed a grayish yellow tone, obviously with intent to deceive. "Poor devil!" said Tulacque.

"You see," said Paradis, "we not only take 'em to get killed, but mess them about first!"

"It's for their good, any way!"

"Eh oui, and us too, it's for our good!"

Towards evening soldiers arrived. From all sides they flowed towards the station. Deep-voiced non-coms. ran in front of the files. They were stemming the tide of men and massing them along the barriers or in railed squares—pretty well everywhere. The men piled their arms, dropped their knapsacks, and not being free to go out, waited, buried side by side in shadow.

The arrivals followed each other in volume that grew as the twilight deepened. Along with the troops, the motors flowed up, and soon there was an unbroken roar. Limousines glided through an enormous sea of lorries, little, middling, and big. All these cleared aside, wedged themselves in, subsided in their appointed places. A vast hum of voices and mingled noises arose from the ocean of men and vehicles that beat upon the approaches to the station and began in places to filter through.

"That's nothing yet," said Cocon, The Man of Figures. "At Army Corps Headquarters alone there are thirty officers' motors; and you don't know," he added, "how many trains of fifty trucks it takes to entrain all the Corpsmen and all the box of tricks—except, of course, the lorries, that'll join the new sector on their feet? Don't guess, flat-face. It takes ninety."

"Great Scott! And there are thirty-three Corps?"

"There are thirty-nine, lousy one!"

The turmoil increases; the station becomes still more populous. As far as the eye can make out a shape or the ghost of a shape, there is a hurly-burly of movement as lively as a panic. All the hierarchy of the non-coms. expand themselves and go into action, pass and repass like meteors, wave their bright-striped arms, and multiply the commands and counter-commands that are carried by the worming orderlies and cyclists, the former tardy, the latter maneuvering in quick dashes, like fish in water.

Here now is evening, definitely. The blots made by the uniforms of the poilus grouped about the hillocks of rifles become indistinct, and blend with the ground; and then their mass is betrayed only by the glow of pipes and cigarettes. In some places on the edge of the clusters, the little bright points festoon the gloom like illuminated streamers in a merry-making street.

Over this confused and heaving expanse an amalgam of voices rises like the sea breaking on the shore: and above this unending murmur, renewed commands, shouts, the din of a shot load or of one transferred, the crash of steam-hammers redoubling their dull endeavors, and the roaring of boilers.

In the immense obscurity, surcharged with men and with all things, lights begin everywhere to appear. These are the flash-lamps of officers and detachment leaders, and the cyclists' acetylene lamps, whose intensely white points zigzag hither and thither and reveal an outer zone of pallid resurrection.

An acetylene searchlight blazes blindingly out and depicts a dome of daylight. Other beams pierce and rend the universal gray.

Then does the station assume a fantastic air. Mysterious shapes spring up and adhere to the sky's dark blue. Mountains come into view, rough-modeled, and vast as the ruins of a town. One can see the beginning of unending rows of objects, finally plunged in night. One guesses what the great bulks may be whose outermost outlines flash forth from a black abyss of the unknown.

On our left, detachments of cavalry and infantry move ever forward like a ponderous flood. We hear the diffused obscurity of voices. We see some ranks delineated by a flash of phosphorescent light or a ruddy glimmering, and we listen to long-drawn trails of noise.

Up the gangways of the vans whose gray trunks and black mouths one sees by the dancing and smoking flame of torches, artillerymen are leading horses. There are appeals and shouts, a frantic trampling of conflict, and the angry kicking of some restive animal—insulted by its guide—against the panels of the van where he is cloistered.

Not far away, they are putting wagons on to railway trucks. Swarming humanity surrounds a hill of trusses of fodder. A scattered multitude furiously attacks great strata of bales.

"That's three hours we've been on our pins," sighs Paradis.

"And those, there, what are they?" In some snatches of light we see a group of goblins, surrounded by glowworms and carrying strange instruments, come out and then disappear.

"That's the searchlight section," says Cocon.

"You've got your considering cap on, camarade; what's it about?"

"There are four Divisions, at present, in an Army Corps," replies Cocon; "the number changes, sometimes it is three, sometimes five. Just now, it's four. And each of our Divisions," continues the mathematical one, whom our squad glories in owning, "includes three R.I.—regiments of infantry; two B.C.P.—battalions of chasseurs pied; one R.T.I.—regiment of territorial infantry—without counting the special regiments, Artillery, Engineers, Transport, etc., and not counting either Headquarters of the D.I. and the departments not brigaded but attached directly to the D.I. A regiment of the line of three battalions occupies four trains, one for H.Q., the machine-gun company, and the C.H.R. (compagnie hors rang, and one to each battalion. All the troops won't entrain here. They'll entrain in echelons along the line according to the position of the quarters and the period of reliefs."

"I'm tired," says Tulacque. "We don't get enough solids to eat, mark you. We stand up because it's the fashion, but we've no longer either force or freshness."

"I've been getting information," Cocon goes on; "the troops—the real troops—will only entrain as from midnight. They are still mustered here and there in the villages ten kilometers round about. All the departments of the Army Corps will first set off, and the E.N.E.—elements non endivisionnes," Cocon obligingly explains, "that is, attached directly to the A.C. Among the E.N.E. you won't see the Balloon Department nor the Squadron—they're too big goods, and they navigate on their own, with their staff and officers and hospitals. The chasseurs regiment is another of these E.N.E."

"There's no regiment of chasseurs," says Barque, thoughtlessly, "it's battalions. One says 'such and such a battalion of chasseurs.'"

We can see Cocon shrugging his shoulders in the shadows, and his glasses cast a scornful gleam. "Think so, duck-neb? Then I'll tell you, since you're so clever, there are two—foot chasseurs and horse chasseurs."

"Gad! I forgot the horsemen," says Barque.

"Only them!" Cocon said. "In the E.N.E. of the Army Corps, there's the Corps Artillery, that is to say, the central artillery that's additional to that of the divisions. It includes the H.A.—heavy artillery; the T.A.—trench artillery; the A.D.—artillery depot, the armored cars, the anti-aircraft batteries—do I know, or don't I? There's the Engineers; the Military Police—to wit, the service of cops on foot and slops on horseback; the Medical Department; the Veterinary ditto; a squadron of the Draught Corps; a Territorial regiment for the guards and fatigues at H.Q.—Headquarters; the Service de l'Intendance, and the supply column. There's also the drove of cattle, the Remount Depot, the Motor Department—talk about the swarm of soft jobs I could tell you about in an hour if I wanted to!—the Paymaster that controls the pay-offices and the Post, the Council of War, the Telegraphists, and all the electrical lot. All those have chiefs, commandants, sections and sub-sections, and they're rotten with clerks and orderlies of sorts, and all the bally box of tricks. You can see from here the sort of job the C.O. of a Corp's got!"

At this moment we were surrounded by a party of soldiers carrying boxes in addition to their equipment, and parcels tied up in paper that they bore reluctantly and anon placed on the ground, puffing.

"Those are the Staff secretaries. They are a part of the H.Q.—Headquarters—that is to say, a sort of General's suite. When they're flitting, they lug about their chests of records, their tables, their registers, and all the dirty oddments they need for their writing. Tiens! see that, there; it's a typewriter those two are carrying, the old papa and the little sausage, with a rifle threaded through the parcel. They're in three offices, and there's also the dispatch-riders' section, the Chancellerie, the A.C.T.S.—Army Corps Topographical Section—that distributes maps to the Divisions, and makes maps and plans from the aviators and the observers and the prisoners. It's the officers of all the departments who, under the orders of two colonels, form the Staff of the Army Corps. But the H.Q., properly so called, which also includes orderlies, cooks, storekeepers, workpeople, electricians, police, and the horsemen of the Escort, is bossed by a commandant."

At this moment we receive collectively a tremendous bump. "Hey, look out! Out of the way!" cries a man, by way of apology, who is being assisted by several others to push a cart towards the wagons. The work is hard, for the ground slopes up, and so soon as they cease to buttress themselves against the cart and adhere to the wheels, it slips back. The sullen men crush themselves against it in the depth of the gloom, grinding their teeth and growling, as though they fell upon some monster.

Barque, all the while rubbing his back, questions one of the frantic gang: "Think you're going to do it, old duckfoot?"

"Nom de Dieu!" roars he, engrossed in his job, "mind these setts! You're going to wreck the show!" With a sudden movement he jostles Barque again, and this time turns round on him: "What are you doing there, dung-guts, numskull?"

"Non, it can't be that you're drunk?" Barque retorts. "'What am I doing here?' It's good, that! Tell me, you lousy gang, wouldn't you like to do it too!"

"Out of the way!" cries a new voice, which precedes some men doubled up under burdens incongruous, but apparently overwhelming.

One can no longer remain anywhere. Everywhere we are in the way. We go forward, we scatter, we retire in the turmoil.

"In addition, I tell you," continues Cocon, tranquil as a scientist, "there are the Divisions, each organized pretty much like an Army Corps—"

"Oui, we know it; miss the deal!"

"He makes a fine to-do about it all, that mountebank in the horse-box on casters. What a mother-in-law he'd make!"

"I'll bet that's the Major's wrong-headed horse, the one that the vet said was a calf in process of becoming a cow."

"It's well organized, all the same, all that, no doubt about it," says Lamuse admiringly, forced back by a wave of artillerymen carrying boxes.

"That's true," Marthereau admits; "to get all this lot on the way, you've not got to be a lot of turnip-heads nor a lot of custards—Bon Dieu, look where you're putting your damned boots, you black-livered beast!"

"Talk about a flitting! When I went to live at Marcoussis with my family, there was less fuss than this. But then I'm not built that way myself."

We are silent; and then we hear Cocon saying, "For the whole French Army that holds the lines to go by—I'm not speaking of those who are fixed up at the rear, where there are twice as many men again, and services like the ambulance that cost nine million francs and can clear you seven thousand cases a day—to see them go by in trains of sixty coaches each, following each other without stopping, at intervals of a quarter of an hour, it would take forty days and forty nights."

"Ah!" they say. It is too much effort for their imagination; they lose interest and sicken of the magnitude of these figures. They yawn, and with watering eyes they follow, in the confusion of haste and shouts and smoke, of roars and gleams and flashes, the terrible line of the armored train that moves in the distance, with fire in the sky behind it.

On Leave

EUDORE sat down awhile, there by the roadside well, before taking the path over the fields that led to the trenches, his hands crossed over one knee, his pale face uplifted. He had no mustache under his nose—only a little flat smear over each corner of his mouth. He whistled, and then yawned in the face of the morning till the tears came.

An artilleryman who was quartered on the edge of the wood—over there where a line of horses and carts looked like a gypsies' bivouac—came up, with the well in his mind, and two canvas buckets that danced at the end of his arms in time with his feet. In front of the sleepy unarmed soldier with a bulging bag he stood fast.

"On leave?"

"Yes," said Eudore; "just back."

"Good for you," said the gunner as he made off.

"You've nothing to grumble at—with six days' leave in your water-bottle!"

And here, see, are four more men coming down the road, their gait heavy and slow, their boots turned into enormous caricatures of boots by reason of the mud. As one man they stopped on espying the profile of Eudore.

"There's Eudore! Hello, Eudore! hello, the old sport! You're back then!" they cried together, as they hurried up and offered him hands as big and ruddy as if they were hidden in woolen gloves.

"Morning, boys," said Eudore.

"Had a good time? What have you got to tell us, my boy?"

"Yes," replied Eudore, "not so bad."

"We've been on wine fatigue, and we've finished. Let's go back together, pas?"

In single file they went down the embankment of the road—arm in arm they crossed the field of gray mud, where their feet fell with the sound of dough being mixed in the kneading-trough.

"Well, you've seen your wife, your little Mariette—the only girl for you—that you could never open your jaw without telling us a tale about her, eh?"

Eudore's wan face winced.

"My wife? Yes, I saw her, sure enough, but only for a little while—there was no way of doing any better—but no luck, I admit, and that's all about it."

"How's that?"

"How? You know that we live at Villers-l'Abbaye, a hamlet of four houses neither more nor less, astraddle over the road. One of those houses is our cafe, and she runs it, or rather she is running it again since they gave up shelling the village.

"Now then, with my leave coming along, she asked for a permit to Mont-St-Eloi, where my old folks are, and my permit was for Mont-St-Eloi too. See the move?

"Being a little woman with a head-piece, you know, she had applied for her permit long before the date when my leave was expected. All the same, my leave came before her permit. Spite o' that I set off—for one doesn't let his turn in the company go by, eh? So I stayed with the old people, and waited. I like 'em well enough, but I got down in the mouth all the same. As for them, it was enough that they could see me, and it worried them that I was bored by their company-how else could it be? At the end of the sixth day—at the finish of my leave, and the very evening before returning—a young man on a bicycle, son of the Florence family, brings me a letter from Mariette to say that her permit had not yet come—"

"Ah, rotten luck," cried the audience.

"And that," continued Eudore, "there was only one thing to do.—I was to get leave from the mayor of Mont-St-Eloi, who would get it from the military, and go myself at full speed to see her at Villers."

"You should have done that the first day, not the sixth!"

"So it seems, but I was afraid we should cross and me miss her—y'see, as soon as I landed, I was expecting her all the time, and every minute I fancied I could see her at the open door. So I did as she told me."

"After all, you saw her?"

"Just one day—or rather, just one night."

"Quite sufficient!" merrily said Lamuse, and Eudore the pale and serious shook his head under the shower of pointed and perilous jests that followed.

"Shut your great mouths for five minutes, chaps."

"Get on with it, petit."

"There isn't a great lot of it," said Eudore.

"Well, then, you were saying you had got a hump with your old people?"

"Ah, yes. They had tried their best to make up for Mariette—with lovely rashers of our own ham, and plum brandy, and patching up my linen, and all sorts of little spoiled-kid tricks—and I noticed they were still slanging each other in the old familiar way! But you talk about a difference! I always had my eye on the door to see if some time or other it wouldn't get a move on and turn into a woman. So I went and saw the mayor, and set off, yesterday, towards two in the afternoon—towards fourteen o'clock I might well say, seeing that I had been counting the hours since the day before! I had just one day of my leave left then.

"As we drew near in the dusk, through the carriage window of the little railway that still keeps going down there on some fag-ends of line, I recognized half the country, and the other half I didn't. Here and there I got the sense of it, all at once, and it came back all fresh to me, and melted away again, just as if it was talking to me. Then it shut up. In the end we got out, and I found—the limit, that was—that we had to pad the hoof to the last station.

"Never, old man, have I been in such weather. It had rained for six days. For six days the sky washed the earth and then washed it again. The earth was softening and shifting, and filling up the holes and making new ones."

"Same here—it only stopped raining this morning."

"It was just my luck. And everywhere there were swollen new streams, washing away the borders of the fields as though they were lines on paper. There were hills that ran with water from top to bottom. Gusts of wind sent the rain in great clouds flying and whirling about, and lashing our hands and faces and necks.

"So you bet, when I had tramped to the station, if some one had pulled a really ugly face at me, it would have been enough to make me turn back.

"But when we did get to the place, there were several of us—some more men on leave—they weren't bound for Villers, but they had to go through it to get somewhere else. So it happened that we got there in a lump—five old cronies that didn't know each other.

"I could make out nothing of anything. They've been worse shelled over there than here, and then there was the water everywhere, and it was getting dark.

"I told you there are only four houses in the little place, only they're a good bit off from each other. You come to the lower end of a slope. I didn't know too well where I was, no more than my pals did, though they belonged to the district and had some notion of the lay of it—and all the less because of the rain falling in bucketsful.

"It got so bad that we couldn't keep from hurrying and began to run. We passed by the farm of the Alleux—that's the first of the houses—and it looked like a sort of stone ghost. Bits of walls like splintered pillars standing up out of the water; the house was shipwrecked. The other farm, a little further, was as good as drowned dead.

"Our house is the third. It's on the edge of the road that runs along the top of the slope. We climbed up, facing the rain that beat on us in the dusk and began to blind us—the cold and wet fairly smacked us in the eye, flop!—and broke our ranks like machine-guns.

"The house! I ran like a greyhound—like an African attacking. Mariette! I could see her with her arms raised high in the doorway behind that fine curtain of night and rain—of rain so fierce that it drove her back and kept her shrinking between the doorposts like a statue of the Virgin in its niche. I just threw myself forward, but remembered to give my pals the sign to follow me. The house swallowed the lot of us. Mariette laughed a little to see me, with a tear in her eye. She waited till we were alone together and then laughed and cried all at once. I told the boys to make themselves at home and sit down, some on the chairs and the rest on the table.

"'Where are they going, ces messieurs?' asked Manette.

"'We are going to Vauvelles.'

"'Jesus!' she said, 'you'll never get there. You can't do those two miles and more in the night, with the roads washed away, and swamps everywhere. You mustn't even try to.'

"'Well, we'll go on to-morrow, then; only we must find somewhere to pass the night.'

"'I'll go with you,' I said, 'as far as the Pendu farm—they're not short of room in that shop. You'll snore in there all right, and you can start at daybreak.'

"'Right! let's get a move on so far.'

"We went out again. What a downpour! We were wet past bearing. The water poured into our socks through the boot-soles and by the trouser bottoms, and they too were soaked through and through up to the knees. Before we got to this Pendu, we meet a shadow in a big black cloak, with a lantern. The lantern is raised, and we see a gold stripe on the sleeve, and then an angry face.

"'What the hell are you doing there?' says the shadow, drawing back a little and putting one fist on his hip, while the rain rattled like hail on his hood.

"'They're men on leave for Vauvelles—they can't set off again to-night—they would like to sleep in the Pendu farm.'

"'What do you say? Sleep here?—This is the police station—I am the officer on guard and there are Boche prisoners in the buildings.' And I'll tell you what he said as well—'I must see you hop it from here in less than two seconds. Bonsoir.'

"So we right about face and started back again—stumbling as if we were boozed, slipping, puffing, splashing and bespattering ourselves. One of the boys cried to me through the wind and rain, 'We'll go back with you as far as your home, all the same. If we haven't a house we've time enough.'

"'Where will you sleep?'

"'Oh, we'll find somewhere, don't worry, for the little time we have to kill here.'

"'Yes, we'll find somewhere, all right,' I said. 'Come in again for a minute meanwhile—I won't take no—and Mariette sees us enter once more in single file, all five of us soaked like bread in soup.

"So there we all were, with only one little room to go round in and go round again—the only room in the house, seeing that it isn't a palace.

"'Tell me, madame,' says one of our friends, 'isn't there a cellar here?'

"'There's water in it,' says Mariette; 'you can't see the bottom step and it's only got two.'

"'Damn,' says the man, 'for I see there's no loft, either.'

"After a minute or two he gets up: 'Good-night, old pal,' he says to me, and they get their hats on.

"'What, are you going off in weather like this, boys?'

"'Do you think,' says the old sport, 'that we're going to spoil your stay with your wife?'

"'But, my good man—'

"'But me no buts. It's nine o'clock, and you've got to take your hook before day. So good-night. Coming, you others?'

"'Rather,' say the boys. 'Good-night all.'

"There they are at the door and opening it. Mariette and me, we look at each other—but we don't move. Once more we look at each other, and then we sprang at them. I grabbed the skirt of a coat and she a belt—all wet enough to wring out.

"'Never! We won't let you go—it can't be done.'

"'But—'

"'But me no buts,' I reply, while she locks the door."

"Then what?" asked Lamuse.

"Then? Nothing at all," replied Eudore. "We just stayed like that, very discreetly—all the night—sitting, propped up in the corners, yawning—like the watchers over a dead man. We made a bit of talk at first. From time to time some one said, 'Is it still raining?' and went and had a look, and said, 'It's still raining'—we could hear it, by the way. A big chap who had a mustache like a Bulgarian fought against sleeping like a wild man. Sometimes one or two among the crowd slept, but there was always one to yawn and keep an eye open for politeness, who stretched himself or half got up so that he could settle more comfortably.

"Mariette and me, we never slept. We looked at each other, but we looked at the others as well, and they looked at us, and there you are.

"Morning came and cleaned the window. I got up to go and look outside. The rain was hardly less. In the room I could see dark forms that began to stir and breathe hard. Mariette's eyes were red with looking at me all night. Between her and me a soldier was filling his pipe and shivering.

"Some one beats a tattoo on the window, and I half open it. A silhouette with a streaming hat appears, as though carried and driven there by the terrible force of the blast that came with it, and asks—

"'Hey, in the cafe there! Is there any coffee to be had?'

"'Coming, sir, coming,' cried Mariette.

"She gets up from her chair, a little benumbed. Without a word she looks at her self in our bit of a mirror, touches her hair lightly, and says quite simply, the good lass—

"'I am going to make coffee for everybody.'

"When that was drunk off, we had all of us to go. Besides, customers turned up every minute.

"'Hey, la p'tite mere,' they cried, shoving their noses in at the half-open window, 'let's have a coffee—or three—or four'—'and two more again,' says another voice.

"We go up to Mariette to say good-by. They knew they had played gooseberry that night most damnably, but I could see plainly that they didn't know if it would be the thing to say something about it or just let it drop altogether.

"Then the Bulgarian made up his mind: 'We've made a hell of a mess of it for you, eh, ma p'tite dame?'

"He said that to show he'd been well brought up, the old sport.

"Mariette thanks him and offers him her hand—'That's nothing at all, sir. I hope you'll enjoy your leave.'

"And me, I held her tight in my arms and kissed her as long as I could—half a minute—discontented—my God, there was reason to be—but glad that Mariette had not driven the boys out like dogs, and I felt sure she liked me too for not doing it.

"'But that isn't all,' said one of the leave men, lifting the skirt of his cape and fumbling in his coat pocket; 'that's not all. What do we owe you for the coffees?'

"'Nothing, for you stayed the night with me; you are my guests.'

"'Oh, madame, we can't have that!'

"And how they set to to make protests and compliments in front of each other! Old man, you can say what you like—we may be only poor devils, but it was astonishing, that little palaver of good manners.

"'Come along! Let's be hopping it, eh?'

"They go out one by one. I stay till the last. Just then another passer-by begins to knock on the window—another who was dying for a mouthful of coffee. Mariette by the open door leaned forward and cried, 'One second!'

"Then she put into my arms a parcel that she had ready. 'I had bought a knuckle of ham—it was for supper—for us—for us two—and a liter of good wine. But, ma foi! when I saw there were five of you, I didn't want to divide it out so much, and I want still less now. There's the ham, the bread, and the wine. I give them to you so that you can enjoy them by yourself, my boy. As for them, we have given them enough,' she says.

"Poor Mariette," sighs Eudore. "Fifteen months since I'd seen her. And when shall I see her again? Ever?—It was jolly, that idea of hers. She crammed all that stuff into my bag—"

He half opens his brown canvas pouch.

"Look, here they are! The ham here, and the bread, and there's the booze. Well, seeing it's there, you don't know what we're going to do with it? We're going to share it out between us, eh, old pals?"

The Anger of Volpatte

WHEN Volpatte arrived from his sick-leave, after two months' absence, we surrounded him. But he was sullen and silent, and tried to get away.

"Well, what about it? Volpatte, have you nothing to tell us?"

"Tell us all about the hospital and the sick-leave, old cock, from the day when you set off in your bandages, with your snout in parenthesis! You must have seen something of the official shops. Speak then, nome de Dieu!"

"I don't want to say anything at all about it," said Volpatte.

"What's that? What are you talking about?"

"I'm fed up—that's what I am! The people back there, I'm sick of them—they make me spew, and you can tell 'em so!"

"What have they done to you?"

"A lot of sods, they are!" says Volpatte.

There he was, with his head as of yore, his ears "stuck on again" and his Mongolian cheekbones—stubbornly set in the middle of the puzzled circle that besieged him; amid we felt that the mouth fast closed on ominous silence meant high pressure of seething exasperation in the depth of him.

Some words overflowed from him at last. He turned round—facing towards the rear and the bases—and shook his fist at infinite space. "There are too many of them," he said between his teeth, "there are too many!" He seemed to be threatening and repelling a rising sea of phantoms.

A little later, we questioned him again, knowing well that his anger could not thus be retained within, and that the savage silence would explode at the first chance.

It was in a deep communication trench, away back, where we had come together for a meal after a morning spent in digging. Torrential rain was falling. We were muddled and drenched and hustled by the flood, and we ate standing in single file, without shelter, under the dissolving sky. Only by feats of skill could we protect the bread and bully from the spouts that flowed from every point in space; and while we ate we put our hands and faces as much as possible under our cowls. The rain rattled and bounced and streamed on our limp woven armor, and worked with open brutality or sly secrecy into ourselves and our food. Our feet were sinking farther and farther, taking deep root in the stream that flowed along the clayey bottom of the trench. Some faces were laughing, though their mustaches dripped. Others grimaced at the spongy bread and flabby meat, or at the missiles which attacked their skin from all sides at every defect in their heavy and miry armor-plate.

Barque, who was hugging his mess-tin to his heart, bawled at Volpatte: "Well then, a lot of sods, you say, that you've seen down there where you've been?"

"For instance?" cried Blaire, while a redoubled squall shook and scattered his words; "what have you seen in the way of sods?"

"There are—" Volpatte began, "and then—there are too many of them, nom de Dieu! There are—"

He tried to say what was the matter with him, but could only repeat, "There are too many of them!" oppressed and panting. He swallowed a pulpy mouthful of bread as if there went with it the disordered and suffocating mass of his memories.

"Is it the shirkers you want to talk about?"

"By God!" He had thrown the rest of his beef over the parapet, and this cry, this gasp, escaped violently from his mouth as if from a valve.

"Don't worry about the soft-job brigade, old cross-patch," advised Barque, banteringly, but not without some bitterness. "What good does it do?"

Concealed and huddled up under the fragile and unsteady roof of his oiled hood, while the water poured down its shining slopes, and holding his empty mess-tin out for the rain to clean it, Volpatte snarled, "I'm not daft—not a bit of it—and I know very well there've got to be these individuals at the rear. Let them have their dead-heads for all I care—but there's too many of them, and they're all alike, and all rotters, voila!"

Relieved by this affirmation, which shed a little light on the gloomy farrago of fury he was loosing among us, Volpatte began to speak in fragments across the relentless sheets of rain—

"At the very first village they sent me to, I saw duds, and duds galore, and they began to get on my nerves. All sorts of departments and sub-departments and managements and centers and offices and committees—you're no sooner there than you meet swarms of fools, swarms of different services that are only different in name—enough to turn your brain. I tell you, the man that invented the names of all those committees, he was wrong in his head.

"So could I help but be sick of it? Ah, mon vieux," said our comrade, musing, "all those individuals fiddle-faddling and making believe down there, all spruced up with their fine caps and officers' coats and shameful boots, that gulp dainties and can put a dram of best brandy down their gullets whenever they want, and wash themselves oftener twice than once, and go to church, and never stop smoking, and pack themselves up in feathers at night to read the newspaper—and then they say afterwards, 'I've been in the war!'"

One point above all had got hold of Volpatte and emerged from his confused and impassioned vision: "All those soldiers, they haven't to run away with their table-tools and get a bite any old way—they've got to be at their ease—they'd rather go and sit themselves down with some tart in the district, at a special reserved table, and guzzle vegetables, and the fine lady puts their crockery out all square for them on the dining-table, and their pots of jam and every other blasted thing to eat; in short, the advantages of riches and peace in that doubly-damned hell they call the Rear!"

Volpatte's neighbor shook his head under the torrents that fell from heaven and said, "So much the better for them."

"I'm not crazy—" Volpatte began again.

"P'raps, but you're not fair."

Volpatte felt himself insulted by the word. He started, and raised his head furiously, and the rain, that was waiting for the chance, took him plump in the face. "Not fair—me? Not fair—to those dung-hills?"

"Exactly, monsieur," the neighbor replied; "I tell you that you play hell with them and yet you'd jolly well like to be in the rotters' place."

"Very likely—but what does that prove, rump-face? To begin with, we, we've been in danger, and it ought to be our turn for the other. But they're always the same, I tell you; and then there's young men there, strong as bulls and poised like wrestlers, and then—there are too many of them! D'you hear? It's always too many, I say, because it is so."

"Too many? What do you know about it, vilain? These departments and committees, do you know what they are?"

"I don't know what they are," Volpatte set off again, "but I know—"

"Don't you think they need a crowd to keep all the army's affairs going?"

"I don't care a damn, but—"

"But you wish it was you, eh?" chaffed the invisible neighbor, who concealed in the depth of the hood on which the reservoirs of space were emptying either a supreme indifference or a cruel desire to take a rise out of Volpatte.

"I can't help it," said the other, simply.

"There's those that can help it for you," interposed the shrill voice of Barque; "I knew one of 'em—"

"I, too, I've seen 'em!" Volpatte yelled with a desperate effort through the storm. "Tiens! not far from the front, don't know where exactly, where there's an ambulance clearing-station and a sous-intendance—I met the reptile there."

The wind, as it passed over us, tossed him the question, "What was it?"

At that moment there was a lull, and the weather allowed Volpatte to talk after a fashion. He said: "He took me round all the jumble of the depot as if it was a fair, although he was one of the sights of the place. He led me along the passages and into the dining-rooms of houses and supplementary barracks. He half opened doors with labels on them, and said, 'Look here, and here too—look!' I went inspecting with him, but he didn't go back, like I did, to the trenches, don't fret yourself, and he wasn't coming back from them either, don't worry! The reptile, the first time I saw him he was walking nice and leisurely in the yard—'I'm in the Expenses Department,' he says. We talked a bit, and the next day he got an orderly job so as to dodge getting sent away, seeing it was his turn to go since the beginning of the war.

"On the step of the door where he'd laid all night on a feather bed, he was polishing the pumps of his monkey master—beautiful yellow pumps—rubbing 'em with paste, fairly glazing 'em, my boy. I stopped to watch him, and the chap told me all about himself. Mon vieux, I don't remember much more of the stuffing that came out of his crafty skull than I remember of the History of France and the dates we whined at school.

Never, I tell you, bad be been sent to the front, although he was Class
1903, and a lusty devil at that, he was. Danger and dog-tiredness and all
the ugliness of war—not for him, but for the others, oui. He knew damned
well that if he set foot in the firing-line, the line would see that the beast
got it, so he ran like hell from it, and stopped where he was. He said
they'd tried all ways to get him, but he'd given the slip to all the captains,
all the colonels, all the majors, and they were all damnably mad with him.
He told me about it. How did he work it? He'd sit down all of a sudden,
put on a stupid look, do the scrim-shanker stunt, and flop like a bundle of
dirty linen. 'I've got a sort of general fatigue,' he'd blubber. They didn't
know how to take him, and after a bit they just let him drop—everybody
was fit to spew on him. And he changed his tricks according to the
circumstances, d'you catch on? Sometimes he had something wrong with
his foot—he was damned clever with his feet. And then he contrived
things, and he knew one head from another, and how to take his
opportunities. He knew what's what, he did. You could see him go and
slip in like a pretty poilu among the depot chaps, where the soft jobs were,
and stay there; and then he'd put himself out no end to be useful to the
pals. He'd get up at three o'clock in the morning to make the juice, go and
fetch the water while the others were getting their grub. At last, he'd
wormed himself in everywhere, he came to be one of the family, the rotter,
the carrion. He did it so he wouldn't have to do it. He seemed to me like
an individual that would have earned five quid honestly with the same
work and bother that he puts into forging a one-pound note. But there,
he'll get his skin out of it all right, he will. At the front he'd be lost sight
of in the throng of it, but he's not so stupid. Be damned to them, he says,
that take their grub on the ground, and be damned to them still more when
they're under it. When we've all done with fighting, he'll go back home
and he'll say to his friends and neighbors, 'Here I am safe and sound,' and
his pals'll be glad, because be's a good sort, with engaging manners,
contemptible creature that he is, and—and this is the most stupid thing of
all—but he takes you in and you swallow him whole, the son of a bug.

"And then, those sort of beings, don't you believe there's only one of
them. There are barrels of 'em in every depot, that hang on and writhe
when their time comes to go, and they say, 'I'm not going,' and they don't
go, and they never succeed in driving them as far as the front."

"Nothing new in all that," said Barque, "we know it, we know it!"

"Then there are the offices," Volpatte went on, engrossed in his story of travel; "whole houses and streets and districts. I saw that my little corner in the rear was only a speck, and I had full view of them. Non, I'd never have believed there'd be so many men on chairs while war was going on—"

A hand protruded from the rank and made trial of space—"No more sauce falling"—"Then we're going out, bet your life on it." So "March!" was the cry.

The storm held its peace. We filed off in the long narrow swamp stagnating in the bottom of the trench where the moment before it had shaken under slabs of rain. Volpatte's grumbling began again amidst our sorry stroll and the eddies of floundering feet. I listened to him as I watched the shoulders of a poverty-stricken overcoat swaying in front of me, drenched through and through. This time Volpatte was on the track of the police—

"The farther you go from the front the more you see of them."

"Their battlefield is not the same as ours."

Tulacque had an ancient grudge against them. "Look," he said, "how the bobbies spread themselves about to get good lodgings and good food, and then, after the drinking regulations, they dropped on the secret wine-sellers. You saw them lying in wait, with a corner of an eye on the shop-doors, to see if there weren't any poilus slipping quietly out, two-faced that they are, leering to left and to right and licking their mustaches."

"There are good ones among 'em. I knew one in my country, the Cote d'Or, where I—"

"Shut up!" was Tulacque's peremptory interruption; "they're all alike. There isn't one that can put another right."

"Yes, they're lucky," said Volpatte, "but do you think they're contented? Not a bit; they grouse. At least," he corrected himself, "there was one I met, and he was a grouser. He was devilish bothered by the drill-manual. 'It isn't worth while to learn the drill instruction,' he said, 'they're always changing it. F'r instance, take the department of military police; well, as soon as you've got the gist of it, it's something else. Ah, when will this war be over?' he says."

"They do what they're told to do, those chaps," ventured Eudore.

"Surely. It isn't their fault at all. It doesn't alter the fact that these professional soldiers, pensioned and decorated in the time when we're only civvies, will have made war in a damned funny way."

"That reminds me of a forester that I saw as well," said Volpatte, "who played hell about the fatigues they put him to. 'It's disgusting,' the fellow said to me, 'what they do with us. We're old non-coms., soldiers that have done four years of service at least. We're paid on the higher scale, it's true, but what of that? We are Officials, and yet they humiliate us. At H.Q. they set us to cleaning, and carrying the dung away. The civilians see the treatment they inflict on us, and they look down on us. And if you look like grousing, they'll actually talk about sending you off to the trenches, like foot-soldiers! What's going to become of our prestige? When we go back to the parishes as rangers after the war—if we do come back from it—the people of the villages and forests will say, "Ah, it was you that was sweeping the streets at X—!" To get back our prestige, compromised by human injustice and ingratitude, I know well,' he says, 'that we shall have to make complaints, and make complaints and make 'em with all our might, to the rich and to the influential!' he says."

"I knew a gendarme who was all right," said Lamuse. "'The police are temperate enough in general,' he says, 'but there are always dirty devils everywhere, pas? The civilian is really afraid of the gendarme,' says he, 'and that's a fact; and so, I admit it, there are some who take advantage of it, and those ones—the tag-rag of the gendarmerie—know where to get a glass or two. If I was Chief or Brigadier, I'd screw 'em down; not half I wouldn't,' he says; 'for public opinion,' he says again, 'lays the blame on the whole force when a single one with a grievance makes a complaint.'"

"As for me," says Paradis, "one of the worst days of my life was once when I saluted a gendarme, taking him for a lieutenant, with his white stripes. Fortunately—I don't say it to console myself, but because it's probably true—fortunately, I don't think he saw me."

A silence. "Oui, 'vidently," the men murmured; "but what about it? No need to worry."

A little later, when we were seated along a wall, with our backs to the stones, and our feet plunged and planted in the ground, Volpatte continued unloading his impressions.

"I went into a big room that was a Depot office—bookkeeping department, I believe. It swarmed with tables, and people in it like in a market. Clouds of talk. All along the walls on each side and in the middle, personages sitting in front of their spread-out goods like waste-paper merchants. I put in a request to be put back into my regiment, and they said to me, 'Take your damned hook, and get busy with it.' I lit on a sergeant, a little chap with airs, spick as a daisy, with a gold-rimmed spy-glass—eye-glasses with a tape on them. He was young, but being a re-enlisted soldier, he had the right not to go to the front. I said to him, 'Sergeant!' But he didn't hear me, being busy slanging a secretary—it's unfortunate, mon garcon,' he was saying; 'I've told you twenty times that you must send one notice of it to be carried out by the Squadron Commander, Provost of the C.A., and one by way of advice, without signature, but making mention of the signature, to the Provost of the Force Publique d'Amiens and of the centers of the district, of which you have the list—in envelopes, of course, of the general commanding the district. It's very simple,' he says.

"I'd drawn back three paces to wait till he'd done with jawing. Five minutes after, I went up to the sergeant. He said to me, 'My dear sir, I have not the time to bother with you; I have many other matters to attend to.' As a matter of fact, he was all in a flummox in front of his typewriter, the chump, because he'd forgotten, he said, to press on the capital-letter lever, and so, instead of underlining the heading of his page, he'd damn well scored a line of 8's in the middle of the top. So he couldn't hear anything, and he played hell with the Americans, seeing the machine came from there.

"After that, he growled against another woolly-leg, because on the memorandum of the distribution of maps they hadn't put the names of the Ration Department, the Cattle Department, and the Administrative Convoy of the 328th D.I.

"Alongside, a fool was obstinately trying to pull more circulars off a jellygraph than it would print, doing his damnedest to produce a lot of ghosts that you could hardly read. Others were talking: 'Where are the

Parisian fasteners?' asked a toff. And they don't call things by their proper
names: 'Tell me now, if you please, what are the elements quartered at
X—?' The elements! What's all that sort of babble?" asked Volpatte.

"At the end of the big table where these fellows were that I've
mentioned and that I'd been to, and the sergeant floundering about behind
a hillock of papers at the top of it and giving orders, a simpleton was
doing nothing but tap on his blotting-pad with his hands. His job, the mug,
was the department of leave-papers, and as the big push had begun and all
leave was stopped, he hadn't anything to do—'Capital!' he says.

"And all that, that's one table in one room in one department in one
depot. I've seen more, and then more, and more and more again. I don't
know, but it's enough to drive you off your nut, I tell you."

"Have they got brisques?"

"Not many there, but in the department of the second line every one had
'em. You had museums of 'em there—whole Zoological Gardens of
stripes."

"Prettiest thing I've seen in the way of stripes," said Tulacque, "was a
motorist, dressed in cloth that you'd have said was satin, with new stripes,
and the leathers of an English officer, though a second-class soldier as he
was. With his finger on his cheek, he leaned with his elbows on that fine
carriage adorned with windows that he was the valet de chambre of. He'd
have made you sick, the dainty beast. He was just exactly the poilu that
you see pictures of in the ladies' papers—the pretty little naughty papers."

Each has now his memories, his tirade on this much-excogitated subject
of the shirkers, and all begin to overflow and to talk at once. A hubbub
surrounds the foot of the mean wall where we are heaped like bundles,
with a gray, muddy, and trampled spectacle lying before us, laid waste by
rain.

"—orderly in waiting to the Road Department, then at the Bakery, then
cyclist to the Revictualing Department of the Eleventh Battery."

"—every morning he had a note to take to the Service de l'Intendance,
to the Gunnery School, to the Bridges Department, and in the evening to
the A.D. and the A.T.—that was all."

"—when I was coming back from leave,' said that orderly, 'the women
cheered us at all the level-crossing gates that the train passed.' 'They took
you for soldiers,' I said."

"—'Ah,' I said, 'you're called up, then, are you?' 'Certainly,' he says to me, 'considering that I've been a round of meetings in America with a Ministerial deputation. P'raps it's not exactly being called up, that? Anyway, mon ami,' he says, 'I don't pay any rent, so I must be called up.' 'And me—'"

"To finish," cries Volpatte, silencing the hum with his authority of a traveler returned from "down there," "to finish, I saw a whole legion of 'em all together at a blow-out. For two days I was a sort of helper in the kitchen of one of the centers of the C.O.A., 'cos they couldn't let me do nothing while waiting for my reply, which didn't hurry, seeing they'd sent another inquiry and a super-inquiry after it, and the reply had too many halts to make in each office, going and coming.

"In short, I was cook in the shop. Once I waited at table, seeing that the head cook had just got back from leave for the fourth time and was tired. I saw and I heard those people every time I went into the dining-room, that was in the Prefecture, and all that hot and illuminated row got into my head. They were only auxiliaries in there, but there were plenty of the armed service among the number, too. They were almost all old men, with a few young ones besides, sitting here and there.

"I'd begun to get about enough of it when one of the broomsticks said, 'The shutters must be closed; it's more prudent.' My boy, they were a lump of a hundred and twenty-five miles from the firing-line, but that pock-marked puppy he wanted to make believe there was danger of bombardment by aircraft—"

"And there's my cousin," said Tulacque, fumbling, "who wrote to me—Look, here's what he says: 'Mon cher Adolphe, here I am definitely settled in Paris as attache to Guard-Room 60. While you are down there. I must stay in the capital at the mercy of a Taube or a Zeppelin!'"

The phrase sheds a tranquil delight abroad, and we assimilate it like a tit-bit, laughing.

"After that," Volpatte went on, "those layers of soft-jobbers fed me up still more. As a dinner it was all right—cod, seeing it was Friday, but prepared like soles a la Marguerite—I know all about it. But the talk!—"

"They call the bayonet Rosalie, don't they?"

"Yes, the padded luneys. But during dinner these gentlemen talked above all about themselves. Every one, so as to explain why he wasn't somewhere else, as good as said (but all the while saying something else and gorging like an ogre), 'I'm ill, I'm feeble, look at me, ruin that I am. Me, I'm in my dotage.' They were all seeking inside themselves to find diseases to wrap themselves up in—'I wanted to go to the war, but I've a rupture, two ruptures, three ruptures.' Ah, non, that feast!—'The orders that speak of sending everybody away,' explained a funny man, 'they're like the comedies,' he explained, 'there's always a last act to clear up all the jobbery of the others. That third act is this paragraph, "Unless the requirements of the Departments stand in the way."' There was one that told this tale, 'I had three friends that I counted on to give me a lift up. I was going to apply to them; but, one after another, a little before I put my request, they were killed by the enemy; look at that,' he says, 'I've no luck!' Another was explaining to another that, as for him, he would very much have liked to go, but the surgeon-major had taken him round the waist to keep him by force in the depot with the auxiliary. 'Eh bien,' he says, 'I resigned myself. After all, I shall be of greater value in putting my intellect to the service of the country than in carrying a knapsack.' And him that was alongside said, 'Oui,' with his headpiece feathered on top. He'd jolly well consented to go to Bordeaux at the time when the Boches were getting near Paris, and then Bordeaux became the stylish place; but afterwards he returned firmly to the front—to Paris—and said something like this, 'My ability is of value to France; it is absolutely necessary that I guard it for France.'

"They talked about other people that weren't there—of the commandant who was getting an impossible temper, and they explained that the more imbecile he got the harsher he got; and the General that made unexpected inspections with the idea of kicking all the soft-jobbers out, but who'd been laid up for eight days, very ill—'he's certainly going to die; his condition no longer gives rise to any uneasiness,' they said, smoking the cigarettes that Society swells send to the depots for the soldiers at the front. 'D'you know,' they said, 'little Frazy, who is such a nice boy, the cherub, he's at last found an excuse for staying behind. They wanted some cattle slaughterers for the abattoir, and he's enlisted himself in there for protection, although he's got a University degree and in spite of being an attorney's clerk. As for Flandrin's son, he's succeeded in getting himself attached to the roadmenders.—Roadmender, him? Do you think they'll let him stop so?' 'Certain sure,' replies one of the cowardly milksops. 'A road-mender's job is for a long time.'

"Talk about idiots," Marthereau growls.

"And they were all jealous, I don't know why, of a chap called Bourin. Formerly he moved in the best Parisian circles. He lunched and dined in the city. He made eighteen calls a day, and fluttered about the drawing-rooms from afternoon tea till daybreak. He was indefatigable in leading cotillons, organizing festivities, swallowing theatrical shows, without counting the motoring parties, and all the lot running with champagne. Then the war came. So he's no longer capable, the poor boy, of staying on the look-out a bit late at an embrasure, or of cutting wire. He must stay peacefully in the warm. And then, him, a Parisian, to go into the provinces and bury himself in the trenches! Never in this world! 'I realize, too,' replied an individual, 'that at thirty-seven I've arrived at the age when I must take care of myself!' And while the fellow was saying that, I was thinking of Dumont the gamekeeper, who was forty-two, and was done in close to me on Hill 132, so near that after he got the handful of bullets in his head, my body shook with the trembling of his."

"And what were they like with you, these thieves?"

"To hell with me, it was, but they didn't show it too much, only now and again when they couldn't hold themselves in. They looked at me out of the corner of their eyes, and took damn good care not to touch me in passing, for I was still war-mucky.

"It disgusted me a bit to be in the middle of that heap of good-for-nothings, but I said to myself, 'Come, it's only for a bit, Firmin.' There was just one time that I very near broke out with the itch, and that was when one of 'em said, 'Later, when we return, if we do return.'—NO! He had no right to say that. Sayings like that, before you let them out of your gob, you've got to earn them; it's like a decoration. Let them get cushy jobs, if they like, but not play at being men in the open when they've damned well run away. And you hear 'em discussing the battles, for they're in closer touch than you with the big bugs and with the way the war's managed; and afterwards, when you return, if you do return, it's you that'll be wrong in the middle of all that crowd of humbugs, with the poor little truth that you've got.

"Ah, that evening, I tell you, all those heads in the reek of the light, the foolery of those people enjoying life and profiting by peace! It was like a ballet at the theater or the make-believe of a magic lantern. There were—there were—there are a hundred thousand more of them," Volpatte at last concluded in confusion.

But the men who were paying for the safety of the others with their strength and their lives enjoyed the wrath that choked him, that brought him to bay in his corner, and overwhelmed him with the apparitions of shirkers.

"Lucky he doesn't start talking about the factory hands who've served their apprenticeship in the war, and all those who've stayed at home under the excuse of National Defense, that was put on its feet in five secs!" murmured Tirette; "he'd keep us going with them till Doomsday."

"You say there are a hundred thousand of them, flea-bite," chaffed Barque. "Well, in 1914—do you hear me?—Millerand, the War Minister, said to the M.P.'s, 'There are no shirkers.'"

"Millerand!" growled Volpatte. "I tell you, I don't know the man; but if he said that, he's a dirty sloven, sure enough!"

"One is always," said Bertrand, "a shirker to some one else."

"That's true; no matter what you call yourself, you'll always—always—find worse blackguards and better blackguards than yourself."

"All those that never go up to the trenches, or those who never go into the first line, and even those who only go there now and then, they're shirkers, if you like to call 'em so, and you'd see how many there are if they only gave stripes to the real fighters."

"There are two hundred and fifty to each regiment of two battalions," said Cocon.

"There are the orderlies, and a bit since there were even the servants of the adjutants."—"The cooks and the under-cooks."—"The sergeant-majors, and the quartermaster-sergeants, as often as not."—"The mess corporals and the mess fatigues."—"Some office-props and the guard of the colors."—"The baggage-masters." "The drivers, the laborers, and all the section, with all its non-coms., and even the sappers."—"The cyclists." "Not all of them."—"Nearly all the Red Cross service."—"Not the stretcher-bearers, of course; for they've not only got a devilish rotten job, but they live with the companies, and when attacks are on they charge with their stretchers; but the hospital attendants."

"Nearly all parsons, especially at the rear. For, you know, parsons with knapsacks on, I haven't seen a devil of a lot of 'em, have you?"

"Nor me either. In the papers, but not here."

"There are some, it seems."—"Ah!"

"Anyway, the common soldier's taken something on in this war."

"There are others that are in the open. We're not the only ones."

"We are!" said Tulacque, sharply; "we're almost the only ones!"

He added, "You may say—I know well enough what you'll tell me—that it was the motor lorries and the heavy artillery that brought it off at Verdun. It's true, but they've got a soft job all the same by the side of us. We're always in danger, against their once, and we've got the bullets and the bombs, too, that they haven't. The heavy artillery reared rabbits near their dug-outs, and they've been making themselves omelettes for eighteen months. We are really in danger. Those that only get a bit of it, or only once, aren't in it at all. Otherwise, everybody would be. The nursemaid strolling the streets of Paris would be, too, since there are the Taubes and the Zeppelins, as that pudding-head said that the pal was talking about just now."

"In the first expedition to the Dardanelles, there was actually a chemist wounded by a shell. You don't believe me, but it's true all the same—an officer with green facings, wounded!"

"That's chance, as I wrote to Mangouste, driver of a remount horse for the section, that got wounded—but it was done by a motor lorry."

"That's it, it's like that. After all, a bomb can tumble down on a pavement, in Paris or in Bordeaux."

"Oui, oui; so it's too easy to say, 'Don't let's make distinctions in danger!' Wait a bit. Since the beginning, there are some of those others who've got killed by an unlucky chance; among us there are some that are still alive by a lucky chance. It isn't the same thing, that, seeing that when you're dead, it's for a long time."

"Yes," says Tirette, "but you're getting too venomous with your stories of shirkers. As long as we can't help it, it's time to turn over. I'm thinking of a retired forest-ranger at Cherey, where we were last month, who went about the streets of the town spying everywhere to rout out some civilian of military age, and he smelled out the dodgers like a mastiff. Behold him pulling up in front of a sturdy goodwife that had a mustache, and he only sees her mustache, so he bullyrags her—'Why aren't you at the front, you?'"

"For my part," says Pepin, "I don't fret myself about the shirkers or the semi-shirkers, it's wasting one's time; but where they get on my nerves, it's when they swank. I'm of Volpatte's opinion. Let 'em shirk, good, that's human nature; but afterwards they shouldn't say, 'I've been a soldier.' Take the engages, for instance—"

"That depends on the engages. Those who have offered for the infantry without conditions, I look up to those men as much as to those that have got killed; but the engages in the departments or special arms, even in the heavy artillery, they begin to get my back up. We know 'em! When they're doing the agreeable in their social circle, they'll say, 'I've offered for the war.'—'Ah, what a fine thing you have done; of your own free will you have defied the machine-guns! '—'Well, yes, madame la marquise, I'm built like that!' Eh, get out of it, humbug!"

"Oui, it's always the same tale. They wouldn't be able to say in the drawing-rooms afterwards, 'Tenez, here I am; look at me for a voluntary engage!'"

"I know a gentleman who enlisted in the aerodromes. He had a fine uniform—he'd have done better to offer for the Opera-Comique. What am I saying—'he'd have done better?' He'd have done a damn sight better, oui. At least he'd have made other people laugh honestly, instead of making them laugh with the spleen in it."

"They're a lot of cheap china, fresh painted, and plastered with ornaments and all sorts of falderals, but they don't go under fire."

"If there'd only been people like those, the Boches would be at Bayonne."

"When war's on, one must risk his skin, eh, corporal?"

"Yes," said Bertrand, "there are some times when duty and danger are exactly the same thing; when the country, when justice and liberty are in danger, it isn't in taking shelter that you defend them. On the contrary, war means danger of death and sacrifice of life for everybody, for everybody; no one is sacred. One must go for it, upright, right to the end, and not pretend to do it in a fanciful uniform. These services at the bases, and they're necessary, must be automatically guaranteed by the really weak and the really old."

"Besides, there are too many rich and influential people who have shouted, 'Let us save France!—and begin by saving ourselves!' On the declaration of war, there was a big rush to get out of it, that's what there was, and the strongest succeeded. I noticed myself, in my little corner, it was especially those that jawed most about patriotism previously. Anyway, as the others were saying just now, if they get into a funk-hole, the worst filthiness they can do is to make people believe they've run risks. 'Cos those that have really run risks, they deserve the same respect as the dead."

"Well, what then? It's always like that, old man; you can't change human nature."

"It can't be helped. Grouse, complain? Tiens! talking about complaining, did you know Margoulin?"

"Margoulin? The good sort that was with us, that they left to die at le Crassier because they thought he was dead?"

"Well, he wanted to make a complaint. Every day he talked about protesting against all those things to the captain and the commandant. He'd say after breakfast, 'I'll go and say it as sure as that pint of wine's there.' And a minute later, 'If I don't speak, there's never a pint of wine there at all.' And if you were passing later you'd hear him again, 'Tiens! is that a pint of wine there? Well, you'll see if I don't speak! Result—he said nothing at all. You'll say, 'But he got killed.' True, but previously he had God's own time to do it two thousand times if he'd dared."

"All that, it makes me ill," growled Blaire, sullen, but with a flash of fury.

"We others, we've seen nothing—seeing that we don't see anything—but if we did see—!"

"Old chap," Volpatte cried, "those depots—take notice of what I say—you'd have to turn the Seine, the Garonne, the Rhone and the Loire into them to clean them. In the interval, they're living, and they live well, and they go to doze peacefully every night, every night!"

The soldier held his peace. In the distance he saw the night as they would pass it—cramped up, trembling with vigilance in the deep darkness, at the bottom of the listening-hole whose ragged jaws showed in black outline all around whenever a gun hurled its dawn into the sky.

Bitterly said Cocon: "All that, it doesn't give you any desire to die."

"Yes, it does," some one replies tranquilly. "Yes, it does. Don't exaggerate, old kipper-skin."

Argoval

THE twilight of evening was coming near from the direction of the country, and a gentle breeze, soft as a whisper, came with it.

In the houses alongside this rural way—a main road, garbed for a few paces like a main street—the rooms whose pallid windows no longer fed them with the limpidity of space found their own light from lamps and candles, so that the evening left them and went outside, and one saw light and darkness gradually changing places.

On the edge of the village, towards the fields, some unladen soldiers were wandering, facing the breeze. We were ending the day in peace, and enjoying that idle ease whose happiness one only realizes when one is really weary. It was fine weather, we were at the beginning of rest, and dreaming about it. Evening seemed to make our faces bigger before it darkened them, and they shone with the serenity of nature.

Sergeant Suilhard came to me, took my arm, and led me away. "Come," he said, "and I'll show you something."

The approaches to the village abounded in rows of tall and tranquil trees, and we followed them along. Under the pressure of the breeze their vast verdure yielded from time to time in slow majestic movements.

Suilhard went in front of me. He led me into a deep lane, which twisted about between high banks; and on each side grew a border of bushes, whose tops met each other. For some moments we walked in a bower of tender green. A last gleam of light, falling aslant across the lane, made points of bright yellow among the foliage, and round as gold coins. "This is pretty," I said.

He said nothing, but looked aside and hard. Then he stopped. "It must be there."

He made me climb up a bit of a track to a field, a great quadrangle within tall trees, and full of the scent of hay.

"Tiens!" I said, looking at the ground, "it's all trampled here; there's been something to do."

"Come," said Suilhard to me. He led me into the field, not far from its gate. There was a group of soldiers there, talking in low voices. My companion stretched out his hand. "It's there," he said.

A very short post, hardly a yard high, was implanted a few paces from the hedge, composed just there of young trees. "It was there," he said, "that they shot a soldier of the 204th this morning. They planted that post in the night. They brought the chap here at dawn, and these are the fellows of his squad who killed him. He tried to dodge the trenches. During relief he stayed behind, and then went quietly off to quarters. He did nothing else; they meant, no doubt, to make an example of him."

We came near to the conversation of the others. "No, no, not at all," said one. "He wasn't a ruffian, he wasn't one of those toughs that we all know. We all enlisted together. He was a decent sort, like ourselves, no more, no less—a bit funky, that's all. He was in the front line from the beginning, he was, and I've never seen him boozed, I haven't."

"Yes, but all must be told. Unfortunately for him, there was a 'previous conviction.' There were two, you know, that did the trick—the other got two years. But Cajard, because of the sentence he got in civil life couldn't benefit by extenuating circumstances. He'd done some giddy-goat trick in civil life, when he was drunk."

"You can see a little blood on the ground if you look," said a stooping soldier.

"There was the whole ceremonial," another went on, "from A to Z—the colonel on horseback, the degradation; then they tied him to the little post, the cattle-stoup. He had to be forced to kneel or sit on the ground with a similar post."

"It's past understanding," said a third, after a silence, "if it wasn't for the example the sergeant spoke about."

On the post the soldiers had scrawled inscriptions and protests. A croix de guerre, cut clumsily of wood, was nailed to it, and read: "A. Cajard, mobilized in August, 1914, in gratitude to France."

Returning to quarters I met Volpatte, still surrounded and talking. He was relating some new anecdotes of his journey among the happy ones.

The Dog

THE weather was appalling. Water and wind attacked the passers-by; riddled, flooded, and upheaved the roads.

I was returning from fatigue to our quarters at the far end of the village. The landscape that morning showed dirty yellow through the solid rain, and the sky was dark as a slated roof. The downpour flogged the horse-trough as with birchen rods. Along the walls, human shapes went in shrinking files, stooping, abashed, splashing.

In spite of the rain and the cold and bitter wind, a crowd had gathered in front of the door of the barn where we were lodging. All close together and back to back, the men seemed from a distance like a great moving sponge. Those who could see, over shoulders and between heads, opened their eyes wide and said, "He has a nerve, the boy!" Then the inquisitive ones broke away, with red noses and streaming faces, into the down-pour that lashed and the blast that bit, and letting the hands fall that they had upraised in surprise, they plunged them in their pockets.

In the center, and running with rain, abode the cause of the gathering—Fouillade, bare to the waist and washing himself in abundant water. Thin as an insect, working his long slender arms in riotous frenzy, he soaped and splashed his head, neck, and chest, down to the upstanding gridirons of his sides. Over his funnel-shaped cheeks the brisk activity had spread a flaky beard like snow, and piled on the top of his head a greasy fleece that the rain was puncturing with little holes.

By way of a tub, the patient was using three mess-tins which he had filled with water—no one knew how—in a village where there was none; and as there was no clean spot anywhere to put anything down in that universal streaming of earth and sky, he thrust his towel into the waistband of his trousers, while the soap went back into his pocket every time he used it.

They who still remained wondered at this heroic gesticulation in the face of adversity, and said again, as they wagged their heads, "It's a disease of cleanliness he's got."

"You know he's going to be carpeted, they say, for that affair of the shell-hole with Volpatte." And they mixed the two exploits together in a muddled way, that of the shell-hole, and the present, and looked on him as the hero of the moment, while he puffed, sniffled, grunted, spat, and tried to dry himself under the celestial shower-bath with rapid rubbing and as a measure of deception; then at last he resumed his clothes.

After his wash, Fouillade feels cold. He turns about and stands in the doorway of the barn that shelters us. The arctic blast discolors and disparages his long face, so hollow and sunburned; it draws tears from his eyes, and scatters them on the cheeks once scorched by the mistral; his nose, too, weeps increasingly.

Yielding to the ceaseless bite of the wind that grips his ears in spite of the muffler knotted round his head, and his calves in spite of the yellow puttees with which his cockerel legs are enwound, he reenters the barn, but comes out of it again at once, rolling ferocious eyes, and muttering oaths with the accent one hears in that corner of the land, over six hundred miles from here, whence he was driven by war.

So he stands outside, erect, more truly excited than ever before in these northern scenes. And the wind comes and steals into him, and comes again roughly, shaking and maltreating his scarecrow's slight and flesh-less figure.

Ye gods! It is almost uninhabitable, the barn they have assigned to us to live in during this period of rest. It is a collapsing refuge, gloomy and leaky, confined as a well. One half of it is under water—we see rats swimming in it—and the men are crowded in the other half. The walls, composed of laths stuck together with dried mud, are cracked, sunken, holed in all their circuit, and extensively broken through above. The night we got here—until the morning—we plugged as well as we could the openings within reach, by inserting leafy branches and hurdles. But the higher holes, and those in the roof, still gaped and always. When dawn hovers there, weakling and early, the wind for contrast rushes in and blows round every side with all its strength, and the squad endures the hustling of an everlasting draught.

When we are there, we remain upright in the ruined obscurity, groping, shivering, complaining.

Fouillade, who has come in once more, goaded by the cold, regrets his ablutions. He has pains in his loins and back. He wants something to do, but what?

Sit down? Impossible; it is too dirty inside there. The ground and the paving-stones are plastered with mud; the straw scattered for our sleeping is soaked through, by the water that comes through the holes and by the boots that wipe themselves with it. Besides, if you sit down, you freeze; and if you lie on the straw, you are troubled by the smell of manure, and sickened by the vapors of ammonia. Fouillade contents himself by looking at his place, and yawning wide enough to dislocate his long jaw, further lengthened by a goatee beard where you would see white hairs if the daylight were really daylight.

"The other pals and boys," said Marthereau, "they're no better off than we are. After breakfast I went to see a jail-bird of the 11th on the farm near the hospital. You've to clamber over a wall by a ladder that's too short—talk about a scissor-cut!" says Marthereau, who is short in the leg; "and when once you're in the hen-run and rabbit-hutch you're shoved and poked by everybody and a nuisance to 'em all. You don't know where to put your pasties down. I vamoosed from there, and sharp."

"For my part," says Cocon, "I wanted to go to the blacksmith's when we'd got quit of grubbing, to imbibe something hot, and pay for it. Yesterday he was selling coffee, but some bobbies called there this morning, so the good man's got the shakes, and he's locked his door."

Lamuse has tried to clean his rifle. But one cannot clean his rifle here, even if he squats on the ground near the door, nor even if he takes away the sodden tent-cloth, hard and icy, which hangs across the doorway like a stalactite; it is too dark. "And then, old chap, if you let a screw fall, you may as well hang yourself as try to find it, 'specially when your fists are frozen silly."

"As for me, I ought to be sewing some things, but—what cheer!"

One alternative remains—to stretch oneself on the straw, covering the head with handkerchief or towel to isolate it from the searching stench of fermenting straw, and sleep. Fouillade, master of his time to-day, being on neither guard nor fatigues, decides. He lights a taper to seek among his belongings, and unwinds the coils of his comforter, and we see his emaciated shape, sculptured in black relief, folding and refolding it.

"Potato fatigue, inside there, my little lambs!" a sonorous voice bellows at the door. The hooded shape from which it comes is Sergeant Henriot. He is a malignant sort of simpleton, and though all the while joking in clumsy sympathy he supervises the evacuation of quarters with a sharp eye for the evasive malingerer.

Outside, on the streaming road in the perpetual rain, the second section is scattered, also summoned and driven to work by the adjutant. The two sections mingle together. We climb the street and the hillock of clayey soil where the traveling kitchen is smoking.

"Now then, my lads, get on with it; it isn't a long job when everybody sets to—Come—what have you got to grumble about, you? That does no good."

Twenty minutes later we return at a trot. As we grope about in the barn, we cannot touch anything but what is sodden and cold, and the sour smell of wet animals is added to the vapor of the liquid manure that our beds contain.

We gather again, standing, around the props that hold the barn up, and around the rills that fall vertically from the holes in the roof—faint columns which rest on vague bases of splashing water. "Here we are again!" we cry.

Two lumps in turn block the doorway, soaked with the rain that drains from them—Lamuse and Barque, who have been in quest of a brasier, and now return from the expedition empty-handed, sullen and vicious. "Not a shadow of a fire-bucket, and what's more, no wood or coal either, not for a fortune." It is impossible to have any fire. "If I can't get any, no one can," says Barque, with a pride which a hundred exploits justify.

We stay motionless, or move slowly in the little space we have, aghast at so much misery. "Whose is the paper?"

"It's mine," says Becuwe.

"What does it say? Ah, zut, one can't read in this darkness!"

"It says they've done everything necessary now for the soldiers, to keep them warm in the trenches. They've got all they want, and blankets and shirts and brasiers and fire-buckets and bucketsful of coal; and that it's like that in the first-line trenches."

"Ah, damnation!" growl some of the poor prisoners of the barn, and they shake their fists at the emptiness without and at the newspaper itself.

But Fouillade has lost interest in what they say. He has bent his long Don Quixote carcase down in the shadow, and outstretched the lean neck that looks as if it were braided with violin strings. There is something on the ground that attracts him.

It is Labri, the other squad's dog, an uncertain sort of mongrel sheep-dog, with a lopped tail, curled up on a tiny litter of straw-dust. Fouillade looks at Labri, and Labri at him. Becuwe comes up and says, with the intonation of the Lille district, "He won't eat his food; the dog isn't well. Hey, Labri, what's the matter with you? There's your bread and meat; eat it up; it's good when it's in your bucket. He's poorly. One of these mornings we shall find him dead."

Labri is not happy. The soldier to whom he is entrusted is hard on him, and usually ill-treats him—when he takes any notice of him at all. The animal is tied up all day. He is cold and ill and left to himself. He only exists. From time to time, when there is movement going on around him, he has hopes of going out, rises and stretches himself, and bestirs his tail to incipient demonstration. But he is disillusioned, and lies down again, gazing past his nearly full mess-tin.

He is weary, and disgusted with life. Even if he has escaped the bullet or bomb to which he is as much exposed as we, he will end by dying here. Fouillade puts his thin hand on the dog's head, and it gazes at him again. Their two glances are alike—the only difference is that one comes from above and the other from below.

Fouillade sits down also—the worse for him!—in a corner, his hands covered by the folds of his greatcoat, his long legs doubled up like a folding bed. He is dreaming, his eyes closed under their bluish lids; there is something that he sees again. It is one of those moments when the country from which he is divided assumes in the distance the charms of reality—the perfumes and colors of l'Herault, the streets of Cette. He sees so plainly and so near that he hears the noise of the shallops in the Canal du Midi, and the unloading at the docks; and their call to him is distinctly clear.

Above the road where the scent of thyme and immortelles is so strong that it is almost a taste in the mouth, in the heart of the sunshine whose winging shafts stir the air into a warmed and scented breeze, on Mont St. Clair, blossoms and flourishes the home of his folks. Up there, one can see with the same glance where the Lake of Thau, which is green like glass, joins hands with the Mediterranean Sea, which is azure; and sometimes one can make out as well, in the depths of the indigo sky, the carven phantoms of the Pyrenees.

There was he born, there he grew up, happy and free. There he played, on the golden or ruddy ground; played—even—at soldiers. The eager joy of wielding a wooden saber flushed the cheeks now sunken and seamed. He opens his eyes, looks about him, shakes his head, and falls upon regret for the days when glory and war to him were pure, lofty, and sunny things.

The man puts his hand over his eyes, to retain the vision within. Nowadays, it is different.

It was up there in the same place, later, that he came to know Clemence. She was just passing, the first time, sumptuous with sunshine, and so fair that the loose sheaf of straw she carried in her arms seemed to him nut-brown by contrast. The second time, she had a friend with her, and they both stopped to watch him. He heard them whispering, and turned towards them. Seeing themselves discovered, the two young women made off, with a sibilance of skirts, and giggles like the cry of a partridge.

And it was there, too, that he and she together set up their home. Over its front travels a vine, which he coddled under a straw hat, whatever the season. By the garden gate stands the rose-tree that he knows so well—it never used its thorns except to try to hold him back a little as he went by.

Will he return again to it all? Ah, he has looked too deeply into the profundity of the past not to see the future in appalling accuracy. He thinks of the regiment, decimated at each shift; of the big knocks and hard he has had and will have, of sickness, and of wear—

He gets up and snorts, as though to shake off what was and what will be. He is back in the middle of the gloom, and is frozen and swept by the wind, among the scattered and dejected men who blindly await the evening. He is back in the present, and he is shivering still.

Two paces of his long legs make him butt into a group that is talking—by way of diversion or consolation—of good cheer.

"At my place," says one, "they make enormous loaves, round ones, big as cart-wheels they are!" And the man amuses himself by opening his eyes wide, so that he can see the loaves of the homeland.

"Where I come from," interposes the poor Southerner, "holiday feasts last so long that the bread that's new at the beginning is stale at the end!"

"There's a jolly wine—it doesn't look much, that little wine where I come from; but if it hasn't fifteen degrees of alcohol it hasn't anything!"

Fouillade speaks then of a red wine which is almost violet, which stands dilution as well as if it had been brought into the world to that end.

"We've got the jurancon wine," said a Bearnais, "the real thing, not what they sell you for jurancon, which comes from Paris; indeed, I know one of the makers."

"If it comes to that," said Fouillade, "in our country we've got muscatels of every sort, all the colors of the rainbow, like patterns of silk stuff. You come home with me some time, and every day you shall taste a nonsuch, my boy."

"Sounds like a wedding feast," said the grateful soldier.

So it comes about that Fouillade is agitated by the vinous memories into which he has plunged, which recall to him as well the dear perfume of garlic on that far-off table. The vapors of the blue wine in big bottles, and the liqueur wines so delicately varied, mount to his head amid the sluggish and mournful storm that fills the barn.

Suddenly he calls to mind that there is settled in the village where they are quartered a tavern-keeper who is a native of Beziers, called Magnac. Magnac had said to him, "Come and see me, mon camarade, one of these mornings, and we'll drink some wine from down there, we will! I've several bottles of it, and you shall tell me what you think of it."

This sudden prospect dazzles Fouillade. Through all his length runs a thrill of delight, as though he had found the way of salvation. Drink the wine of the South—of his own particular South, even—drink much of it—it would be so good to see life rosy again, if only for a day! Ah yes, he wants wine; and he gets drunk in a dream.

But as he goes out he collides at the entry with Corporal Broyer, who is running down the street like a peddler, and shouting at every opening, "Morning parade!"

The company assembles and forms in squares on the sticky mound where the traveling kitchen is sending soot into the rain. "I'll go and have a drink after parade," says Fouillade to himself.

And he listens listlessly, full of his plan, to the reading of the report. But carelessly as he listens, he hears the officer read, "It is absolutely forbidden to leave quarters before 5 p.m. and after 8 p.m.," and he hears the captain, without noticing the murmur that runs round the poilus, add this comment on the order: "This is Divisional Headquarters. However many there are of you, don't show yourselves. Keep under cover. If the General sees you in the street, he will have you put to fatigues at once. He must not see a single soldier. Stay where you are all day in your quarters. Do what you like as long as no one sees you—no one!"

We go back into the barn.

Two o'clock. It is three hours yet, and then it will be totally dark, before one may risk going outside without being punished.

Shall we sleep while waiting? Fouillade is sleepy no longer; the hope of wine has shaken him up. And then, if one sleeps in the day, he will not sleep at night. No! To lie with your eyes open is worse than a nightmare. The weather gets worse; wind and rain increase, without and within.

Then what? If one may not stand still, nor sit down, nor lie down, nor go for a stroll, nor work—what?

Deepening misery settles on the party of benumbed and tired soldiers. They suffer to the bone, nor know what to do with their bodies. "Nom de Dieu, we're badly off!" is the cry of the derelicts—a lamentation, an appeal for help.

Then by instinct they give themselves up to the only occupation possible to them in there—to walk up and down on the spot, and thus ward off anchylosis.

So they begin to walk quickly to and fro in the scanty place that three strides might compass; they turn about and cross and brush each other, bent forward, hands pocketed—tramp, tramp. These human beings whom the blast cuts even among their straw are like a crowd of the wretched wrecks of cities who await, under the lowering sky of winter, the opening of some charitable institution. But no door will open for them—unless it Le four days hence, one evening at the end of the rest, to return to the trenches.

Alone in a corner, Cocon cowers. He is tormented by lice; but weakened by the cold and wet he has not the pluck to change his linen; and he sits there sullen, unmoving—and devoured.

As five o'clock draws near, in spite of all, Fouillade begins again to intoxicate himself with his dream of wine, and he waits, with its gleam in his soul. What time is it?—A quarter to five.—Five minutes to five.—Now!

He is outside in black night. With great splashing skips he makes his way towards the tavern of Magnac, the generous and communicative Biterrois. Only with great trouble does he find the door in the dark and the inky rain. By God, there is no light! Great God again, it is closed! The gleam of a match that his great lean hand covers like a lamp-shade shows him the fateful notice—"Out of Bounds." Magnac, guilty of some transgression, has been banished into gloom and idleness!

Fouillade turns his back on the tavern that has become the prison of its lonely keeper. He will not give up his dream. He will go somewhere else and have vin ordinaire, and pay for it, that's all. He puts his hand in his pocket to sound his purse; it is there. There ought to be thirty-seven sous in it, which will not run to the wine of Prou, but—

But suddenly he starts, stops dead, and smites himself on the forehead. His long-drawn face is contracted in a frightful grimace, masked by the night. No, he no longer has thirty-seven sous, fool that he is! He has forgotten the tin of sardines that he bought the night before—so disgusting did he find the dark macaroni of the soldiers' mess—and the drinks he stood to the cobbler who put him some nails in his boots.

Misery! There could not be more than thirteen sous left!

To get as elevated as one ought, and to avenge himself on the life of the moment, he would certainly need—damn'ation—a liter and a half, In this place, a liter of red ordinary costs twenty-one sous. It won't go.

His eyes wander around him in the darkness, looking for some one. Perhaps there is a pal somewhere who will lend him money, or stand him a liter.

But who—who? Not Becuwe, he has only a marraine who sends him tobacco and note-paper every fortnight. Not Barque, who would not toe the line; nor Blaire, the miser—he wouldn't understand. Not Biquet, who seems to have something against him; nor Pepin who himself begs, and never pays, even when he is host. Ah, if Volpatte were there! There is Mesnil Andre, but he is actually in debt to Fouillade on account of several drinks round. Corporal Bertrand? Following on a remark of Fouillade's, Bertrand told him to go to the devil, and now they look at each other sideways. Farfadet? Fouillade hardly speaks a word to him in the ordinary way. No, he feels that he cannot ask this of Farfadet. And then—a thousand thunders!—what is the use of seeking saviors in one's imagination? Where are they, all these people, at this hour?

Slowly he goes back towards the barn. Then mechanically he turns and goes forward again, with hesitating steps. He will try, all the same. Perhaps he can find convivial comrades. He approaches the central part of the village just when night has buried the earth.

The lighted doors and windows of the taverns shine again in the mud of the main street. There are taverns every twenty paces. One dimly sees the heavy specters of soldiers, mostly in groups, descending the street. When a motor-car comes along, they draw aside to let it pass, dazzled by the head-lights, and bespattered by the liquid mud that the wheels hurl over the whole width of the road.

The taverns are full. Through the steamy windows one can see they are packed with compact clouds of helmeted men. Fouillade goes into one or two, on chance. Once over the threshold, the dram-shop's tepid breath, the light, the smell and the hubbub, affect him with longing. This gathering at tables is at least a fragment of the past in the present.

He looks from table to table, and disturbs the groups as he goes up to scrutinize all the merrymakers in the room. Alas, he knows no one! Elsewhere, it is the same; he has no luck. In vain he has extended his neck and sent his desperate glances in search of a familiar head among the uniformed men who in clumps or couples drink and talk or in solitude write. He has the air of a cadger, and no one pays him heed.

Finding no soul to come to his relief, he decides to invest at least what he has in his pocket. He slips up to the counter. "A pint of wine—and good."

"White?"

"Eh, oui."

"You, mon garcon, you're from the South," says the landlady, handing him a little full bottle and a glass, and gathering his twelve sous.

He places himself at the corner of a table already overcrowded by four drinkers who are united in a game of cards. He fills the glass to the brim and empties it, then fills it again.

"Hey, good health to you! Don't drink the tumbler!" yelps in his face a man who arrives in the dirty blue jumper of fatigues, and displays a heavy cross-bar of eyebrows across his pale face, a conical head, and half a pound's weight of ears. It is Harlingue, the armorer.

It is not very glorious to be seated alone before a pint in the presence of a comrade who gives signs of thirst. But Fouillade pretends not to understand the requirements of the gentleman who dallies in front of him with an engaging smile, and he hurriedly empties his glass. The other turns his back, not without grumbling that "they're not very generous, but on the contrary greedy, these Southerners."

Fouillade has put his chin on his fists, and looks unseeing at a corner of the room where the crowded poilus elbow, squeeze, and jostle each other to get by.

It was pretty good, that swig of white wine, but of what use are those few drops in the Sahara of Fouillade? The blues did not far recede, and now they return.

The Southerner rises and goes out, with his two glasses of wine in his stomach and one sou in his pocket. He plucks up courage to visit one more tavern, to plumb it with his eyes, and by way of excuse to mutter, as he leaves the place, "Curse him! He's never there, the animal!"

Then he returns to the barn, which still—as always—whistles with wind and water. Fouillade lights his candle, and by the glimmer of the flame that struggles desperately to take wing and fly away, he sees Labri. He stoops low, with his light over the miserable dog—perhaps it will die first. Labri is sleeping, but feebly, for he opens an eye at once, and his tail moves.

The Southerner strokes him, and says to him in a low voice, "It can't be helped, it—" He will not say more to sadden him, but the dog signifies appreciation by jerking his head before closing his eyes again. Fouillade rises stiffly, by reason of his rusty joints, and makes for his couch. For only one thing more he is now hoping—to sleep, that the dismal day may die, that wasted day, like so many others that there will be to endure stoically and to overcome, before the last day arrives of the war or of his life.

The Doorway

"IT's foggy. Would you like to go?"

It is Poterloo who asks, as he turns towards me and shows eyes so blue that they make his fine, fair head seem transparent.

Poterloo comes from Souchez, and now that the Chasseurs have at last retaken it, he wants to see again the village where he lived happily in the days when he was only a man.

It is a pilgrimage of peril; not that we should have far to go—Souchez is just there. For six months we have lived and worked in the trenches almost within hail of the village. We have only to climb straight from here on to the Bethune road along which the trench creeps, the road honeycombed underneath by our shelters, and descend it for four or five hundred yards as it dips down towards Souchez. But all that ground is under regular and terrible attention. Since their recoil, the Germans have constantly sent huge shells into it. Their thunder shakes us in our caverns from time to time, and we see, high above the scarps, now here now there, the great black geysers of earth and rubbish, and the piled columns of smoke, as high as churches. Why do they bombard Souchez? One cannot say why, for there is no longer anybody or anything in the village so often taken and retaken, that we have so fiercely wrested from each other.

But this morning a dense fog enfolds us, and by favor of the great curtain that the sky throws over the earth one might risk it. We are sure at least of not being seen. The fog hermetically closes the perfected retina of the Sausage that must be somewhere up there, enshrouded in the white wadding that raises its vast wall of partition between our lines and those observation posts of Lens and Angres, whence the enemy spies upon us.

"Right you are!" I say to Poterloo.

Adjutant Barthe, informed of our project, wags his head up and down, and lowers his eyelids in token that he does not see.

We hoist ourselves out of the trench, and behold us both, upright, on the Bethune road!

It is the first time I have walked there during the day. I have never seen it, except from afar, the terrible road that we have so often traveled or crossed in leaps, bowed down in the darkness, and under the whistling of missiles.

"Well, are you coming, old man?"

After some paces, Poterloo has stopped in the middle of the road, where the fog like cotton-wool unravels itself into pendent fragments, and there he dilates his sky-blue eyes and half opens his scarlet mouth.

"Ah, la, la! Ah, la, la!" he murmurs. When I turn to him he points to the road, shakes his head and says, "This is it, Bon Dieu, to think this is it! This bit where we are, I know it so well that if I shut my eyes I can see it as it was, exactly. Old chap, it's awful to see it again like that. It was a beautiful road, planted all the way along with big trees.

"And now, what is it? Look at it—a sort of long thing without a soul—sad, sad. Look at these two trenches on each side, alive; this ripped-up paving, bored with funnels; these trees uprooted, split, scorched, broken like faggots, thrown all ways, pierced by bullets—look, this pock-marked pestilence, here! Ah, my boy, my boy, you can't imagine how it is disfigured, this road!" And he goes forward, seeing some new amazement at every step.

It is a fantastic road enough, in truth. On both sides of it are crouching armies, and their missiles have mingled on it for a year and a half. It is a great disheveled highway, traveled only by bullets and by ranks and files of shells, that have furrowed and upheaved it, covered it with the earth of the fields, scooped it and laid bare its bones. It might be under a curse; it is a way of no color, burned and old, sinister and awful to see.

"If you'd only known it—how clean and smooth it was!" says Poterloo. "All sorts of trees were there, and leaves, and colors—like butterflies; and there was always some one passing on it to give good-day to some good woman rocking between two baskets, or people shouting to each other in a chaise, with the good wind ballooning their smocks. Ah, how happy life was once on a time!"

He dives down to the banks of the misty stream that follows the roadway towards the land of parapets. Stooping, he stops by some faint swellings of the ground on which crosses are fixed—tombs, recessed at intervals into the wall of fog, like the Stations of the Cross in a church.

I call him—we shall never get there at such a funeral pace. Allons!

We come to a wide depression in the land, I in front and Poterloo lagging behind, his head confused and heavy with thought as he tries in vain to exchange with inanimate things his glances of recognition. Just there the road is lower, a fold secretes it from the side towards the north. On this sheltered ground there is a little traffic.

Along the hazy, filthy, and unwholesome space, where withered grass is embedded in black mud, there are rows of dead. They are carried there when the trenches or the plain are cleared during the night. They are waiting—some of them have waited long—to be taken back to the cemeteries after dark.

We approach them slowly. They are close against each other, and each one indicates with arms or legs some different posture of stiffened agony. There are some with half-moldy faces, the skin rusted, or yellow with dark spots. Of several the faces are black as tar, the lips hugely distended—the heads of negroes blown out in goldbeaters' skin. Between two bodies, protruding uncertainly from one or the other, is a severed wrist, ending with a cluster of strings.

Others are shapeless larvae of pollution, with dubious items of equipment pricking up, or bits of bone. Farther on, a corpse has been brought in in such a state that they have been obliged—so as not to lose it on the way—to pile it on a lattice of wire which was then fastened to the two ends of a stake. Thus was it carried in the hollow of its metal hammock, and laid there. You cannot make out either end of the body; alone, in the heap that it makes, one recognizes the gape of a trouser-pocket. An insect goes in and out of it.

Around the dead flutter letters that have escaped from pockets or cartridge pouches while they were being placed on the ground. Over one of these bits of white paper, whose wings still beat though the mud ensnares them, I stoop slightly and read a sentence—"My dear Henry, what a fine day it is for your birthday!" The man is on his belly; his loins are rent from hip to hip by a deep furrow; his head is half turned round; we see a sunken eye; and on temples, cheek and neck a kind of green moss is growing.

A sickening atmosphere roams with the wind around these dead and the heaped-up debris, that lies about them—tent-cloth or clothing in stained tatters, stiff with dried blood, charred by the scorch of the shell, hardened, earthy and already rotting, quick with swarming and questing things. It troubles us. We look at each other and shake our heads, nor dare admit aloud that the place smells bad. All the same, we go away slowly.

Now come breaking out of the fog the bowed backs of men who are joined together by something they are carrying. They are Territorial stretcher-bearers with a new corpse. They come up with their old wan faces, toiling, sweating, and grimacing with the effort. To carry a dead man in the lateral trenches when they are muddy is a work almost beyond human power. They put down the body, which is dressed in new clothes.

"It's not long since, now, that he was standing," says one of the bearers. "It's two hours since he got his bullet in the head for going to look for a Boche rifle in the plain. He was going on leave on Wednesday and wanted to take a rifle home with him. He is a sergeant of the 405th, Class 1914. A nice lad, too."

He takes away the handkerchief that is over the face. It is quite young, and seems to sleep, except that an eyeball has gone, the cheek looks waxen, and a rosy liquid has run over the nostrils, mouth, and eyes.

The body strikes a note of cleanliness in the charnel-house, this still pliant body that lolls its head aside when it is moved as if to lie better; it gives a childish illusion of being less dead than the others. But being less disfigured, it seems more pathetic, nearer to one, more intimate, as we look. And had we said anything in the presence of all that heap of beings destroyed, it would have been "Poor boy!"

We take the road again, which at this point begins to slope down to the depth where Souchez lies. Under our feet in the whiteness of the fog it appears like a valley of frightful misery. The piles of rubbish, of remains and of filthiness accumulate on the shattered spine of the road's paving and on its miry borders in final confusion. The trees bestrew the ground or have disappeared, torn away, their stumps mangled. The banks of the road are overturned and overthrown by shell-fire. All the way along, on both sides of this highway where only the crosses remain standing, are trenches twenty times blown in and re-hollowed, cavities—some with passages into them—hurdles on quagmires.

The more we go forward, the more is everything turned terribly inside out, full of putrefaction, cataclysmic. We walk on a surface of shell fragments, and the foot trips on them at every step. We go among them as if they were snares, and stumble in the medley of broken weapons or bits of kitchen utensils, of water-bottles, fire-buckets, sewing-machines, among the bundles of electrical wiring, the French and German accouterments all mutilated and encrusted in dried mud, and among the sinister piles of clothing, stuck together with a reddish-brown cement. And one must look out, too, for the unexploded shells, which everywhere protrude their noses or reveal their flanks or their bases, painted red, blue, and tawny brown.

"That's the old Boche trench, that they cleared out of in the end." It is choked up in some places, in others riddled with shell-holes. The sandbags have been torn asunder and gutted; they are crumbled, emptied, scattered to the wind. The wooden props and beams arc splintered, and point all ways. The dug-outs are filled to the brim with earth and with—no one knows what. It is all like the dried bed of a river, smashed, extended, slimy, that both water and men have abandoned. In one place the trench has been simply wiped out by the guns. The wide fosse is blocked, and remains no more than a field of new-turned earth, made of holes symmetrically bored side by side, in length and in breadth.

I point out to Poterloo this extraordinary field, that would seem to have been traversed by a giant plow. But he is absorbed to his very vitals in the metamorphosis of the country's face.

He indicates a space in the plain with his finger, and with a stupefied air, as though he came out of a dream—"The Red Tavern!" It is a flat field, carpeted with broken bricks.

And what is that, there? A milestone? No, it is not a milestone. It is a head, a black head, tanned and polished. The mouth is all askew, and you can see something of the mustache bristling on each side—the great head of a carbonized cat. The corpse—it is German—is underneath, buried upright.

"And that?" It is a ghastly collection containing an entirely white skull, and then, six feet away, a pair of boots, and between the two a heap of frayed leather and of rags, cemented by brown mud.

"Come on, there's less fog already. We must hurry."

A hundred yards in front of us, among the more transparent waves of fog that are changing places with us and hide us less and less, a shell whistles and bursts. It has fallen in the spot we are just nearing. We are descending, and the gradient is less steep. We go side by side. My companion says nothing, but looks to right and to left. Then he stops again, as he did at the top of the road. I hear his faltering voice, almost inaudible—"What's this! We're there—this is it—"

In point of fact we have not left the plain, the vast plain, seared and barren—but we are in Souchez!

The village has disappeared, nor have I seen a village go so completely. Ablain-Saint-Nazaire, and Carency, these still retained some shape of a place, with their collapsed and truncated houses, their yards heaped high with plaster and tiles. Here, within the framework of slaughtered trees that surrounds us as a spectral background in the fog, there is no longer any shape. There is not even an end of wall, fence, or porch that remains standing; and it amazes one to discover that there are paving-stones under the tangle of beams, stones, and scrap-iron. This—here—was a street.

It might have been a dirty and boggy waste near a big town, whose rubbish of demolished buildings and its domestic refuse had been shot here for years, till no spot was empty. We plunge into a uniform layer of dung and debris, and make but slow and difficult progress. The bombardment has so changed the face of things that it has diverted the course of the millstream, which now runs haphazard and forms a pond on the remains of the little place where the cross stood.

Here are several shell-holes where swollen horses are rotting; in others the remains of what were once human beings are scattered, distorted by the monstrous injury of shells.

Here, athwart the track we are following, that we ascend as through an avalanche or inundation of ruin, under the unbroken melancholy of the sky, here is a man stretched out as if he slept, but he has that close flattening against the ground which distinguishes a dead man from a sleeper. He is a dinner-fatigue man, with a chaplet of loaves threaded over a belt, and a bunch of his comrades' water-bottles slung on his shoulder by a skein of straps. It must have been only last night that the fragment of a shell caught him in the back. No doubt we are the first to find him, this unknown soldier secretly dead. Perhaps he will be scattered before others find him, so we look for his identity disc—it is stuck in the clotted blood where his right hand stagnates. I copy down the name that is written in letters of blood.

Poterloo lets me do it by myself—he is like a sleepwalker. He looks, and looks in despair, everywhere. He seeks endlessly among those evanished and eviscerated things; through the void he gazes to the haze of the horizon. Then he sits down on a beam, having first sent flying with a kick a saucepan that lay on it, and I sit by his side. A light drizzle is falling. The fog's moisture is resolving in little drops that cover everything with a slight gloss. He murmurs, "Ah, la, la!"

He wipes his forehead and raises imploring eyes to me. He is trying to make out and take in the destruction of all this corner of the earth, and the mournfulness of it. He stammers disjointed remarks and interjections. He takes off his great helmet and his head is smoking. Then he says to me with difficulty, "Old man, you cannot imagine, you cannot, you cannot—"

He whispers: "The Red Tavern, where that—where that Boche's head is, and litters of beastliness all around, that sort of cesspool—it was on the edge of the road, a brick house and two out-buildings alongside—how many times, old man, on the very spot where we stood, how many times, there, the good woman who joked with me on her doorstep, I've given her good-day as I wiped my mouth and looked towards Souchez that I was going back to! And then, after a few steps, I've turned round to shout some nonsense to her! Oh, you cannot imagine! But that, now, that!" He makes an inclusive gesture to indicate all the emptiness that surrounds him.

"We mustn't stay here too long, old chap. The fog's lifting, you know."
He stands up with an effort—"Allons."
The most serious part is yet to come. His house—
He hesitates, turns towards the east, goes. "It's there—no, I've passed it. It's not there. I don't know where it is—or where it was. Ah, misery, misery!" He wrings his hands in despair and staggers in the middle of the medley of plaster and bricks. Then, bewildered by this encumbered plain of lost landmarks, he looks questioningly about in the air, like a thoughtless child, like a madman. He is looking for the intimacy of the bedrooms scattered in infinite space, for their inner form and their twilight now cast upon the winds!

After several goings and comings, he stops at one spot and draws back a little—"It was there, I'm right. Look—it's that stone there that I knew it by. There was a vent-hole there, you can see the mark of the bar of iron that was over the hole before it disappeared."

Sniffling he reflects, and gently shaking his head as though he could not stop it: "It is when you no longer have anything that you understand how happy you were. Ah, how happy we were!"

He comes up to me and laughs nervously: "It's out of the common, that, eh? I'm sure you've never seen yourself like it—can't find the house where you've always lived since—since always—"

He turns about, and it is he who leads me away:

"Well, let's leg it, since there is nothing. Why spend a whole hour looking at places where things were? Let's be off, old man."

We depart—the only two living beings to be seen in that unreal and miasmal place, that village which bestrews the earth and lies under our feet.

We climb again. The weather is clearing and the fog scattering quickly. My silent comrade, who is making great strides with lowered head, points out a field: "The cemetery," he says; "it was there before it was everywhere, before it laid hold on everything without end, like a plague."

Half-way, we go more slowly, and Poterloo comes close to me-"You know, it's too much, all that. It's wiped out too much—all my life up to now. It makes me afraid—it is so completely wiped out."

"Come; your wife's in good health, you know; your little girl, too."

He looks at me comically: "My wife—I'll tell you something; my wife—"

"Well?"

"Well, old chap, I've seen her again."

"You've seen her? I thought she was in the occupied country?"

"Yes, she's at Lens, with my relations. Well, I've seen her—ah, and then, after all, zut!—I'll tell you all about it. Well, I was at Lens, three weeks ago. It was the eleventh; that's twenty days since."

I look at him, astounded. But he looks like one who is speaking the truth. He talks in sputters at my side, as we walk in the increasing light—

"They told us—you remember, perhaps—but you weren't there, I believe—they told us the wire had got to be strengthened in front of the Billard Trench. You know what that means, eh? They hadn't been able to do it till then. As soon as one gets out of the trench he's on a downward slope, that's got a funny name."

"The Toboggan."

"Yes, that's it; and the place is as bad by night or in fog as in broad daylight, because of the rifles trained on it before hand on trestles, and the machine-guns that they point during the day. When they can't see any more, the Boches sprinkle the lot.

"They took the pioneers of the C.H.R., but there were some missing, and they replaced 'em with a few poilus. I was one of 'em. Good. We climb out. Not a single rifle-shot! 'What does it mean?' we says, and behold, we see a Boche, two Boches, three Boches, coming out of the ground—the gray devils!—and they make signs to us and shout 'Kamarad!' 'We're Alsatians,' they says, coming more and more out of their communication trench—the International. 'They won't fire on you, up there,' they says; 'don't be afraid, friends. Just let us bury our dead.' And behold us working aside of each other, and even talking together since they were from Alsace. And to tell the truth, they groused about the war and about their officers. Our sergeant knew all right that it was forbidden to talk with the enemy, and they'd even read it out to us that we were only to talk to them with our rifles. But the sergeant he says to himself that this is God's own chance to strengthen the wire, and as long as they were letting us work against them, we'd just got to take advantage of it.

"Then behold one of the Boches that says, 'There isn't perhaps one of you that comes from the invaded country and would like news of his family?'

"Old chap, that was a bit too much for me. Without thinking if I did right or wrong, I went up to him and I said, 'Yes, there's me.' The Boche asks me questions. I tell him my wife's at Lens with her relations, and the little one, to. He asks where she's staying. I explain to him, and he says he can see it from there. 'Listen,' he says, 'I'll take her a letter, and not only that, but I'll bring you an answer.' Then all of a sudden he taps his forehead, the Boche, and comes close to me—'Listen, my friend, to a lot better still. If you like to do what I say, you shall see your wife, and your kids as well, and all the lot, sure as I see you.' He tells me, to do it, I've only got to go with him at a certain time with a Boche greatcoat and a shako that he'll have for me. He'd mix me up in a coal-fatigue in Lens, and we'd go to our house. I could go and have a look on condition that I laid low and didn't show myself, and he'd be responsible for the chaps of the fatigue, but there were non-coms. in the house that he wouldn't answer for—and, old chap, I agreed!"

"That was serious."

"Yes, for sure, it was serious. I decided all at once, without thinking and without wishing to think, seeing I was dazzled with the idea of seeing my people again; and if I got shot afterwards, well, so much the worse—but give and take. The supply of law and demand they call it, don't they?

"My boy, it all went swimmingly. The only hitch was they had such hard work to find a shako big enough, for, as you know, I'm well off for head. But even that was fixed up. They raked me out in the end a lousebox big enough to hold my head. I've already some Boche boots—those that were Caron's, you know. So, behold us setting off in the Boche trenches—and they're most damnably like ours—with these good sorts of Boche comrades, who told me in very good French—same as I'm speaking—not to fret myself.

"There was no alarm, nothing. Getting there came off all right. Everything went off so sweet and simple that I fancied I must be a defaulting Boche. We got to Lens at nightfall. I remember we passed in front of La Perche and went down the Rue du Quatorze-Juillet. I saw some of the townsfolk walking about in the streets like they do in our quarters. I didn't recognize them because of the evening, nor them me, because of the evening too, and because of the seriousness of things. It was so dark you couldn't put your finger into your eye when I reached my folk's garden.

"My heart was going top speed. I was all trembling from head to foot as if I were only a sort of heart myself. And I had to hold myself back from carrying on aloud, and in French too, I was so happy and upset. The Kamarad says to me, 'You go, pass once, then another time, and look in at the door and the window. Don't look as if you were looking. Be careful.' So I get hold of myself again, and swallow my feelings all at a gulp. Not a bad sort, that devil, seeing he'd have had a hell of a time if I'd got nailed.

"At our place, you know, same as everywhere in the Pas de Calais, the outside doors of the houses are cut in two. At the bottom, it's a sort of barrier, half-way up your body; and above, you might call it a shutter. So you can shut the bottom half and be one-half private.

"The top half was open, and the room, that's the dining-room, and the kitchen as well, of course, was lighted up and I heard voices.

"I went by with my neck twisted sideways. There were heads of men and women with a rosy light on them, round the round table and the lamp. My eyes fell on her, on Clotilde. I saw her plainly. She was sitting between two chaps, non-coms., I believe, and they were talking to her. And what was she doing? Nothing; she was smiling, and her face was prettily bent forward and surrounded with a light little framework of fair hair, and the lamp gave it a bit of a golden look.

"She was smiling. She was contented. She had a look of being well off, by the side of the Boche officer, and the lamp, and the fire that puffed an unfamiliar warmth out on me. I passed, and then I turned round, and passed again. I saw her again, and she was always smiling. Not a forced smile, not a debtor's smile, non, a real smile that came from her, that she gave. And during that time of illumination that I passed in two senses, I could see my baby as well, stretching her hands out to a great striped simpleton and trying to climb on his knee; and then, just by, who do you think I recognized? Madeleine Vandaert, Vandaert's wife, my pal of the 19th, that was killed at the Maine, at Montyon.

"She knew he'd been killed because she was in mourning. And she, she was having good fun, and laughing outright, I tell you—and she looked at one and the other as much as to say, 'I'm all right here!'

"Ah, my boy, I cleared out of that, and butted into the Kamarads that were waiting to take me back. How I got back I couldn't tell you. I was knocked out. I went stumbling like a man under a curse, and if any-body had said a wrong word to me just then—! I should have shouted out loud; I should have made a row, so as to get killed and be done with this filthy life!

"Do you catch on? She was smiling, my wife, my Clotilde, at this time in the war! And why? Have we only got to be away for a time for us not to count any more? You take your damned hook from home to go to the war, and everything seems finished with; and they worry for a while that you're gone, but bit by bit you become as if you didn't exist, they can do without you to be as happy as they were before, and to smile. Ah, Christ! I'm not talking of the other woman that was laughing, but my Clotilde, mine, who at that chance moment when I saw her, whatever you may say, was getting on damned well without me!

"And then, if she'd been with friends or relations; but no, actually with Boche officers! Tell me, shouldn't I have had good reason to jump into the room, fetch her a couple of swipes, and wring the neck of the other old hen in mourning?

"Yes, yes; I thought of doing it. I know all right I was getting violent, I was getting out of control.

"Mark me. I don't want to say more about it than I have said. She's a good lass, Clotilde. I know her, and I've confidence in her. I'm not far wrong, you know. If I were done in, she'd cry all the tears in her body to begin with. She thinks I'm alive, I admit, but that isn't the point. She can't prevent herself from being; well off, and contented, and letting herself go, when she's a good fire, a good lamp, and company, whether I'm there or not—"

I led Poterloo away: "You exaggerate, old chap; you're getting absurd notions, come." We had walked very slowly and were still at the foot of the hill. The fog was becoming like silver as it prepared for departure. Sunshine was very near.

Poterloo looked up and said, "We'll go round by the Carency road and go in at the back." We struck off at an angle into the fields. At the end of a few minutes he said to me, "I exaggerate, you think? You say that I exaggerate?" He reflected. "Ah!" Then he added, with the shaking of the head that had hardly left him all the morning, "What about it? All the same, it's a fact—"

We climbed the slope. The cold had become tepidity. Arrived on a little plateau—"Let's sit here again before going in," he proposed. He sat down, heavy with the world of thought that entangled him. His forehead was wrinkled. Then he turned towards me with an awkward air, as if he were going to beg some favor: "Tell me, mate, I'm wondering if I'm right."

But after looking at me, he looked at everything else, as though he would rather consult them than me.

A transformation was taking place in the sky and on the earth. The fog was hardly more than a fancy. Distances revealed themselves. The narrow plain, gloomy and gray, was getting bigger, chasing its shadows away, and assuming color. The light was passing over it from east to west like sails.

And down there at our very feet, by the grace of distance and of light, we saw Souchez among the trees—the little place arose again before our eyes, new-born in the sunshine!

"Am I right?" repeated Poterloo, more faltering, more dubious.

Before I could speak he replied to himself, at first almost in a whisper, as the light fell on him—"She's quite young, you know; she's twenty-six. She can't hold her youth in, it's coming out of her all over, and when she's resting in the lamp-light and the warmth, she's got to smile; and even if she burst out laughing, it would just simply be her youth, singing in her throat. It isn't on account of others, if truth were told; it's on account of herself. It's life. She lives. Ah, yes, she lives, and that's all. It isn't her fault if she lives. You wouldn't have her die? Very well, what do you want her to do? Cry all day on account of me and the Boches? Grouse? One can't cry all the time, nor grouse for eighteen months. Can't be done. It's too long, I tell you. That's all there is to it."

He stops speaking to look at the view of Notre-Dame-de-Lorette, now wholly illuminated.

"Same with the kid; when she found herself alongside a simpleton that doesn't tell her to go and play with herself, she ends by wanting to get on his knee. Perhaps she'd prefer that it was her uncle or a friend or her father—perhaps—but she tries it on all the same with the only man that's always there, even if it's a great hog in spectacles.

"Ah," he cries, as he gets up and comes gesticulating before me. "There's a good answer one could give me. If I didn't come back from the war, I should say, 'My lad, you've gone to smash, no more Clotilde, no more love! You'll be replaced in her heart sooner or later; no getting round it; your memory, the portrait of you that she carries in her, that'll fade bit by bit and another'll come on top of it, and she'll begin another life again.' Ah, if I didn't come back!"

He laughs heartily. "But I mean to come back. Ah, yes! One must be there. Otherwise—I must be there, look you," he says again more seriously; "otherwise, if you're not there, even if you're dealing with saints and angels, you'll be at fault in the end. That's life. But I am there." He laughs. "Well, I'm a little there, as one might say!"

I get up too, and tap him on the shoulder. "You're right, old pal, it'll all come to an end."

He rubs his hands and goes on talking. "Yes, by God! it'll all finish, don't worry. Oh, I know well there'll be hard graft before it's finished, and still more after. We've got to work, and I don't only mean work with the arms.

"It'll be necessary to make everything over again. Very well, we'll do it. The house? Gone. The garden? Nowhere. All right, we'll rebuild the house, we'll remake the garden. The less there is the more we'll make over again. After all, it's life, and we're made to remake, eh? And we'll remake our life together, and happiness. We'll make the days again; we'll remake the nights.

"And the other side, too. They'll make their world again. Do you know what I say?—perhaps it won't be as long as one thinks—"

"Tiens! I can see Madeleine Vandaert marrying another chap. She's a widow; but, old man, she's been a widow eighteen months. Do you think it's not a big slice, that, eighteen months? They even leave off wearing mourning, I believe, about that time! People don't remember that when they say 'What a strumpet she is,' and when, in effect, they ask her to commit suicide. But mon vieux, one forgets. One is forced to forget. It isn't the people that make you forget; you do it yourself; it's just forgetfulness, mind you. I find Madeleine again all of a sudden, and to see her frivvling there it broke me up as much as if her husband had been killed yesterday—it's natural. But it's a devil of a long time since he got spiked, poor lad. It's a long time since, it's too long since. People are no longer the same. But, mark you, one must come back, one must be there! We shall be there, and we shall be busy with beginning again!"

On the way, he looks and winks, cheered up by finding a peg on which to hang his ideas. He says—"I can see it from here, after the war, all the Souchez people setting themselves again to work and to life—what a business! Tiens, Papa Ponce, for example, the back-number! He was so pernickety that you could see him sweeping the grass in his garden with a horsehair brush, or kneeling on his lawn and trimming the turf with a pair of scissors. Very well, he'll treat himself to that again! And Madame Imaginaire, that lived in one of the last houses towards the Chateau de Carleul, a large woman who seemed to roll along the ground as if she'd got casters under her big circular petticoats. She had a child every year, regular, punctual—a proper machine-gun of kids. Very well, she'll take that occupation up again with all her might."

He stops and ponders, and smiles a very little—almost within himself: "Tiens, I'll tell you; I noticed—it isn't very important, this," he insists, as though suddenly embarrassed by the triviality of this parenthesis—"but I noticed (you notice it in a glance when you're noticing something else) that it was cleaner in our house than in my time—"

We come on some little rails in the ground, climbing almost hidden in the withered grass underfoot. Poterloo points out with his foot this bit of abandoned track, and smiles; "That, that's our railway. It was a cripple, as you may say; that means something that doesn't move. It didn't work very quickly. A snail could have kept pace with it. We shall remake it. But certainly it won't go any quicker. That can't be allowed!"

When we reached the top of the hill, Poterloo turned round and threw a last look over the slaughtered places that we had just visited. Even more than a minute ago, distance recreated the village across the remains of trees shortened and sliced that now looked like young saplings. Better even than just now, the sun shed on that white and red accumulation of mingled material an appearance of life and even an illusion of meditation. Its very stones seemed to feel the vernal revival. The beauty of sunshine heralded what would be, and revealed the future. The face of the watching soldier, too, shone with a glamour of reincarnation, and the smile on it was born of the springtime and of hope. His rosy cheeks and blue eyes seemed brighter than ever.

We go down into the communication trench and there is sunshine there. The trench is yellow, dry, and resounding. I admire its finely geometrical depth, its shovel-smoothed and shining flanks; and I find it enjoyable to hear the clean sharp sound of our feet on the hard ground or on the caillebotis—little gratings of wood, placed end to end and forming a plankway.

I look at my watch. It tells me that it is nine o'clock, and it shows me, too, a dial of delicate color where the sky is reflected in rose-pink and blue, and the fine fret-work of bushes that are planted there above the marges of the trench.

And Poterloo and I look at each other with a kind of confused delight. We are glad to see each other, as though we were meeting after absence! He speaks to me, and though I am quite familiar with the singsong accent of the North, I discover that he is singing.

We have had bad days and tragic nights in the cold and the rain and the mud. Now, although it is still winter, the first fine morning shows and convinces us that it will soon be spring once more. Already the top of the trench is graced by green young grass, and amid its new-born quivering some flowers are awakening. It means the end of contracted and constricted days. Spring is coming from above and from below. We inhale with joyful hearts; we are uplifted.

Yes, the bad days are ending. The war will end, too, que diable! And no doubt it will end in the beautiful season that is coming, that already illumines us, whose zephyrs already caress us.

A whistling sound—tiens, a spent bullet! A bullet? Nonsense—it's a blackbird! Curious how similar the sound was! The blackbirds and the birds of softer song, the countryside and the pageant of the seasons, the intimacy of dwelling-rooms, arrayed in light—Oh! the war will end soon; we shall go back for good to our own; wife, children, or to her who is at once wife and child, and we smile towards them in this young glory that already unites us again.

At the forking of the two trenches, in the open and on the edge, here is something like a doorway. Two posts lean one upon the other, with a confusion of electric wires between them, hanging down like tropical creepers. It looks well. You would say it was a theatrical contrivance or scene. A slender climbing plant twines round one of the posts, and as you follow it with your glance, you see that it already dares to pass from one to the other.

Soon, passing along this trench whose grassy slopes quiver like the flanks of a fine horse, we come out into our own trench on the Bethune road, and here is our place. Our comrades are there, in clusters. They are eating, and enjoying the goodly temperature.

The meal finished, we clean our aluminium mess-tins or plates with a morsel of bread. "Tiens, the sun's going!" It is true; a cloud has passed over and hidden it. "It's going to splash, my little lads," says Lamuse "that's our luck all over! Just as we are going off!"

"A damned country!" says Fouillade. In truth this Northern climate is not worth much. It drizzles and mizzles, reeks and rains. And when there is any sun it soon disappears in the middle of this great damp sky.

Our four days in the trenches are finished, and the relief will commence at nightfall. Leisurely we get ready for leaving. We fill and put aside the knapsacks and bags. We give a rub to the rifles and wrap them up.

It is already four o'clock. Darkness is falling quickly, and we grow indistinct to each other. "Damnation. Here's the rain!" A few drops and then the downpour. Oh, la, la, la! We don our capes and tent-cloths. We go back unto the dug-out, dabbling, and gathering mud on our knees, hands, and elbows, for the bottom of the trench is getting sticky. Once inside, we have hardly time to light a candle, stuck on a bit of stone, and to shiver all round—"Come on, en route!"

We hoist ourselves into the wet and windy darkness outside. I can dimly see Poterloo's powerful shoulders; in the ranks we are always side by side. When we get going I call to him, "Are you there, old chap?"—"Yes, in front of you," he cries to me, turning round. As he turns he gets a buffet in the face from wind and rain, but he laughs. His happy face of the morning abides with him. No downpour shall rob him of the content that he carries in his strong and steadfast heart; no evil night put out the sunshine that I saw possess his thoughts some hours ago.

We march, and jostle each other, and stumble. The rain is continuous, and water runs in the bottom of the trench. The floor-gratings yield as the soil becomes soaked; some of them slope to right or left and we skid on them. In the dark, too, one cannot see them, so we miss them at the turnings and put our feet into holes full of water.

Even in the grayness of the night I will not lose sight of the slaty shine of Poterloo's helmet, which streams like a roof under the torrent, nor of the broad back that is adorned with a square of glistening oilskin. I lock my step in his, and from time to time I question him and he answers me—always in good humor, always serene and strong.

When there are no more of the wooden floor-gratings, we tramp in the thick mud. It is dark now. There is a sudden halt and I am thrown on Poterloo. Up higher we hear half-angry reproaches—"What the devil, will you get on? We shall get broken up!"

"I can't get my trotters unstuck!" replies a pitiful voice.

The engulfed one gets clear at last, and we have to run to overtake the rest of the company. We begin to pant and complain, and bluster against those who are leading. Our feet go down haphazard; we stumble and hold ourselves up by the wails, so that our hands are plastered with mud. The march becomes a stampede, full of the noise of metal things and of oaths.

In redoubled rain there is a second halt; some one has fallen, and the hubbub is general. He picks himself up and we are off again. I exert myself to follow Poterloo's helmet closely that gleams feebly in the night before my eyes, and I shout from time to time, "All right?"—"Yes, yes, all right," he replies, puffing and blowing, and his voice always singsong and resonant.

Our knapsacks, tossed in this rolling race under the assault of the elements, drag and hurt our shoulders.

The trench is blocked by a recent landslide, and we plunge unto it. We have to tear our feet out of the soft and clinging earth, lifting them high at each step. Then, when this crossing is laboriously accomplished, we topple down again into the slippery stream, in the bottom of which are two narrow ruts, boot-worn, which hold one's foot like a vice, and there are pools into which it goes with a great splash. In one place we must stoop very low to pass under a heavy and glutinous bridge that crosses the trench, and we only get through with difficulty. It obliges us to kneel in the mud, to flatten ourselves on the ground, and to crawl on all fours for a few paces. A little farther there are evolutions to perform as we grasp a post that the sinking of the ground has set aslope across the middle of the fairway.

We come to a trench-crossing. "Allons, forward! Look out for yourselves, boys!" says the adjutant, who has flattened himself in a corner to let us pass and to speak to us. "This is a bad spot."

"We're done up," shouts a voice so hoarse that I cannot identify the speaker.

"Damn! I've enough of it, I'm stopping here," groans another, at the end of his wind and his muscle.

"What do you want me to do?" replies the adjutant, "No fault of mine, eh? Allons, get a move on, it's a bad spot—it was shelled at the last relief!"

We go on through the tempest of wind and water. We seem to be going ever down and down, as in a pit. We slip and tumble, butt into the wall of the trench, into which we drive our elbows hard, so as to throw ourselves upright again. Our going is a sort of long slide, on which we keep up just how and where we can. What matters is to stumble only forward, and as straight as possible.

Where are we? I lift my head, in spite of the billows of rain, out of this gulf where we are struggling. Against the hardly discernible background of the buried sky, I can make out the rim of the trench; and there, rising before my eyes all at once and towering over that rim, is something like a sinister doorway, made of two black posts that lean one upon the other, with something hanging from the middle like a torn-off scalp. It is the doorway.

"Forward! Forward!"

I lower my head and see no more; but again I hear the feet that sink in the mud and come out again, the rattle of the bayonets, the heavy exclamations, and the rapid breathing.

Once more there is a violent back-eddy. We pull up sharply, and again I am thrown upon Poterloo and lean on his back, his strong back and solid, like the trunk of a tree, like healthfulness and like hope. He cries to me, "Cheer up, old man, we're there!"

We are standing still. It is necessary to go hack a little—Nom de Dieu!—no, we are moving on again!

Suddenly a fearful explosion falls on us. I tremble to my skull; a metallic reverberation fills my head; a scorching and suffocating smell of sulphur pierces my nostrils. The earth has opened in front of me. I feel myself lifted and hurled aside—doubled up, choked, and half blinded by this lightning and thunder. But still my recollection is clear; and in that moment when I looked wildly and desperately for my comrade-in-arms, I saw his body go up, erect and black, both his arms outstretched to their limit, and a flame in the place of his head!

The Big Words

BARQUE notices that I am writing. He comes towards me on all fours through the straw and lifts his intelligent face to me, with its reddish forelock and the little quick eyes over which circumflex accents fold and unfold them-selves. His mouth is twisting in all directions, by reason of a tablet of chocolate that he crunches and chews, while he holds the moist stump of it in his fist.

With his mouth full, and wafting me the odor of a sweetshop, he stammers—"Tell me, you writing chap, you'll be writing later about soldiers, you'll be speaking of us, eh?"

"Why yes, sonny, I shall talk about you, and about the boys, and about our life."

"Tell me, then"—he indicates with a nod the papers on which I have been making notes. With hovering pencil I watch and listen to him. He has a question to put to me—"Tell me, then, though you needn't if you don't want—there's something I want to ask you. This is it; if you make the common soldiers talk in your book, are you going to make them talk like they do talk, or shall you put it all straight—into pretty talk? It's about the big words that we use. For after all, now, besides falling out sometimes and blackguarding each other, you'll never hear two poilus open their heads for a minute without saying and repeating things that the printers wouldn't much like to print. Then what? If you don't say 'em, your portrait won't be a lifelike one it's as if you were going to paint them and then left out one of the gaudiest colors wherever you found it. All the same, it isn't usually done."

"I shall put the big words in their place, dadda, for they're the truth."

"But tell me, if you put 'em in, won't the people of your sort say you're swine, without worrying about the truth?"

"Very likely, but I shall do it all the same, without worrying about those people."

"Do you want my opinion? Although I know nothing about books, it's brave to do that, because it isn't usually done, and it'll be spicy if you dare do it—but you'll find it hard when it comes to it, you're too polite. That's just one of the faults I've found in you since we've known each other;

that, and also that dirty habit you've got, when they're serving brandy out to us, you pretend it'll do you harm, and instead of giving your share to a pal, you go and pour it on your head to wash your scalp."

Of Burdens

AT the end of the yard of the Muets farm, among the outbuildings, the barn gapes like a cavern. It is always caverns for us, even in houses! When you have crossed the yard, where the manure yields underfoot with a spongy sound or have gone round it instead on the narrow paved path of difficult equilibrium, and when you have arrived at the entrance to the barn, you can see nothing at all.

Then, if you persist, you make out a misty hollow where equally misty and dark lumps are asquat or prone or wandering from one corner to another. At the back, on the right and on the left, the pale gleams of two candles, each with the round halo of a distant moon allow you at last to make out the human shape of these masses, whose mouths emit either steam or thick smoke.

Our hazy retreat, which I allow carefully to swallow me whole, is a scene of excitement this evening. We leave for the trenches to-morrow morning, and the nebulous tenants of the barn are beginning to pack up.

Although darkness falls on my eyes and chokes them as I come in from the pallid evening, I still dodge the snares spread over the ground by water-bottles, mess-tins and weapons, but I butt full into the loaves that are packed together exactly in the middle, like the paving of a yard. I reach my corner. Something alive is there with a huge back, fleecy and rounded, squatting and stooping over a collection of little things that glitter on the ground, and I tap the shoulder upholstered in sheepskin. The being turns round, and by the dull and fitful gleam of a candle which a bayonet stuck in the ground upholds, I see one half of a face, an eye, the end of a mustache, and the corner of a half-open mouth. It growls in a friendly way, and resumes the inspection of its possessions.

"What are you doing there?"

"I'm fixing things, and clearing up."

The quasi-brigand who appears to be checking his booty, is my comrade Volpatte. He has folded his tent-cloth in four and placed it on his bed—that is, on the truss of straw assigned to him—and on this carpet he has emptied and displayed the contents of his pockets.

And it is quite a shop that he broods over with a housewife's solicitous eyes, watchful and jealous, lest some one walks over him. With my eye I tick off his copious exhibition.

Alongside his handkerchief, pipe, tobacco-pouch (which also contains a note-book), knife, purse, and pocket pipe-lighter, which comprise the necessary and indispensable groundwork, here are two leather laces twisted like earthworms round a watch enclosed in a case of transparent celluloid, which has curiously dulled and blanched with age. Then a little round mirror, and another square one; this last, though broken, is of better quality, and bevel-edged. A flask of essence of turpentine, a flask of mineral oil nearly empty, and a third flask, empty. A German belt-plate, bearing the device, "Gott mit uns"; a dragoon's tassel of similar origin; half wrapped in paper, an aviator's arrow in the form of a steel pencil and pointed like a needle; folding scissors and a combined knife and fork of similar pliancy; a stump of pencil and one of candle; a tube of aspirin, also containing opium tablets, and several tin boxes.

Observing that my inspection of his personal possessions is detailed, Volpatte helps me to identify certain items—

"That, that's a leather officer's glove. I cut the fingers off to stop up the mouth of my blunderbuss with; that, that's telephone wire, the only thing to fasten buttons on your greatcoat with if you want 'em to stay there; and here, inside here, d'you know what that is? White thread, good stuff, not what you're put off with when they give you new things, a sort of macaroni au fromage that you pull out with a fork; and there's a set of needles on a post-card. The safety-pins, they're there, separate."

"And here, that's the paper department. Quite a library."

There is indeed a surprising collection of papers among the things disgorged by Volpatte's pockets—the violet packet of writing-paper, whose unworthy printed envelope is out at heels; an Army squad-book, of which the dirty and desiccated binding, like the skin of an old tramp, has perished and shrunk all over: a note-book with a chafed moleskin cover, and packed with papers and photographs, those of his wife and children enthroned in the middle.

Out of this bundle of yellowed and darkened papers Volpatte extracts this photograph and shows it to me once more. I renew acquaintance with Madame Volpatte and her generous bosom, her mild and mellow features;

and with the two little boys in white collars, the elder slender, the younger round as a ball.

"I've only got photos of old people," says Biquet, who is twenty years old. He shows us a portrait holding it close to the candle, of two aged people who look at us with the same well-behaved air as Volpatte's children.

"I've got mine with me, too," says another; "I always stick to the photo of the nestlings."

"Course! Every man carries his crowd along," adds another.

"It's funny," Barque declares, "a portrait wears itself out just with being looked at. You haven't got to gape at it too often, or be too long about it; in the long run, I don't know what happens, but the likeness mizzles."

"You're right," says Blaire, "I've found it like that too, exactly."

"I've got a map of the district as well, among my papers," Volpatte continues. He unfolds it to the light. Illegible and transparent at the creases, it looks like one of those window-blinds made of squares sewn together.

"I've some newspaper too"—he unfolds a newspaper article upon poilus—"and a book"—a twopence-half-penny novel, called Twice a Maid—"Tiens, another newspaper cutting from the Etampes Bee. Don't know why I've kept that, but there must be a reason somewhere. I'll think about it when I have time. And then, my pack of cards, and a set of draughts, with a paper board and the pieces made of sealing-wax."

Barque comes up, regards the scene, and says, "I've a lot more things than that in my pockets." He addresses himself to Volpatte. "Have you got a Boche pay-book, louse-head, some phials of iodine, and a Browning? I've all that, and two knives."

"I've no revolver," says Volpatte, "nor a Boche pay-book, but I could have had two knives or even ten knives; but I only need one."

"That depends," says Barque. "And have you any mechanical buttons, fathead?"

"I haven't any," cries Becuwe.

"The private can't do without 'em," Lamuse asserts. "Without them, to make your braces stick to your breeches, the game's up."

"And I've always got in my pocket," says Blaire, "so's they're within reach, my case of rings." He brings it cut, wrapped up in a gas-mask bag, and shakes it. The files ring inside, and we hear the jingle of aluminium rings in the rough.

"I've always got string," says Biquet, "that's the useful stuff!"

"Not so useful as nails," says Pepin, and he shows three in his hand, big, little, and average.

One by one the others come to join in the conversation, to chaffer and cadge. We are getting used to the half-darkness. But Corporal Salavert, who has a well-earned reputation for dexterity, makes a banging lamp with a candle and a tray, the latter contrived from a Camembert box and some wire. We light up, and around its illumination each man tells what he has in his pockets, with parental preferences and bias.

"To begin with, how many have we?"

"How many pockets? Eighteen," says some one—Cocon, of course, the man of figures.

"Eighteen pockets! You're codding, rat-nose," says big Lamuse.

"Exactly eighteen," replies Cocon. "Count them, if you're as clever as all that."

Lamuse is willing to be guided by reason in the matter, and putting his two hands near the light so as to count accurately, he tells off his great brick-red fingers: Two pockets in the back of the greatcoat; one for the first-aid packet, which is used for tobacco; two inside the greatcoat in front; two outside it on each side, with flaps; three in the trousers, and even three and a half, counting the little one in front.

"I'll bet a compass on it," says Farfadet.

"And I, my bits of tinder."

"I," says Tirloir, "I'll bet a teeny whistle that my wife sent me when she said, 'If you're wounded in the battle you must whistle, so that your comrades will come and save your life.'"

We laugh at the artless words. Tulacque intervenes, and says indulgently to Tiloir, "They don't know what war is back there; and if you started talking about the rear, it'd be you that'd talk rot."

"We won't count that pocket," says Salavert, "it's too small. That makes ten."

"In the jacket, four. That only makes fourteen after all."

"There are the two cartridge pockets, the two new ones that fasten with straps."

"Sixteen," says Salavert.

"Now, blockhead and son of misery, turn my jacket back. You haven't counted those two pockets. Now then, what more do you want? And yet they're just in the usual place. They're your civilian pockets, where you shoved your nose-rag, your tobacco, and the address where you'd got to deliver your parcel when you were a messenger."

"Eighteen!" says Salavert, as grave as a judge. "There are eighteen, and no mistake; that's done it."

At this point in the conversation, some one makes a series of noisy stumbles on the stones of the threshold with the sound of a horse pawing the ground—and blaspheming. Then, after a silence, the barking of a sonorous and authoritative voice—"Hey, inside there! Getting ready? Everything must be fixed up this evening and packed tight and solid, you know. Going into the first line this time, and we may have a hot time of it."

"Right you are, right you are, mon adjutant." heedless voices answer.

"How do you write 'Arnesse'?" asks Benech, who is on all fours, at work with a pencil and an envelope. While Cocon spells "Ernest" for him and the voice of the vanished adjutant is heard afar repeating his harangue, Blaire picks up the thread, and says—

"You should always, my children—listen to what I'm telling you—put your drinking-cup in your pocket. I've tried to stick it everywhere else, but only the pocket's really practical, you take my word. If you're in marching order, or if you've doffed your kit to navigate the trenches either, you've always got it under your fist when chances come, like when a pal who's got some gargle, and feels good towards you says, 'Lend us your cup,' or a peddling wine-seller, either. My young bucks, listen to what I tell you; you'll always find it good—put your cup in your pocket."

"No fear," says Lamuse, "you won't see me put my cup in my pocket; damned silly idea, no more or less. I'd a sight sooner sling it on a strap with a hook."

"Fasten it on a greatcoat button, like the gas-helmet bag, that's a lot better; for suppose you take off your accouterments and there's any wine passing, you look soft."

"I've got a Boche drinking-cup," says Barque; "it's flat, so it goes into a side pocket if you like, or it goes very well into a cartridge-pouch, once you've fired the damn things off or pitched them into a bag."

"A Boche cup's nothing special," says Pepin; "it won't stand up, it's just lumber."

"You wait and see, maggot-snout," says Tirette, who is something of a psychologist. "If we attack this time, same as the adjutant seemed to hint, perhaps you'll find a Boche cup, and then it'll be something special!"

"The adjutant may have said that," Eudore observes, "but he doesn't know."

"It holds more than a half-pint, the Boche cup," remarks Cocon, "seeing that the exact capacity of the half-pint is marked in the cup three-quarters way up; and it's always good for you to have a big one, for if you've got a cup that only just holds a half-pint, then so that you can get your half-pint of coffee or wine or holy water or what not, it's get to be filled right up, and they don't ever do it at serving-out, and if they do, you spill it."

"I believe you that they don't fill it," says Paradis, exasperated by the recollection of that ceremony. "The quartermaster-sergeant, he pours it with his blasted finger in your cup and gives it two raps on its bottom. Result, you get a third, and your cup's in mourning with three black bands on top of each other."

"Yes," says Barque, "that's true; but you shouldn't have a cup too big either, because the chap that's pouring it out for you, he suspects you, and let's it go in damned drops, and so as not to give you more than your measure he gives you less, and you can whistle for it, with your tureen in your fists."

Volpatte puts back in his pockets, one by one, the items of his display. When he came to the purse, he looked at it with an air of deep compassion.

"He's damnably flat, poor chap!" He counted the contents. "Three francs! My boy, I most set about feathering this nest again or I shall be stony when we get back."

"You're not the only one that's broken-backed in the treasury."

"The soldier spends more than he earns, and don't you forget it. I wonder what'd become of a man that only had his pay?"

Paradis replies with concise simplicity, "He'd kick the bucket."

"And see here, look what I've got in my pocket and never let go of"—Pepin, with merry eyes, shows us some silver table-things. "They belonged," he says, "to the ugly trollop where we were quartered at Grand-Rozoy."

"Perhaps they still belong to her?"

Pepin made an uncertain gesture, in which pride mingled with modesty; then, growing bolder, he smiled and said, "I knew her, the old sneak. Certainly, she'll spend the rest of her life looking in every corner for her silver things."

"For my part," says Volpatte, "I've never been able to rake in more than a pair of scissors. Some people have the luck. I haven't. So naturally I watch 'em close, though I admit I've no use for 'em."

"I've pinched a few bits of things here and there, but what of it? The sappers have always left me behind in the matter of pinching; so what about it?"

"You can do what you like, you're always got at by some one in your turn, eh, my boy? Don't fret about it."

"I keep my wife's letters," says Blaire.

"And I send mine back to her."

"And I keep them, too. Here they are." Eudore exposes a packet of worn and shiny paper, whose grimy condition the twilight modestly veils. "I keep them. Sometimes I read them again. When I'm cold and humpy, I read 'em again. It doesn't actually warm you up, but it seems to."

There must be a deep significance in the curious expression, for several men raise their heads and say, "Yes, that's so."

By fits and starts the conversation goes on in the bosom of this fantastic barn and the great moving shadows that cross it; night is heaped up in its corners, and pointed by a few scattered and sickly candles.

I watch these busy and burdened flitters come and go, outline themselves strangely, then stoop and slide down to the ground; they talk to themselves and to each other, their feet are encumbered by the litter. They are showing their riches to each other. "Tiens, look!"—"Great!" they reply enviously.

What they have not got they want. There are treasures among the squad long coveted by all; the two-liter water-bottle, for instance, preserved by Barque, that a skillful rifle-shot with a blank cartridge has stretched to the capacity of two and a half liters; and Bertrand's famous great knife with the horn handle.

Among the heaving swarm there are sidelong glances that skim these curiosities, and then each man resumes "eyes right," devotes himself to his belongings, and concentrates upon getting it in order.

They are mournful belongings, indeed. Everything made for the soldier is commonplace, ugly, and of bad quality; from his cardboard boots, attached to the uppers by a criss-cross of worthless thread, to his badly cut, badly shaped, and badly sewn clothes, made of shoddy and transparent cloth—blotting-paper—that one day of sunshine fades and an hour of rain wets through, to his emaciated leathers, brittle as shavings and torn by the buckle spikes, to his flannel underwear that is thinner than cotton, to his straw-like tobacco.

Marthereau is beside me, and he points to our comrades: "Look at them, these poor chaps gaping into their bags o' tricks. You'd say it was a mothers' meeting, ogling their kids. Hark to 'em. They're calling for their knick-knacks. Tiens, that one, the times he says 'My knife!' same as if he was calling 'Lon,' or 'Charles,' or 'Dolphus.' And you know it's impossible for them to make their load any less. Can't be did. It isn't that they don't want—our job isn't one that makes us any stronger, eh? But they can't. Too proud of 'em."

The burdens to be borne are formidable, and one knows well enough, parbleu, that every item makes them more severe, each little addition is one bruise more.

For it is not merely a matter of what one buries in his pockets and pouches. To complete the burden there is what one carries on his back. The knapsack is the trunk and even the cupboard; and the old soldier is familiar with the art of enlarging it almost miraculously by the judicious disposal of his household goods and provisions. Besides the regulation and obligatory contents—two tins of pressed beef, a dozen biscuits, two tablets of coffee and two packets of dried soup, the bag of sugar, fatigue smock, and spare boots—we find a way of getting in some pots of jam, tobacco, chocolate, candles, soft-soled shoes; and even soap, a spirit lamp, some solidified spirit, and some woolen things. With the blanket, sheet, tentcloth, trenching-tool, water-bottle, and an item of the field-cooking kit, the burden gets heavier and taller and wider, monumental and crushing.

And my neighbor says truly that every time he reaches his goal after some miles of highway and communication trenches, the poilu swears hard that the next time he'll leave a heap of things behind and give his shoulders a little relief from the yoke of the knapsack. But every time he is preparing for departure, he assumes again the same overbearing and almost superhuman load; he never lets it go, though he curses it always.

"There are some bad boys," says Lamuse, "among the shirkers, that find a way of keeping something in the company wagon or the medical van. I know one that's got two shirts and a pair of drawers in an adjutant's canteen—but, you see, there's two hundred and fifty chaps in the company, and they're all up to the dodge and not many of 'em can profit by it; it's chiefly the non-coms.; the more stripes they've got, the easier it is to plant their luggage, not forgetting that the commandant visits the wagons sometimes without warning and fires your things into the middle of the road if he finds 'em in a horse-box where they've no business—Be off with you!—not to mention the bully-ragging and the clink."

"In the early days it was all right, my boy. There were some chaps—I've seen 'em—who stuck their bags and even their knapsacks in baby-carts and pushed 'em along the road."

"Ah, not half! Those were the good times of the war. But all that's changed."

Volpatte, deaf to all the talk, muffled in his blanket as if in a shawl which makes him look like an old witch, revolves round an object that lies on the ground. "I'm wondering," lie says, addressing no one, "whether to take away this damned tin stove. It's the only one in the squad and I've always carried it. Oui, but it leaks like a cullender." He cannot decide, and makes a really pathetic picture of separation.

Barque watches him obliquely, and makes fun of him. We hear him say, "Senile dodderer!" But he pauses in his chaffing to say, "After all, if we were in his shoes we should be equally fatheaded."

Volpatte postpones his decision till later. "I'll see about it in the morning, when I'm loading the camel's back."

After the inspection and recharging of pockets, it is the turn of the bags, and then of the cartridge-pouches, and Barque holds forth on the way to make the regulation two hundred cartridges go into the three pouches. In the lump it is impossible. They must be unpacked and placed side by side upright, head against foot. Thus can one cram each pouch without leaving any space, and make himself a waistband that weighs over twelve pounds.

Rifles have been cleaned already. One looks to the swathing of the breech and the plugging of the muzzle, precautions which trench-dirt renders indispensable.

How every rifle can easily be recognized is discussed. "I've made some nicks in the sling. See, I've cut into the edge."

"I've twisted a bootlace round the top of the sling, and that way, I can tell it by touch as well as seeing."

"I use a mechanical button. No mistake about that. In the dark I can find it at once and say, 'That's my pea-shooter. Because, you know, there are some boys that don't bother themselves; they just roll around while the pals are cleaning theirs, and then they're devilish quick at putting a quiet fist on a popgun that's been cleaned; and then after they've even the cheek to go and say, 'Mon capitaine, I've got a rifle that's a bit of all right.' I'm not on in that act. It's the D system, my old wonder—a damned dirty dodge, and there are times when I'm fed up with it, and more."

And thus, though their rifles are all alike, they are as different as their handwriting.

"It's curious and funny," says Marthereau to me "we're going up to the trenches to-morrow, and there's nobody drunk yet, nor that way inclined. Ah, I don't say," he concedes at once, "but what those two there aren't a bit fresh, nor a little elevated; without being absolutely blind, they're somewhat boozed, pr'aps—"

"It's Poitron and Poilpot, of Broyer's squad."

They are lying down and talking in a low voice. We can make out the round nose of one, which stands out equally with his mouth, close by a candle, and with his hand, whose lifted finger makes little explanatory signs, faithfully followed by the shadow it casts.

"I know how to light a fire, but I don't know how to light it again when it's gone out," declares Poitron.

"Ass!" says Poilpot, "if you know how to light it you know how to relight it, seeing that if you light it, it's because it's gone out, and you might say that you're relighting it when you're lighting it."

"That's all rot. I'm not mathematical, and to hell with the gibberish you talk. I tell you and I tell you again that when it comes to lighting a fire, I'm there, but to light it again when it's gone out, I'm no good. I can't speak any straighter than that."

I do not catch the insistent retort of Poilpot, but—"But, you damned numskull," gurgles Poitron, "haven't I told you thirty times that I can't? You must have a pig's head, anyway!"

Marthereau confides to me, "I've heard about enough of that." Obviously he spoke too soon just now.

A sort of fever, provoked by farewell libations, prevails in the wretched straw-spread hole where our tribe—some upright and hesitant, others kneeling and hammering like colliers—is mending, stacking, and subduing its provisions, clothes, and tools. There is a wordy growling, a riot of gesture. From the smoky glimmers, rubicund faces start forth in relief, and dark hands move about in the shadows like marionettes. In the barn next to ours, and separated from it only by a wall of a man's height, arise tipsy shouts. Two men in there have fallen upon each other with fierce violence and anger. The air is vibrant with the coarsest expressions the human ear ever hears. But one of the disputants, a stranger from another squad, is ejected by the tenants, and the flow of curses from the other grows feebler and expires.

"Same as us," says Marthereau with a certain pride, "they hold themselves in!"

It is true. Thanks to Bertrand, who is possessed by a hatred of drunkenness, of the fatal poison that gambles with multitudes, our squad is one of the least befouled by wine and brandy.

They are shouting and singing and talking all around. And they laugh endlessly, for in the human mechanism laughter is the sound of wheels that work, of deeds that are done.

One tries to fathom certain faces that show up in provocative relief among this menagerie of shadows, this aviary of reflections. But one cannot. They are visible, but you can see nothing in the depth of them.

"Ten o'clock already, friends," says Bertrand. "We'll finish the camel's humps off to-morrow. Time for by-by." Each one then slowly retires to rest, but the jabbering hardly pauses. Man takes all things easily when he is under no obligation to hurry. The men go to and fro, each with some object in his hand, and along the wall I watch Eudore's huge shadow gliding, as he passes in front of a candle with two little bags of camphor hanging from the end of his fingers.

Lamuse is throwing himself about in search of a good position; he seems ill at ease. To-day, obviously, and whatever his capacity may be, he has eaten too much.

"Some of us want to sleep! Shut them up, you lot of louts!" cries Mesnil Joseph from his litter.

This entreaty has a subduing effect for a moment, but does not stop the burble of voices nor the passing to and fro.

"We're going up to-morrow, it's true," says Paradis, "and in the evening we shall go into the first line. But nobody's thinking about it. We know it, and that's all."

Gradually each has regained his place. I have stretched myself on the straw, and Marthereau wraps himself up by my side.

Enter an enormous bulk, taking great pains not to make a noise. It is the field-hospital sergeant, a Marist Brother, a huge bearded simpleton in spectacles. When he has taken off his greatcoat and appears in his jacket, you are conscious that he feels awkward about showing his legs. We see that it hurries discreetly, this silhouette of a bearded hippopotamus. He blows, sighs, and mutters.

Marthereau indicates him with a nod of his bead, and says to me, "Look at him. Those chaps have always got to be talking fudge. When we ask him what he does in civil life, he won't say 'I'm a school teacher' he says, leering at you from under his specs with the half of his eyes, 'I'm a professor.' When he gets up very early to go to mass, he says, 'I've got belly-ache, I must go and take a turn round the corner and no mistake.'"

A little farther off, Papa Ramure is talking of his homeland: "Where I live, it's just a bit of a hamlet, no great shakes. There's my old man there, seasoning pipes all day long; whether he's working or resting, he blows his smoke up to the sky or into the smoke of the stove."

I listen to this rural idyll, and it takes suddenly a specialized and technical character: "That's why he makes a paillon. D'you know what a paillon is? You take a stalk of green corn and peel it. You split it in two

and then in two again, and you have different sizes. Then with a thread
and the four slips of straw, he goes round the stem of his pipe—"

The lesson ceases abruptly, there being no apparent audience.

There are only two candles alight. A wide wing of darkness overspreads
the prostrate collection of men.

Private conversation still flickers along the primitive dormitory, and
some fragments of it reach my ears. Just now, Papa Ramure is abusing the
commandant.

"The commandant, old man, with his four bits of gold string, I've
noticed he don't know how to smoke. He sucks all out at his pipes, and he
burns 'em. It isn't a mouth he's got in his head, it's a snout. The wood
splits and scorches, and instead of being wood, it's coal. Clay pipes,
they'll stick it better, but he roasts 'em brown all the same. Talk about a
snout! So, old man, mind what I'm telling you, he'll come to what doesn't
ever happen often; through being forced to get white-hot and baked to the
marrow, his pipe'll explode in his nose before everybody. You'll see."

Little by little, peace, silence, and darkness take possession of the barn
and enshroud the hopes and the sighs of its occupants. The lines of
identical bundles formed by these beings rolled up side by side in their
blankets seem a sort of huge organ, which sends forth diversified snoring.

With his nose already in his blanket, I hear Marthereau talking to me
about himself: "I'm a buyer of rags, you know," he says, "or to put it
better, a rag merchant. But me, I'm wholesale; I buy from the little
rag-and-bone men of the streets, and I have a shop—a warehouse mind
you!—which I use as a depot. I deal in all kinds of rags, from linen to
jam-pots, but principally brush-handles, sacks, and old shoes; and
naturally, I make a specialty of rabbit-skins."

And a little later I still hear him: "As for me, little and queer-shaped as I
am, all the same I can carry a bin of two hundred pounds' weight to the
warehouse, up the steps, and my feet in sabots. Once I had a to-do with a
person—"

"What I can't abide," cries Fouillade, all of a sudden, "is the exercises
and marches they give us when we're resting. My back's mincemeat, and I
can't get a snooze even, I'm that cramped."

There is a metallic noise in Volpatte's direction. He has decided to take
the stove, though he chides it constantly for the fatal fault of its
perforations.

One who is but half asleep groans, "Oh, la, la! When will this war
finish!"

A cry of stubborn and mysterious rebellion bursts forth—"They'd take
the very skin off us!"

There follows a single, "Don't fret yourself!" as darkly inconsequent as
the cry of revolt.

I wake up a long time afterwards, as two o'clock is striking; and in a
pallor of light which doubtless comes from the moon, I see the agitated
silhouette of Pinegal. A cock has crowed afar. Pinegal raises himself
halfway to a sitting position, and I hear his husky voice: "Well now, it's
the middle of the night, and there's a cock loosing his jaw. He's blind
drunk, that cock." He laughs, and repeats, "He's blind, that cock," and he
twists himself again into the woolens, and resumes his slumber with a
gurgle in which snores are mingled with merriment.

Cocon has been wakened by Pinegal. The man of figures therefore
thinks aloud, and says: "The squad had seventeen men when it set off for
the war. It has seventeen also at present, with the stop-gaps. Each man has
already worn out four greatcoats, one of the original blue, and three
cigar-smoke blue, two pairs of trousers and six pairs of boots. One must
count two rifles to each man, but one can't count the overalls. Our
emergency rations have been renewed twenty-three times. Among us
seventeen, we've been mentioned fourteen times in Army Orders, of
which two were to the Brigade, four to the Division, and one to the Army.
Once we stayed sixteen days in the trenches without relief. We've been
quartered and lodged in forty-seven different villages up to now. Since the
beginning of the campaign, twelve thousand men have passed through the
regiment, which consists of two thousand."

A strange lisping noise interrupts him. It comes from Blaire, whose new
ivories prevent him from talking as they also prevent him from eating. But
he puts them in every evening, and retains them all night with fierce
determination, for he was promised that in the end he would grow
accustomed to the object they have put into his head.

I raise myself on my elbow, as on a battlefield, and look once more on the beings whom the scenes and happenings of the times have rolled up all together. I look at them all, plunged in the abyss of passive oblivion, some of them seeming still to be absorbed in their pitiful anxieties, their childish instincts, and their slave-like ignorance.

The intoxication of sleep masters me. But I recall what they have done and what they will do; and with that consummate picture of a sorry human night before me, a shroud that fills our cavern with darkness, I dream of some great unknown light.

The Egg

WE were badly off, hungry and thirsty; and in these wretched quarters there was nothing!

Something had gone wrong with the revictualing department and our wants were becoming acute. Where the sorry place surrounded them, with its empty doors, its bones of houses, and its bald-headed telegraph posts, a crowd of hungry men were grinding their teeth and confirming the absence of everything:—"The juice has sloped and the wine's up the spout, and the bully's zero. Cheese? Nix. Napoo jam, napoo butter on skewers."

"We've nothing, and no error, nothing; and play hell as you like, it doesn't help."

"Talk about rotten quarters! Three houses with nothing inside but draughts and damp."

"No good having any of the filthy here, you might as well have only the skin of a bob in your purse, as long as there's nothing to buy."

"You might be a Rothschild, or even a military tailor, but what use'd your brass be?"

"Yesterday there was a bit of a cat mewing round where the 7th are. I feel sure they've eaten it."

"Yes, there was; you could see its ribs like rocks on the sea-shore."

"There were some chaps," says Blaire, "who bustled about when they got here and managed to find a few bottles of common wine at the bacca-shop at the corner of the street."

"Ah, the swine! Lucky devils to be sliding that down their necks."

"It was muck, all the same, it'd make your cup as black as your baccy-pipe."

"There are some, they say, who've swallowed a fowl."

"Damn," says Fouillade.

"I've hardly had a bite. I had a sardine left, and a little tea in the bottom of a bag that I chewed up with some sugar."

"You can't even have a bit of a drunk—it's off the map."

"And that isn't enough either, even when you're not a big eater and you're got a communication trench as flat as a pancake."

"One meal in two days—a yellow mess, shining like gold, no broth and no meat—everything left behind."

"And worst of all we've nothing to light a pipe with."

"True, and that's misery. I haven't a single match. I had several bits of ends, but they've gone. I've hunted in vain through all the pockets of my flea-case—nix. As for buying them it's hopeless, as you say."

"I've got the head of a match that I'm keeping." It is a real hardship indeed, and the sight is pitiful of the poilus who cannot light pipe or cigarette but put them away in their pockets and stroll in resignation. By good fortune, Tirloir has his petrol pipe-lighter and it still contains a little spirit. Those who are aware of it gather round him, bringing their pipes packed and cold. There is not even any paper to light, and the flame itself must be used until the remaining spirit in its tiny insect's belly is burned.

As for me, I've been lucky, and I see Paradis wandering about, his kindly face to the wind, grumbling and chewing a bit of wood. "Tiens," I say to him, "take this."

"A box of matches!" he exclaims amazed, looking at it as one looks at a jewel. "Egad! That's capital! Matches!"

A moment later we see him lighting his pipe, his face saucily sideways and splendidly crimsoned by the reflected flame, and everybody shouts, "Paradis' got some matches!"

Towards evening I meet Paradis near the ruined triangle of a house-front at the corner of the two streets of this most miserable among villages.

He beckons to me. "Hist!" He has a curious and rather awkward air.

"I say," he says to me affectionately, but looking at his feet, "a bit since, you chucked me a box of flamers. Well, you're going to get a bit of your own back for it. Here!"

He puts something in my hand. "Be careful!" he whispers, "it's fragile!"

Dazzled by the resplendent purity of his present, hardly even daring to believe my eyes, I see—an egg!

An Idyll

"REALLY and truly," said Paradis, my neighbor in the ranks, "believe me or not, I'm knocked out—I've never before been so paid on a march as I have been with this one, this evening."

His feet were dragging, and his square shoulders bowed under the burden of the knapsack, whose height and big irregular outline seemed almost fantastic. Twice he tripped and stumbled.

Paradis is tough. But he had been running up and down the trench all night as liaison man while the others were sleeping, so he had good reason to be exhausted and to growl "Quoi? These kilometers must be made of india-rubber, there's no way out of it."

Every three steps he hoisted his knapsack roughly up with a hitch of his hips, and panted under its dragging; and all the heap that he made with his bundles tossed and creaked like an overloaded wagon.

"We're there," said a non-com.

Non-coms. always say that, on every occasion. But—in spite of the non-com.'s declaration—we were really arriving in a twilight village which seemed to be drawn in white chalk and heavy strokes of black upon the blue paper of the sky, where the sable silhouette of the church—a pointed tower flanked by two turrets more slender and more sharp—was that of a tall cypress.

But the soldier, even when he enters the village where he is to be quartered, has not reached the end of his troubles. It rarely happens that either the squad or the section actually lodges in the place assigned to them, and this by reason of misunderstandings and cross purposes which tangle and disentangle themselves on the spot; and it is only after several quarter-hours of tribulation that each man is led to his actual shelter of the moment.

So after the usual wanderings we were admitted to our night's lodging—a roof supported by four posts, and with the four quarters of the compass for its walls. But it was a good roof—an advantage which we could appreciate. It was already sheltering a cart and a plow, and we settled ourselves by them. Paradis, who had fumed and complained without ceasing during the hour we had spent in tramping to and fro, threw down his knapsack and then himself, and stayed there awhile, weary to the utmost, protesting that his limbs were benumbed, that the soles of his feet were painful, and indeed all the rest of him.

But now the house to which our hanging roof was subject, the house which stood just in front of us, was lighted up. Nothing attracts a soldier in the gray monotony of evening so much as a window whence beams the star of a lamp.

"Shall we have a squint?" proposed Volpatte.

"So be it," said Paradis. He gets up gradually, and hobbling with weariness, steers himself towards the golden window that has appeared in the gloom, and then towards the door. Volpatte follows him, and I Volpatte.

We enter, and ask the old man who has let us in and whose twinkling head is as threadbare as an old hat, if he has any wine to sell.

"No," replies the old man, shaking his head, where a little white fluff crops out in places.

"No beer? No coffee? Anything at all—"

"No, mes amis, nothing of anything. We don't belong here; we're refugees, you know."

"Then seeing there's nothing, we'll be off." We right-about face. At least we have enjoyed for a moment the warmth which pervades the house and a sight of the lamp. Already Volpatte has gained the threshold and his back is disappearing in the darkness.

But I espy an old woman, sunk in the depths of a chair in the other corner of the kitchen, who appears to have some busy occupation.

I pinch Paradis' arm. "There's the belle of the house. Shall we pay our addresses to her?"

Paradis makes a gesture of lordly indifference. He has lost interest in women—all those he has seen for a year and a half were not for him; and moreover, even when they would like to be his, he is equally uninterested.

"Young or old—pooh!" he says to me, beginning to yawn. For want of something to do and to lengthen the leaving, he goes up to the goodwife. "Good-evening, gran'ma," he mumbles, finishing his yawn.

"Good-evening, mes enfants," quavers the old dame. So near, we see her in detail. She is shriveled, bent and bowed in her old bones, and the whole of her face is white as the dial of a clock.

And what is she doing? Wedged between her chair and the edge of the
table she is trying to clean some boots. It is a heavy task for her infantile
hands; their movements are uncertain, and her strokes with the brush
sometimes go astray. The boots, too, are very dirty indeed.

Seeing that we are watching her, she whispers to us that she must polish
them well, and this evening too, for they are her little girl's boots, who is a
dressmaker in the town and goes off first thing in the morning.

Paradis has stooped to look at the boots more closely, and suddenly he
puts his hand out towards them. "Drop it, gran'ma; I'll spruce up your
lass's trotter-cases for you in three secs."

The old woman lodges an objection by shaking her head and her
shoulders. But Paradis takes the boots with authority, while the
grandmother, paralyzed by her weakness, argues the question and opposes
us with shadowy protest.

Paradis has taken a boot in each hand; he holds them gingerly and looks
at them for a moment, and you would even say that he was squeezing them
a little.

"Aren't they small!" he says in a voice which is not what we hear in the
usual way.

He has secured the brushes as well, and sets himself to wielding them
with zealous carefulness. I notice that he is smiling, with his eyes fixed on
his work.

Then, when the mud has gone from the boots, he takes some polish on
the end of the double-pointed brush and caresses them with it intently.

They are dainty boots—quite those of a stylish young lady; rows of
little buttons shine on them.

"Not a single button missing," he whispers to me, and there is pride in
his tone.

He is no longer sleepy; he yawns no more. On the contrary, his lips are
tightly closed; a gleam of youth and spring-time lights up his face; and he
who was on the point of going to sleep seems just to have woke up.

And where the polish has bestowed a beautiful black his fingers move
over the body of the boot, which opens widely in the upper part and
betrays—ever such a little—the lower curves of the leg. His fingers, so
skilled in polishing, are rather awkward all the same as they turn the boots
over and turn them again, as he smiles at them and ponders—profoundly

and afar—while the old woman lifts her arms in the air and calls me to witness "What a very kind soldier!" he is.

It is finished. The boots are cleaned and finished off in style; they are like mirrors. Nothing is left to do.

He puts them on the edge of the table, very carefully, as if they were saintly relics; then at last his hands let them go. But his eyes do not at once leave them. He looks at them, and then lowering his head, he looks at his own boots. I remember that while he made this comparison the great lad—a hero by destiny, a Bohemian, a monk—smiled once more with all his heart.

The old woman was showing signs of activity in the depths of her chair; she had an idea. "I'll tell her! She shall thank you herself, monsieur! Hey, Josephine!" she cried, turning towards a door.

But Paradis stopped her with an expansive gesture which I thought magnificent. "No, it's not worth while, gran'ma; leave her where she is. We're going. We won't trouble her, allez!"

Such decision sounded in his voice that it carried authority, and the old woman obediently sank into inactivity and held her peace.

We went away to our bed under the wall-less roof, between the arms of the plow that was waiting for us. And then Paradis began again to yawn; but by the light of the candle in our crib, a full minute later, I saw that the happy smile remained yet on his face.

In the Sap

IN the excitement of a distribution of letters from which the squad were returning—some with the delight of a letter, some with the semi-delight of a postcard, and others with a new load (speedily reassumed) of expectation and hope—a comrade comes with a brandished newspaper to tell us an amazing story—"Tu sais, the weasel-faced ancient at Gauchin?"

"The old boy who was treasure-seeking?"

"Well, he's found it!"

"Gerraway!"

"It's just as I tell you, you great lump! What would you like me to say to you? Mass? Don't know it. Anyway, the yard of his place has been bombed, and a chest full of money was turned up out of the ground near a wall. He got his treasure full on the back. And now the parson's quietly cut in and talks about claiming credit for the miracle."

We listen open-mouthed. "A treasure—well! well! The old bald-head!"

The sudden revelation plunges us in an abyss of reflection. "And to think how damned sick we were of the old cackler when he made such a song about his treasure and dinned it into our ears!"

"We were right enough down there, you remember, when we were saying 'One never knows.' Didn't guess how near we were to being right, either."

"All the same, there are some things you can be sure of," says Farfadet, who as soon as Gauchin was mentioned had remained dreaming and distant, as though a lovely face was smiling on him. "But as for this," he added, "I'd never have believed it either! Shan't I find him stuck up, the old ruin, when I go back there after the war!"

"They want a willing man to help the sappers with a job," says the big adjutant.

"Not likely!" growl the men, without moving.

"It'll be of use in relieving the boys," the adjutant goes on.

With that the grumbling ceases, and several heads are raised. "Here!" says Lamuse.

"Get into your harness, big 'un, and come with me." Lamuse buckles on his knapsack, rolls up his blanket, and fetters his pouches. Since his seizure of unlucky affection was allayed, he has become more melancholy than before, and although a sort of fatality makes him continually stouter, he has become engrossed and isolated, and rarely speaks.

In the evening something comes along the trench, rising and falling according to the lumps and holes in the ground; a shape that seems in the shadows to be swimming, that outspreads its arms sometimes, as though appealing for help. It is Lamuse.

He is among us again, covered with mold and mud. He trembles and streams with sweat, as one who is afraid. His lips stir, and he gasps, before they can shape a word.

"Well, what is there?" we ask him vainly.

He collapses in a corner among us and prostrates himself. We offer him wine, and he refuses it with a sign. Then he turns towards me and beckons me with a movement of his head.

When I am by him he whispers to me, very low, and as if in church, "I have seen Eudoxie again." He gasps for breath, his chest wheezes, and with his eyeballs fast fixed upon a nightmare, he says, "She was putrid."

"It was the place we'd lost," Lamuse went on, "and that the Colonials took again with the bayonet ten days ago.

"First we made a hole for the sap, and I was in at it, since I was scooping more than the others I found myself in front. The others were widening and making solid behind. But behold I find a jumble of beams. I'd lit on an old trench, caved in, 'vidently; half caved in—there was some space and room. In the middle of those stumps of wood all mixed together that I was lifting away one by one from in front of me, there was something like a big sandbag in height, upright, and something on the top of it hanging down.

"And behold a plank gives way, and the queer sack falls on me, with its weight on top. I was pegged down, and the smell of a corpse filled my throat—on the top of the bundle there was a head, and it was the hair that I'd seen hanging down.

"You understand, one couldn't see very well; but I recognized the hair 'cause there isn't any other like it in the world, and then the rest of the face, all stove in and moldy, the neck pulped, and all the lot dead for a month perhaps. It was Eudoxie, I tell you.

"Yes, it was the woman I could never go near before, you know—that I only saw a long way off and couldn't ever touch, same as diamonds. She used to run about everywhere, you know. She used even to wander in the lines. One day she must have stopped a bullet, and stayed there, dead and lost, until the chance of this sap.

"You clinch the position? I was forced to hold her up with one arm as well as I could, and work with the other. She was trying to fall on me with all her weight. Old man, she wanted to kiss me, and I didn't want—it was terrible. She seemed to be saying to me, 'You wanted to kiss me, well then, come, come now!' She had on her—she had there, fastened on, the remains of a bunch of flowers, and that was rotten, too, and the posy stank in my nose like the corpse of some little beast.

"I had to take her in my arms, in both of them, and turn gently round so that I could put her down on the other side. The place was so narrow and pinched that as we turned, for a moment, I hugged her to my breast and couldn't help it. With all my strength, old chap, as I should have hugged her once on a time if she'd have let me.

"I've been half an hour cleaning myself from the touch of her and the smell that she breathed on me in spite of me and in spite of herself. Ah, lucky for me that I'm as done up as a wretched cart-horse!"

He turns over on his belly, clenches his fists, and slumbers, with his face buried in the ground and his dubious dream of passion and corruption.

A Box of Matches

IT is five o'clock in the evening. Three men are seen moving in the bottom of the gloomy trench. Around their extinguished fire in the dirty excavation they are frightful to see, black and sinister. Rain and negligence have put their fire out, and the four cooks are looking at the corpses of brands that are shrouded in ashes and the stumps of wood whence the flame has flown.

Volpatte staggers up to the group and throws down the black mass that he had on his shoulder. "I've pulled it out of a dug-out where it won't show much."

"We have wood," says Blaire, "but we've got to light it. Otherwise, how are we going to cook this cab-horse?"

"It's a fine piece," wails a dark-faced man, "thin flank. In my belief, that's the best bit of the beast, the flank."

"Fire?" Volpatte objects, "there are no more matches, no more anything."

"We must have fire," growls Poupardin, whose indistinct bulk has the proportions of a bear as he rolls and sways in the dark depths of our cage.

"No two ways about it, we've got to have it," Pepin agrees. He is coming out of a dug-out like a sweep out of a chimney. His gray mass emerges and appears, like night upon evening.

"Don't worry; I shall get some," declares Blaire in a concentrated tone of angry decision. He has not been cook long, and is keen to show himself quite equal to adverse conditions in the exercise of his functions.

He spoke as Martin Cesar used to speak when he was alive. His aim is to resemble the great legendary figure of the cook who always found ways for a fire, just as others, among the non-coms., would fain imitate Napoleon.

"I shall go if it's necessary and fetch every bit of wood there is at Battalion H.Q. I shall go and requisition the colonel's matches—I shall go—"

"Let's go and forage." Poupardin leads the way. His face is like the bottom of a saucepan that the fire has gradually befouled. As it is cruelly cold, he is wrapped up all over. He wears a cape which is half goatskin and half sheepskin, half brown and half whitish, and this twofold skin of tints geometrically cut makes him like some strange occult animal.

Pepin has a cotton cap so soiled and so shiny with grease that it might be made of black silk. Volpatte, inside his Balaklava and his fleeces, resembles a walking tree-trunk. A square opening betrays a yellow face at the top of the thick and heavy bark of the mass he makes, which is bifurcated by a couple of legs.

"Let's look up the 10th. They've always got the needful. They're on the Pylones road, beyond the Boyau-Neuf."

The four alarming objects get under way, cloud-shape, in the trench that unwinds itself sinuously before them like a blind alley, unsafe, unlighted, and unpaved. It is uninhabited, too, in this part, being a gangway between the second lines and the first lines.

In the dusty twilight two Moroccans meet the fire-questing cooks. One has the skin of a black boot and the other of a yellow shoe. Hope gleams in the depths of the cooks' hearts.

"Matches, boys?"

"Napoo," replies the black one, and his smile reveals his long crockery-like teeth in his cigar-colored mouth of moroccan leather.

In his turn the yellow one advances and asks, "Tobacco? A bit of tobacco?" And he holds out his greenish sleeve and his great hard paw, in which the cracks are full of brown dirt, and the nails purplish.

Pepin growls, rummages in his clothes, and pulls out a pinch of tobacco, mixed with dust, which he hands to the sharpshooter.

A little farther they meet a sentry who is half asleep—in the middle of the evening—on a heap of loose earth. The drowsy soldier says, "It's to the right, and then again to the right, and then straight forward. Don't go wrong about it."

They march—for a long time. "We must have come a long way," says Volpatte, after half an hour of fruitless paces and encloistered loneliness.

"I say, we're going downhill a hell of a lot, don't you think?" asks Blaire.

"Don't worry, old duffer," scoffs Pepin, "but if you've got cold feet you can leave us to it."

Still we tramp on in the falling night. The ever-empty trench—a desert of terrible length—has taken a shabby and singular appearance. The parapets are in ruins; earthslides have made the ground undulate in hillocks.

An indefinite uneasiness lays hold of the four huge fire-hunters, and increases as night overwhelms them in this monstrous road.

Pepin, who is leading just now, stands fast and holds up his hand as a signal to halt. "Footsteps," they say in a sobered tone.

Then, and in the heart of them, they are afraid. It was a mistake for them all to leave their shelter for so long. They are to blame. And one never knows.

"Get in there, quick, quick!" says Pepin, pointing to a right-angled cranny on the ground level.

By the test of a hand, the rectangular shadow is proved to be the entry to a funk-hole. They crawl in singly; and the last one, impatient, pushes the others; they become an involuntary carpet in the dense darkness of the hole.

A sound of steps and of voices becomes distinct and draws nearer. From the mass of the four men who tightly hung up the burrow, tentative hands are put out at a venture. All at once Pepin murmurs in a stifled voice, "What's this?"

"What?" ask the others, pressed and wedged against him.

"Clips!" says Pepin under his breath, "Boche cartridge-clips on the shelf! We're in the Boche trench!"

"Let's hop it." Three men make a jump to get out.

"Look out, bon Dieu! Don't stir!—footsteps—"

They hear some one walking, with the quick step of a solitary man. They keep still and hold their breath. With their eyes fixed on the ground level, they see the darkness moving on the right, and then a shadow with legs detaches itself, approaches, and passes. The shadow assumes an outline. It is topped by a helmet covered with a cloth and rising to a point. There is no other sound than that of his passing feet.

Hardly has the German gone by when the four cooks, with no concerted plan and with a single movement, burst forth, jostling each other, run like madmen, and hurl themselves on him.

"Kamerad, messieurs!" he says.

But the blade of a knife gleams and disappears. The man collapses as if he would plunge into the ground. Pepin seizes the helmet as the Boche is failing and keeps it in his hand.

"Let's leg it," growls the voice of Poupardin.

"Got to search him first!"

They lift him and turn him over, and set the soft, damp and warm body up again. Suddenly he coughs.

"He isn't dead!"—"Yes, he is dead; that's the air."

They shake him by the pockets; with hasty breathing the four black men stoop over their task. "The helmet's mine," says Pepin. "It was me that knifed him, I want the helmet."

They tear from the body its pocket-book of still warm papers, its field-glass, purse, and leggings.

"Matches!" shouts Blaire, shaking a box, "he's got some!"

"Ah, the fool that you are!" hisses Volpatte.

"Now let's be off like hell." They pile the body in a corner and break into a run, prey to a sort of panic, and regardless of the row their disordered flight makes.

"It's this way!—This way!—Hurry, lads—for all you're worth!"

Without speaking they dash across the maze of the strangely empty trench that seems to have no end.

"My wind's gone," says Blaire, "I'm—" He staggers and stops.

"Come on, buck up, old chap," gasps Pepin, hoarse and breathless. He takes him by the sleeve and drags him forward like a stubborn shaft-horse.

"We're right!" says Poupardin suddenly. "Yes, I remember that tree. It's the Pylones road!"

"Ah!" wails Blaire, whose breathing is shaking him like an engine. He throws himself forward with a last impulse—and sits down on the ground.

"Halt!" cries a sentry—"Good Lord!" he stammers as he sees the four poilus. "Where the—where are you coming from, that way?"

They laugh, jump about like puppets, full-blooded and streaming with perspiration, blacker than ever in the night. The German officer's helmet is gleaming in the hands of Pepin. "Oh, Christ!" murmurs the sentry, with gaping mouth, "but what's been up?"

An exuberant reaction excites and bewitches them. All talk at once. In haste and confusion they act again the drama which hardly yet they realize is over. They had gone wrong when they left the sleepy sentry and had taken the International Trench, of which a part is ours and another part German. Between the French and German sections there is no barricade or division. There is merely a sort of neutral zone, at the two ends of which sentries watch ceaselessly. No doubt the German watcher was not at his post, or likely he hid himself when he saw the four shadows, or perhaps be doubled back and had not time to bring up reinforcements. Or perhaps, too, the German officer had strayed too far ahead in the neutral zone. In short, one understands what happened without understanding it.

"The funny part of it," says Pepin, "is that we knew all about that, and never thought to be careful about it when we set off."

"We were looking for matches," says Volpatte.

"And we've got some!" cries Pepin. "You've not lost the flamers, old broomstick?"

"No damned fear!" says Blaire; "Boche matches are better stuff than ours. Besides, they're all we've got to light our fire! Lose my box? Let any one try to pinch it off me!"

"We're behind time—the soup-water'll be freezing. Hurry up, so far. Afterwards there'll be a good yarn to tell in the sewer where the boys are, about what we did to the Boches."

Bombardment

WE are in the flat country, a vast mistiness, but above it is dark blue. The end of the night is marked by a little falling snow which powders our shoulders and the folds in our sleeves. We are marching in fours, hooded. We seem in the turbid twilight to be the wandering survivors of one Northern district who are trekking to another.

We have followed a road and have crossed the ruins of Ablain-Saint-Nazaire. We have had confused glimpses of its whitish heaps of houses and the dim spider-webs of its suspended roofs. The village is so long that although full night buried us in it we saw its last buildings beginning to pale in the frost of dawn. Through the grating of a cellar on the edge of this petrified ocean's waves, we made out the fire kept going by the custodians of the dead town. We have paddled in swampy fields, lost ourselves in silent places where the mud seized us by the feet, we have dubiously regained our balance and our bearings again on another road, the one which leads from Carency to Souchez. The tall bordering poplars are shivered and their trunks mangled; in one place the road is an enormous colonnade of trees destroyed. Then, marching with us on both sides, we see through the shadows ghostly dwarfs of trees, wide-cloven like spreading palms; botched and jumbled into round blocks or long strips; doubled upon themselves, as if they knelt. From time to time our march is disordered and bustled by the yielding of a swamp. The road becomes a marsh which we cross on our heels, while our feet make the sound of sculling. Planks have been laid in it here and there. Where they have so far sunk in the mud as to proffer their edges to us we slip on them. Sometimes there is enough water to float them, and then under the weight of a man they splash and go under, and the man stumbles or falls, with frenzied imprecations.

It must be five o'clock. The stark and affrighting scene unfolds itself to our eyes, but it is still encircled by a great fantastic ring of mist and of darkness. We go on and on without pause, and come to a place where we can make out a dark hillock, at the foot of which there seems to be some lively movement of human beings.

"Advance by twos," says the leader of the detachment. "Let each team of two take alternately a plank and a hurdle." We load ourselves up. One of the two in each couple assumes the rifle of his partner as well as his own. The other with difficulty shifts and pulls out from the pile a long plank, muddy and slippery, which weighs full eighty pounds, or a hurdle of leafy branches as big as a door, which he can only just keep on his back as he bends forward with his hands aloft and grips its edges.

We resume our march, very slowly and very ponderously, scattered over the now graying road, with complaints and heavy curses which the effort strangles in our throats. After about a hundred yards, the two men of each team exchange loads, so that after two hundred yards, in spite of the bitter blenching breeze of early morning, all but the non-coms. are running with sweat.

Suddenly a vivid star expands down yonder in the uncertain direction that we are taking—a rocket. Widely it lights a part of the sky with its milky nimbus, blots out the stars, and then falls gracefully, fairy-like.

There is a swift light opposite us over there; a flash and a detonation. It is a shell! By the flat reflection that the explosion instantaneously spreads over the lower sky we see a ridge clearly outlined in front of us from east to west, perhaps half a mile away.

That ridge is ours—so much of it as we can see from here and up to the top of it, where our troops are. On the other slope, a hundred yards from our first line, is the first German line. The shell fell on the summit, in our lines; it is the others who are firing. Another shell another and yet another plant trees of faintly violet light on the top of the rise, and each of them dully illumines the whole of the horizon.

Soon there is a sparkling of brilliant stars and a sudden jungle of fiery plumes on the hill; and a fairy mirage of blue and white hangs lightly before our eyes in the full gulf of night.

Those among us who must devote the whole buttressed power of their arms and legs to prevent their greasy loads from sliding off their backs and to prevent themselves from sliding to the ground, these neither see nor hear anything. The others, sniffing and shivering with cold, wiping their noses with limp and sodden handkerchiefs, watch and remark, cursing the obstacles in the way with fragments of profanity. "It's like watching fireworks," they say.

And to complete the illusion of a great operatic scene, fairy-like but sinister, before which our bent and black party crawls and splashes, behold a red star, and then a green; then a sheaf of red fire, very much tardier. In our ranks, as the available half of our pairs of eyes watch the display, we cannot help murmuring in idle tones of popular admiration, "Ah, a red one!"—"Look, a green one!" It is the Germans who are sending up signals, and our men as well who are asking for artillery support.

Our road turns and climbs again as the day at last decides to appear. Everything looks dirty. A layer of stickiness, pearl-gray and white, covers the road, and around it the real world makes a mournful appearance. Behind us we leave ruined Souchez, whose houses are only flat heaps of rubbish and her trees but humps of bramble-like slivers. We plunge into a hole on our left, the entrance to the communication trench. We let our loads fall in a circular enclosure prepared for them, and both hot and frozen we settled in the trench and wait our hands abraded, wet, and stiff with cramp.

Buried in our holes up to the chin, our chests heaving against the solid bulk of the ground that protects us, we watch the dazzling and deepening drama develop. The bombardment is redoubled. The trees of light on the ridge have melted into hazy parachutes in the pallor of dawn, sickly heads of Medusae with points of fire; then, more sharply defined as the day expands, they become bunches of smoke-feathers, ostrich feathers white and gray, which come suddenly to life on the jumbled and melancholy soil of Hill 119, five or six hundred yards in front of us, and then slowly fade away. They are truly the pillar of fire and the pillar of cloud, circling as one and thundering together. On the flank of the bill we see a party of men running to earth. One by one they disappear, swallowed up in the adjoining anthills.

Now, one can better make out the form of our "guests." At each shot a tuft of sulphurous white underlined in black forms sixty yards up in the air, unfolds and mottles itself, and we catch in the explosion the whistling of the charge of bullets that the yellow cloud hurls angrily to the ground. It bursts in sixfold squalls, one after another—bang, bang, bang, bang, bang, bang. It is the 77 mm. gun.

We disdain the 77 mm. shrapnel, in spite of the fact that Blesbois was killed by one of them three days ago. They nearly always burst too high.

Barque explains it to us, although we know it well: "One's chamber-pot protects one's nut well enough against the bullets. So they can destroy your shoulder and damn well knock you down, but they don't spread you about. Naturally, you've got to be fly, all the same. Got to be careful you don't lift your neb in the air as long as they're buzzing about, nor put your hand out to see if it's raining. Now, our 75 mm.—"

"There aren't only the 77's," Mesnil Andre broke in, "there's all damned sorts. Spell those out for me—" Those are shrill and cutting whistles, trembling or rattling; and clouds of all shapes gather on the slopes yonder whose vastness shows through them, slopes where our men are in the depths of the dug-outs. Gigantic plumes of faint fire mingle with huge tassels of steam, tufts that throw out straight filaments, smoky feathers that expand as they fall—quite white or greenish-gray, black or copper with gleams of gold, or as if blotched with ink.

The two last explosions are quite near. Above the battered ground they take shape like vast balls of black and tawny dust; and as they deploy and leisurely depart at the wind's will, having finished their task, they have the outline of fabled dragons.

Our line of faces on the level of the ground turns that way, and we follow them with our eyes from the bottom of the trench in the middle of this country peopled by blazing and ferocious apparitions, these fields that the sky has crushed.

"Those, they're the 150 mm. howitzers."—"They're the 210's, calf-head."—"There go the regular guns, too; the hogs! Look at that one!" It was a shell that burst on the ground and threw up earth and debris in a fan-shaped cloud of darkness. Across the cloven land it looked like the frightful spitting of some volcano, piled up in the bowels of the earth.

A diabolical uproar surrounds us. We are conscious of a sustained crescendo, an incessant multiplication of the universal frenzy. A hurricane of hoarse and hollow banging, of raging clamor, of piercing and beast-like screams, fastens furiously with tatters of smoke upon the earth where we are buried up to our necks, and the wind of the shells seems to set it heaving and pitching.

"Look at that," bawls Barque, "and me that said they were short of munitions!"

"Oh, la, la! We know all about that! That and the other fudge the newspapers squirt all over us!"

A dull crackle makes itself audible amidst the babel of noise. That slow rattle is of all the sounds of war the one that most quickens the heart.

"The coffee-mill! One of ours, listen. The shots come regularly, while the Boches' haven't got the same length of time between the shots; they go crack—crack-crack-crack—crack-crack—crack—"

"Don't cod yourself, crack-pate; it isn't an unsewing-machine at all; it's a motor-cycle on the road to 31 dugout, away yonder."

"Well, I think it's a chap up aloft there, having a look round from his broomstick," chuckles Pepin, as he raises his nose and sweeps the firmament in search of an aeroplane.

A discussion arises, but one cannot say what the noise is, and that's all. One tries in vain to become familiar with all those diverse disturbances. It even happened the other day in the wood that a whole section mistook for the hoarse howl of a shell the first notes of a neighboring mule as he began his whinnying bray.

"I say, there's a good show of sausages in the air this morning," says Lamuse. Lifting our eyes, we count them.

"There are eight sausages on our side and eight on the Boches'," says Cocon, who has already counted them.

There are, in fact, at regular intervals along the horizon, opposite the distance-dwindled group of captive enemy balloons, the eight long hovering eyes of the army, buoyant and sensitive, and joined to the various headquarters by living threads.

"They see us as we see them. How the devil can one escape from that row of God Almighties up there?"

There's our reply!

Suddenly, behind our backs, there bursts the sharp and deafening stridor of the 75's. Their increasing crackling thunder arouses and elates us. We shout with our guns, and look at each other without hearing our shouts—except for the curiously piercing voice that comes from Barque's great mouth—amid the rolling of that fantastic drum whose every note is the report of a cannon.

Then we turn our eyes ahead and outstretch our necks, and on the top of the hill we see the still higher silhouette of a row of black infernal trees whose terrible roots are striking down into the invisible slope where the enemy cowers.

While the "75" battery continues its barking a hundred yards behind us—the sharp anvil-blows of a huge hammer, followed by a dizzy scream of force and fury—a gigantic gurgling dominates the devilish oratorio; that, also, is coming from our side. "It's a gran'pa, that one!"

The shell cleaves the air at perhaps a thousand yards above us; the voice of its gun covers all as with a pavilion of resonance. The sound of its travel is sluggish, and one divines a projectile bigger-boweled, more enormous than the others. We can hear it passing and declining in front with the ponderous and increasing vibration of a train that enters a station under brakes; then, its heavy whine sounds fainter. We watch the hill opposite, and after several seconds it is covered by a salmon-pink cloud that the wind spreads over one-half of the horizon. "It's a 220 mm."

"One can see them," declares Volpatte, "those shells, when they come out of the gun. If you're in the right line, you can even see them a good long away from the gun."

Another follows: "There! Look, look! Did you see that one? You didn't look quick enough, you missed it. Get a move on! Look, another! Did you see it?"

"I did not see it."—"Ass! Got to be a bedstead for you to see it! Look, quick, that one, there! Did you see it, unlucky good-for-nothing?"—"I saw it; is that all?"

Some have made out a small black object, slender and pointed as a blackbird with folded wings, pricking a wide curve down from the zenith.

"That weighs 240 lb., that one, my old bug," says Volpatte proudly, "and when that drops on a funk-hole it kills everybody inside it. Those that aren't picked off by the explosion are struck dead by the wind of it, or they're gas-poisoned before they can say 'ouf!'"

"The 270 mm. shell can be seen very well, too—talk about a bit of iron—when the howitzer sends it up—allez, off you go!"

"And the 155 Rimailho, too; but you can't see that one because it goes too straight and too far; the more you look for it the more it vanishes before your eyes."

In a stench of sulphur amid black powder, of burned stuffs and calcined earth which roams in sheets about the country, all the menagerie is let loose and gives battle. Bellowings, roarings, growlings, strange and savage; feline caterwaulings that fiercely rend your ears and search your belly, or the long-drawn piercing hoot like the siren of a ship in distress. At times, even, something like shouts cross each other in the air-currents, with curious variation of tone that make the sound human. The country is bodily lifted in places and falls back again. From one end of the horizon to the other it seems to us that the earth itself is raging with storm and tempest.

And the greatest guns, far away and still farther, diffuse growls much subdued and smothered, but you know the strength of them by the displacement of air which comes and raps you on the ear.

Now, behold a heavy mass of woolly green which expands and hovers over the bombarded region and draws out in every direction. This touch of strangely incongruous color in the picture summons attention, and all we encaged prisoners turn our faces towards the hideous outcrop.

"Gas, probably. Let's have our masks ready."—"The hogs!"

"They're unfair tricks, those," says Farfadet.

"They're what?" asks Barque jeeringly.

"Why, yes, they're dirty dodges, those gases—"

"You make me tired," retorts Barque, "with your fair ways and your unfair ways. When you've seen men squashed, cut in two, or divided from top to bottom, blown into showers by an ordinary shell, bellies turned inside out and scattered anyhow, skulls forced bodily into the chest as if by a blow with a club, and in place of the head a bit of neck, oozing currant jam of brains all over the chest and back—you've seen that and yet you can say 'There are clean ways!'"

"Doesn't alter the fact that the shell is allowed, it's recognized—"

"Ah, la, la! I'll tell you what—you make me blubber just as much as you make me laugh!" And he turns his back.

"Hey, look out, boys!"

We strain our eyes, and one of us has thrown himself flat on the ground; others look instinctively and frowning towards the shelter that we have not time to reach, and during these two seconds each one bends his head. It is a grating noise as of huge scissors which comes near and nearer to us, and ends at last with a ringing crash of unloaded iron.

That ore fell not far from us—two hundred yards away, perhaps. We crouch in the bottom of the trench and remain doubled up while the place where we are is lashed by a shower of little fragments.

"Don't want this in my tummy, even from that distance," says Paradis, extracting from the earth of the trench wall a morsel that has just lodged there. It is like a bit of coke, bristling with edged and pointed facets, and he dances it in his hand so as not to burn himself.

There is a hissing noise. Paradis sharply bows his head and we follow suit. "The fuse!—it has gone over." The shrapnel fuse goes up and then comes down vertically; but that of the percussion shell detaches itself from the broken mass after the explosion and usually abides buried at the point of contact, but at other times it flies off at random like a big red-hot pebble. One must beware of it. It may hurl itself on you a very long time after the detonation and by incredible paths, passing over the embankment and plunging into the cavities.

"Nothing so piggish as a fuse. It happened to me once—"

"There's worse things," broke in Bags of the 11th, "The Austrian shells, the 130's and the 74's. I'm afraid of them. They're nickel-plated, they say, but what I do know, seeing I've been there, is they come so quick you can't do anything to dodge them. You no sooner hear em snoring than they burst on you.

"The German 105's, neither, you haven't hardly the time to flatten yourself. I once got the gunners to tell me all about them."

"I tell you, the shells from the naval guns, you haven't the time to hear 'em. Got to pack yourself up before they come."

"And there's that new shell, a dirty devil, that breaks wind after it's dodged into the earth and out of it again two or three times in the space of six yards. When I know there's one of them about, I want to go round the corner. I remember one time—"

"That's all nothing, my lads," said the new sergeant, stopping on his way past, "you ought to see what they chucked us at Verdun, where I've come from. Nothing but whoppers, 380's and 420's and 244's. When you've been shelled down there you know all about it—the woods are sliced down like cornfields, the dug-outs marked and burst in even when they've three thicknesses of beams, all the road-crossings sprinkled, the roads blown into the air and changed into long heaps of smashed convoys and wrecked guns, corpses twisted together as though shoveled up. You could see thirty chaps laid out by one shot at the cross-roads; you could see fellows whirling around as they went up, always about fifteen yards, and bits of trousers caught and stuck on the tops of the trees that were left. You could see one of these 380's go into a house at Verdun by the roof, bore through two or three floors, and burst at the bottom, and all the damn lot's got to go aloft; and in the fields whole battalions would scatter and lie flat under the shower like poor little defenseless rabbits. At every step on the ground in the fields you'd got lumps as thick as your arm and as wide as that, and it'd take four poilus to lift the lump of iron. The fields looked as if they were full of rocks. And that went on without a halt for months on end, months on end!" the sergeant repeated as he passed on, no doubt to tell again the story of his souvenirs somewhere else.

"Look, look, corporal, those chaps over there—are they soft in the head?" On the bombarded position we saw dots of human beings emerge hurriedly and run towards the explosions.

"They're gunners," said Bertrand; "as soon as a shell's burst they sprint and rummage for the fuse is the hole, for the position of the fuse gives the direction of its battery, you see, by the way it's dug itself in; and as for the distance, you've only got to read it—it's shown on the range-figures cut on the time-fuse which is set just before firing."

"No matter—they're off their onions to go out under such shelling."

"Gunners, my boy," says a man of another company who was strolling in the trench, "are either quite good or quite bad. Either they're trumps or they're trash. I tell you—"

"That's true of all privates, what you're saying."

"Possibly; but I'm not talking to you about all privates; I'm talking to you about gunners, and I tell you too that—"

"Hey, my lads! Better find a hole to dump yourselves in, before you get one on the snitch!"

The strolling stranger carried his story away, and Cocon, who was in a perverse mood, declared: "We can be doing our hair in the dug-out, seeing it's rather boring outside."

"Look, they're sending torpedoes over there!" said Paradis, pointing. Torpedoes go straight up, or very nearly so, like larks, fluttering and rustling; then they stop, hesitate, and come straight down again, heralding their fall in its last seconds by a "baby-cry" that we know well. From here, the inhabitants of the ridge seem like invisible players, lined up for a game with a ball.

"In the Argonne," says Lamuse, "my brother says in a letter that they get turtle-doves, as he calls them. They're big heavy things, fired off very close. They come in cooing, really they do, he says, and when they break wind they don't half make a shindy, he says."

"There's nothing worse than the mortar-toad, that seems to chase after you and jump over the top of you, and it bursts in the very trench, just scraping over the bank."

"Tiens, tiens, did you hear it?" A whistling was approaching us when suddenly it ceased. The contrivance has not burst. "It's a shell that cried off," Paradis asserts. And we strain our ears for the satisfaction of hearing—or of not hearing—others.

Lamuse says: "All the fields and the roads and the villages about here, they're covered with dud shells of all sizes—ours as well, to say truth. The ground must be full of 'em, that you can't see. I wonder how they'll go on, later, when the time comes to say, 'That's enough of it, let's start work again.'"

And all the time, in a monotony of madness, the avalanche of fire and iron goes on; shrapnel with its whistling explosion and its overcharged heart of furious metal and the great percussion shells, whose thunder is that of the railway engine which crashes suddenly into a wall, the thunder of loaded rails or steel beams, toppling down a declivity. The air is now glutted and viewless, it is crossed and recrossed by heavy blasts, and the murder of the earth continues all around, deeply and more deeply, to the limit of completion.

There are even other guns which now join in—they are ours. Their report is like that of the 75's, but louder, and it has a prolonged and resounding echo, like thunder reverberating among mountains.

"They're the long 120's. They're on the edge of the wood half a mile away. Fine guns, old man, like gray-hounds. They're slender and fine-nosed, those guns—you want to call them 'Madame.' They're not like the 220's—they're all snout, like coal-scuttles, and spit their shells out from the bottom upwards. The 120's get there just the same, but among the teams of artillery they look like kids in bassinettes."

Conversation languishes; here and there are yawns. The dimensions and weight of this outbreak of the guns fatigue the mind. Our voices flounder in it and are drowned.

"I've never seen anything like this for a bombardment," shouts Barque.

"We always say that," replies Paradis.

"Just so," bawls Volpatte. "There's been talk of an attack lately; I should say this is the beginning of something."

The others say simply, "Ah!"

Volpatte displays an intention of snatching a wink of sleep. He settles himself on the ground with his back against one wall of the trench and his feet buttressed against the other wall.

We converse together on divers subjects. Biquet tells the story of a rat he has seen: "He was cheeky and comical, you know. I'd taken off my trotter-cases, and that rat, he chewed all the edge of the uppers into embroidery. Of course, I'd greased 'em."

Volpatte, who is now definitely out of action, moves and says, "I can't get to sleep for your gabbling."

"You can't make me believe, old fraud," says Marthereau, "that you can raise a single snore with a shindy like this all round you."

Volpatte replies with one.

Fall in! March!

We are changing our spot. Where are they taking us to? We have no idea. The most we know is that we are in reserve, and that they may take us round to strengthen certain points in succession, or to clear the communication trenches, in which the regulation of passing troops is as complicated a job, if blocks and collisions are to be avoided, as it is of the trains in a busy station. It is impossible to make out the meaning of the immense maneuver in which the rolling of our regiment is only that of a little wheel, nor what is going on in all the huge area of the sector. But, lost in the network of deeps where we go and come without end, weary, harassed and stiff-jointed by prolonged halts, stupefied by noise and delay, poisoned by smoke, we make out that our artillery is becoming more and more active; the offensive seems to have changed places.

Halt! A fire of intense and incredible fury was threshing the parapets of the trench where we were halted at the moment: "Fritz is going it strong; he's afraid of an attack, he's going dotty. Ah, isn't he letting fly!"

A heavy hail was pouring over us, hacking terribly at atmosphere and sky, scraping and skimming all the plain.

I looked through a loophole and saw a swift and strange vision. In front of us, a dozen yards away at most, there were motionless forms outstretched side by side—a row of mown-down soldiers—and the countless projectiles that hurtled from all sides were riddling this rank of the dead!

The bullets that flayed the soil in straight streaks amid raised slender stems of cloud were perforating and ripping the bodies so rigidly close to the ground, breaking the stiffened limbs, plunging into the wan and vacant faces, bursting and bespattering the liquefied eyes; and even did that file of corpses stir and budge out of line under the avalanche.

We could hear the blunt sound of the dizzy copper points as they pierced cloth and flesh, the sound of a furious stroke with a knife, the harsh blow of a stick upon clothing. Above us rushed jets of shrill whistling, with the declining and far more serious hum of ricochets. And we bent our heads under the enormous flight of noises and voices.

"Trench must be cleared—Gee up!" We leave this most infamous corner of the battlefield where even the dead are torn, wounded, and slain anew.

We turn towards the right and towards the rear. The communication trench rises, and at the top of the gully we pass in front of a telephone station and a group of artillery officers and gunners. Here there is a further halt. We mark time, and hear the artillery observer shout his commands, which the telephonist buried beside him picks up and repeats: "First gun, same sight; two-tenths to left; three a minute!"

Some of us have risked our heads over the edge of the bank and have glimpsed for the space of the lightning's flash all the field of battle round which our company has uncertainly wandered since the morning. I saw a limitless gray plain, across whose width the wind seemed to be driving faint and thin waves of dust, pierced in places by a more pointed billow of smoke.

Where the sun and the clouds trail patches of black and of white, the immense space sparkles dully from point to point where our batteries are firing, and I saw it one moment entirely spangled with short-lived flashes. Another minute, part of the field grew dark under a steamy and whitish film, a sort of hurricane of snow.

Afar, on the evil, endless, and half-ruined fields, caverned like cemeteries, we see the slender skeleton of a church, like a bit of torn paper; and from one margin of the picture to the other, dim rows of vertical marks, close together and underlined, like the straight strokes of a written page—these are the roads and their trees. Delicate meandering lines streak the plain backward and forward and rule it in squares, and these windings are stippled with men.

We can make out some fragments of lines made up of these human points who have emerged from the hollowed streaks and are moving on the plain in the horrible face of the flying firmament. It is difficult to believe that each of those tiny spots is a living thing with fragile and quivering flesh, infinitely unarmed in space, full of deep thoughts, full of far memories and crowded pictures. One is fascinated by this scattered dust of men as small as the stars in the sky.

Poor unknowns, poor fellow-men, it is your turn to give battle. Another time it will be ours. Perhaps to-morrow it will be ours to feel the heavens burst over our heads or the earth open under our feet, to be assailed by the prodigious plague of projectiles, to be swept away by the blasts of a tornado a hundred thousand times stronger than the tornado.

They urge us into the rearward shelters. For our eyes the field of death vanishes. To our ears the thunder is deadened on the great anvil of the clouds. The sound of universal destruction is still. The squad surrounds itself with the familiar noises of life, and sinks into the fondling littleness of the dug-outs.

Under Fire

RUDELY awakened in the dark, I open my eyes: "What? What's up?"

"Your turn on guard—it's two o'clock in the morning," says Corporal Bertrand at the opening into the hole where I am prostrate on the floor. I hear him without seeing him.

"I'm coming," I growl, and shake myself, and yawn in the little sepulchral shelter. I stretch my arms, and my hands touch the soft and cold clay. Then I cleave the heavy odor that fills the dug-out and crawl out in the middle of the dense gloom between the collapsed bodies of the sleepers. After several stumbles and entanglements among accouterments, knapsacks and limbs stretched out in all directions, I put my hand on my rifle and find myself upright in the open air, half awake and dubiously balanced, assailed by the black and bitter breeze.

Shivering, I follow the corporal; he plunges in between the dark embankments whose lower ends press strangely and closely on our march. He stops; the place is here. I make out a heavy mass half-way up the ghostly wall which comes loose and descends from it with a whinnying yawn, and I hoist myself into the niche which it had occupied.

The moon is hidden by mist, but a very weak and uncertain light overspreads the scene, and one's sight gropes its way. Then a wide strip of darkness, hovering and gliding up aloft, puts it out. Even after touching the breastwork and the loophole in front of my face I can hardly make them out, and my inquiring hand discovers, among an ordered deposit of things, a mass of grenade handles.

"Keep your eye skinned, old chap," says Bertrand in a low voice. "Don't forget that our listening-post is in front there on the left. Allons, so long." His steps die away, followed by those of the sleepy sentry whom I am relieving.

Rifle-shots crackle all round. Abruptly a bullet smacks the earth of the wall against which I am leaning. I peer through the loophole. Our line runs along the top of the ravine, and the land slopes downward in front of me, plunging into an abyss of darkness where one can see nothing. One's sight ends always by picking out the regular lines of the stakes of our wire entanglements, planted on the shore of the waves of night, and here and there the circular funnel-like wounds of shells, little, larger, or enormous, and some of the nearest occupied by mysterious lumber. The wind blows in my face, and nothing else is stirring save the vast moisture that drain from it. It is cold enough to set one shivering in perpetual motion. I look upwards, this way and that; everything is borne down by dreadful gloom. I might be derelict and alone in the middle of a world destroyed by a cataclysm.

There is a swift illumination up above—a rocket. The scene in which I am stranded is picked out in sketchy incipience around me. The crest of our trench stands forth, jagged and dishevelled, and I see, stuck to the outer wall every five paces like upright caterpillars, the shadows of the watchers. Their rifles are revealed beside them by a few spots of light. The trench is shored with sandbags. It is widened everywhere, and in many places ripped up by landslides. The sandbags, piled up and dislodged, appear in the starlike light of the rocket like the great dismantled stones of ancient ruined buildings. I look through the loophole, and discern in the misty and pallid atmosphere expanded by the meteor the rows of stakes and even the thin lines of barbed wire which cross and recross between the posts. To my seeing they are like strokes of a pen scratched upon the pale and perforated ground. Lower down, the ravine is filled with the motionless silence of the ocean of night.

I come down from my look-out and steer at a guess towards my neighbor in vigil, and come upon him with outstretched hand. "Is that you?" I say to him in a subdued voice, though I don't know him.

"Yes," he replies, equally ignorant who I am, blind like myself. "It's quiet at this time," he adds "A bit since I thought they were going to attack, and they may have tried it on, on the right, where they chucked over a lot of bombs. There's been a barrage of 75's—vrrrran, vrrrran—Old man, I said to myself, 'Those 75's, p'raps they've good reason for firing. If they did come out, the Boches, they must have found something.' Tiens, listen, down there, the bullets buffing themselves!"

He opens his flask and takes a draught, and his last words, still subdued, smell of wine: "Ah, la, la! Talk about a filthy war! Don't you think we should be a lot better at home!—Hullo! What's the matter with the ass?" A rifle has rung out beside us, making a brief and sudden flash of phosphorescence. Others go off here and there along our line. Rifle-shots are catching after dark.

We go to inquire of one of the shooters, guessing our way through the solid blackness that has fallen again upon us like a roof. Stumbling, and thrown anon on each other, we reach the man and touch him—"Well, what's up?"

He thought he saw something moving, but there is nothing more. We return through the density, my unknown neighbor and I, unsteady, and laboring along the narrow way of slippery mud, doubled up as if we each carried a crushing burden. At one point of the horizon and then at another all around, a gun sounds, and its heavy din blends with the volleys of rifle-fire, redoubled one minute and dying out the next, and with the clusters of grenade-reports, of deeper sound than the crack of Lebel or Mauser, and nearly like the voice of the old classical rifles. The wind has again increased; it is so strong that one must protect himself against it in the darkness; masses of huge cloud are passing in front of the moon.

So there we are, this man and I, jostling without knowing each other, revealed and then hidden from each other in sudden jerks by the flashes of the guns, oppressed by the opacity, the center of a huge circle of fires that appear and disappear in the devilish landscape.

"We're under a curse," says the man.

We separate, and go each to his own loophole, to weary our eyes upon invisibility. Is some frightful and dismal storm about to break? But that night it did not. At the end of my long wait, with the first streaks of day, there was even a lull.

Again I saw, when the dawn came down on us like a stormy evening, the steep banks of our crumbling trench as they came to life again under the sooty scarf of the low-hanging clouds, a trench dismal and dirty, infinitely dirty, humped with debris and filthiness. Under the livid sky the sandbags are taking the same hue, and their vaguely shining and rounded shapes are like the bowels and viscera of giants, nakedly exposed upon the earth.

In the trench-wall behind me, in a hollowed recess, there is a heap of horizontal things like logs. Tree-trunks? No, they are corpses.

As the call of birds goes up from the furrowed ground, as the shadowy fields are renewed, and the light breaks and adorns each blade of grass, I look towards the ravine. Below the quickening field and its high surges of earth and burned hollows, beyond the bristling of stakes, there is still a lifeless lake of shadow, and in front of the opposite slope a wall of night still stands.

Then I turn again and look upon these dead men whom the day is gradually exhuming, revealing their stained and stiffened forms. There are four of them. They are our comrades, Lamuse, Barque, Biquet, and little Eudore. They rot there quite near us, blocking one half of the wide, twisting, and muddy furrow that the living must still defend.

They have been laid there as well as may be, supporting and crushing each other. The topmost is wrapped in a tent-cloth. Handkerchiefs had been placed on the faces of the others; but in brushing against them in the dark without seeing them, or even in the daytime without noticing them, the handkerchiefs have fallen, and we are living face to face with these dead, heaped up there like a wood-pile.

It was four nights ago that they were all killed together. I remember the night myself indistinctly—it is like a dream. We were on patrol—they, I, Mesnil Andre, and Corporal Bertrand; and our business was to identify a new German listening-post marked by the artillery observers. We left the trench towards midnight and crept down the slope in line, three or four paces from each other. Thus we descended far into the ravine, and saw, lying before our eyes, the embankment of their International Trench. After we had verified that there was no listening-post in this slice of the ground we climbed back, with infinite care. Dimly I saw my neighbors to right and left, like sacks of shadow, crawling, slowly sliding, undulating and rocking in the mud and the murk, with the projecting needle in front of a rifle. Some bullets whistled above us, but they did not know we were there, they were not looking for us. When we got within sight of the mound of our line, we took a breather for a moment; one of us let a sigh go, another spoke. Another turned round bodily, and the sheath of his bayonet rang out against a stone. Instantly a rocket shot redly up from the International Trench. We threw ourselves flat on the ground, closely, desperately, and waited there motionless, with the terrible star hanging

over us and flooding us with daylight, twenty-five or thirty yards from our
trench. Then a machine-gun on the other side of the ravine swept the zone
where we were. Corporal Bertrand and I had had the luck to find in front
of us, just as the red rocket went up and before it burst into light, a
shell-hole, where a broken trestle was steeped in the mud. We flattened
ourselves against the edge of the hole, buried ourselves in the mud as
much as possible, and the poor skeleton of rotten wood concealed us. The
jet of the machine-gun crossed several times. We heard a piercing whistle
in the middle of each report, the sharp and violent sound of bullets that
went into the earth, and dull and soft blows as well, followed by groans,
by a little cry, and suddenly by a sound like the heavy snoring of a sleeper,
a sound which slowly ebbed. Bertrand and I waited, grazed by the
horizontal hail of bullets that traced a network of death an inch or so
above us and sometimes scraped our clothes, driving us still deeper into
the mud, nor dared we risk a movement which might have lifted a little
some part of our bodies. The machine-gun at last held its peace in an
enormous silence. A quarter of an hour later we two slid out of the
shell-hole, and crawling on our elbows we fell at last like bundles into our
listening-post. It was high time, too, for at that moment the moon shone
out. We were obliged to stay in the bottom of the trench till morning, and
then till evening, for the machine-gun swept the approaches without
pause. We could not see the prostrate bodies through the loop-holes of the
post, by reason of the steepness of the ground—except, just on the level of
our field of vision, a lump which appeared to be the back of one of them.
In the evening, a sap was dug to reach the place where they had fallen.
The work could not be finished in one night and was resumed by the
pioneers the following night, for, overwhelmed with fatigue, we could no
longer keep from falling asleep.

Awaking from a leaden sleep, I saw the four corpses that the sappers
had reached from underneath, hooking and then hauling them into the sap
with ropes. Each of them had several adjoining wounds, bullet-holes an
inch or so apart—the mitrailleuse had fired fast. The body of Mesnil
Andre was not found, and his brother Joseph did some mad escapades in
search of it. He went out quite alone into No Man's Land, where the
crossed fire of machine-guns swept it three ways at once and constantly.
In the morning, dragging himself along like a slug, he showed over the

bank a face black with mud and horribly wasted. They pulled him in again, with his face scratched by barbed wire, his hands bleeding, with heavy clods of mud in the folds of his clothes, and stinking of death. Like an idiot be kept on saying, "He's nowhere." He buried himself in a corner with his rifle, which he set himself to clean without hearing what was said to him, and only repeating "He's nowhere."

It is four nights ago since that night, and as the dawn comes once again to cleanse the earthly Gehenna, the bodies are becoming definitely distinct.

Barque in his rigidity seems immoderately long, his arms lie closely to the body, his chest has sunk, his belly is hollow as a basin. With his head upraised by a lump of mud, he looks over his feet at those who come up on the left; his face is dark and polluted by the clammy stains of disordered hair, and his wide and scalded eyes are heavily encrusted with blackened blood. Eudore seems very small by contrast, and his little face is completely white, so white as to remind you of the be-flowered face of a pierrot, and it is touching to see that little circle of white paper among the gray and bluish tints of the corpses. The Breton Biquet, squat and square as a flagstone, appears to be under the stress of a huge effort; he might be trying to uplift the misty darkness; and the extreme exertion overflows upon the protruding cheek-bones and forehead of his grimacing face, contorts it hideously, sets the dried and dusty hair bristling, divides his jaws in a spectral cry, and spreads wide the eyelids from his lightless troubled eyes, his flinty eyes; and his hands are contracted in a clutch upon empty air.

Barque and Biquet were shot in the belly; Eudore in the throat. In the dragging and carrying they were further injured. Big Lamuse, at last bloodless, had a puffed and creased face, and the eyes were gradually sinking in their sockets, one more than the other. They have wrapped him in a tent-cloth, and it shows a dark stain where the neck is. His right shoulder has been mangled by several bullets, and the arm is held on only by strips of the sleeve and by threads that they have put in since. The first night he was placed there, this arm hung outside the heap of dead, and the yellow hand, curled up on a lump of earth, touched passers-by in the face; so they pinned the arm to the greatcoat.

A pestilential vapor begins to hover about the remains of these beings with whom we lived so intimately and suffered so long.

When we see them we say, "They are dead, all four"; but they are too far disfigured for us to say truly, "It is they," and one must turn away from the motionless monsters to feel the void they have left among us and the familiar things that have been wrenched away.

Men of other companies or regiments, strangers who come this way by day—by night one leans unconsciously on everything within reach of the hand, dead or alive-give a start when faced by these corpses flattened one on the other in the open trench. Sometimes they are angry—"What are they thinking about to leave those stiffs there?"—"It's shameful." Then they add, "It's true they can't be taken away from there." And they were only buried in the night.

Morning has come. Opposite us we see the other slope of the ravine, Hill 119, an eminence scraped, stripped, and scratched, veined with shaken trenches and lined with parallel cuttings that vividly reveal the clay and the chalky soil. Nothing is stirring there; and our shells that burst in places with wide spouts of foam like huge billows seem to deliver their resounding blows upon a great breakwater, ruined and abandoned.

My spell of vigil is finished, and the other sentinels, enveloped in damp and trickling tent-cloths, with their stripes and plasters of mud and their livid jaws, disengage themselves from the soil wherein they are molded, bestir themselves, and come down. For us, it is rest until evening.

We yawn and stroll. We see a comrade pass and then another. Officers go to and fro, armed with periscopes and telescopes. We feel our feet again, and begin once more to live. The customary remarks cross and clash; and were it not for the dilapidated outlook, the sunken lines of the trench that buries us on the hillside, and the veto on our voices, we might fancy ourselves in the rear lines. But lassitude weighs upon all of us, our faces are jaundiced and the eyelids reddened; through long watching we look as if we had been weeping. For several days now we have all of us been sagging and growing old.

One after another the men of my squad have made a confluence at a curve in the trench. They pile themselves where the soil is only chalky, and where, above the crust that bristles with severed roots, the excavations have exposed some beds of white stones that had lain in the darkness for over a hundred thousand years.

There in the widened fairway, Bertrand's squad beaches itself. It is much reduced this time, for beyond the losses of the other night, we no longer have Poterloo, killed in a relief, nor Cadilhac, wounded in the leg by a splinter the same evening as Poterloo, nor Tirioir nor Tulacque who have been sent back, the one for dysentery, and the other for pneumonia, which is taking an ugly turn—as he says in the postcards which he sends us as a pastime from the base hospital where he is vegetating.

Once more I see gathered and grouped, soiled by contact with the earth and dirty smoke, the familiar faces and poses of those who have not been separated since the beginning, chained and riveted together in fraternity. But there is less dissimilarity than at the beginning in the appearance of the cave-men.

Papa Blaire displays in his well-worn mouth a set of new teeth, so resplendent that one can see nothing in all his poor face except those gayly-dight jaws. The great event of these foreign teeth's establishment, which he is taming by degrees and sometimes uses for eating, has profoundly modified his character and his manners. He is rarely besmeared with grime, he is hardly slovenly. Now that he has become handsome he feels it necessary to become elegant. For the moment he is dejected, because—a miracle—he cannot wash himself. Deeply sunk in a corner, he half opens a lack-luster eye, bites and masticates his old soldier's mustache—not long ago the only ornament on his face—and from time to time spits out a hair.

Fouillade is shivering, cold-smitten, or yawns, depressed and shabby. Marthereau has not changed at all. He is still as always well-bearded, his eye round and blue, and his legs so short that his trousers seem to be slipping continually from his waist and dropping to his feet. Cocon is always Cocon by the dried and parchment-like head wherein sums are working; but a recurrence of lice, the ravages of which we see overflowing on to his neck and wrists, has isolated him for a week now in protracted tussles which leave him surly when he returns among us. Paradis retains unimpaired the same quantum of good color and good temper; he is unchanging, perennial. We smile when he appears in the distance, placarded on the background of sandbags like a new poster. Nothing has changed in Pepin either, whom we can just see taking a stroll—we can tell him behind by his red-and-white squares of an oilcloth draught-board, and in front by his blade-like face and the gleam of a knife in his cold gray look. Nor has Volpatte changed, with his leggings, his shouldered blanket, and his face of a Mongolian tatooed with dirt; nor Tirette, although he has been worried for some time by blood-red streaks in his eyes—for some unknown and mysterious reason. Farfadet keeps himself aloof, in pensive expectation. When the post is being given out he awakes from his reverie to go so far, and then retires into himself. His clerkly hands indite numerous and careful postcards. He does not know of Eudoxie's end. Lamuse said no more to any one of the ultimate and awful embrace in which he clasped her body. He regretted—I knew it—his whispered confidence to me that evening, and up to his death he kept the horrible affair sacred to himself, with tenacious bashfulness. So we see Farfadet continuing to live his airy existence with the living likeness of that fair hair, which he only leaves for the scarce monosyllables of his contact with us. Corporal Bertrand has still the same soldierly and serious mien among us; he is always ready with his tranquil smile to answer all questions with lucid explanations, to help each of us to do his duty.

We are chatting as of yore, as not long since. But the necessity of speaking in low tones distinguishes our remarks and imposes on them a lugubrious tranquillity.

Something unusual has happened. For the last three months the sojourn of each unit in the first-line trenches has been four days. Yet we have now been five days here and there is no mention of relief. Some rumors of early attack are going about, brought by the liaison men and those of the fatigue-party that renews our rations every other night—without regularity or guarantee. Other portents are adding themselves to the whispers of offensive—the stopping of leave, the failure of the post, the obvious change in the officers, who are serious and closer to us. But talk on this subject always ends with a shrug of the shoulders; the soldier is never warned what is to be done with him; they put a bandage on his eyes, and only remove it at the last minute. So, "We shall see."—"We can only wait."

We detach ourselves from the tragic event foreboded. Is this because of the impossibility of a complete understanding, or a despondent unwillingness to decipher those orders that are sealed letters to us, or a lively faith that one will pass through the peril once more? Always, in spite of the premonitory signs and the prophecies that seem to be coming true, we fall back automatically upon the cares of the moment and absorb ourselves in them—hunger, thirst, the lice whose crushing ensanguines all our nails, the great weariness that saps us all.

"Seen Joseph this morning?" says Volpatte. "He doesn't look very grand, poor lad."

"He'll do something daft, certain sure. He's as good as a goner, that lad, mind you. First chance he has he'll jump in front of a bullet. I can see he will."

"It'd give any one the pip for the rest of his natural. There were six brothers of 'em, you know; four of 'em killed; two in Alsace, one in Champagne, one in Argonne. If Andre's killed he's the fifth."

"If he'd been killed they'd have found his body—they'd have seen it from the observation-post; you can't lose the rump and the thighs. My idea is that the night they went on patrol he went astray coming back—crawled right round, poor devil, and fell right into the Boche lines."

"Perhaps he got sewn up in their wire."

"I tell you they'd have found him if he'd been done in; you know jolly well the Boches wouldn't have brought the body in. And we looked everywhere. As long as he's not been found you can take it from me that he's got away somewhere on his feet, wounded or unwounded."

This so logical theory finds favor, and now it is known that Mesnil Andre is a prisoner there is less interest in him. But his brother continues to be a pitiable object—"Poor old chap, he's so young!" And the men of the squad look at him secretly.

"I've got a twist!" says Cocon suddenly. The hour of dinner has gone past and we are demanding it. There appears to be only the remains of what was brought the night before.

"What's the corporal thinking of to starve us? There he is—I'll go and get hold of him. Hey, corporal! Why can't you get us something to eat?"—"Yes, yes—something to eat!" re-echoes the destiny of these eternally hungry men.

"I'm coming," says bustling Bertrand, who keeps going both day and night.

"What then?" says Pepin, always hot-headed. "I don't feel like chewing macaroni again; I shall open a tin of meat in less than two secs?" The daily comedy of dinner steps to the front again in this drama.

"Don't touch your reserve rations!" says Bertrand; "as soon as I'm back from seeing the captain I'll get you something."

When he returns he brings and distributes a salad of potatoes and onions, and as mastication proceeds our features relax and our eyes become composed.

For the ceremony of eating, Paradis has hoisted a policeman's hat. It is hardly the right place or time for it, but the hat is quite new, and the tailor, who promised it for three months ago, only delivered it the day we came up. The pliant two-cornered hat of bright blue cloth on his flourishing round head gives him the look of a pasteboard gendarme with red-painted cheeks. Nevertheless, all the while he is eating, Paradis looks at me steadily. I go up to him. "You've a funny old face."

"Don't worry about it," he replies. "I want a chat with you. Come with me and see something."

His hand goes out to his half-full cup placed beside his dinner things; he hesitates, and then decides to put his wine in a safe place down his gullet, and the cup in his pocket. He moves off and I follow him.

In passing he picks up his helmet that gapes on the earthen bench. After a dozen paces he comes close to me and says in a low voice and with a queer air, without looking at me—as he does when he is upset—"I know where Mesnil Andre is. Would you like to see him? Come, then."

So saying, he takes off his police hat, folds and pockets it. and puts on his helmet. He sets off again and I follow him without a word.

He leads me fifty yards farther, towards the place where our common dug-out is, and the footbridge of sandbags under which one always slides with the impression that the muddy arch will collapse on one's back. After the footbridge, a hollow appears in the wall of the trench, with a step made of a hurdle stuck fast in the clay. Paradis climbs there, and motions to me to follow him on to the narrow and slippery platform. There was recently a sentry's loophole here, and it has been destroyed and made again lower down with a couple of bullet-screens. One is obliged to stoop low lest his head rise above the contrivance.

Paradis says to me, still in the same low voice, "It's me that fixed up those two shields, so as to see—for I'd got an idea, and I wanted to see. Put your eye to this—"

"I don't see anything; the hole's stopped up. What's that lump of cloth?"

"It's him," says Paradis.

Ah! It was a corpse, a corpse sitting in a hole, and horribly near—

Having flattened my face against the steel plate and glued my eye to the hole in the bullet-screen, I saw all of it. He was squatting, the head hanging forward between the legs, both arms placed on his knees, his hands hooked and half closed. He was easily identifiable—so near, so near!—in spite of his squinting and lightless eyes, by the mass of his muddy beard and the distorted mouth that revealed the teeth. He looked as if he were both smiling and grimacing at his rifle, stuck straight up in the mud before him. His outstretched hands were quite blue above and scarlet underneath, crimsoned by a damp and hellish reflection.

It was he, rain-washed and besmeared with a sort of scum, polluted and dreadfully pale, four days dead, and close up to our embankment into which the shell-hole where he had burrowed had bitten. We had not found him because he was too near!

Between this derelict dead in its unnatural solitude and the men who inhabited the dug-out there was only a slender partition of earth, and I realize that the place in it where I lay my head corresponds to the spot buttressed by this dreadful body.

I withdraw my face from the peep-hole and Paradis and I exchange glances. "Mustn't tell him yet," my companion whispers. "No, we mustn't, not at once—" "I spoke to the captain about rooting him out, and he said, too, 'we mustn't mention it now to the lad.'" A light breath of wind goes by. "I can smell it!"—"Rather!" The odor enters our thoughts and capsizes our very hearts.

"So now," says Paradis, "Joseph's left alone, out of six brothers. And I'll tell you what—I don't think he'll stop long. The lad won't take care of himself—he'll get himself done in. A lucky wound's got to drop on him from the sky, otherwise he's corpsed. Six brothers—it's too bad, that!

Don't you think it's too bad?" He added, "It's astonishing that he was so near us."

"His arm's just against the spot where I put my head."

"Yes," says Paradis, "his right arm, where there's a wrist-watch."

The watch—I stop short—is it a fancy, a dream? It seems to me—yes, I am sure now—that three days ago, the night when we were so tired out, before I went to sleep I heard what sounded like the ticking of a watch and even wondered where it could come from.

"It was very likely that watch you heard all the same, through the earth," says Paradis, whom I have told some of my thoughts; "they go on thinking and turning round even when the chap stops. Damn, your own ticker doesn't know you—it just goes quietly on making little circles."

I asked, "There's blood on his hands; but where was he hit?"

"Don't know; in the belly, I think; I thought there was something dark underneath him. Or perhaps in the face—did you notice the little stain on the cheek?"

I recall the hairy and greenish face of the dead man. "Yes, there was something on the cheek. Yes, perhaps it went in there—"

"Look out!" says Paradis hurriedly, "there he is! We ought not to have stayed here."

But we stay all the same, irresolutely wavering, as Mesnil Joseph comes straight up to us. Never did he seem so frail to us. We can see his pallor afar off, his oppressed and unnatural expression; he is bowed as be walks, and goes slowly, borne down by endless fatigue and his immovable notion.

"What's the matter with your face?" he asks me—he has seen me point out to Paradis the possible entry of the bullet. I pretend not to understand and then make some kind of evasive reply. All at once I have a torturing idea—the smell! It is there, and there is no mistaking it. It reveals a corpse; and perhaps he will guess rightly.

It seems to me that he has suddenly smelt the sign—the pathetic, lamentable appeal of the dead. But he says nothing, continues his solitary walk, and disappears round the corner.

"Yesterday," says Paradis to me, "he came just here, with his mess-tin full of rice that he didn't want to eat. Just as if he knew what he was doing, the fool stops here and talks of pitching the rest of his food over the bank, just on the spot where—where the other was. I couldn't stick that, old chap. I grabbed his arm just as he chucked the rice into the air, and it flopped down here in the trench. Old man, he turned round on me in a rage and all red in the face, 'What the hell's up with you now?' he says. I looked as fat-headed as I could, and mumbled some rot about not doing it on purpose. He shrugs his shoulders, and looks at me same as if I was dirt. He goes off, saying to himself, 'Did you see him, the blockhead?' He's bad-tempered, you know, the poor chap, and I couldn't complain. 'All right, all right,' he kept saying; and I didn't like it, you know, because I did wrong all the time, although I was right."

We go back together in silence and re-enter the dugout where the others are gathered. It is an old headquarters post, and spacious. Just as we slide in, Paradis listens. "Our batteries have been playing extra hell for the last hour, don't you think?"

I know what he means, and reply with an empty gesture, "We shall see, old man, we shall see all right!"

In the dug-out, to an audience of three, Tirette is again pouring out his barrack-life tales. Marthereau is snoring in a corner; he is close to the entry, and to get down we have to stride over his short legs, which seem to have gone back into his trunk. A group of kneeling men around a folded blanket are playing with cards—

"My turn!"—"40, 42—48—49!—Good!"

"Isn't he lucky, that game-bird; it's imposs', I've got stumped three times I want nothing more to do with you. You're skinning me this evening, and you robbed me the other day, too, you infernal fritter!"—"What did you revoke for, mugwump?"—"I'd only the king, nothing else."

"All the same," murmurs some one who is eating in a corner, "this Camembert, it cost twenty-five sous, but you talk about muck! Outside there's a layer of sticky glue, and inside it's plaster that breaks."

Meanwhile Tirette relates the outrages inflicted on him during his twenty-one days of training owing to the quarrelsome temper of a certain major: "A great hog he was, my boy, everything rotten on this earth. All the lot of us looked foul when he went by or when we saw him in the officers' room spread out on a chair that you couldn't see underneath him, with his vast belly and huge cap, and circled round with stripes from top to bottom, like a barrel—he was hard on the private! They called him Loeb—a Boche, you see!"

"I knew him!" cried Paradis; "when war started he was declared unfit for active service, naturally. While I was doing my term he was a dodger already—but he dodged round all the street corners to pinch you—you got a day's clink for an unbuttoned button, and he gave it you over and above if there was some bit of a thing about you that wasn't quite O.K.—and everybody laughed. He thought they were laughing at you, and you knew they were laughing at him, but you knew it in vain, you were in it up to your head for the clink."

"He had a wife," Tirette goes on, "the old—"

"I remember her, too," Paradis exclaimed. "You talk about a bitch!"

"Some of 'em drag a little pug-dog about with 'em, but him, he trailed that yellow minx about everywhere, with her broom-handle hips and her wicked look. It was her that worked the old sod up against us. He was more stupid than wicked, but as soon as she was there he got more wicked than stupid. So you bet they were some nuisance—"

Just then, Marthereau wakes up from his sleep by the entry with a half-groan. He straightens himself up, sitting on his straw like a gaol-bird, and we see his bearded silhouette take the vague outline of a Chinese, while his round eye rolls and turns in the shadows. He is looking at his dreams of a moment ago. Then he passes his hand over his eyes and—as if it had some connection with his dream—recalls the scene that night when we came up to the trenches—"For all that," he says, in a voice weighty with slumber and reflection, "there were some half-seas-over that night! Ah, what a night! All those troops, companies and whole regiments, yelling and surging all the way up the road! In the thinnest of the dark you could see the jumble of poilus that went on and up—like the sea itself, you'd say—and carrying on across all the convoys of artillery and ambulance wagons that we met that night. I've never seen so many, so many convoys in the night, never!" Then he deals himself a thump on the chest, settles down again in self-possession, groans, and says no more.

Blaire's voice rises, giving expression to the haunting thought that wakes in the depths of the men: "It's four o'clock. It's too late for there to be anything from our side."

One of the gamesters in the other corner yelps a question at another: "Now then? Are you going to play or aren't you, worm-face?"

Tirette continues the story of his major: "Behold one day they'd served us at the barracks with some suetty soup. Old man, a disease, it was! So a chap asks to speak to the captain, and holds his mess-tin up to his nose."

"Numskull!" some one shouts in the other corner. "Why didn't you trump, then?"

"'Ah, damn it,' said the captain, 'take it away from my nose, it positively stinks.'"

"It wasn't my game," quavers a discontented but unconvinced voice.

"And the captain, he makes a report to the major. But behold the major, mad as the devil, he butts in shaking the paper in his paw: 'What's this?' he says. 'Where's the soup that has caused this rebellion, that I may taste it?' They bring him some in a clean mess-tin and he sniffs it. 'What now!' he says, 'it smells good. They damned well shan't have it then, rich soup like this!'"

"Not your game! And he was leading, too! Bungler! It's unlucky, you know."

"Then at five o'clock as we were coming out of barracks, our two marvels butt in again and plank themselves in front of the swaddies coming out, trying to spot some little thing not quite so, and he said, 'Ah, my bucks, you thought you'd score off me by complaining of this excellent soup that I have consumed myself along with my partner here; just wait and see if I don't get even with you. Hey, you with the long hair, the tall artist, come here a minute!' And all the time the beast was jawing, his bag-o'-bones—as straight and thin as a post—went 'oui, oui' with her head."

"That depends; if he hadn't a trump, it's another matter."

"But all of a sudden we see her go white as a sheet, she puts her fist on her tummy and she shakes like all that, and then suddenly, in front of all the fellows that filled the square, she drops her umbrella and starts spewing!"

"Hey, listen!" says Paradis, sharply, "they're shouting in the trench. Don't you hear? Isn't it 'alarm!' they're shouting?"

"Alarm? Are you mad?"

The words were hardly said when a shadow comes in through the low doorway of our dug-out and cries—"Alarm, 22nd! Stand to arms!"

A moment of silence and then several exclamations. "I knew it," murmurs Paradis between his teeth, and he goes on his knees towards the opening into the molehill that shelters us. Speech then ceases and we seem to be struck dumb. Stooping or kneeling we bestir ourselves; we buckle on our waist-belts; shadowy arms dart from one side to another; pockets are rummaged. And we issue forth pell-mell, dragging our knapsacks behind us by the straps, our blankets and pouches.

Outside we are deafened. The roar of gunfire has increased a hundredfold, to left, to right, and in front of us. Our batteries give voice without ceasing.

"Do you think they're attacking?" ventures a man. "How should I know?" replies another voice with irritated brevity.

Our jaws are set and we swallow our thoughts, hurrying, bustling, colliding, and grumbling without words.

A command goes forth—"Shoulder your packs."—"There's a counter-command—" shouts an officer who runs down the trench with great strides, working his elbows, and the rest of his sentence disappears with him. A counter-command! A visible tremor has run through the files, a start which uplifts our heads and holds us all in extreme expectation.

But no; the counter-order only concerns the knapsacks. No pack; but the blanket rolled round the body, and the trenching-tool at the waist. We unbuckle our blankets, tear them open and roll them up. Still no word is spoken; each has a steadfast eye and the mouth forcefully shut. The corporals and sergeants go here and there, feverishly spurring the silent haste in which the men are bowed: "Now then, hurry up! Come, come, what the hell are you doing? Will you hurry, yes or no?"

A detachment of soldiers with a badge of crossed axes on their sleeves clear themselves a fairway and swiftly delve holes in the wall of the trench. We watch them sideways as we don our equipment.

"What are they doing, those chaps?"—"It's to climb up by."

We are ready. The men marshal themselves, still silently, their blankets crosswise, the helmet-strap on the chin, leaning on their rifles. I look at their pale, contracted, and reflective faces. They are not soldiers, they are men. They are not adventurers, or warriors, or made for human slaughter, neither butchers nor cattle. They are laborers and artisans whom one recognizes in their uniforms. They are civilians uprooted, and they are ready. They await the signal for death or murder; but you may see, looking at their faces between the vertical gleams of their bayonets, that they are simply men.

Each one knows that he is going to take his head, his chest, his belly, his whole body, and all naked, up to the rifles pointed forward, to the shells, to the bombs piled and ready, and above all to the methodical and almost infallible machine-guns—to all that is waiting for him yonder and is now so frightfully silent—before he reaches the other soldiers that he must kill. They are not careless of their lives, like brigands, nor blinded by passion like savages. In spite of the doctrines with which they have been cultivated they are not inflamed. They are above instinctive excesses. They are not drunk, either physically or morally. It is in full consciousness, as in full health and full strength, that they are massed there to hurl themselves once more into that sort of madman's part imposed on all men by the madness of the human race. One sees the thought and the fear and the farewell that there is in their silence, their stillness, in the mask of tranquillity which unnaturally grips their faces. They are not the kind of hero one thinks of, but their sacrifice has greater worth than they who have not seen them will ever be able to understand.

They are waiting; a waiting that extends and seems eternal. Now and then one or another starts a little when a bullet, fired from the other side, skims the forward embankment that shields us and plunges into the flabby flesh of the rear wall.

The end of the day is spreading a sublime but melancholy light on that strong unbroken mass of beings of whom some only will live to see the night. It is raining—there is always rain in my memories of all the tragedies of the great war. The evening is making ready, along with a vague and chilling menace; it is about to set for men that snare that is as wide as the world.

New orders are peddled from mouth to mouth. Bombs strung on wire hoops are distributed—"Let each man take two bombs!"

The major goes by. He is restrained in his gestures, in undress, girded, undecorated. We hear him say, "There's something good, mes enfants, the Boches are clearing out. You'll get along all right, eh?"

News passes among us like a breeze. "The Moroccans and the 21st Company are in front of us. The attack is launched on our right."

The corporals are summoned to the captain, and return with armsful of steel things. Bertrand is fingering me; he hooks something on to a button of my greatcoat. It is a kitchen knife. "I'm putting this on to your coat," he says.

"Me too!" says Pepin.

"No," says Bertrand, "it's forbidden to take volunteers for these things."

"Be damned to you!" growls Pepin.

We wait, in the great rainy and shot-hammered space that has no other boundary than the distant and tremendous cannonade. Bertrand has finished his distribution and returns. Several soldiers have sat down, and some of them are yawning.

The cyclist Billette slips through in front of us, carrying an officer's waterproof on his arm and obviously averting his face. "Hullo, aren't you going too?" Cocon cries to him.

"No, I'm not going," says the other. "I'm in the 17th. The Fifth Battalion's not attacking!"

"Ah, they've always got the luck, the Fifth. They've never got to fight like we have!" Billette is already in the distance, and a few grimaces follow his disappearance.

A man arrives running, and speaks to Bertrand, and then Bertrand turns to us—

"Up you go," he says, "it's our turn."

All move at once. We put our feet on the steps made by the sappers, raise ourselves, elbow to elbow, beyond the shelter of the trench, and climb on to the parapet.

Bertrand is out on the sloping ground. He covers us with a quick glance, and when we are all there he says, "Allons, forward!"

Our voices have a curious resonance. The start has been made very quickly, unexpectedly almost, as in a dream. There is no whistling sound in the air. Among the vast uproar of the guns we discern very clearly this surprising silence of bullets around us—

We descend over the rough and slippery ground with involuntary gestures, helping ourselves sometimes with the rifle. Mechanically the eye fastens on some detail of the declivity, of the ruined ground, on the sparse and shattered stakes pricking up, at the wreckage in the holes. It is unbelievable that we are upright in full daylight on this slope where several survivors remember sliding along in the darkness with such care, and where the others have only hazarded furtive glances through the loopholes. No, there is no firing against us. The wide exodus of the battalion out of the ground seems to have passed unnoticed! This truce is full of an increasing menace, increasing. The pale light confuses us.

On all sides the slope is covered by men who, like us, are bent on the descent. On the right the outline is defined of a company that is reaching the ravine by Trench 97—an old German work in ruins. We cross our wire by openings. Still no one fires on us. Some awkward ones who have made false steps are getting up again. We form up on the farther side of the entanglements and then set ourselves to topple down the slope rather faster—there is an instinctive acceleration in the movement. Several bullets arrive at last among us. Bertrand shouts to us to reserve our bombs and wait till the last moment.

But the sound of his voice is carried away. Abruptly, across all the width of the opposite slope, lurid flames burst forth that strike the air with terrible detonations. In line from left to right fires emerge from the sky and explosions from the ground. It is a frightful curtain which divides us from the world, which divides us from the past and from the future. We stop, fixed to the ground, stupefied by the sudden host that thunders from every side; then a simultaneous effort uplifts our mass again and throws it swiftly forward. We stumble and impede each other in the great waves of smoke. With harsh crashes and whirlwinds of pulverized earth, towards the profundity into which we hurl ourselves pell-mell, we see craters opened here and there, side by side, and merging in each other. Then one knows no longer where the discharges fall. Volleys are let loose so monstrously resounding that one feels himself annihilated by the mere sound of the downpoured thunder of these great constellations of destruction that form in the sky. One sees and one feels the fragments passing close to one's head with their hiss of red-hot iron plunged in water. The blast of one explosion so burns my hands that I let my rifle fall. I pick it up again, reeling, and set off in the tawny-gleaming tempest with lowered head, lashed by spirits of dust and soot in a crushing downpour like volcanic lava. The stridor of the bursting shells hurts your ears, beats you on the neck, goes through your temples, and you cannot endure it without a cry. The gusts of death drive us on, lift us up, rock us to and fro. We leap, and do not know whither we go. Our eyes are blinking and weeping and obscured. The view before us is blocked by a flashing avalanche that fills space.

It is the barrage fire. We have to go through that whirlwind of fire and those fearful showers that vertically fall. We are passing through. We are through it, by chance. Here and there I have seen forms that spun round and were lifted up and laid down, illumined by a brief reflection from over yonder. I have glimpsed strange faces that uttered some sort of cry—you could see them without hearing them in the roar of annihilation. A brasier full of red and black masses huge and furious fell about me, excavating the ground, tearing it from under my feet, throwing me aside like a bouncing toy. I remember that I strode over a smoldering corpse, quite black, with a tissue of rosy blood shriveling on him; and I remember, too, that the skirts of the greatcoat flying next to me had caught fire, and left a trail of smoke behind. On our right, all along Trench 97, our glances were drawn and dazzled by a rank of frightful flames, closely crowded against each other like men.

Forward!

Now, we are nearly running. I see some who fall solidly flat, face forward, and others who founder meekly, as though they would sit down on the ground. We step aside abruptly to avoid the prostrate dead, quiet and rigid, or else offensive, and also—more perilous snares!—the wounded that hook on to you, struggling.

The International Trench! We are there. The wire entanglements have been torn up into long roots and creepers, thrown afar and coiled up, swept away and piled in great drifts by the guns. Between these big bushes of rain-damped steel the ground is open and free.

The trench is not defended. The Germans have abandoned it, or else a first wave has already passed over it. Its interior bristles with rifles placed against the bank. In the bottom are scattered corpses. From the jumbled litter of the long trench, hands emerge that protrude from gray sleeves with red facings, and booted legs. In places the embankment is destroyed and its woodwork splintered—all the flank of the trench collapsed and fallen into an indescribable mixture. In other places, round pits are yawning. And of all that moment I have best retained the vision of a whimsical trench covered with many-colored rags and tatters. For the making of their sandbags the Germans had used cotton and woolen stuffs of motley design pillaged from some house-furnisher's shop; and all this hotch-potch of colored remnants, mangled and frayed, floats and flaps and dances in our faces.

We have spread out in the trench. The lieutenant, who has jumped to the other side, is stooping and summoning us with signs and shouts—"Don't stay there; forward, forward!"

We climb the wall of the trench with the help of the sacks, of weapons, and of the backs that are piled up there. In the bottom of the ravine the soil is shot-churned, crowded with jetsam, swarming with prostrate bodies. Some are motionless as blocks of wood; others move slowly or convulsively. The barrage fire continues to increase its infernal discharge behind us on the ground that we have crossed. But where we are at the foot of the rise it is a dead point for the artillery.

A short and uncertain calm follows. We are less deafened and look at each other. There is fever in the eyes, and the cheek-bones are blood-red. Our breathing snores and our hearts drum in our bodies.

In haste and confusion we recognize each other, as if we had met again face to face in a nightmare on the uttermost shores of death. Some hurried words are cast upon this glade in hell—"It's you!" —"Where's Cocon?"—"Don't know."—"Have you seen the captain?"—"No."—"Going strong?"—"Yes."

The bottom of the ravine is crossed and the other slope rises opposite. We climb in Indian file by a stairway rough-hewn in the ground: "Look out!" The shout means that a soldier half-way up the steps has been struck in the loins by a shell-fragment; he falls with his arms forward, bareheaded, like the diving swimmer. We can see the shapeless silhouette of the mass as it plunges into the gulf. I can almost see the detail of his blown hair over the black profile of his face.

We debouch upon the height. A great colorless emptiness is outspread before us. At first one can see nothing but a chalky and stony plain, yellow and gray to the limit of sight. No human wave is preceding ours; in front of us there is no living soul, but the ground is peopled with dead—recent corpses that still mimic agony or sleep, and old remains already bleached and scattered to the wind, half assimilated by the earth.

As soon as our pushing and jolted file emerges, two men close to me are hit, two shadows are hurled to the ground and roll under our feet, one with a sharp cry, and the other silently, as a felled ox. Another disappears with the caper of a lunatic, as if he had been snatched away. Instinctively we close up as we hustle forward—always forward—and the wound in our line closes of its own accord. The adjutant stops, raises his sword, lets it fall, and drops to his knees. His kneeling body slopes backward in jerks, his helmet drops on his heels, and he remains there, bareheaded, face to the sky. Hurriedly the rush of the rank has split open to respect his immobility.

But we cannot see the lieutenant. No more leaders then—Hesitation checks the wave of humanity that begins to beat on the plateau. Above the trampling one hears the hoarse effort of our lungs. "Forward!" cries some soldier, and then all resume the onward race to perdition with increasing speed.

"Where's Bertrand?" comes the laborious complaint of one of the foremost runners. "There! Here!" He had stooped in passing over a wounded man, but he leaves him quickly, and the man extends his arms towards him and seems to sob.

It is just at the moment when he rejoins us that we hear in front of us, coming from a sort of ground swelling, the crackle of a machine-gun. It is a moment of agony—more serious even than when we were passing through the flaming earthquake of the barrage. That familiar voice speaks to us across the plain, sharp and horrible. But we no longer stop. "Go on, go on!"

Our panting becomes hoarse groaning, yet still we hurl ourselves toward the horizon.

"The Boches! I see them!" a man says suddenly. "Yes—their heads, there—above the trench—it's there, the trench, that line. It's close, Ah, the hogs!"

We can indeed make out little round gray caps which rise and then drop on the ground level, fifty yards away, beyond a belt of dark earth, furrowed and humped. Encouraged they spring forward, they who now form the group where I am. So near the goal, so far unscathed, shall we not reach it? Yes, we will reach it! We make great strides and no longer hear anything. Each man plunges straight ahead, fascinated by the terrible trench, bent rigidly forward, almost incapable of turning his head to right or to left. I have a notion that many of us missed their footing and fell to the ground. I jump sideways to miss the suddenly erect bayonet of a toppling rifle. Quite close to me, Farfadet jostles me with his face bleeding, throws himself on Volpatte who is beside me and clings to him. Volpatte doubles up without slackening his rush and drags him along some paces, then shakes him off without looking at him and without knowing who he is, and shouts at him in a breaking voice almost choked with exertion: "Let me go, let me go, nom de Dieu! They'll pick you up directly—don't worry."

The other man sinks to the ground, and his face, plastered with a scarlet mask and void of all expression, turns in every direction; while Volpatte, already in the distance, automatically repeats between his teeth, "Don't worry," with a steady forward gaze on the line.

A shower of bullets spirts around me, increasing the number of those who suddenly halt, who collapse slowly, defiant and gesticulating, of those who dive forward solidly with all the body's burden, of the shouts, deep, furious, and desperate, and even of that hollow and terrible gasp when a man's life goes bodily forth in a breath. And we who are not yet stricken, we look ahead, we walk and we run, among the frolics of the death that strikes at random into our flesh.

The wire entanglements—and there is one stretch of them intact. We go along to where it has been gutted into a wide and deep opening. This is a colossal funnel-hole, formed of smaller funnels placed together, a fantastic volcanic crater, scooped there by the guns.

The sight of this convulsion is stupefying; truly it seems that it must have come from the center of the earth. Such a rending of virgin strata puts new edge on our attacking fury, and none of us can keep from shouting with a solemn shake of the head—even just now when words are but painfully torn from our throats—"Ah, Christ! Look what hell we've given 'em there! Ah, look!"

Driven as if by the wind, we mount or descend at the will of the hollows and the earthy mounds in the gigantic fissure dug and blackened and burned by furious flames. The soil clings to the feet and we tear them out angrily. The accouterments and stuffs that cover the soft soil, the linen that is scattered about from sundered knapsacks, prevent us from sticking fast in it, and we are careful to plant our feet in this debris when we jump into the holes or climb the hillocks.

Behind us voices urge us—"Forward, boys, forward, nome de Dieu!"

"All the regiment is behind us!" they cry. We do not turn round to see, but the assurance electrifies our rush once more.

No more caps are visible behind the embankment of the trench we are nearing. Some German dead are crumbling in front of it, in pinnacled heaps or extended lines. We are there. The parapet takes definite and sinister shape and detail; the loopholes—we are prodigiously, incredibly close!

Something falls in front of us. It is a bomb. With a kick Corporal Bertrand returns it so well that it rises and bursts just over the trench.

With that fortunate deed the squad reaches the trench.

Pepin has hurled himself flat on the ground and is involved with a corpse. He reaches the edge and plunges in—the first to enter. Fouillade, with great gestures and shouts, jumps into the pit almost at the same moment that Pepin rolls down it. Indistinctly I see—in the time of the lightning's flash—a whole row of black demons stooping and squatting for the descent, on the ridge of the embankment, on the edge of the dark ambush.

A terrible volley bursts point-blank in our faces, flinging in front of us a sudden row of flames the whole length of the earthen verge. After the stunning shock we shake ourselves and burst into devilish laughter—the discharge has passed too high. And at once, with shouts and roars of salvation, we slide and roll and fall alive into the belly of the trench!

We are submerged in a mysterious smoke, and at first I can only see blue uniforms in the stifling gulf. We go one way and then another, driven by each other, snarling and searching. We turn about, and with our hands encumbered by knife, bombs, and rifle, we do not know at first what to do.

"They're in their funk-holes, the swine!" is the cry. Heavy explosions are shaking the earth—underground, in the dug-outs. We are all at once divided by huge clouds of smoke so thick that we are masked and can see nothing more. We struggle like drowning men through the acrid darkness of a fallen fragment of night. One stumbles against barriers of cowering clustered beings who bleed and howl in the bottom. Hardly can one make out the trench walls, straight up just here and made of white sandbags, which are everywhere torn like paper. At one time the heavy adhesive reek sways and lifts, and one sees again the swarming mob of the attackers. Torn out of the dusty picture, the silhouette of a hand-to-hand struggle is drawn in fog on the wall, it droops and sinks to the bottom. I hear several shrill cries of "Kamarad!" proceeding from a pale-faced and gray-clad group in the huge corner made by a rending shell. Under the inky cloud the tempest of men flows back, climbs towards the right, eddying, pitching and falling, along the dark and ruined mole.

And suddenly one feels that it is over. We see and hear and understand that our wave, rolling here through the barrage fire, has not encountered an equal breaker. They have fallen back on our approach. The battle has dissolved in front of us. The slender curtain of defenders has crumbled into the holes, where they are caught like rats or killed. There is no more resistance, but a void, a great void. We advance in crowds like a terrible array of spectators.

And here the trench seems all lightning-struck. With its tumbled white walls it might be just here the soft and slimy bed of a vanished river that has left stony bluffs, with here and there the flat round hole of a pool, also dried up; and on the edges, on the sloping banks and in the bottom, there is a long trailing glacier of corpses—a dead river that is filled again to overflowing by the new tide and the breaking wave of our company. In the smoke vomited by dug-outs and the shaking wind of subterranean explosions, I come upon a compact mass of men hooked onto each other who are describing a wide circle. Just as we reach them the entire mass breaks up to make a residue of furious battle. I see Blaire break away, his helmet hanging on his neck by the chin-strap and his face flayed, and uttering a savage yell. I stumble upon a man who is crouching at the entry to a dug-out. Drawing back from the black hatchway, yawning and treacherous, he steadies himself with his left hand on a beam. In his right hand and for several seconds he holds a bomb which is on the point of exploding. It disappears in the hole, bursts immediately, and a horrible human echo answers him from the bowels of the earth. The man seizes another bomb.

Another man strikes and shatters the posts at the mouth of another dug-out with a pickax he has found there, causing a landslide, and the entry is blocked. I see several shadows trampling and gesticulating over the tomb.

Of the living ragged band that has got so far and has reached this long-sought trench after dashing against the storm of invincible shells and bullets launched to meet them, I can hardly recognize those whom I know, just as though all that had gone before of our lives had suddenly become very distant. There is some change working in them. A frenzied excitement is driving them all out of themselves.

"What are we stopping here for?" says one, grinding his teeth.

"Why don't we go on to the next?" a second asks me in fury. "Now we're here, we'd be there in a few jumps!'

"I, too, I want to go on."—"Me, too. Ah, the hogs!" They shake themselves like banners. They carry the luck of their survival as it were glory; they are implacable, uncontrolled, intoxicated with themselves.

We wait and stamp about in the captured work, this strange demolished way that winds along the plain and goes from the unknown to the unknown.

Advance to the right!

We begin to flow again in one direction. No doubt it is a movement planned up there, back yonder, by the chiefs. We trample soft bodies underfoot, some of which are moving and slowly altering their position; rivulets and cries come from them. Like posts and heaps of rubbish, corpses are piled anyhow on the wounded, and press them down, suffocate them, strangle them. So that I can get by, I must push at a slaughtered trunk of which the neck is a spring of gurgling blood.

In the cataclysm of earth and of massive wreckage blown up and blown out, above the hordes of wounded and dead that stir together, athwart the moving forest of smoke implanted in the trench and in all its environs, one no longer sees any face but what is inflamed, blood-red with sweat, eyes flashing. Some groups seem to be dancing as they brandish their knives. They are elated, immensely confident, ferocious.

The battle dies down imperceptibly. A soldier says, "Well, what's to be done now?" ft flares up again suddenly at one point. Twenty yards away in the plain, in the direction of a circle that the gray embankment makes, a cluster of rifle-shots crackles and hurls its scattered missiles around a hidden machine-gun, that spits intermittently and seems to be in difficulties.

Under the shadowy wing of a sort of yellow and bluish nimbus I see men encircling the flashing machine and closing in on it. Near to me I make out the silhouette of Mesnil Joseph, who is steering straight and with no effort of concealment for the spot whence the barking explosions come in jerky sequence.

A flash shoots out from a corner of the trench between us two. Joseph halts, sways, stoops, and drops on one knee. I run to him and he watches me coming. "It's nothing—my thigh. I can crawl along by myself." He seems to have become quiet, childish, docile; and sways slowly towards the trench.

I have still in my eyes the exact spot whence rang the shot that hit him, and I slip round there by the left, making a detour. No one there. I only meet another of our squad on the same errand—Paradis.

We are bustled by men who are carrying on their shoulders pieces of iron of all shapes. They block up the trench and separate us. "The machine-gun's taken by the 7th," they shout, "it won't bark any more. It was a mad devil—filthy beast! Filthy beast!"

"What's there to do now?"—"Nothing."

We stay there, jumbled together, and sit down. The living have ceased to gasp for breath, the dying have rattled their last, surrounded by smoke and lights and the din of the guns that rolls to all the ends of the earth. We no longer know where we are. There is neither earth nor sky—nothing but a sort of cloud. The first period of inaction is forming in the chaotic drama, and there is a general slackening in the movement and the uproar.

The cannonade grows less; it still shakes the sky as a cough shakes a man, but it is farther off now. Enthusiasm is allayed, and there remains only the infinite fatigue that rises and overwhelms us, and the infinite waiting that begins over again.

Where is the enemy? He has left his dead everywhere, and we have seen rows of prisoners. Yonder again there is one, drab, ill-defined and smoky, outlined against the dirty sky. But the bulk seem to have dispersed afar. A few shells come to us here and there blunderingly, and we ridicule them. We are saved, we are quiet, we are alone, in this desert where an immensity of corpses adjoins a line of the living.

Night has come. The dust has flown away, but has yielded place to shadow and darkness over the long-drawn multitude's disorder. Men approach each other, sit down, get up again and walk about, leaning on each other or hooked together. Between the dug-outs, which are blocked by the mingled dead, we gather in groups and squat. Some have laid their rifles on the ground and wander on the rim of the trench with their arms balancing; and when they come near we can see that they are blackened and scorched, their eyes are red and slashed with mud. We speak seldom, but are beginning to think.

We see the stretcher-bearers, whose sharp silhouettes stoop and grope; they advance linked two and two together by their long burdens. Yonder on our right one hears the blows of pick and shovel.

I wander into the middle of this gloomy turmoil. In a place where the embankment has crushed the embankment of the trench into a gentle slope, some one is seated. A faint light still prevails. The tranquil attitude of this man as he looks reflectively in front of him is sculptural and striking. Stooping, I recognize him as Corporal Bertrand. He turns his face towards me, and I feel that he is looking at me through the shadows with his thoughtful smile.

"I was coming to look for you," he says; "they're organizing a guard for the trench until we've got news of what the others have done and what's going on in front. I'm going to put you on double sentry with Paradis, in a listening-post that the sappers have just dug."

We watch the shadows of the passers-by and of those who are seated, outlined in inky blots, bowed and bent in diverse attitudes under the gray sky, all along the ruined parapet. Dwarfed to the size of insects and worms, they make a strange and secret stirring among these shadow-hidden lands where for two years war has caused cities of soldiers to wander or stagnate over deep and boundless cemeteries.

Two obscure forms pass in the dark, several paces from us; they are talking together in low voices—"You bet, old chap, instead of listening to him, I shoved my bayonet into his belly so that I couldn't haul it out."

"There were four in the bottom of the hole. I called to 'em to come out, and as soon as one came out I stuck him. Blood ran down me up to the elbow and stuck up my sleeves."

"Ah!" the first speaker went on, "when we are telling all about it later, if we get back, to the other people at home, by the stove and the candle, who's going to believe it? It's a pity, isn't it?"

"I don't care a damn about that, as long as we do get back," said the other; "I want the end quickly, and only that."

Bertrand was used to speak very little ordinarily, and never of himself. But he said, "I've got three of them on my hands. I struck like a madman. Ah, we were all like beasts when we got here!"

He raised his voice and there was a restrained tremor in it: "it was necessary," he said, "it was necessary, for the future's sake."

He crossed his arms and tossed his head: "The future!" he cried all at once as a prophet might. "How will they regard this slaughter, they who'll live after us, to whom progress—which comes as sure as fate—will at last restore the poise of their conscience? How will they regard these exploits which even we who perform them don't know whether one should compare them with those of Plutarch's and Corneille's heroes or with those of hooligans and apaches?

"And for all that, mind you," Bertrand went on, "there is one figure that has risen above the war and will blaze with the beauty and strength of his courage—"

I listened, leaning on a stick and towards him, drinking in the voice that came in the twilight silence from the lips that so rarely spoke. He cried with a clear voice—"Liebknecht!"

He stood up with his arms still crossed. His face, as profoundly serious as a statue's, drooped upon his chest. But he emerged once again from his marble muteness to repeat, "The future, the future! The work of the future will be to wipe out the present, to wipe it out more than we can imagine, to wipe it out like something abominable and shameful. And yet—this present—it had to be, it had to be! Shame on military glory, shame on armies, shame on the soldier's calling, that changes men by turns into stupid victims or ignoble brutes. Yes, shame. That's the true word, but it's too true; it's true in eternity, but it's not yet true for us. It will be true when there is a Bible that is entirely true, when it is found written among the other truths that a purified mind will at the same time let us understand. We are still lost, still exiled far from that time. In our time of to-day, in these moments, this truth is hardly more than a fallacy, this sacred saying is only blasphemy!"

A kind of laugh came from him, full of echoing dreams—"To think I once told them I believed in prophecies, just to kid them!"

I sat down by Bertrand's side. This soldier who had always done more than was required of him and survived notwithstanding, stood at that moment in my eyes for those who incarnate a lofty moral conception, who have the strength to detach themselves from the hustle of circumstances, and who are destined, however little their path may run through a splendor of events, to dominate their time.

"I have always thought all those things," I murmured.

"Ah!" said Bertrand. We looked at each other without a word, with a little surprised self-communion. After this full silence he spoke again. "It's time to start duty; take your rifle and come."

From our listening-post we see towards the east a light spreading like a conflagration, but bluer and sadder than buildings on fire. It streaks the sky above a long black cloud which extends suspended like the smoke of an extinguished fire, like an immense stain on the world. It is the returning morning.

It is so cold that we cannot stand still in spite of our fettering fatigue. We tremble and shiver and shed tears, and our teeth chatter. Little by little, with dispiriting tardiness, day escapes from the sky into the slender framework of the black clouds. All is frozen, colorless and empty; a deathly silence reigns everywhere. There is rime and snow under a burden of mist. Everything is white. Paradis moves—a heavy pallid ghost, for we two also are all white. I had placed my shoulder-bag on the other side of the parapet, and it looks as if wrapped in paper. In the bottom of the hole a little snow floats, fretted and gray in the black foot-bath. Outside the hole, on the piled-up things, in the excavations, upon the crowded dead, snow rests like muslin.

Two stooping protuberant masses are crayoned on the mist; they grow darker as they approach and hail us. They are the men who come to relieve us. Their faces are ruddy and tearful with cold, their cheek-bones like enameled tiles; but their greatcoats are not snow-powdered, for they have slept underground.

Paradis hoists himself out. Over the plain I follow his Father Christmas back and the duck-like waddle of the boots that pick up white-felted soles. Bending deeply forward we regain the trench; the footsteps of those who replaced us are marked in black on the scanty whiteness that covers the ground.

Watchers are standing at intervals in the trench, over which tarpaulins are stretched on posts here and there, figured in white velvet or mottled with rime, and forming great irregular tents; and between the watchers are squatting forms who grumble and try to fight against the cold, to exclude it from the meager fireside of their own chests, or who are simply frozen. A dead man has slid down, upright and hardly askew, with his feet in the trench and his chest and arms resting on the bank. He was clasping the earth when life left him. His face is turned skyward and is covered with a leprosy of ice, the eyelids are white as the eyes, the mustache caked with hard slime. Other bodies are sleeping, less white than that one; the snowy stratum is only intact on lifeless things.

"We must sleep." Paradis and I are looking for shelter, a hole where we may hide ourselves and shut our eyes. "It can't be helped if there are stiffs in the dugouts," mutters Paradis; "in a cold like this they'll keep, they won't be too bad." We go forward, so weary that we can only see the ground.

I am alone. Where is Paradis? He must have lain down in some hole, and perhaps I did not hear his call. I meet Marthereau. "I'm looking where I can sleep, I've been on guard," he says.

"I, too; let's look together."

"What's all the row and to-do?" says Marthereau. A mingled hubbub of trampling and voices overflows from the communication trench that goes off here. "The communication trenches are full of men. Who are you?"

One of those with whom we are suddenly mixed up replies, "We're the Fifth Battalion." The newcomers stop. They are in marching order. The one that spoke sits down for a breathing space on the curves of a sand-bag that protrudes from the line. He wipes his nose with the back of his sleeve.

"What are you doing here? Have they told you to come?"

"Not half they haven't told us. We're coming to attack. We're going yonder, right up." With his head he indicates the north. The curiosity with which we look at them fastens on to a detail. "You've carried everything with you?"—"We chose to keep it, that's all."

"Forward!" they are ordered. They rise and proceed, incompletely awake, their eyes puffy, their wrinkles underlined. There are young men among them with thin necks and vacuous eyes, and old men; and in the middle, ordinary ones. They march with a commonplace and pacific step. What they are going to do seems to us, who did it last night, beyond human strength. But still they go away towards the north.

"The revally of the damned," says Marthereau.

We make way for them with a sort of admiration and a sort of terror. When they have passed, Marthereau wags his head and murmurs, "There are some getting ready, too, on the other side, with their gray uniforms. Do you think those chaps are feeling it about the attack? Then why have they come? It's not their doing, I know, but it's theirs all the same, seeing they're here.—I know, I know, but it's odd, all of it."

The sight of a passer-by alters the course of his ideas: "Tiens, there's Truc, the big one, d'you know him? Isn't he immense and pointed, that chap! As for me, I know I'm not quite hardly big enough; but him, he goes too far. He always knows what's going on, that two-yarder! For savvying everything, there's nobody going to give him the go-by! I'll go and chivvy him about a funk-hole."

"If there's a rabbit-hole anywhere?" replies the elongated passer-by, leaning on Marthereau like a poplar tree, "for sure, my old Caparthe, certainly. Tiens, there"—and unbending his elbow he makes an indicative gesture like a flag-signaler—"'Villa von Hindenburg.' and there, 'Villa Glucks auf.' If that doesn't satisfy you, you gentlemen are hard to please.

P'raps there's a few lodgers in the basement, but not noisy lodgers, and you can talk out aloud in front of them, you know!"

"Ah, nom de Dieu!" cried Marthereau a quarter of an hour after we had established ourselves in one of these square-cut graves, "there's lodgers he didn't tell us about, that frightful great lightning-rod, that infinity!" His eyelids were just closing, but they opened again and he scratched his arms and thighs: "I want a snooze! It appears it's out of the question. Can't resist these things."

We settled ourselves to yawning and sighing, and finally we lighted a stump of candle, wet enough to resist us although covered with our hands; and we watched each other yawn.

The German dug-out consisted of several rooms. We were against a partition of ill-fitting planks; and on the other side, in Cave No. 2, some men were also awake. We saw light trickle through the crannies between the planks and heard rumbling voices. "It's the other section," said Marthereau.

Then we listened, mechanically. "When I was off on leave," boomed an invisible talker, "we had the hump at first, because we were thinking of my poor brother who was missing in March—dead, no doubt—and of my poor little Julien, of Class 1915, killed in the October attacks. And then bit by bit, her and me, we settled down to be happy at being together again, you see. Our little kid, the last, a five-year-old, entertained us a treat. He wanted to play soldiers with me, and I made a little gun for him. I explained the trenches to him; and he, all fluttering with delight like a bird, he was shooting at me and yelling. Ah, the damned young gentleman, he did it properly! He'll make a famous poilu later! I tell you, he's quite got the military spirit!"

A silence; then an obscure murmur of talk, in the midst of which we catch the name of Napoleon; then another voice, or the same, saying, "Wilhelm, he's a stinking beast to have brought this war on. But Napoleon, he was a great man!"

Marthereau is kneeling in front of me in the feeble and scanty rays of our candle, in the bottom of this dark ill-enclosed hole where the cold shudders through at intervals, where vermin swarm and where the sorry crowd of living men endures the faint but musty savor of a tomb; and Marthereau looks at me. He still hears, as I do, the unknown soldier who said, "Wilhelm is a stinking beast, but Napoleon was a great man," and who extolled the martial ardor of the little boy still left to him. Marthereau droops his arms and wags his weary head—and the shadow of the double gesture is thrown on the partition by the lean light in a sudden caricature.

"Ah!" says my humble companion, "we're all of us not bad sorts, and we're unlucky, and we're poor devils as well. But we're too stupid, we're too stupid!"

Again he turns his eyes on me. In his bewhiskered and poodle-like face I see his fine eyes shining in wondering and still confused contemplation of things which he is setting himself to understand in the innocence of his obscurity.

We come out of the uninhabitable shelter; the weather has bettered a little; the snow has melted, and all is soiled anew. "The wind's licked up the sugar," says Marthereau.

I am deputed to accompany Mesnil Joseph to the refuge on the Pylones road. Sergeant Henriot gives me charge of the wounded man and hands me his clearing order. "If you meet Bertrand on the way," says Henriot, "tell him to look sharp and get busy, will you?" Bertrand went away on liaison duty last night and they have been waiting for him for an hour; the captain is getting impatient and threatens to lose his temper.

I get under way with Joseph, who walks very slowly, a little paler than usual, and still taciturn. Now and again he halts, and his face twitches. We follow the communication trenches, and a comrade appears suddenly. It is Volpatte, and he says, "I'm going with you to the foot of the hill." As he is off duty, he is wielding a magnificent twisted walking-stick, and he shakes in his hand like castanets the precious pair of scissors that never leaves him.

All three of us come out of the communication trench when the slope of the land allows us to do it without danger of bullets—the guns are not firing. As soon as we are outside we stumble upon a gathering of men. It is raining. Between the heavy legs planted there like little trees on the gray plain in the mist we see a dead man. Volpatte edges his way in to the horizontal form upon which these upright ones are waiting; then he turns round violently and shouts to us, "It's Pepin!"

"Ah!" says Joseph, who is already almost fainting. He leans on me and we draw near. Pepin is full length, his feet and hands bent and shriveled, and his rain-washed face is swollen and horribly gray.

A man who holds a pickax and whose sweating face is full of little black trenches, recounts to us the death of Pepin: "He'd gone into a funk-hole where the Boches had planked themselves, and behold no one knew he was there and they smoked the hole to make sure of cleaning it out, and the poor lad, they found him after the operation, corpsed, and all pulled out like a cat's innards in the middle of the Boche cold meat that he'd stuck—and very nicely stuck too, I may say, seeing I was in business as a butcher in the suburbs of Paris."

"One less to the squad!" says Volpatte as we go away.

We are now on the edge of the ravine at the spot where the plateau begins that our desperate charge traversed last evening, and we cannot recognize it. This plain, which had then seemed to me quite level, though it really slopes, is an amazing charnel-house. It swarms with corpses, and might be a cemetery of which the top has been taken away.

Groups of men are moving about it, identifying the dead of last evening and last night, turning the remains over, recognizing them by some detail in spite of their faces. One of these searchers, kneeling, draws from a dead hand an effaced and mangled photograph—a portrait killed.

In the distance, black shell-smoke goes up in scrolls, then detonates over the horizon. The wide and stippled flight of an army of crows sweeps the sky.

Down below among the motionless multitude, and identifiable by their wasting and disfigurement, there are zouaves, tirailleurs, and Foreign Legionaries from the May attack. The extreme end of our lines was then on Berthonval Wood, five or six kilometers from here. In that attack, which was one of the most terrible of the war or of any war, those men got here in a single rush. They thus formed a point too far advanced in the wave of attack, and were caught on the flanks between the machine-guns posted to right and to left on the lines they had overshot. It is some months now since death hollowed their eyes and consumed their cheeks, but even in those storm-scattered and dissolving remains one can identify the havoc of the machine-guns that destroyed them, piercing their backs and loins and severing them in the middle. By the side of heads black and waxen as

Egyptian mummies, clotted with grubs and the wreckage of insects, where white teeth still gleam in some cavities, by the side of poor darkening stumps that abound like a field of old roots laid bare, one discovers naked yellow skulls wearing the red cloth fez, whose gray cover has crumbled like paper. Some thigh-bones protrude from the heaps of rags stuck together with reddish mud; and from the holes filled with clothes shredded and daubed with a sort of tar, a spinal fragment emerges. Some ribs are scattered on the soil like old cages broken; and close by, blackened leathers are afloat, with water-bottles and drinking-cups pierced and flattened. About a cloven knapsack, on the top of some bones and a cluster of bits of cloth and accouterments, some white points are evenly scattered; by stooping one can see that they are the finger and toe constructions of what was once a corpse.

Sometimes only a rag emerges from long mounds to indicate that some human being was there destroyed, for all these unburied dead end by entering the soil.

The Germans, who were here yesterday, abandoned their soldiers by the side of ours without interring them—as witness these three putrefied corpses on the top of each other, in each other, with their round gray caps whose red edge is hidden with a gray band, their yellow-gray jackets, and their green faces. I look for the features of one of them. From the depth of his neck up to the tufts of hair that stick to the brim of his cap is just an earthy mass, the face become an anthill, and two rotten berries in place of the eyes. Another is a dried emptiness flat on its belly, the back in tatters that almost flutter, the hands, feet, and face enrooted in the soil.

"Look! It's a new one, this—"

In the middle of the plateau and in the depth of the rainy and bitter air, on the ghastly morrow of this debauch of slaughter, there is a head planted in the ground, a wet and bloodless head, with a heavy beard.

It is one of ours, and the helmet is beside it. The distended eyelids permit a little to be seen of the dull porcelain of his eyes, and one lip shines like a slug in the shapeless beard. No doubt he fell into a shell-hole, which was filled up by another shell, burying him up to the neck like the cat's-head German of the Red Tavern at Souchez.

"I don't know him," says Joseph, who has come up very slowly and speaks with difficulty.

"I recognize him," replies Volpatte.

"That bearded man?" says Joseph.

"He has no beard. Look—" Stooping, Volpatte passes the end of his stick under the chin of the corpse and breaks off a sort of slab of mud in which the head was set, a slab that looked like a beard. Then he picks up the dead man's helmet and puts it on his head, and for a moment holds before the eyes the round handles of his famous scissors so as to imitate spectacles.

"Ah!" we all cried together, "it's Cocon!"

When you hear of or see the death of one of those who fought by your side and lived exactly the same life, you receive a direct blow in the flesh before even understanding. It is truly as if one heard of his own destruction. It is only later that one begins to mourn.

We look at the hideous head that is murder's jest, the murdered head already and cruelly effacing our memories of Cocon. Another comrade less. We remain there around him, afraid.

"He was—"

We should like to speak a little, but do not know what to say that would be sufficiently serious or telling or true.

"Come," says Joseph, with an effort, wholly engrossed by his severe suffering, "I haven't strength enough to be stopping all the time."

We leave poor Cocon, the ex-statistician, with a last look, a look too short and almost vacant.

"One cannot imagine—" says Volpatte.

No, one cannot imagine. All these disappearances at once surpass the imagination. There are not enough survivors now. But we have vague idea of the grandeur of these dead. They have given all; by degrees they have given all their strength, and finally they have given themselves, en bloc. They have outpaced life, and their effort has something of superhuman perfection.

"Tiens, he's just been wounded, that one, and yet—" A fresh wound is moistening the neck of a body that is almost a skeleton.

"It's a rat," says Volpatte. "The stiffs are old ones, but the rats talk to 'em. You see some rats laid out—poisoned, p'raps—near every body or under it. Tiens, this poor old chap shall show us his." He lifts up the foot of the collapsed remains and reveals two dead rats.

"I should like to find Farfadet again," says Volpatte. "I told him to wait just when we started running and he clipped hold of me. Poor lad, let's hope he waited!"

So he goes to and fro, attracted towards the dead by a strange curiosity; and these, indifferent, bandy him about from one to another, and at each step he looks on the ground. Suddenly he utters a cry of distress. With his hand he beckons us as he kneels to a dead man.

Bertrand!

Acute emotion grips us. He has been killed; he, too, like the rest, he who most towered over us by his energy and intelligence. By virtue of always doing his duty, he has at last got killed. He has at last found death where indeed it was.

We look at him, and then turn away from the sight and look upon each other.

The shock of his loss is aggravated by the spectacle that his remains present, for they are abominable to see. Death has bestowed a grotesque look and attitude on the man who was so comely and so tranquil. With his hair scattered over his eyes, his mustache trailing in his mouth, and his face swollen—he is laughing. One eye is widely open, the other shut, and the tongue lolls out. His arms are outstretched in the form of a cross: the hands open, the fingers separated. The right leg is straight. The left, whence flowed the hemorrhage that made him die, has been broken by a shell; it is twisted into a circle, dislocated, slack, invertebrate. A mournful irony has invested the last writhe of his agony with the appearance of a clown's antic.

We arrange him, and lay him straight, and tranquillize the horrible masks. Volpatte has taken a pocket-book from him and places it reverently among his own papers, by the side of the portrait of his own wife and children. That done, he shakes his head: "He—he was truly a good sort, old man. When he said anything, that was the proof that it was true. Ah, we needed him badly!"

"Yes," I said, "we had need of him always."

"Ah, la, la!" murmurs Volpatte, and he trembles. Joseph repeats in a weak voice, "Ah, nom de Dieu! Ah, nom de Dieu!"

The plateau is as covered with people as a public square; fatigue-parties in detachments, and isolated men. Here and there, the stretcher-bearers are beginning (patiently and in a small way) their huge and endless task.

Volpatte leaves us, to return to the trench and announce our new losses, and above all the great gap left by Bertrand. He says to Joseph, "We shan't lose sight of you, eh? Write us a line now and again—just, 'All goes well; signed, Camembert,' eh?" He disappears among the people who cross each other's path in the expanse now completely possessed by a mournful and endless rain.

Joseph leans on me and we go down into the ravine. The slope by which we descend is known as the Zouaves' Cells. In the May attack, the Zouaves had all begun to dig themselves individual shelters, and round these they were exterminated. Some are still seen, prone on the brim of an incipient hole, with their trenching-tools in their fleshless hands or looking at them with the cavernous hollows where shrivel the entrails of eyes. The ground is so full of dead that the earth-falls uncover places that bristle with feet, with half-clothed skeletons, and with ossuaries of skulls placed side by side on the steep slope like porcelain globe-jars.

In the ground here there are several strata of dead and in many places the delving of the shells has brought out the oldest and set them out in display on the top of the new ones. The bottom of the ravine is completely carpeted with debris of weapons, clothing, and implements. One tramples shell fragments, old iron, loaves and even biscuits that have fallen from knapsacks and are not yet dissolved by the rain. Mess-tins, pots of jam, and helmets are pierced and riddled by bullets—the scrapings and scum of a hell-broth; and the dislocated posts that survive are stippled with holes.

The trenches that run in this valley have a look of earthquake crevasses, and as if whole tombs of uncouth things had been emptied on the ruins of the earth's convulsion. And there, where no dead are, the very earth is cadaverous.

We follow the International Trench, still fluttering with rainbow rags—a shapeless trench which the confusion of torn stuffs invests with an air of a trench assassinated—to a place where the irregular and winding ditch forms an elbow. All the way along, as far as an earthwork barricade that blocks the way, German corpses are entangled and knotted as in a torrent of the damned, some of them emerging from muddy caves in the middle of a bewildering conglomerate of beams, ropes, creepers of iron, trench-rollers, hurdles, and bullet-screens. At the barrier itself, one corpse stands upright, fixed in the other dead, while another, planted in the same spot, stands obliquely in the dismal place, the whole arrangement looking like part of a big wheel embedded in the mud, or the shattered sail of a windmill. And over all this, this catastrophe of flesh and filthiness, religious images are broadcast, post-cards, pious pamphlets, leaflets on which prayers are written in Gothic lettering—they have scattered themselves in waves from gutted clothing. The paper words seem to bedeck with blossom these shores of pestilence, this Valley of Death, with their countless pallors of barren lies.

I seek a solid footway to guide Joseph in—his wound is paralyzing him by degrees, and he feels it extending throughout his body. While I support him, and he is looking at nothing, I look upon the ghastly upheaval through which we are escaping.

A German sergeant is seated, here where we tread, supported by the riven timbers that once formed the shelter of a sentry. There is a little hole under his eye; the thrust of a bayonet has nailed him to the planks through his face. In front of him, also sitting, with his elbows on his knees and his fists on his chin, there is a man who has all the top of his skull taken off like a boiled egg. Beside them—an awful watchman!—the half of a man is standing, a man sliced in two from scalp to stomach, upright against the earthen wall. I do not know where the other half of this human post may be, whose eye hangs down above and whose bluish viscera curl spirally round his leg.

Down below, one's foot detaches itself from a matrix of blood, stiffened with French bayonets that have been bent, doubled, and twisted by the force of the blow. Through a gap in the mutilated wall one espies a recess where the bodies of soldiers of the Prussian Guard seem to kneel in the pose of suppliants, run through from behind, with blood-stained gaps, impaled. Out of this group they have pulled to its edge a huge Senegalese tirailleur, who, petrified in the contorted position where death seized him, leans upon empty air and holds fast by his feet, staring at his two severed wrists. No doubt a bomb had exploded in his hands; and since all his face is alive, he seems to be gnawing maggots.

"It was here," says a passing soldier of an Alpine regiment, "that they did the white flag trick; and as they'd got Africans to deal with, you bet they got it hot!—Tiens, there's the white flag itself that these dunghills used."

He seizes and shakes a long handle that lies there. A square of white stuff is nailed to it, and unfolds itself innocently.

A procession of shovel-bearers advances along the battered trench. They have an order to shovel the earth into the relics of the trenches, to stop everything up, so that the bodies may be buried on the spot. Thus these helmeted warriors will here perform the work of the redresser of wrongs as they restore their full shape to the fields and make level the cavities already half filled by cargoes of invaders.

Some one calls me from the other side of the trench, a man sitting on the ground and leaning against a stake. It is Papa Ramure. Through his unbuttoned greatcoat and jacket I see bandages around his chest. "The ambulance men have been to tuck me up," he says, in a weak and stertorous voice, "but they can't take me away from here before evening. But I know all right that I'm petering out every minute."

He jerks his head. "Stay a bit," he asks me. He is much moved, and the tears are flowing. He offers his hand and holds mine. He wants to say a lot of things to me and almost to make confession. "I was a straight man before the war," he says, with trickling tears; "I worked from morning to night to feed my little lot. And then I came here to kill Boches. And now, I've got killed. Listen, listen, listen, don't go away, listen to me—"

"I must take Joseph back—he's at the end of his strength. I'll come back afterwards."

Ramure lifted his streaming eyes to the wounded man. "Not only living, but wounded! Escaped from death! Ah, some women and children are lucky! All right, take him, take him, and come back—I hope I shall be waiting for you—"

Now we must climb the other slope of the ravine, and we enter the deformed and maltreated ditch of the old Trench 97.

Suddenly a frantic whistling tears the air and there is a shower of shrapnel above us. Meteorites flash and scatter in fearful flight in the heart of the yellow clouds. Revolving missiles rush through the heavens to break and burn upon the bill, to ransack it and exhume the old bones of men; and the thundering flames multiply themselves along an even line.

It is the barrage fire beginning again. Like children we cry, "Enough, enough!"

In this fury of fatal engines, this mechanical cataclysm that pursues us through space, there is something that surpasses human strength and will, something supernatural. Joseph, standing with his hand in mine, looks over his shoulder at the storm of rending explosions. He bows his head like an imprisoned beast, distracted: "What, again! Always, then!" he growls; "after all we've done and all we've seen—and now it begins again! Ah, non, non!"

He falls on his knees, gasps for breath, and throws a futile look of full hatred before him and behind him. He repeats, "It's never finished, never!"

I take him by the arm and raise him. "Come; it'll be finished for you."

We must dally there awhile before climbing, so I will go and bring back Ramure in extremis, who is waiting for me. But Joseph clings to me, and then I notice a movement of men about the spot where I left the dying man. I can guess what it means; it is no longer worth while to go there.

The ground of the ravine where we two are closely clustered to abide the tempest is quivering, and at each shot we feel the deep simoom of the shells. But in the hole where we are there is scarcely any risk of being hit. At the first lull, some of the men who were also waiting detach themselves and begin to go up; stretcher-bearers redouble their huge efforts to carry a body and climb, making one think of stubborn ants pushed back by successive grains of sand; wounded men and liaison men move again.

"Let's go on," says Joseph, with sagging shoulders, as he measures the hill with his eye—the last stage of his Gethsemane.

There are trees here; a row of excoriated willow trunks, some of wide countenance, and others hollowed and yawning, like coffins on end. The scene through which we are struggling is rent and convulsed, with hills and chasms, and with such somber swellings as if all the clouds of storm had rolled down here. Above the tortured earth, this stampeded file of trunks stands forth against a striped brown sky, milky in places and obscurely sparkling—a sky of agate.

Across the entry to Trench 97 a felled oak twists his great body, and a corpse stops up the trench. Its head and legs are buried in the ground. The dirty water that trickles in the trench has covered it with a sandy glaze, and through the moist deposit the chest and belly bulge forth, clad in a shirt. We stride over the frigid remains, slimy and pale, that suggest the belly of a stranded crocodile; and it is difficult to do so, by reason of the soft and slippery ground. We have to plunge our hands up to the wrists in the mud of the wall.

At this moment an infernal whistle falls on us and we bend like bushes. The shell bursts in the air in front of us, deafening and blinding, and buries us under a horribly sibilant mountain of dark smoke. A climbing soldier has churned the air with his arms and disappeared, hurled into some hole. Shouts have gone up and fallen again like rubbish. While we are looking, through the great black veil that the wind tears from the ground and dismisses into the sky, at the bearers who are putting down a stretcher, running to the place of the explosion and picking up something inert—I recall the unforgettable scene when my brother-in-arms, Poterloo, whose heart was so full of hope, vanished with his arms outstretched in the flame of a shell.

We arrive at last on the summit, which is marked as with a signal by a wounded and frightful man. He is upright in the wind, shaken but upright, enrooted there. In his uplifted and wind-tossed cape we see a yelling and convulsive face. We pass by him, and he is like a sort of screaming tree.

We have arrived at our old first line, the one from which we set off for the attack. We sit down on a firing-step with our backs to the holes cut for our exodus at the last minute by the sappers. Euterpe, the cyclist, passes and gives us good-day. Then he turns in his tracks and draws from the cuff of his coat-sleeve an envelope, whose protruding edge had conferred a white stripe on him.

"It's you, isn't it," he says to me, "that takes Biquet's letters that's dead?"—"Yes."—"Here's a returned one; the address has hopped it."

The envelope was exposed, no doubt, to rain on the top of a packet, and the address is no longer legible among the violet mottlings on the dried and frayed paper. Alone there survives in a corner the address of the sender. I pull the letter out gently—"My dear mother"—Ah, I remember!

Biquet, now lying in the open air in the very trench where we are halted, wrote that letter not long ago in our quarters at Gauchin-l'Abbe, one flaming and splendid afternoon, in reply to a letter from his mother, whose fears for him had proved groundless and made him laugh—"You think I'm in the cold and rain and danger. Not at all; on the contrary, all that's finished. It's hot, we're sweating, and we've nothing to do only to stroll about in the sunshine. I laughed to read your letter—"

I return to the frail and damaged envelope the letter which, if chance had not averted this new irony, would have been read by the old peasant woman at the moment when the body of her son is a wet nothing in the cold and the storm, a nothing that trickles and flows like a dark spring on the wall of the trench.

Joseph has leaned his head backwards. His eyes close for a moment, his mouth half opens, and his breathing is fitful.

"Courage!" I say to him, and he opens his eyes again.

"Ah!" he replies, "it isn't to me you should say that. Look at those chaps, there, they're going back yonder, and you too, you're going back. It all has to go on for you others. Ah, one must be really strong to go on, to go on!"

The Refuge

FROM this point onwards we are in sight of the enemy observation-posts, and must no longer leave the communication trenches. First we follow that of the Pylones road. The trench is cut along the side of the road, and the road itself is wiped out; so are its trees. Half of it, all the way along, has been chewed and swallowed by the trench; and what is left of it has been invaded by the earth and the grass, and mingled with the fields in the fullness of time. At some places in the trench—there, where a sandbag has burst and left only a muddy cell—you may see again on the level of your eyes the stony ballast of the ex-road, cut to the quick, or even the roots of the bordering trees that have been cut down to embody in the trench wall. The latter is as slashed and uneven as if it were a wave of earth and rubbish and dark scum that the immense plain has spat out and pushed against the edge of the trench.

We arrive at a junction of trenches, and on the top of the maltreated hillock which is outlined on the cloudy grayness, a mournful signboard stands crookedly in the wind. The trench system becomes still more cramped and close, and the men who are flowing towards the clearing-station from all parts of the sector multiply and throng in the deep-dug ways.

These lamentable lanes are staked out with corpses. At uneven intervals their walls are broken into by quite recent gaps, extending to their full depth, by funnelholes of fresh earth which trespass upon the unwholesome land beyond, where earthy bodies are squatting with their chins on their knees or leaning against the wall as straight and silent as the rifles which wait beside them. Some of these standing dead turn their blood-bespattered faces towards the survivors; others exchange their looks with the sky's emptiness.

Joseph halts to take breath. I say to him as to a child, "We're nearly there, we're nearly there."

The sinister ramparts of this way of desolation contract still more. They impel a feeling of suffocation, of a nightmare of falling which oppresses and strangles: and in these depths where the walls seem to be coming nearer and closing in, you are forced to halt, to wriggle a path for yourself, to vex and disturb the dead, to be pushed about by the endless disorder of the files that flow along these hinder trenches, files made up of messengers, of the maimed, of men who groan and who cry aloud, who hurry frantically, crimsoned by fever or pallid and visibly shaken by pain.

All this throng at last pulls up and gathers and groans at the crossways where the burrows of the Refuge open out.

A doctor is trying with shouts and gesticulations to keep a little space clear from the rising tide that beats upon the threshold of the shelter, where he applies summary bandages in the open air; they say he has not ceased to do it, nor his helpers either, all the night and all the day, that he is accomplishing a superhuman task.

When they leave his hands, some of the wounded are swallowed up by the black hole of the Refuge; others are sent back to the bigger clearing-station contrived in the trench on the Bethune road.

In this confined cavity formed by the crossing of the ditches, in the bottom of a sort of robbers' den, we waited two hours, buffeted, squeezed, choked and blinded, climbing over each other like cattle, in an odor of blood and butchery. There are faces that become more distorted and emaciated from minute to minute. One of the patients can no longer hold back his tears; they come in floods, and as he shakes his head he sprinkles his neighbors. Another, bleeding like a fountain, shouts, "Hey, there! have a look at me!" A young man with burning eyes yells like a soul in hell, "I'm on fire!" and he roars and blows like a furnace.

Joseph is bandaged. He thrusts a way through to me and holds out his hand: "It isn't serious, it seems; good-by," he says.

At once we are separated in the mob. With my last glance I see his wasted face and the vacant absorption in his trouble as he is meekly led away by a Divisional stretcher-bearer whose hand is on his shoulder; and suddenly I see him no more. In war, life separates us just as death does, without our having even the time to think about it.

They tell me not to stay there, but to go down into the Refuge to rest before returning. There are two entries, very low and very narrow, on the level of the ground. This one is flush with the mouth of a sloping gallery, narrow as the conduit of a sewer. In order to penetrate the Refuge, one must first turn round and work backwards with bent body into the shrunken pipe, and here the feet discover steps. Every three paces there is a deep step.

Once inside you have a first impression of being trapped—that there is not room enough either to descend or climb out. As you go on burying yourself in the gulf, the nightmare of suffocation continues that you progressively endured as you advanced along the bowels of the trenches before foundering in here. On all sides you bump and scrape yourself, you are clutched by the tightness of the passage, you are wedged and stuck. I have to change the position of my cartridge pouches by sliding them round the belt and to take my bags in my arms against my chest. At the fourth step the suffocation increases still more and one has a moment of agony; little as one may lift his knee for the rearward step, his back strikes the roof. In this spot it is necessary to go on all fours, still backwards. As you go down into the depth, a pestilent atmosphere and heavy as earth buries you. Your hands touch only the cold, sticky and sepulchral clay of the wall, which bears you down on all sides and enshrouds you in a dismal solitude; its blind and moldy breath touches your face. On the last steps, reached after long labor, one is assailed by a hot, unearthly clamor that rises from the hole as from a sort of kitchen.

When you reach at last the bottom of this laddered sap that elbows and compresses you at every step, the evil dream is not ended, for you find yourself in a lone but very narrow cavern where gloom reigns, a mere corridor not more than five feet high. If you cease to stoop and to walk with bended knees, your head violently strikes the planks that roof the Refuge, and the newcomers are heard to growl—more or less forcefully, according to their temper and condition—"Ah, lucky I've got my tin hat on:"

One makes out the gesture of some one who is squatting in an angle. It is an ambulance man on guard, whose monotone says to each arrival, "Take the mud off your boots before going in." So you stumble into an accumulating pile of mud; it entangles you at the foot of the steps on this threshold of hell.

In the hubbub of lamentation and groaning, in the strong smell of a countless concentration of wounds, in this blinking cavern of confused and unintelligible life, I try first to get my bearings. Some weak candle flames are shining along the Refuge, but they only relieve the darkness in the spots where they pierce it. At the farthest end faint daylight appears, as it might to a dungeon prisoner at the bottom of an oubliette. This obscure vent-hole allows one to make out some big objects ranged along the corridor; they are low stretchers, like coffins. Around and above them one then dimly discerns the movement of broken and drooping shadows, and the stirring of ranks and groups of specters against the walls.

I turn round. At the end opposite that where the faraway light leaks through, a mob is gathered in front of a tent-cloth which reaches from the ceiling to the ground, and thus forms an apartment, whose illumination shines through the oily yellow material. In this retreat, anti-tetanus injections are going on by the light of an acetylene lamp. When the cloth is lifted to allow some one to enter or leave, the glare brutally besplashes the disordered rags of the wounded stationed in front to await their treatment. Bowed by the ceiling, seated, kneeling or groveling, they push each other in the desire not to lose their turn or to steal some other's, and they bark like dogs, "My turn!"—"Me!"—"Me!" In this corner of modified conflict the tepid stinks of acetylene and bleeding men are horrible to swallow.

I turn away from it and seek elsewhere to find a place where I may sit down. I go forward a little, groping, still stooping and curled up, and my hands in front.

By grace of the flame which a smoker holds over his pipe I see a bench before me, full of beings. My eyes are growing accustomed to the gloom that stagnates in the cave, and I can make out pretty well this row of people whose bandages and swathings dimly whiten their beads and limbs. Crippled, gashed, deformed, motionless or restless, fast fixed in this kind of barge, they present an incongruous collection of suffering and misery.

One of them cries out suddenly, half rises, and then sits down again. His neighbor, whose greatcoat is torn and his head bare, looks at him and says to him—"What's the use of worrying?"

And he repeats the sentence several times at random, gazing straight in front of him, his hands on his knees. A young man in the middle of the seat is talking to himself. He says that he is an aviator. There are burns down one side of his body and on his face. In his fever he is still burning; it seems to him that he is still gnawed by the pointed flames that leaped from his engine. He is muttering, "Gott mit uns!" and then, "God is with us!"

A zouave with his arm in a sling, who sits awry and seems to carry his shoulder like a torturing burden, speaks to him: "You're the aviator that fell, aren't you?"

"I've seen—things," replies the flying-man laboriously.

"I too, I've seen some!" the soldier interrupts; "some people couldn't stick it, to see what I've seen."

"Come and sit here," says one of the men on the seat to me, making room as he speaks. "Are you wounded?"

"No; I brought a wounded man here, and I'm going back."

"You're worse than wounded then; come and sit down."

"I was mayor in my place," explains one of the sufferers, "but when I go back no one will know me again, it's so long now that I've been in misery."

"Four hours now have I been stuck on this bench," groans a sort of mendicant, whose shaking hand holds his helmet on his knees like an alms-bowl, whose head is lowered and his back rounded.

"We're waiting to be cleared, you know," I am informed by a big man who pants and sweats—all the bulk of him seems to be boiling. His mustache hangs as if it had come half unstuck through the moisture of his face. He turns two big and lightless eyes on me, and his wound is not visible.

"That's so," says another; "all the wounded of the Brigade come and pile themselves up here one after another, without counting them from other places. Yes, look at it now; this hole here, it's the midden for the whole Brigade."

"I'm gangrened, I'm smashed, I'm all in bits inside," droned one who sat with his head in his hands and spoke through his fingers; "yet up to last week I was young and I was clean. They've changed me. Now, I've got nothing but a dirty old decomposed body to drag along."

"Yesterday," says another, "I was twenty-six years old. And now how old am I?" He tries to get up, so as to show us his shaking and faded face, worn out in a night, to show us the emaciation, the depression of cheeks and eye-sockets, and the dying flicker of light in his greasy eye.

"It hurts!" humbly says some one invisible.

"What's the use of worrying?" repeats the other mechanically.

There was a silence, and then the aviator cried, "The padres were trying on both sides to hide their voices."

"What's that mean?" said the astonished zouave.

"Are you taking leave of 'em, old chap?" asked a chasseur wounded in the hand and with one arm bound to his body, as his eyes left the mummified limb for a moment to glance at the flying-man.

The latter's looks were distraught; he was trying to interpret a mysterious picture which everywhere he saw before his eyes—"Up there, from the sky, you don't see much, you know. Among the squares of the fields and the little heaps of the villages the roads run like white cotton. You can make out, too, some hollow threads that look as if they'd been traced with a pin-point and scratched through fine sand. These nets that festoon the plain with regularly wavy marks, they're the trenches. Last Sunday morning I was flying over the firing-line. Between our first lines and their first lines, between their extreme edges, between the fringes of the two huge armies that are up against each other, looking at each other and not seeing, and waiting—it's not very far; sometimes forty yards, sometimes sixty. To me it looked about a stride, at the great height where I was planing. And behold I could make out two crowds, one among the Boches, and one of ours, in these parallel lines that seemed to touch each other; each was a solid, lively lump, and all around 'em were dots like grains of black sand scattered on gray sand, and these hardly budged—it didn't look like an alarm! So I went down several turns to investigate.

"Then I understood. It was Sunday, and there were two religious services being held under my eyes—the altar, the padre, and all the crowd of chaps. The more I went down the more I could see that the two things were alike—so exactly alike that it looked silly. One of the services—whichever you like—was a reflection of the other, and I wondered if I was seeing double. I went down lower; they didn't fire at me. Why? I don't know at all. Then I could hear. I heard one murmur, one only. I could only gather a single prayer that came up to me en bloc, the sound of a single chant that passed by me on its way to heaven. I went to and fro in space to listen to this faint mixture of hymns that blended together just the same although they were one against the other; and the more they tried to get on top of each other, the more they were blended together up in the heights of the sky where I was floating.

"I got some shrapnel just at the moment when, very low down, I made out the two voices from the earth that made up the one—'Gott mit uns!' and 'God is with us!'—and I flew away."

The young man shook his bandage-covered head; he seemed deranged by the recollection. "I said to myself at the moment, 'I must be mad!'"

"It's the truth of things that's mad," said the zouave.

With his eyes shining in delirium, the narrator sought to express and convey the deep disturbing idea that was besieging him, that he was struggling against.

"Now think of it!" he said. "Fancy those two identical crowds yelling things that are identical and yet opposite, these identical enemy cries! What must the good God think about it all? I know well enough that He knows everything, but even if He knows everything, He won't know what to make of it."

"Rot!" cried the zouave.

"He doesn't care a damn for us, don't fret yourself."

"Anyway, what is there funny about it? That doesn't prevent people from quarreling with each other—and don't they! And rifle-shots speak jolly well the same language, don't they?"

"Yes," said the aviator, "but there's only one God. It isn't the departure of prayers that I don't understand; it's their arrival."

The conversation dropped.

"There's a crowd of wounded laid out in there," the man with the dull eyes said to me, "and I'm wondering all ways how they got 'em down here. It must have been a terrible job, tumbling them in here."

Two Colonials, hard and lean, supporting each other like tipsy men, butted into us and recoiled, looking on the ground for some place to fall on.

"Old chap, in that trench I'm telling you of," the hoarse voice of one was relating, "we were three days without rations, three full days without anything—anything. Willy-nilly, we had to drink our own water, and no help for it."

The other explained that once on a time he had cholera. "Ah, that's a dirty business—fever, vomiting, colics; old man, I was ill with that lot!"

"And then, too," suddenly growled the flying-man, still fierce to pursue the answer to the gigantic conundrum, "what is this God thinking of to let everybody believe like that that He's with them? Why does He let us all—all of us—shout out side by side, like idiots and brutes, 'God is with us!'—'No, not at all, you're wrong; God is with us'?"

A groan arose from a stretcher, and for a moment fluttered lonely in the silence as if it were an answer.

Then, "I don't believe in God," said a pain-racked voice; "I know He doesn't exist—because of the suffering there is. They can tell us all the clap-trap they like, and trim up all the words they can rind and all they can make up, but to say that all this innocent suffering could come from a perfect God, it's damned skull-stuffing."

"For my part," another of the men on the seat goes on, "I don't believe in God because of the cold. I've seen men become corpses bit by bit, just simply with cold. If there was a God of goodness, there wouldn't be any cold. You can't get away from that."

"Before you can believe in God, you've got to do away with everything there is. So we've got a long way to go!"

Several mutilated men, without seeing each other, combine in head-shakes of dissent "You're right," says another, "you're right."

These men in ruins, vanquished in victory, isolated and scattered, have the beginnings of a revelation. There come moments in the tragedy of these events when men are not only sincere, but truth-telling, moments when you see that they and the truth are face to face.

"As for me," said a new speaker, "if I don't believe in God, it's—" A fit of coughing terribly continued his sentence.

When the fit passed and his cheeks were purple and wet with tears, some one asked him, "Where are you wounded?"

"I'm not wounded; I'm ill."

"Oh, I see!" they said, in a tone which meant "You're not interesting."

He understood, and pleaded the cause of his illness:

"I'm done in, I spit blood. I've no strength left, and it doesn't come back, you know, when it goes away like that."

"Ah, ah!" murmured the comrades—wavering, but secretly convinced all the same of the inferiority of civilian ailments to wounds.

In resignation he lowered his head and repeated to himself very quietly, "I can't walk any more; where would you have me go?"

A commotion is arising for some unknown reason in the horizontal gulf which lengthens as it contracts from stretcher to stretcher as far as the eye can see, as far as the pallid peep of daylight, in this confused corridor where the poor winking flames of candles redden and seem feverish, and winged shadows cast themselves. The odds and ends of heads and limbs are agitated, appeals and cries arouse each other and increase in number like invisible ghosts. The prostrate bodies undulate, double up, and turn over.

In the heart of this den of captives, debased and punished by pain, I make out the big mass of a hospital attendant whose heavy shoulders rise and fall like a knapsack carried crosswise, and whose stentorian voice reverberates at speed through the cave. "You've been meddling with your bandage again, you son of a lubber, you varmint!" he thunders. "I'll do it up again for you, as long as it's you, my chick, but if you touch it again, you'll see what I'll do to you!"

Behold him then in the obscurity, twisting a bandage round the cranium of a very little man who is almost upright, who has bristling hair and a beard which puffs out in front. With dangling arms, he submits in silence. But the attendant abandons him, looks on the ground and exclaims sonorously, "What the—? Eh, come now, my friend, are you cracked? There's manners for you, to lie down on the top of a patient!" And his capacious hand disengages a second limp body on which the first had extended himself as on a mattress; while the mannikin with the bandaged head alongside, as soon as he is let alone, puts his hands to his head without saying a word and tries once more to remove the encircling lint.

There is an uproar, too, among some shadows that are visible against a luminous background; they seem to be wildly agitated in the gloom of the crypt. The light of a candle shows us several men shaken with their efforts to hold a wounded soldier down on his stretcher. It is a man whose feet are gone. At the end of his legs are terrible bandages, with tourniquets to restrain the hemorrhage. His stumps have bled into the linen wrappings, and he seems to wear red breeches. His face is devilish, shining and sullen, and he is raving. They are pressing down on his shoulders and knees, for this man without feet would fain jump from the stretcher and go away.

"Let me go!" he rattles in breathless, quavering rage. His voice is low, with sudden sonorities, like a trumpet that one tries to blow too softly. "By God, let me go, I tell you! Do you think I'm going to stop here? Allons, let me be, or I'll jump over you on my hands!"

So violently he contracts and extends himself that he pulls to and fro those who are trying to restrain him by their gripping weight, and I can see the zigzags of the candle held by a kneeling man whose other arm engirdles the mutilated maniac, who shouts so fiercely that he wakes up the sleepers and dispels the drowsiness of the rest. On all sides they turn towards him; half rising, they listen to the incoherent lamentations which end by dying in the dark. At the same moment, in another corner, two prostrate wounded, crucified on the ground, so curse each other that one of them has to be removed before the frantic dialogue is broken up.

I go farther away, towards the point where the light from outside comes through among the tangled beams as through a broken grating, and stride over the interminable stretchers that take up all the width of the underground alley whose oppressive confinement chokes me. The human forms prone on the stretchers are now hardly stirring under the Jack-o'-lanterns of the candles; they stagnate in their rattling breath and heavy groans.

On the edge of a stretcher a man is sitting, leaning against the wall. His clothes are torn apart, and in the middle of their darkness appears the white, emaciated breast of a martyr. His head is bent quite back and veiled in shadow, but I can see the beating of his heart.

The daylight that is trickling through at the end, drop by drop, comes in by an earth-fall. Several shells, falling on the same spot, have broken through the heavy earthen roof of the Refuge.

Here, some pale reflections are cast on the blue of the greatcoats, on the shoulders and along the folds. Almost paralyzed by the darkness and their own weakness, a group of men is pressing towards the gap, like dead men half awaking, to taste a little of the pallid air and detach themselves from the sepulcher. This corner at the extremity of the gloom offers itself as a way of escape, an oasis where one may stand upright, where one is lightly, angelically touched by the light of heaven.

"There were some chaps there that were blown to bits when the shells burst," said some one to me who was waiting there in the sickly ray of entombed light. "You talk about a mess! Look, there's the padre hooking down what was blown up."

The huge Red Cross sergeant, in a hunter's chestnut waistcoat which gives him the chest of a gorilla, is detaching the pendent entrails twisted among the beams of the shattered woodwork. For the purpose he is using a rifle with fixed bayonet, since he could not find a stick long enough; and the heavy giant, bald, bearded and asthmatic, wields the weapon awkwardly. He has a mild face, meek and unhappy, and while he tries to catch the remains of intestines in the corners, he mutters a string of "Oh's!" like sighs. His eyes are masked by blue glasses; his breathing is noisy. The top of his head is of puny dimensions, and the huge thickness of his neck has a conical shape. To see him thus pricking and unhanging from the air strips of viscera and rags of flesh, you could take him for a butcher at some fiendish task.

But I let myself fall in a corner with my eyes half closed, seeing hardly anything of the spectacle that lies and palpitates and falls around me. Indistinctly I gather some fragments of sentences—still the horrible monotony of the story of wounds: "Nom de Dieu! In that place I should think the bullets were touching each other."—"His head was bored through from one temple to the other. You could have passed a thread through."

"Those beggars were an hour before they lifted their fire and stopped peppering us." Nearer to me some one gabbles at the end of his story, "When I'm sleeping I dream that I'm killing him over again!"

Other memories are called up and buzz about among the buried wounded; it is like the purring of countless gear-wheels in a machine that turns and turns. And I hear afar him who repeats from his seat, "What's the use of worrying?" in all possible tones, commanding a pitiful, sometimes like a prophet and anon like one shipwrecked; he metrifies with his cry the chorus of choking and plaintive voices that try so terribly to extol their suffering.

Some one comes forward, blindly feeling the wall with his stick, and reaches me. It is Farfadet! I call him, and he turns nearly towards me to tell me that one eye is gone, and the other is bandaged as well. I give him my place, take him by the shoulders and make him sit down. He submits, and seated at the base of the wall waits patiently, with the resignation of his clerkly calling, as if in a waiting-room.

I come to anchor a little farther away, in an empty space where two prostrate men are talking to each other in low voices; they are so near to me that I hear them without listening. They are two soldiers of the Foreign Legion; their helmets and greatcoats are dark yellow.

"It's not worth while to make-believe about it," says one of them banteringly. "I'm staying here this time. It's finished—my bowels are shot through. If I were in a hospital, in a town, they'd operate on me in time, and it might stick up again. But here! It was yesterday I got it. We're two or three hours from the Bethune road, aren't we? And how many hours, think you, from the road to an ambulance where they can operate? And then, when are they going to pick us up? It's nobody's fault, I dare say; but you've got to look facts in the face. Oh, I know it isn't going to be any worse from now than it is, but it can't be long, seeing I've a hole all the way through my parcel of guts. You, your foot'll get all right, or they'll put you another one on. But I'm going to die."

"Ah!" said the other, convinced by the reasoning of his neighbor. The latter goes on—"Listen, Dominique. You've led a bad life. You cribbed things, and you were quarrelsome when drunk. You've dirtied your ticket in the police register, properly."

"I can't say it isn't true, because it is," says the other; "but what have you got to do with it?"

"You'll lead a bad life again after the war, inevitably; and then you'll have bother about that affair of the cooper."

The other becomes fierce and aggressive. "What the hell's it to do with you? Shut your jaw!"

"As for me, I've no more family than you have. I've nobody, except Louise—and she isn't a relation of mine, seeing we're not married. And there are no convictions against me, beyond a few little military jobs. There's nothing on my name."

"Well, what about it? I don't care a damn."

"I'm going to tell you. Take my name. Take it—I give it you; as long as neither of us has any family."

"Your name?"

"Yes; you'll call yourself Leonard Carlotti, that's all. 'Tisn't a big job. What harm can it do you? Straight off, you've no more convictions. They won't hunt you out, and you can be as happy as I should have been if this bullet hadn't gone through my magazine."

"Oh Christ!" said the other, "you'd do that? You'd—that—well, old chap, that beats all!"

"Take it. It's there in my pocket-book in my greatcoat. Go on, take it, and hand yours over to me—so that I can carry it all away with me. You'll be able to live where you like, except where I come from, where I'm known a bit, at Longueville in Tunis. You'll remember that? And anyway, it's written down. You must read it, the pocket-book. I shan't blab to anybody. To bring the trick off properly, mum's the word, absolutely."

He ponders a moment, and then says with a shiver "I'll p'raps tell Louise, so's she'll find I've done the right thing, and think the better of me, when I write to her to say good-by."

But he thinks better of it, and shakes his head with an heroic effort. "No—I shan't let on, even to her. She's her, of course, but women are such chatterers!"

The other man looks at him, and repeats, "Ah, nome de Dieu!"

Without being noticed by the two men I leave the drama narrowly developing in this lamentable corner and its jostling and traffic and hubbub.

Now I touch the composed and convalescent chat of two poor wretches—"Ah, my boy, the affection he had for that vine of his! You couldn't find anything wrong among the branches of it—"

"That little nipper, that wee little kid, when I went out with him, holding his tiny fist, it felt as if I'd got hold of the little warm neck of a swallow, you know."

And alongside this sentimental avowal, here is the passing revelation of another mind: "Don't I know the 547th! Rather! Listen, it's a funny regiment. They've got a poilu in it who's called Petitjean, another called Petitpierre, and another called Petitlouis. Old man, it's as I'm telling you; that's the kind of regiment it is."

As I begin to pick out a way with a view to leaving the cavern, there is a great noise down yonder of a fall and a chorus of exclamations. It is the hospital sergeant who has fallen. Through the breach that he was clearing of its soft and bloody relics, a bullet has taken him in the throat, and he is spread out full length on the ground. His great bewildered eyes are rolling and his breath comes foaming. His mouth and the lower part of his face are quickly covered with a cloud of rosy bubbles. They place his head on a bag of bandages, and the bag is instantly soaked with blood. An attendant cries that the packets of lint will be spoiled, and they are needed. Something else is sought on which to put the head that ceaselessly makes a light and discolored froth. Only a loaf can be found, and it is slid under the spongy hair.

While they hold the sergeant's hand and question him, he only slavers new heaps of bubbles, and we see his great black-bearded head across this rosy cloud. Laid out like that, he might be a deep-breathing marine monster, and the transparent red foam gathers and creeps up to his great hazy eyes, no longer spectacled.

Then his throat rattles. It is a childish rattle, and he dies moving his head to right and to left as though he were trying very gently to say "No."

Looking on the enormous inert mass, I reflect that he was a good man. He had an innocent and impressionable heart. How I reproach myself that I sometimes abused him for the ingenuous narrowness of his views, and for a certain clerical impertinence that he always had! And how glad I am in this distressing scene—yes, happy enough to tremble with joy—that I restrained myself from an angry protest when I found him stealthily reading a letter I was writing, a protest that would unjustly have wounded him! I remember the time when he exasperated me so much by his dissertation on France and the Virgin Mary. It seemed impossible to me that he could utter those thoughts sincerely. Why should he not have been sincere? Has he not been really killed today? I remember, too, certain deeds of devotion, the kindly patience of the great man, exiled in war as in life—and the rest does not matter. His ideas themselves are only trivial details compared with his heart—which is there on the ground in ruins in this corner of Hell. With what intensity I lamented this man who was so far asunder from me in everything!

Then fell the thunder on us! We were thrown violently on each other by the frightful shaking of the ground and the walls. It was as if the overhanging earth had burst and hurled itself down. Part of the armor-plate of beams collapsed, enlarging the hole that already pierced the cavern. Another shock—another pulverized span fell in roaring destruction. The corpse of the great Red Cross sergeant went rolling against the wall like the trunk of a tree. All the timber in the long frame-work of the cave, those heavy black vertebrae, cracked with an ear-splitting noise, and all the prisoners in the dungeon shouted together in horror.

Blow after blow, the explosions resound and drive us in all directions as the bombardment mangles and devours the sanctuary of pierced and diminished refuge. As the hissing flight of shells hammers and crushes the gaping end of the cave with its thunderbolts, daylight streams in through the clefts. More sharply now, and more unnaturally, one sees the flushed faces and those pallid with death, the eyes which fade in agony or burn with fever, the patched-up white-bound bodies, the monstrous bandages. All that was hidden rises again into daylight. Haggard, blinking and distorted, in face of the flood of iron and embers that the hurricanes of light bring with them, the wounded arise and scatter and try to take flight. All the terror-struck inhabitants roll about in compact masses across the miserable tunnel, as if in the pitching hold of a great ship that strikes the rocks.

The aviator, as upright as he can get and with his neck on the ceiling, waves his arms and appeals to God, asks Him what He is called, what is His real name. Overthrown by the blast and cast upon the others, I see him who, bare of breast and his clothes gaping like a wound, reveals the heart of a Christ. The greatcoat of the man who still monotonously repeats, "What's the use of worrying?" now shows itself all green, bright green, the effect of the picric acid no doubt released by the explosion that has staggered his brain. Others—the rest, indeed—helpless and maimed, move and creep and cringe, worm themselves into the corners. They are like moles, poor, defenseless beasts, hunted by the hellish hounds of the guns.

The bombardment slackens, and ends in a cloud of smoke that still echoes the crashes, in a quivering and burning after-damp. I pass out through the breach; and still surrounded and entwined in the clamor of despair, I arrive under the free sky, in the soft earth where mingled planks and legs are sunk. I catch myself on some wreckage; it is the embankment of the trench. At the moment when I plunge into the communication trenches they are visible a long way; they are still gloomily stirring, still filled by the crowd that overflows from the trenches and flows without end towards the refuges. For whole days, for whole nights, you will see the long rolling streams of men plucked from the fields of battle, from the plain over there that also has feelings of its own, though it bleeds and rots without end.

Going About

WE have been along the Boulevard de la Republique and then the Avenue Gambetta, and now we are debouching into the Place du Commerce. The nails in our polished boots ring on the pavements of the capital. It is fine weather, and the shining sky glistens and flashes as if we saw it through the frames of a greenhouse; it sets a-sparkle all the shop-fronts in the square. The skirts of our well-brushed greatcoats have been let down, and as they are usually fastened back, you can see two squares on the floating lappets where the cloth is bluer.

Our sauntering party halts and hesitates for a moment in front of the Cafe de la Sous-Prefecture, also called the Grand-Cafe.

"We have the right to go in!" says Volpatte.

"Too many officers in there," replies Blaire, who has lifted his chin over the guipure curtains in which the establishment is dressed up and risked a glance through the window between its golden letters.

"Besides," says Paradis, "we haven't seen enough yet."

We resume our walk and, simple soldiers that we are, we survey the sumptuous shops that encircle the Place du Commerce; the drapers, the stationers, the chemists, and—like a General's decorated uniform—the display of the jeweler. We have put forth our smiles like ornaments, for we are exempt from all duty until the evening, we are free, we are masters of our own time. Our steps are gentle and sedate; our empty and swinging hands are also promenading, to and fro.

"No doubt about it, you get some good out of this rest," remarks Paradis.

It is an abundantly impressive city which expands before our steps. One is in touch with life, with the life of the people, the life of the Rear, the normal life. How we used to think, down yonder, that we should never get here!

We see gentlemen, ladies, English officers, aviators-recognizable afar by their slim elegance and their decorations—soldiers who are parading their scraped clothes and scrubbed skins and the solitary ornament of their engraved identity discs, flashing in the sunshine on their greatcoats; and these last risk themselves carefully in the beautiful scene that is clear of all nightmares.

We make exclamations as they do who come from afar: "Talk about a crowd!" says Tirette in wonder. "Ah, it's a wealthy town!" says Blaire.

A work-girl passes and looks at us. Volpatte gives me a jog with his elbow and swallows her with his eyes, then points out to me two other women farther away who are coming up, and with beaming eye he certifies that the town is rich in femininity—"Old man, they are plump!" A moment ago Paradis had a certain timidity to overcome before he could approach a cluster of cakes of luxurious lodging, and touch and eat them; and every minute we are obliged to halt in the middle of the pavement and wait for Blaire, who is attracted and detained by the displays of fancy jumpers and caps, neck-ties in pale blue drill, slippers as red and shiny as mahogany. Blaire has reached the final height of his transformation. He who held the record for negligence and grime is certainly the best groomed of us all, especially since the further complication of his ivories, which were broken in the attack and had to be remade. He affects an off-hand demeanor. "He looks young and youthful," says Marthereau.

We find ourselves suddenly face to face with a toothless creature who smiles to the depth of her throat. Some black hair bristles round her hat. Her big, unpleasant features, riddled with pock-marks, recalls the ill-painted faces that one sees on the coarse canvas of a traveling show. 'She's beautiful,' says Volpatte. Marthereau, at whom she smiled, is dumb with shock.

Thus do the poilus converse who are suddenly placed under the spell of a town. More and more they rejoice in the beautiful scene, so neat and incredibly clean. They resume possession of life tranquil and peaceful, of that conception of comfort and even of happiness for which in the main houses were built.

"We should easily get used to it again, you know, old man, after all!"

Meanwhile a crowd is gathered around an outfitter's shop-window where the proprietor has contrived, with the aid of mannikins in wood and wax, a ridiculous tableau. On a groundwork of little pebbles like those in an aquarium, there is a kneeling German, in a suit so new that the creases are definite, and punctuated with an Iron Cross in cardboard. He holds up his two wooden pink hands to a French officer, whose curly wig makes a

cushion for a juvenile cap, who has bulging, crimson cheeks, and whose
infantile eye of adamant looks somewhere else. Beside the two personages
lies a rifle bar-rowed from the odd trophies of a box of toys. A card gives
the title of the animated group—"Kamarad!"

"Ah, damn it, look!"

We shrug our shoulders at sight of the puerile contrivance, the only
thing here that recalls to us the gigantic war raging somewhere under the
sky. We begin to laugh bitterly, offended and even wounded to the quick
in our new impressions. Tirette collects himself, and some abusive
sarcasm rises to his lips; but the protest lingers and is mute by reason of
our total transportation, the amazement of being somewhere else.

Our group is then espied by a very stylish and rustling lady, radiant in
violet and black silk and enveloped in perfumes. She puts out her little
gloved hand and touches Volpatte's sleeve and then Blaire's shoulder, and
they instantly halt, gorgonized by this direct contact with the fairy-like
being.

"Tell me, messieurs, you who are real soldiers from the front, you have
seen that in the trenches, haven't you?"

"Er—yes—yes." reply the two poor fellows, horribly frightened and
gloriously gratified.

"Ah!" the crowd murmurs, "did you hear? And they've been there, they
have!"

When we find ourselves alone again on the flagged perfection of the
pavement, Volpatte and Blaire look at each other and shake their heads.

"After all," says Volpatte, "it is pretty much like that you know!"

"Why, yes, of course!"

And these were their first words of false swearing that day.

We go into the Cafe de l'Industrie et des Fleurs. A roadway of matting
clothes the middle of the floor. Painted all the way along the walls, all the
way up the square pillars that support the roof, and on the front of the
counter, there is purple convolvulus among great scarlet poppies and roses
like red cabbages.

"No doubt about it, we've got good taste in France," says Tirette.

"The chap that did all that had a cartload of patience," Blaire declares
as he looks at the rainbow embellishments.

"In these places," Volpatte adds, "the pleasure of drinking isn't the only one."

Paradis informs us that he knows all about cafes. On Sundays formerly, he frequented cafes as beautiful as this one and even more beautiful. Only, he explains, that was a long time ago, and he has lost the flavor that they've got. He indicates a little enameled wash-hand basin hanging on the wall and decorated with flowers: "There's where one can wash his hands." We steer politely towards the basin. Volpatte signs to Paradis to turn the tap, and says, "Set the waterworks going!"

Then all six of us enter the saloon, whose circumference is already adorned with customers, and install ourselves at a table.

"We'll have six currant-vermouths, shall we?"

"We could very easily get used to it again, after all," they repeat.

Some civilians leave their places and come near us. They whisper, "They've all got the Croix de Guerre, Adolphe, you see—"—"Those are real poilus!"

Our comrades overhear, and now they only talk among themselves abstractedly, with their ears elsewhere, and an unconscious air of importance appears.

A moment later, the man and woman from whom the remarks proceeded lean towards us with their elbows on the white marble and question us: "Life in the trenches, it's very rough, isn't it?"

"Er—yes—well, of course, it isn't always pleasant."

"What splendid physical and moral endurance you have! In the end you get used to the life, don't you?"

"Why, yes, of course, one gets used to it—one gets used to it all right."

"All the same, it's a terrible existence—and the suffering!" murmurs the lady, turning over the leaves of an illustrated paper which displays gloomy pictures of destruction. "They ought not to publish these things, Adolphe, about the dirt and the vermin and the fatigues! Brave as you are, you must be unhappy?"

Volpatte, to whom she speaks, blushes. He is ashamed of the misery whence he comes, whither he must return. He lowers his head and lies, perhaps without realizing the extent of his mendacity: "No, after all, we're not unhappy, it isn't so terrible as all that!"

The lady is of the same opinion. "I know," she says, "there are compensations! How superb a charge must be, eh? All those masses of men advancing like they do in a holiday procession, and the trumpets playing a rousing air in the fields! And the dear little soldiers that can't be held back and shouting, 'Vive la France!' and even laughing as they die! Ah! we others, we're not in honor's way like you are. My husband is a clerk at the Prefecture, and just now he's got a holiday to treat his rheumatism."

"I should very much have liked to be a soldier," said the gentleman, "but I've no luck. The head of my office can't get on without me."

People go and come, elbowing and disappearing behind each other. The waiters worm their way through with their fragile and sparkling burdens—green, red or bright yellow, with a white border. The grating of feet on the sanded floor mingles with the exclamations of the regular customers as they recognize each other, some standing, others leaning on their elbows, amid the sound of glasses and dominoes pushed along the tables. In the background, around the seductive shock of ivory balls, a crowding circle of spectators emits classical pleasantries.

"Every man to his trade, mon brave," says a man at the other end of the table whose face is adorned with powerful colors, addressing Tirette directly; "you are heroes. On our side, we are working in the economic life of the country. It is a struggle like yours. I am useful—I don't say more useful than you, but equally so."

And I see Tirette through the cigar-smoke making round eyes, and in the hubbub I can hardly hear the reply of his humble and dumbfounded voice—Tirette, the funny man of the squad!—"Yes, that's true; every man to his trade."

Furtively we stole away.

We are almost silent as we leave the Cafe des Fleurs. It seems as if we no longer know how to talk. Something like discontent irritates my comrades and knits their brows. They look as if they are becoming aware that they have not done their duty at an important juncture.

"Fine lot of gibberish they've talked to us, the beasts!" Tirette growls at last with a rancor that gathers strength the more we unite and collect ourselves again.

"We ought to have got beastly drunk to-day!" replies Paradis brutally.

We walk without a word spoken. Then, after a time, "They're a lot of idiots, filthy idiots," Tirette goes on; "they tried to cod us, but I'm not on; if I see them again," he says, with a crescendo of anger, "I shall know what to say to them!"

"We shan't see them again," says Blaire.

"In eight days from now, p'raps we shall be laid out," says Volpatte.

In the approaches to the square we run into a mob of people flowing out from the Hotel de Ville and from another big public building which displays the columns of a temple supporting a pediment. Offices are closing, and pouring forth civilians of all sorts and all ages, and military men both young and old, who seem at a distance to be dressed pretty much like us; but when nearer they stand revealed as the shirkers and deserters of the war, in spite of being disguised as soldiers, in spite of their brisques.

Women and children are waiting for them, in pretty and happy clusters. The commercial people are shutting up their shops with complacent content and a smile for both the day ended and for the morrow, elated by the lively and constant thrills of profits increased, by the growing jingle of the cash-box. They have stayed behind in the heart of their own firesides; they have only to stoop to caress their children. We see them beaming in the first starlights of the street, all these rich folk who are becoming richer, all these tranquil people whose tranquillity increases every day, people who are full, you feel, and in spite of all, of an unconfessable prayer. They all go slowly, by grace of the fine evening, and settle themselves in perfected homes, or in cafes where they are waited upon. Couples are forming, too, young women and young men, civilians or soldiers, with some badge of their preservation embroidered on their collars. They make haste into the shadows of security where the others go, where the dawn of lighted rooms awaits them; they hurry towards the night of rest and caresses.

And as we pass quite close to a ground-floor window which is half open, we see the breeze gently inflate the lace curtain and lend it the light and delicious form of lingerie—and the advancing throng drives us back, poor strangers that we are!

We wander along the pavement, all through the twilight that begins to glow with gold—for in towns Night adorns herself with jewels. The sight of this world has revealed a great truth to us at last, nor could we avoid it: a Difference which becomes evident between human beings, a Difference far deeper than that of nations and with defensive trenches more impregnable; the clean-cut and truly unpardonable division that there is in a country's inhabitants between those who gain and those who grieve, those who are required to sacrifice all, all, to give their numbers and strength and suffering to the last limit, those upon whom the others walk and advance, smile and succeed.

Some items of mourning attire make blots in the crowd and have their message for us, but the rest is of merriment, not mourning.

"It isn't one single country, that's not possible," suddenly says Volpatte with singular precision, "there are two. We're divided into two foreign countries. The Front, over there, where there are too many unhappy, and the Rear, here, where there are too many happy."

"How can you help it? It serves its end—it's the background—but afterwards—"

"Yes, I know; but all the same, all the same, there are too many of them, and they're too happy, and they're always the same ones, and there's no reason—"

"What can you do?" says Tirette.

"So much the worse," adds Blaire, still more simply.

"In eight days from now p'raps we shall have snuffed it!" Volpatte is content to repeat as we go away with lowered heads.

The Fatigue-Party

EVENING is falling upon the trench. All through the day it has been drawing near, invisible as fate, and now it encroaches on the banks of the long ditches like the lips of a wound infinitely great.

We have talked, eaten, slept, and written in the bottom of the trench since the morning. Now that evening is here, an eddying springs up in the boundless crevice; it stirs and unifies the torpid disorder of the scattered men. It is the hour when we arise and work.

Volpatte and Tirette approach each other. "Another day gone by, another like the rest of 'em," says Volpatte, looking at the darkening sky.

"You're off it; our day isn't finished," replies Tirette, whose long experience of calamity has taught him that one must not jump to conclusions, where we are, even in regard to the modest future of a commonplace evening that has already begun.

"Allons! Muster!" We join up with the laggard inattention of custom. With himself each man brings his rifle, his pouches of cartridges, his water-bottle, and a pouch that contains a lump of bread. Volpatte is still eating, with protruding and palpitating cheek. Paradis, with purple nose and chattering teeth, growls. Fouillade trails his rifle along like a broom. Marthereau looks at a mournful handkerchief, rumpled and stiff, and puts it back in his pocket. A cold drizzle is falling, and everybody shivers.

Down yonder we hear a droning chant—"Two shovels, one pick, two shovels, one pick——" The file trickles along to the tool-store, stagnates at the door, and departs, bristling with implements.

"Everybody here? Gee up!" says the sergeant. Downward and rolling, we go forward. We know not where we go. We know nothing, except that the night and the earth are blending in the same abyss.

As we emerge into the nude twilight from the trench, we see it already black as the crater of a dead volcano. Great gray clouds, storm-charged, hang from the sky. The plain, too, is gray in the pallid light; the grass is muddy, and all slashed with water. The things which here and there seem only distorted limbs are denuded trees. We cannot see far around us in the damp reek; besides, we only look downwards at the mud in which we slide—"Porridge!"

Going across country we knead and pound a sticky paste which spreads out and flows back from every step—"Chocolate cream—coffee creams!"

On the stony parts, the wiped-out ruins of roads that have become barren as the fields, the marching troop breaks through a layer of slime into a flinty conglomerate that grates and gives way under our iron-shod soles—"Seems as if we were walking on buttered toast!"

On the slope of a knoll sometimes, the mud is black and thick and deep-rutted, like that which forms around the horse-ponds in villages, and in these ruts there are lakes and puddles and ponds, whose edges seem to be in rags.

The pleasantries of the wags, who in the early freshness of the journey had cried, "Quack, quack," when they went through the water, are now becoming rare and gloomy; gradually the jokers are damped down. The rain begins to fall heavily. The daylight dwindles, and the confusion that is space contracts. The last lingering light welters on the ground and in the water.

A steaming silhouette of men like monks appears through the rain in the west. It is a company of the 204th, wrapped in tent-cloths. As we go by we see the pale and shrunken faces and the dark noses of these dripping prowlers before they disappear. The track we are following through the faint grass of the fields is itself a sticky field streaked with countless parallel ruts, all plowed in the same line by the feet and the wheels of those who go to the front and those who go to the rear.

We have to jump over gaping trenches, and this is not always easy, for the edges have become soft and slippery, and earth-falls have widened them. Fatigue, too, begins to bear upon our shoulders. Vehicles cross our path with a great noise and splashing. Artillery limbers prance by and spray us heavily. The motor lorries are borne on whirling circles of water around the wheels, with spirting tumultuous spokes.

As the darkness increases, the jolted vehicles and the horses' necks and the profiles of the riders with their floating cloaks and slung carbines stand out still more fantastically against the misty floods from the sky. Here, there is a block of ammunition carts of the artillery. The horses are standing and trampling as we go by. We hear the creaking of axles, shouts, disputes, commands which collide, and the roar of the ocean of rain. Over the confused scuffle we can see steam rising from the buttocks of the teams and the cloaks of the horsemen.

"Look out!" Something is laid out on the ground on our right—a row of dead. As we go by, our feet instinctively avoid them and our eyes search them. We see upright boot-soles, outstretched necks, the hollows of uncertain faces, hands half clenched in the air over the dark medley.

We march and march, over fields still ghostly and foot-worn, under a sky where ragged clouds unfurl themselves upon the blackening expanse—which seems to have befouled itself by prolonged contact with so many multitudes of sorry humanity.

Then we go down again into the communication trenches. To reach them we make a wide circuit, so that the rearguard can see the whole company, a hundred yards away, deployed in the gloom, little obscure figures sticking to the slopes and following each other in loose order, with their tools amid their rifles pricking up on each side of their heads, a slender trivial line that plunges in and raises its arms as if in entreaty.

These trenches—still of the second lines—are populous. On the thresholds of the dug-outs, where cart-cloths and skins of animals hang and flap, squatting and bearded men watch our passing with expressionless eyes, as if they were looking at nothing. From beneath other cloths, drawn down to the ground, feet are projected, and snores.

"Nom de Dieu! It's a long way!" the trampers begin to grumble. There is an eddy and recoil in the flow.

"Halt!" The stop is to let others go by. We pile ourselves up, cursing, on the walls of the trench. It is a company of machine-gunners with their curious burdens.

There seems to be no end to it, and the long halts are wearying. Muscles are beginning to stretch. The everlasting march is overwhelming us. We have hardly got going again when we have to recoil once more into a traverse to let the relief of the telephonists go by. We back like awkward cattle, and restart more heavily.

"Look out for the wire!" The telephone wire undulates above the trench, and crosses it in places between two posts. When it is too slack, its curve sags into the trench and catches the rifles of passing men, and the ensnared ones struggle, and abuse the engineers who don't know how to fix up their threads.

Then, as the drooping entanglement of precious wires increases, we shoulder our rifles with the butt in the air, carry the shovels under our arms, and go forward with lowered heads.

Our progress now is suddenly checked, and we only advance step by step, locked in each other. The head of the column must be in difficult case. We reach a spot where failing ground leads to a yawning hole—the Covered Trench. The others have disappeared through the low doorway. "We've got to go into this blackpudding, then?"

Every man hesitates before ingulfing himself in the narrow underground darkness, and it is the total of these hesitations and lingerings that is reflected in the rear sections of the column in the form of wavering, obstruction, and sometimes abrupt shocks.

From our first steps in the Covered Trench, a heavy darkness settles on us and divides us from each other. The damp odor of a swamped cave steals into us. In the ceiling of the earthen corridor that contains us, we can make out a few streaks and holes of pallor—the chinks and rents in the overhead planks. Little streams of water flow freely through them in places, and in spite of tentative groping we stumble on heaped-up timber. Alongside, our knocks discover the dim vertical presence of the supporting beams.

The air in this interminable tunnel is vibrating heavily. It is the searchlight engine that is installed there—we have to pass in front of it.

After we have felt our deep-drowned way for a quarter of an hour, some one who is overborne by the darkness and the wet, and tired of bumping into unknown people, growls, "I don't care—I'm going to light up."

The brilliant beam of a little electric lamp flashes out, and instantly the sergeant bellows, "Ye gods! Who's the complete ass that's making a light? Are you daft? Don't you know it can be seen, you scab, through the roof?"

The flash-lamp, after revealing some dark and oozing walls in its cone of light, retires into the night. "Not much you can't see it!" jeers the man, "and anyway we're not in the first lines." "Ah, that can't be seen!"

The sergeant, wedged into the file and continuing to advance, appears to be turning round as he goes and attempting some forceful observations—"You gallows-bird! You damned dodger!" But suddenly he starts a new roar—"What! Another man smoking now! Holy hell!" This time he tries to halt, but in vain he rears himself against the wall and struggles to stick to it. He is forced precipitately to go with the stream and is carried away among his own shouts, which return and swallow him up, while the cigarette, the cause of his rage, disappears in silence.

The jerky beat of the engine grows louder, and an increasing heat surrounds us. The overcharged air of the trench vibrates more and more as we go forward. The engine's jarring note soon hammers our ears and shakes us through. Still it gets hotter; it is like some great animal breathing in our faces. The buried trench seems to be leading us down and down into the tumult of some infernal workshop, whose dark-red glow is sketching out our huge and curving shadows in purple on the walls.

In a diabolical crescendo of din, of hot wind and of lights, we flow deafened towards the furnace. One would think that the engine itself was hurling itself through the tunnel to meet us, like a frantic motor-cyclist drawing dizzily near with his headlight and destruction.

Scorched and half blinded, we pass in front of the red furnace and the black engine, whose flywheel roars like a hurricane, and we have hardly time to make out the movements of men around it. We shut our eyes, choked by the contact of this glaring white-hot breath.

Now, the noise and the heat are raging behind us and growing feebler, and my neighbor mutters in his beard, "And that idiot that said my lamp would be seen!"

And here is the free air! The sky is a very dark blue, of the same color as the earth and little lighter. The rain becomes worse and worse, and walking is laborious in the heavy slime. The whole boot sinks in, and it is a labor of acute pain to withdraw the foot every time. Hardly anything is left visible in the night, but at the exit from the hole we see a disorder of beams which flounder in the widened trench—some demolished dugout.

Just at this moment, a searchlight's unearthly arm that was swinging through space stops and falls on us, and we find that the tangle of uprooted and sunken posts and shattered framing is populous with dead soldiers. Quite close to me, the head of a kneeling body hangs on its back by an uncertain thread; a black veneer, edged with clotted drops, covers the cheek. Another body so clasps a post in its arms that it has only half fallen. Another, lying in the form of a circle, has been stripped by the shell, and his back and belly are laid bare. Another, outstretched on the edge of the heap, has thrown his hand across our path; and in this place where there no traffic except by night—for the trench is blocked just there by the earth-fall and inaccessible by day—every one treads on that hand. By the searchlight's shaft I saw it clearly, fleshless and worn, a sort of withered fin.

The rain is raging and the sound of its streaming dominates everything—a horror of desolation. We feel the water on our flesh as if the deluge had washed our clothes away.

We enter the open trench, and the embrace of night and storm resumes the sole possession of this confusion of corpses, stranded and cramped on a square of earth as on a raft.

The wind freezes the drops of sweat on our foreheads. It is near midnight. For six hours now we have marched in the increasing burden of the mud. This is the time when the Paris theaters are constellated with electroliers and blossoming with lamps; when they are filled with luxurious excitement, with the rustle of skirts, with merrymaking and warmth; when a fragrant and radiant multitude, chatting, laughing, smiling, applauding, expanding, feels itself pleasantly affected by the cleverly graduated emotions which the comedy evokes, and lolls in contented enjoyment of the rich and splendid pageants of military glorification that crowd the stage of the music-hall.

"Aren't we there? Nom de Dieu, shan't we ever get there?" The groan is breathed by the long procession that tosses about in these crevices of the earth, carrying rifles and shovels and pickaxes under the eternal torrent. We march and march. We are drunk with fatigue, and roll to this side and that. Stupefied and soaked, we strike with our shoulders a substance as sodden as ourselves.

"Halt!"—"Are we there?"—"Ah, yes, we're there!"

For the moment a heavy recoil presses us back and then a murmur runs along: "We've lost ourselves." The truth dawns on the confusion of the wandering horde. We have taken the wrong turn at some fork, and it will be the deuce of a job to find the right way again.

Then, too, a rumor passes from mouth to mouth that a fighting company on its way to the lines is coming up behind us. The way by which we have come is stopped up with men. It is the block absolute.

At all costs we must try to regain the lost trench—which is alleged to be on our left—by trickling through some sap or other. Utterly wearied and unnerved, the men break into gesticulations and violent reproaches. They trudge awhile, then drop their tools and halt. Here and there are compact groups—you can glimpse them by the light of the star-shells—who have let themselves fall to the ground. Scattered afar from south to north, the troop waits in the merciless rain.

The lieutenant who is in charge and has led us astray, wriggles his way along the men in quest of some lateral exit. A little trench appears, shallow and narrow.

"We most go that way, no doubt about it," the officer hastens to say. "Come, forward, boys."

Each man sulkily picks up his burden. But a chorus of oaths and curses rises from the first who enter the little sap: "It's a latrine!"

A disgusting smell escapes from the trench, and those inside halt butt into each other, and refuse to advance. We are all jammed against each other and block up the threshold.

"I'd rather climb out and go in the open!" cries a man. But there are flashes rending the sky above the embankments on all sides, and the sight is so fearsome of these jets of resounding flame that overhang our pit and its swarming shadows that no one responds to the madman's saying.

Willing or unwilling, since we cannot go back, we must even take that way. "Forward into the filth!" cries the leader of the troop. We plunge in, tense with repulsion. Bullets are whistling over. "Lower your heads!" The trench has little depth; one must stoop very low to avoid being hit, and the stench becomes intolerable. At last we emerge into the communication trench that we left in error. We begin again to march. Though we march without end we arrive nowhere.

While we wander on, dumb and vacant, in the dizzy stupefaction of fatigue, the stream which is running in the bottom of the trench cleanses our befouled feet.

The roars of the artillery succeed each other faster and faster, till they make but a single roar upon all the earth. From all sides the gunfire and the bursting shells hurl their swift shafts of light and stripe confusedly the black sky over our heads. The bombardment then becomes so intense that its illumination has no break. In the continuous chain of thunderbolts we can see each other clearly—our helmets streaming like the bodies of fishes, our sodden leathers, the shovel-blades black and glistening; we can even see the pale drops of the unending rain. Never have I seen the like of it; in very truth it is moonlight made by gunfire.

Together there mounts from our lines and from the enemy's such a cloud of rockets that they unite and mingle in constellations; at one moment, to light us on our hideous way, there was a Great Bear of star-shells in the valley of the sky that we could see between the parapets.

We are lost again, and this time we must be close to the first lines; but a depression in this part of the plain forms a sort of basin, overrun by shadows. We have marched along a sap and then back again. In the phosphorescent vibration of the guns, shimmering like a cinematograph, we make out above the parapet two stretcher-bearers trying to cross the trench with their laden stretcher.

The lieutenant, who at least knows the place where he should guide the team of workers, questions them, "Where is the New Trench?"—"Don't know." From the ranks another question is put to them, "How far are we from the Boches?" They make no reply, as they are talking among themselves.

"I'm stopping," says the man in front; "I'm too tired."

"Come, get on with you, nom de Dieu!" says the other in a surly tone and floundering heavily, his arms extended by the stretcher. "We can't step and rust here."

They put the stretcher down on the parapet, the edge of it overhanging the trench, and as we pass underneath we can see the prostrate man's feet. The rain which falls on the stretcher drains from it darkened.

"Wounded?" some one asks down below.

"No, a stiff," growls the bearer this time, "and he weighs twelve stone at least. Wounded I don't mind—for two days and two nights we haven't left off carrying 'em—but it's rotten, breaking yourself up with lugging dead men about." And the bearer, upright on the edge of the bank, drops a foot to the base of the opposite bank across the cavity, and with his legs wide apart, laboriously balanced, he grips the stretcher and begins to draw it across, calling on his companion to help him.

A little farther we see the stooping form of a hooded officer, and as he raises his hand to his face we see two gold lines on his sleeve. He, surely, will tell us the way. But he addresses us, and asks if we have not seen the battery he is looking for. We shall never get there!

But we do, all the same. We finish up in a field of blackness where a few lean posts are bristling. We climb up to it, and spread out in silence. This is the spot.

The placing of us is an undertaking. Four separate times we go forward and then retire, before the company is regularly echeloned along the length of the trench to be dug, before an equal interval is left between each team of one striker and two shovelers. "Incline three paces more—too much—one pace to the rear. Come, one pace to the rear—are you deaf?—Halt! There!"

This adjustment is done by the lieutenant and a noncom. of the Engineers who has sprung up out of the ground. Together or separately they run along the file and give their muttered orders into the men's ears as they take them by the arm, sometimes, to guide them. Though begun in an orderly way, the arrangement degenerates, thanks to the ill temper of the exhausted men, who must continually be uprooting themselves from the spot where the undulating mob is stranded.

"We're in front of the first lines," they whisper round me. "No." murmur other voices, "we're just behind."

No one knows. The rain still falls, though less fiercely than at some moments on the march. But what matters the rain! We have spread ourselves out on the ground. Now that our backs and limbs rest in the yielding mud, we are so comfortable that we are unconcerned about the rain that pricks our faces and drives through to our flesh, indifferent to the saturation of the bed that contains us.

But we get hardly time enough to draw breath. They are not so imprudent as to let us bury ourselves in sleep. We must set ourselves to incessant labor. It is two o'clock of the morning; in four hours more it will be too light for us to stay here. There is not a minute to lose.

"Every man," they say to us, "must dig five feet in length, two and a half feet in width, and two and three-quarter feet in depth. That makes fifteen feet in length for each team. And I advise you to get into it; the sooner it's done, the sooner you'll leave."

We know the pious claptrap. It is not recorded in the annals of the regiment that a trenching fatigue-party ever once got away before the moment when it became absolutely necessary to quit the neighborhood if they were not to be seen, marked and destroyed along with the work of their hands.

We murmur, "Yes, yes—all right; it's not worth saying. Go easy."

But everybody applies himself to the job courageously, except for some invincible sleepers whose nap will involve them later in superhuman efforts.

We attack the first layer of the new line—little mounds of earth, stringy with grass. The ease and speed with which the work begins—like all entrenching work in free soil—foster the illusion that it will soon be finished, that we shall be able to sleep in the cavities we have scooped: and thus a certain eagerness revives.

But whether by reason of the noise of the shovels, or because some men are chatting almost aloud, in spite of reproofs, our activity wakes up a rocket, whose flaming vertical line rattles suddenly on our right.

"Lie down!" Every man flattens himself, and the rocket balances and parades its huge pallor over a sort of field of the dead.

As soon as it is out one hears the men, in places and then all along, detach themselves from their secretive stillness, get up, and resume the task with more discretion.

Soon another star-shell tosses aloft its long golden stalk, and still more brightly illuminates the flat and motionless line of trenchmakers. Then another and another.

Bullets rend the air around us, and we hear a cry, "Some one wounded!" He passes, supported by comrades. We can just see the group of men who are going away, dragging one of their number.

The place becomes unwholesome. We stoop and crouch, and some are scratching at the earth on their knees. Others are working full length; they toil, and turn, and turn again, like men in nightmares. The earth, whose first layer was light to lift, becomes muddy and sticky; it is hard to handle, and clings to the tool like glue. After every shovelful the blade must be scraped.

Already a thin heap of earth is winding along, and each man has the idea of reinforcing the incipient breastwork with his pouch and his rolled-up greatcoat, and he hoods himself behind the slender pile of shadow when a volley comes—

While we work we sweat, and as soon as we stop working we are pierced through by the cold. A spell seems to be cast on us, paralyzing our arms. The rockets torment and pursue us, and allow us but little movement. After every one of them that petrifies us with its light we have to struggle against a task still more stubborn. The hole only deepens into the darkness with painful and despairing tardiness.

The ground gets softer; each shovelful drips and flows, and spreads from the blade with a flabby sound. At last some one cries, "Water!" The repeated cry travels all along the row of diggers—"Water—that's done it!"

"Melusson's team's dug deeper, and there's water. They've struck a swamp."—"No help for it."

We stop in confusion. In the bosom of the night we hear the sound of shovels and picks thrown down like empty weapons. The non-coms. go gropingly after the officer to get instructions. Here and there, with no desire for anything better, some men are going deliciously to sleep under the caress of the rain, under the radiant rockets.

It was very nearly at this minute, as far as I can remember, that the bombardment began again. The first shell fell with a terrible splitting of the air, which seemed to tear itself in two; and other whistles were already converging upon us when its explosion uplifted the ground at the head of the detachment in the heart of the magnitude of night and rain, revealing gesticulations upon a sudden screen of red.

No doubt they had seen us, thanks to the rockets, and had trained their fire on us.

The men hurled and rolled themselves towards the little flooded ditch that they had dug, wedging, burying, and immersing themselves in it, and placed the blades of the shovels over their heads. To right, to left, in front and behind, shells burst so near that every one of them shook us in our bed of clay; and it became soon one continuous quaking that seized the wretched gutter, crowded with men and scaly with shovels, under the strata of smoke and the falling fire. The splinters and debris crossed in all directions with a network of noise over the dazzling field. No second passed but we all thought what some stammered with their faces in the earth, "We're done, this time!"

A little in front of the place where I am, a shape has arisen and cried, "Let's be off!" Prone bodies half rose out of the shroud of mud that dripped in tails and liquid rags from their limbs, and these deathful apparitions cried also, "Let's go!" They were on their knees, on all-fours, crawling towards the way of retreat: "Get on, allez, get on!"

But the long file stayed motionless, and the frenzied complaints were in vain. They who were down there at the end would not budge, and their inactivity immobilized the rest. Some wounded passed over the others, crawling over them as over debris, and sprinkling the whole company with their blood.

We discovered at last the cause of the maddening inactivity of the detachment's tail—"There's a barrage fire beyond."

A weird imprisoned panic seized upon the men with cries inarticulate and gestures stillborn. They writhed upon the spot. But little shelter as the incipient trench afforded, no one dared leave the ditch that saved us from protruding above the level of the ground, no one dared fly from death towards the traverse that should be down there. Great were the risks of the wounded who had managed to crawl over the others, and every moment some were struck and went down again.

Fire and water fell blended everywhere. Profoundly entangled in the supernatural din, we shook from neck to heels. The most hideous of deaths was falling and bounding and plunging all around us in waves of light, its crashing snatched our fearfulness in all directions—our flesh prepared itself for the monstrous sacrifice! In that tense moment of imminent destruction, we could only remember just then how often we had already experienced it, how often undergone this outpouring of iron, and the burning roar of it, and the stench. It is only during a bombardment that one really recalls those he has already endured.

And still, without ceasing, newly-wounded men crept over us, fleeing at any price. In the fear that their contact evoked we groaned again, "We shan't get out of this; nobody will get out of it."

Suddenly a gap appeared in the compressed humanity, and those behind breathed again, for we were on the move.

We began by crawling, then we ran, bowed low in the mud and water that mirrored the flashes and the crimson gleams, stumbling and falling over submerged obstructions, ourselves resembling heavy splashing projectiles, thunder-hurled along the ground. We arrive at the starting-place of the trench we had begun to dig.

"There's no trench—there's nothing."

In truth the eye could discern no shelter in the plain where our work had begun. Even by the stormy flash of the rockets we could only see the plain, a huge and raging desert. The trench could not be far away, for it had brought us here. But which way must we steer to find it?

The rain redoubled. We lingered a moment in mournful disappointment, gathered on a lightning-smitten and unknown shore—and then the stampede.

Some bore to the left, some to the right, some went straight forward—tiny groups that one only saw for a second in the heart of the thundering rain before they were separated by sable avalanches and curtains of flaming smoke.

The bombardment over our heads grew less; it was chiefly over the place where we had been that it was increasing. But it might any minute isolate everything and destroy it.

The rain became more and more torrential—a deluge in the night. The darkness was so deep that the star-shells only lit up slices of water-seamed obscurity, in the depths of which fleeing phantoms came and went and ran round in circles.

I cannot say how long I wandered with the group with which I had remained. We went into morasses. We strained our sight forward in quest of the embankment and the trench of salvation, towards the ditch that was somewhere there, as towards a harbor.

A cry of consolation was heard at last through the vapors of war and the elements—"A trench!" But the embankment of that trench was moving; it was made of men mingled in confusion, who seemed to be coming out and abandoning it.

"Don't stay there, mates!" cried the fugitives; "clear off, don't come near. It's hell—everything's collapsing—the trenches are legging it and the dug-outs are bunged up—the mud's pouring in everywhere. There won't be any trenches by the morning—it's all up with them about here!"

They disappeared. Where? We forgot to ask for some little direction from these men whose streaming shapes had no sooner appeared than they were swallowed up in the dark.

Even our little group crumbled away among the devastation, no longer knowing where they were. Now one, now another, faded into the night, disappearing towards his chance of escape.

We climbed slopes and descended them. I saw dimly in front of me men bowed and hunchbacked, mounting a slippery incline where mud held them back, and the wind and rain repelled them under a dome of cloudy lights.

Then we flowed back, and plunged into a marsh up to our knees. So high must we lift our feet that we walked with a sound of swimming. Each forward stride was an enormous effort which slackened in agony.

It was there that we felt death drawing near. But we beached ourselves at last on a sort of clay embankment that divided the swamp. As we followed the slippery back of this slender island along, I remember that once we had to stoop and steer ourselves by touching some half-buried corpses, so that we should not be thrown down from the soft and sinuous ridge. My hand discovered shoulders and hard backs, a face cold as a helmet, and a pipe still desperately bitten by dead jaws.

As we emerged and raised our heads at a venture we heard the sound of voices not far away. "Voices! Ah, voices!" They sounded tranquil to us, as though they called us by our names, and we all came close together to approach this fraternal murmuring of men.

The words became distinct. They were quite near—in the hillock that we could dimly see like an oasis: and yet we could not hear what they said. The sounds were muddled, and we did not understand them.

"What are they saying?" asked one of us in a curious tone.

Instinctively we stopped trying to find a way in. A doubt, a painful idea was seizing us. Then, clearly enunciated, there rang out these words—"Achtung!—Zweites Geschutz—Schuss—" Farther back, the report of a gun answered the telephonic command.

Horror and stupefaction nailed us to the spot at first—"Where are we? Oh, Christ, where are we?" Turning right about face, slowly in spite of all, borne down anew by exhaustion and dismay, we took flight, as overwhelmed by weariness as if we had many wounds, pulled back by the mud towards the enemy country, and retaining only just enough energy to repel the thought of the sweetness it would have been to let ourselves die.

We came to a sort of great plain. We halted and threw ourselves on the ground on the side of a mound, and leaned back upon it, unable to make another step.

And we moved no more, my shadowy comrades nor I. The rain splashed in our faces, streamed down our backs and chests, ran down from our knees and filled our boots.

We should perhaps be killed or taken prisoners when day came. But we thought no more of anything. We could do no more; we knew no more.

The Dawn

WE are waiting for daylight in the place where we sank to the ground. Sinister and slow it comes, chilling and dismal, and expands upon the livid landscape.

The rain has ceased to fall—there is none left in the sky. The leaden plain and its mirrors of sullied water seem to issue not only from the night but from the sea.

Drowsy or half asleep, sometimes opening our eyes only to close them again, we attend the incredible renewal of light, paralyzed with cold and broken with fatigue.

Where are the trenches?

We see lakes, and between the lakes there are lines of milky and motionless water. There is more water even than we had thought. It has taken everything and spread everywhere, and the prophecy of the men in the night has come true. There are no more trenches; those canals are the trenches enshrouded. It is a universal flood. The battlefield is not sleeping; it is dead. Life may be going on down yonder perhaps, but we cannot see so far.

Swaying painfully, like a sick man, in the terrible encumbering clasp of my greatcoat, I half raise myself to look at it all. There are three monstrously shapeless forms beside me. One of them—it is Paradis, in an amazing armor of mud, with a swelling at the waist that stands for his cartridge pouches—gets up also. The others are asleep, and make no movement.

And what is this silence, too, this prodigious silence? There is no sound, except when from time to time a lump of earth slips into the water, in the middle of this fantastic paralysis of the world. No one is firing. There are no shells, for they would not burst. There are no bullets, either, for the men—

Ah, the men! Where are the men?

We see them gradually. Not far from us there are some stranded and sleeping hulks so molded in mud from head to foot that they are almost transformed into inanimate objects.

Some distance away I can make out others, curled up and clinging like snails all along a rounded embankment, from which they have partly slipped back into the water. It is a motionless rank of clumsy lumps, of bundles placed side by side, dripping water and mud, and of the same color as the soil with which they are blended.

I make an effort to break the silence. To Paradis, who also is looking that way, I say, "Are they dead?"

"We'll go and see presently," he says in a low voice; "stop here a bit yet. We shall have the heart to go there by and by."

We look at each other, and our eyes fall also on the others who came and fell down here. Their faces spell such weariness that they are no longer faces so much as something dirty, disfigured and bruised, with blood-shot eyes. Since the beginning we have seen each other in all manner of shapes and appearances, and yet—we do not know each other.

Paradis turns his head and looks elsewhere.

Suddenly I see him seized with trembling. He extends an arm enormously caked in mud. "There—there—" he says.

On the water which overflows from a stretch particularly cross-seamed and gullied, some lumps are floating, some round-backed reefs.

We drag ourselves to the spot. They are drowned men. Their arms and heads are submerged. On the surface of the plastery liquid appear their backs and the straps of their accouterments. Their blue cloth trousers are inflated, with the feet attached askew upon the ballooning legs, like the black wooden feet on the shapeless legs of marionettes. From one sunken head the hair stands straight up like water-weeds. Here is a face which the water only lightly touches; the head is beached on the marge, and the body disappears in its turbid tomb. The face is lifted skyward. The eyes are two white holes; the mouth is a black hole. The mask's yellow and puffed-up skin appears soft and creased, like dough gone cold.

They are the men who were watching there, and could not extricate themselves from the mud. All their efforts to escape over the sticky escarpment of the trench that was slowly and fatally filling with water only dragged them still more into the depth. They died clinging to the yielding support of the earth.

There, our first lines are; and there, the first German lines, equally silent and flooded. On our way to these flaccid ruins we pass through the

middle of what yesterday was the zone of terror, the awful space on whose
threshold the fierce rush of our last attack was forced to stop, the No
Man's Land which bullets and shells had not ceased to furrow for a year
and a half, where their crossed fire during these latter days had furiously
swept the ground from one horizon to the other.

Now, it is a field of rest. The ground is everywhere dotted with beings
who sleep or who are on the way to die, slowly moving, lifting an arm,
lifting the head.

The enemy trench is completing the process of foundering into itself,
among great marshy undulations and funnel-holes, shaggy with mud: it
forms among them a line of pools and wells. Here and there we can see
the still overhanging banks begin to move, crumble, and fail down. In one
place we can lean against it.

In this bewildering circle of filth there are no bodies. But there, worse
than a body, a solitary arm protrudes, bare and white as a stone, from a
hole which dimly shows on the other side of the water. The man has been
buried in his dug-out and has had only the time to thrust out his arm.

Quite near, we notice that some mounds of earth aligned along the
ruined ramparts of this deep-drowned ditch are human. Are they dead—or
asleep? We do not know; in any case, they rest.

Are they German or French? We do not know. One of them has opened
his eyes, and looks at us with swaying head. We say to him, "French?"—a
nd then, "Deutsch?" He makes no reply, but shuts his eyes again and
relapses into oblivion. We never knew what he was.

We cannot decide the identity of these beings, either by their clothes,
thickly covered with filth, or by their head-dress, for they are bareheaded
or swathed in woolens under their liquid and offensive cowls; or by their
weapons, for they either have no rifles or their hands rest lightly on
something they have dragged along, a shapeless and sticky mass, like to a
sort of fish.

All these men of corpse-like faces who are before us and behind us, at
the limit of their strength, void of speech as of will, all these earth-charged
men who you would say were carrying their own winding-sheets, are as
much alike as if they were naked. Out of the horror of the night
apparitions are issuing from this side and that who are clad in exactly the
same uniform of misery and mud.

It is the end of all. For the moment it is the prodigious finish, the epic cessation of the war.

I once used to think that the worst hell in war was the flame of shells; and then for long I thought it was the suffocation of the caverns which eternally confine us. But it is neither of these. Hell is water.

The wind is rising, and its icy breath goes through our flesh. On the wrecked and dissolving plain, flecked with bodies between its worm-shaped chasms of water, among the islands of motionless men stuck together like reptiles, in this flattening and sinking chaos there are some slight indications of movement. We see slowly stirring groups and fragments of groups, composed of beings who bow under the weight of their coats and aprons of mud, who trail themselves along, disperse, and crawl about in the depths of the sky's tarnished light. The dawn is so foul that one would say the day was already done.

These survivors are migrating across the desolated steppe, pursued by an unspeakable evil which exhausts and bewilders them. They are lamentable objects; and some, when they are fully seen, are dramatically ludicrous, for the whelming mud from which they still take flight has half unclothed them.

As they pass by their glances go widely around. They look at us, and discovering men in us they cry through the wind, "It's worse down yonder than it is here. The chaps are falling into the holes, and you can't pull them out. All them that trod on the edge of a shell-hole last night, they're dead. Down there where we're coming from you can see a head in the ground, working its arms, embedded. There's a hurdle-path that's given way in places and the hurdles have sunk into holes, and it's a man-trap. Where there's no more hurdles there's two yards deep of water. Your rifle? You couldn't pull it out again when you'd stuck it in. Look at those men, there. They've cut off all the bottom half of their great-coats—hard lines on the pockets—to help 'em get clear, and also because they hadn't strength to drag a weight like that. Dumas' coat, we were able to pull it off him, and it weighed a good eighty pounds; we could just lift it, two of us, with both our hands. Look—him with the bare legs; it's taken everything off him, his trousers, his drawers, his boots, all dragged off by the mud. One's never seen that, never."

Scattered and straggling, the herd takes flight in a fever of fear, their feet pulling huge stumps of mud out of the ground. We watch the human flotsam fade away, and the lumps of them diminish, immured in enormous clothes.

We get up, and at once the icy wind makes us tremble like trees. Slowly we veer towards the mass formed by two men curiously joined, leaning shoulder to shoulder, and each with an arm round the neck of the other. Is it the hand-to-hand fight of two soldiers who have overpowered each other in death and still hold their own, who can never again lose their grip? No; they are two men who recline upon each other so as to sleep. As they might not spread themselves on the falling earth that was ready to spread itself on them, they have supported each other, clasping each other's shoulder; and thus plunged in the ground up to their knees, they have gone to sleep.

We respect their stillness, and withdraw from the twin statue of human wretchedness.

Soon we must halt ourselves. We have expected too much of our strength and can go no farther. It is not yet ended. We collapse once more in a churned corner, with a noise as if one shot a load of dung.

From time to time we open our eyes. Some men are steering for us, reeling. They lean over us and speak in low and weary tones. One of them says, "Sie sind todt. Wir bleiben hier." (They're dead. We'll stay here.) The other says, "Ja," like a sigh.

But they see us move, and at once they sink in front of us. The man with the toneless voice says to us in French, "We surrender," and they do not move. Then they give way entirely, as if this was the relief, the end of their torture; and one of them whose face is patterned in mud like a savage tattooed, smiles slightly.

"Stay there," says Paradis, without moving the head that he leans backward upon a hillock; "presently you shall go with us if you want."

"Yes," says the German, "I've had enough." We make no reply, and he says, "And the others too?"

"Yes," says Paradis, "let them stop too, if they like." There are four of them outstretched on the ground. The death-rattle has got one of them. It is like a sobbing song that rises from him. The others then half straighten themselves, kneeling round him, and roll great eyes in their muck-mottled faces. We get up and watch the scene. But the rattle dies out, and the blackened throat which alone in all the big body pulsed like a little bird, is still.

"Er ist todt!" (He's dead) says one of the men, beginning to cry. The others settle themselves again to sleep. The weeper goes to sleep as he weeps.

Other soldiers have come, stumbling, gripped in sudden halts like tipsy men, or gliding along like worms, to take sanctuary here; and we sleep all jumbled together in the common grave.

Waking, Paradis and I look at each other, and remember. We return to life and daylight as in a nightmare. In front of us the calamitous plain is resurrected, where hummocks vaguely appear from their immersion, the steel-like plain that is rusty in places and shines with lines and pools of water, while bodies are strewn here and there in the vastness like foul rubbish, prone bodies that breathe or rot.

Paradis says to me, "That's war."

"Yes, that's it," he repeats in a far-away voice, "that's war. It's not anything else."

He means—and I am with him in his meaning—"More than attacks that are like ceremonial reviews, more than visible battles unfurled like banners, more even than the hand-to-hand encounters of shouting strife, War is frightful and unnatural weariness, water up to the belly, mud and dung and infamous filth. It is befouled faces and tattered flesh, it is the corpses that are no longer like corpses even, floating on the ravenous earth. It is that, that endless monotony of misery, broken, by poignant tragedies; it is that, and not the bayonet glittering like silver, nor the bugle's chanticleer call to the sun!"

Paradis was so full of this thought that he ruminated a memory, and growled, "D'you remember the woman in the town where we went about a bit not so very long ago? She talked some drivel about attacks, and said, 'How beautiful they must be to see!'"

A chasseur who was full length on his belly, flattened out like a cloak, raised his bead out of the filthy background in which it was sunk, and cried, "Beautiful? Oh, hell! It's just as if an ox were to say, 'What a fine sight it must be, all those droves of cattle driven forward to the slaughter-house!'" He spat out mud from his besmeared mouth, and his unburied face was like a beast's.

"Let them say, 'It must be,'" he sputtered in a strange jerky voice, grating and ragged; "that's all right. But beautiful! Oh, hell!"

Writhing under the idea, he added passionately, "It's when they say things like that that they hit us hardest of all!" He spat again, but exhausted by his effort he fell back in his bath of mud, and laid his head in his spittle.

Paradis, possessed by his notion, waved his hand towards the wide unspeakable landscape, and looking steadily on it repeated his sentence, "War is that. It is that everywhere. What are we, we chaps, and what's all this here? Nothing at all. All we can see is only a speck. You've got to remember that this morning there's three thousand kilometers of equal evils, or nearly equal, or worse."

"And then," said the comrade at our side, whom we could not recognize even by his voice, "to-morrow it begins again. It began again the day before yesterday, and all the days before that!"

With an effort as if he was tearing the ground, the chasseur dragged his body out of the earth where he had molded a depression like an oozing coffin, and sat in the hole. He blinked his eyes and tried to shake the balance of mud from his face, and said, "We shall come out of it again this time. And who knows, p'raps we shall come out of it again to-morrow! Who knows?"

Paradis, with his back bent under mats of earth and clay, was trying to convey his idea that the war cannot be imagined or measured in terms of time and space. "When one speaks of the whole war," he said, thinking aloud, "it's as if you said nothing at all—the words are strangled. We're here, and we look at it all like blind men."

A bass voice rolled to us from a little farther away, "No, one cannot imagine it."

At these words a burst of harsh laughter tore itself from some one. "How could you imagine it, to begin with, if you hadn't been there?"

"You'd have to be mad," said the chasseur.

Paradis leaned over a sprawling outspread mass beside him and said, "Are you asleep?"

"No, but I'm not going to budge." The smothered and terror-struck mutter issued instantly from the mass that was covered with a thick and slimy horse-cloth, so indented that it seemed to have been trampled. "I'll tell you why. I believe my belly's shot through. But I'm not sure, and I daren't find out."

"Let's see—"

"No, not yet," says the man. "I'd rather stop on a bit like this."

The others, dragging themselves on their elbows, began to make splashing movements, by way of casting off the clammy infernal covering that weighed them down. The paralysis of cold was passing away from the knot of sufferers, though the light no longer made any progress over the great irregular marsh of the lower plain. The desolation proceeded, but not the day.

Then he who spoke sorrowfully, like a bell, said. "It'll be no good telling about it, eh? They wouldn't believe you; not out of malice or through liking to pull your leg, but because they couldn't. When you say to 'em later, if you live to say it, 'We were on a night job and we got shelled and we were very nearly drowned in mud,' they'll say, 'Ah!' And p'raps they'll say. 'You didn't have a very spicy time on the job.' And that's all. No one can know it. Only us."

"No, not even us, not even us!" some one cried.

"That's what I say, too. We shall forget—we're forgetting already, my boy!"

"We've seen too much to remember."

"And everything we've seen was too much. We're not made to hold it all. It takes its damned hook in all directions. We're too little to hold it."

"You're right, we shall forget! Not only the length of the big misery, which can't be calculated, as you say, ever since the beginning, but the marches that turn up the ground and turn it again, lacerating your feet and wearing out your bones under a load that seems to grow bigger in the sky, the exhaustion until you don't know your own name any more, the tramping and the inaction that grind you, the digging jobs that exceed your strength, the endless vigils when you fight against sleep and watch for an enemy who is everywhere in the night, the pillows of dung and lice—we shall forget not only those, but even the foul wounds of shells and machine-guns, the mines, the gas, and the counter-attacks. At those moments you're full of the excitement of reality, and you've some satisfaction. But all that wears off and goes away, you don't know how and you don't know where, and there's only the names left, only the words of it, like in a dispatch."

"That's true what he says," remarks a man, without moving his head in its pillory of mud. "When I was on leave, I found I'd already jolly well forgotten what had happened to me before. There were some letters from me that I read over again just as if they were a book I was opening. And yet in spite of that, I've forgotten also all the pain I've had in the war. We're forgetting-machines. Men are things that think a little but chiefly forget. That's what we are."

"Then neither the other side nor us'll remember! So much misery all wasted!"

This point of view added to the abasement of these beings on the shore of the flood, like news of a greater disaster, and humiliated them still more.

"Ah, if one did remember!" cried some one.

"If we remembered," said another, "there wouldn't be any more war."

A third added grandly, "Yes, if we remembered, war would be less useless than it is."

But suddenly one of the prone survivors rose to his knees, dark as a great bat ensnared, and as the mud dripped from his waving arms he cried in a hollow voice, "There must be no more war after this!"

In that miry corner where, still feeble unto impotence, we were beset by blasts of wind which laid hold on us with such rude strength that the very ground seemed to sway like sea-drift, the cry of the man who looked as if he were trying to fly away evoked other like cries: "There must be no more war after this!"

The sullen or furious exclamations of these men fettered to the earth, incarnate of earth, arose and slid away on the wind like beating wings—

"No more war! No more war! Enough of it!"

"It's too stupid—it's too stupid," they mumbled.

"What does it mean, at the bottom of it, all this?—all this that you can't even give a name to?"

They snarled and growled like wild beasts on that sort of ice-floe contended for by the elements, in their dismal disguise of ragged mud. So huge was the protest thus rousing them in revolt that it choked them.

"We're made to live, not to be done in like this!"

"Men are made to be husbands, fathers—men, what the devil!—not beasts that hunt each other and cut each other's throats and make themselves stink like all that."

"And yet, everywhere—everywhere—there are beasts, savage beasts or smashed beasts. Look, look!"

I shall never forget the look of those limitless lands wherefrom the water had corroded all color and form, whose contours crumbled on all sides under the assault of the liquid putrescence that flowed across the broken bones of stakes and wire and framing; nor, rising above those things amid the sullen Stygian immensity, can I ever forget the vision of the thrill of reason, logic and simplicity that suddenly shook these men like a fit of madness.

I could see them agitated by this idea—that to try to live one's life on earth and to be happy is not only a right but a duty, and even an ideal and a virtue; that the only end of social life is to make easy the inner life of every one.

"To live!"—"All of us!"—"You!"—"Me!"

"No more war—ah, no!—it's too stupid—worse than that, it's too—"

For a finishing echo to their half-formed thought a saying came to the mangled and miscarried murmur of the mob from a filth-crowned face that I saw arise from the level of the earth—"Two armies fighting each other—that's like one great army committing suicide!"

"And likewise, what have we been for two years now? Incredibly pitiful wretches, and savages as well, brutes, robbers, and dirty devils."

"Worse than that!" mutters he whose only phrase it is.

"Yes, I admit it!"

In their troubled truce of the morning, these men whom fatigue had tormented, whom rain had scourged, whom night-long lightning had convulsed, these survivors of volcanoes and flood began not only to see dimly how war, as hideous morally as physically, outrages common sense, debases noble ideas and dictates all kind of crime, but they remembered how it had enlarged in them and about them every evil instinct save none, mischief developed into lustful cruelty, selfishness into ferocity, the hunger for enjoyment into a mania.

They are picturing all this before their eyes as just now they confusedly pictured their misery. They are crammed with a curse which strives to find a way out and to come to light in words, a curse which makes them to groan and wail. It is as if they toiled to emerge from the delusion and ignorance which soil them as the mud soils them; as if they will at last know why they are scourged.

"Well then?" clamors one.

"Ay, what then?" the other repeats, still more grandly. The wind sets the flooded flats a-tremble to our eyes, and falling furiously on the human masses lying or kneeling and fixed like flagstones and grave-slabs, it wrings new shivering from them.

"There will be no more war," growls a soldier, "when there is no more Germany."

"That's not the right thing to say!" cries another. "It isn't enough. There'll be no more war when the spirit of war is defeated." The roaring of the wind half smothered his words, so he lifted his head and repeated them.

"Germany and militarism"—some one in his anger precipitately cut in—"they're the same thing. They wanted the war and they'd planned it beforehand. They are militarism."

"Militarism—" a soldier began again.

"What is it?" some one asked.

"It's—it's brute force that's ready prepared, and that lets fly suddenly, any minute."

"Yes. To-day militarism is called Germany."

"Yes, but what will it be called to-morrow?"

"I don't know," said a voice serious as a prophet's.

"If the spirit of war isn't killed, you'll have struggle all through the ages."

"We must—one's got to—"

"We must fight!" gurgled the hoarse voice of a man who had lain stiff in the devouring mud ever since our awakening; "we've got to!" His body turned heavily over. "We've got to give all we have, our strength and our skins and our hearts, all our life and what pleasures are left us. The life of prisoners as we are, we've got to take it in both hands. You've got to endure everything, even injustice—and that's the king that's reigning now—and the shameful and disgusting sights we see, so as to come out on top, and win. But if we've got to make such a sacrifice," adds the shapeless man, turning over again, "it's because we're fighting for progress, not for a country; against error, not against a country."

"War must be killed," said the first speaker, "war must be killed in the belly of Germany!"

"Anyway," said one of those who sat enrooted there like a sort of shrub, "anyway, we're beginning to understand why we've got to march away."

"All the same," grumbled the squatting chasseur in his turn, "there are some that fight with quite another idea than that in their heads. I've seen some of 'em, young men, who said, 'To hell with humanitarian ideas'; what mattered to them was nationality and nothing else, and the war was a question of fatherlands—let every man make a shine about his own. They were fighting, those chaps, and they were fighting well."

"They're young, the lads you're talking about; they're young, and we must excuse 'em."

"You can do a thing well without knowing what you are doing."

"Men are mad, that's true. You'll never say that often enough."

"The Jingoes—they're vermin," growled a shadow.

Several times they repeated, as though feeling their way, "War must be killed; war itself."

"That's all silly talk. What diff does it make whether you think this or that? We've got to be winners, that's all."

But the others had begun to cast about. They wanted to know and to see farther than to-day. They throbbed with the effort to beget in themselves some light of wisdom and of will. Some sparse convictions whirled in their minds, and jumbled scraps of creeds issued from their lips.

"Of course—yes—but we must look at facts—you've got to think about the object, old chap."

"The object? To be winners in this war," the pillar-man insisted, "isn't that an object?"

Two there were who replied together, "No!"

At this moment there was a dull noise; cries broke out around us, and we shuddered. A length of earth had detached itself from the hillock on which—after a fashion—we were leaning back, and had completely exhumed in the middle of us a sitting corpse, with its legs out full length. The collapse burst a pool that had gathered on the top of the mound, and the water spread like a cascade over the body and laved it as we looked.

Some one cried, "His face is all black!"

"What is that face?" gasped a voice.

Those who were able drew near in a circle, like frogs. We could not gaze upon the head that showed in low relief upon the trench-wall that the landslide had laid bare. "His face? It isn't his face!" In place of the face we found the hair, and then we saw that the corpse which had seemed to be sitting was broken, and folded the wrong way. In dreadful silence we looked on the vertical back of the dislocated dead, upon the hanging arms, backward curved, and the two outstretched legs that rested on the sinking soil by the points of the toes. Then the discussion began again, revived by this fearful sleeper. As though the corpse was listening they clamored—"No! To win isn't the object. It isn't those others we've got to get at—it's war."

"Can't you see that we've got to finish with war? If we've got to begin again some day, all that's been done is no good. Look at it there!—and it would be in vain. It would be two or three years or more of wasted catastrophe."

"Ah, my boy, if all we've gone through wasn't the end of this great calamity! I value my life; I've got my wife, my family, my home around them; I've got schemes for my life afterwards, mind you. Well, all the same, if this wasn't the end of it, I'd rather die."

"I'm going to die." The echo came at that moment exactly from Paradis' neighbor, who no doubt had examined the wound in his belly. "I'm sorry on account of my children."

"It's on account of my children that I'm not sorry," came a murmur from somewhere else. "I'm dying, so I know what I'm saying, and I say to myself, 'They'll have peace.'"

"Perhaps I shan't die," said another, with a quiver of hope that he could not restrain even in the presence of the doomed, "but I shall suffer. Well, I say, 'more's the pity,' and I even say 'that's all right'; and I shall know how to stick more suffering if I know it's for something."

"Then we'll have to go on fighting after the war?"

"Yes, p'raps—"

"You want more of it, do you?"

"Yes, because I want no more of it," the voice grunted. "And p'raps it'll not be foreigners that we've got to fight?"

"P'raps, yes—"

A still more violent blast of wind shut our eyes and choked us. When it had passed, and we saw the volley take flight across the plain, seizing and shaking its muddy plunder and furrowing the water in the long gaping trenches—long as the grave of an army—we began again.

"After all, what is it that makes the mass and the horror of war?"

"It's the mass of the people."

"But the people—that's us!"

He who had said it looked at me inquiringly.

"Yes," I said to him, "yes, old boy, that's true! It's with us only that they make battles. It is we who are the material of war. War is made up of the flesh and the souls of common soldiers only. It is we who make the plains of dead and the rivers of blood, all of us, and each of us is invisible and silent because of the immensity of our numbers. The emptied towns and the villages destroyed, they are a wilderness of our making. Yes, war is all of us, and all of us together."

"Yes, that's true. It's the people who are war; without them, there would be nothing, nothing but some wrangling, a long way off. But it isn't they who decide on it; it's the masters who steer them."

"The people are struggling to-day to have no more masters that steer them. This war, it's like the French Revolution continuing."

"Well then, if that's so, we're working for the Prussians too?"

"It's to be hoped so," said one of the wretches of the plain.

"Oh, hell!" said the chasseur, grinding his teeth. But he shook his head and added no more.

"We want to look after ourselves! You shouldn't meddle in other people's business," mumbled the obstinate snarler.

"Yes, you should! Because what you call 'other people,' that's just what they're not—they're the same!"

"Why is it always us that has to march away for everybody?"

"That's it!" said a man, and he repeated the words he had used a moment before. "More's the pity, or so much the better."

"The people—they're nothing, though they ought to be everything," then said the man who had questioned me, recalling, though he did not know it, an historic sentence of more than a century ago, but investing it at last with its great universal significance. Escaped from torment, on all fours in the deep grease of the ground, he lifted his leper-like face and looked hungrily before him into infinity.

He looked and looked. He was trying to open the gates of heaven.

"The peoples of the world ought to come to an understanding, through the hides and on the bodies of those who exploit them one way or another. All the masses ought to agree together."

"All men ought to be equal."

The word seems to come to us like a rescue.

"Equal—yes—yes—there are some great meanings for justice and truth. There are some things one believes in, that one turns to and clings to as if they were a sort of light. There's equality, above all."

"There's liberty and fraternity, too."

"But principally equality!"

I tell them that fraternity is a dream, an obscure and uncertain sentiment; that while it is unnatural for a man to hate one whom he does not know, it is equally unnatural to love him. You can build nothing on fraternity. Nor on liberty, either; it is too relative a thing in a society where all the elements subdivide each other by force.

But equality is always the same. Liberty and fraternity are words while equality is a fact. Equality should be the great human formula—social equality, for while individuals have varying values, each must have an equal share in the social life; and that is only just, because the life of one human being is equal to the life of another. That formula is of prodigious importance. The principle of the equal rights of every living being and the sacred will of the majority is infallible and must be invincible; all progress will be brought about by it, all, with a force truly divine. It will bring first the smooth bed-rock of all progress—the settling of quarrels by that justice which is exactly the same thing as the general advantage.

And these men of the people, dimly seeing some unknown Revolution greater than the other, a revolution springing from themselves and already rising, rising in their throats, repeat "Equality!"

It seems as if they were spelling the word and then reading it distinctly on all sides—that there is not upon the earth any privilege, prejudice or injustice that does not collapse in contact with it. It is an answer to all, a word of sublimity. They revolve the idea over and over, and find a kind of perfection in it. They see errors and abuses burning in a brilliant light.

"That would be fine!" said one.

"Too fine to be true!" said another.

But the third said, "It's because it's true that it's fine. It has no other beauty, mind! And it's not because it's fine that it will come. Fineness is not in vogue, any more than love is. It's because it's true that it has to be."

"Then, since justice is wanted by the people, and the people have the power, let them do it."

"They're beginning already!" said some obscure lips.

"It's the way things are running," declared another.

"When all men have made themselves equal, we shall be forced to unite."

"And there'll no longer be appalling things done in the face of heaven by thirty million men who don't wish them."

It is true, and there is nothing to reply to it. What pretended argument or shadow of an answer dare one oppose to it—"There'll no longer be the things done in the face of heaven by thirty millions of men who don't want to do them!"

Such is the logic that I hear and follow of the words, spoken by these pitiful fellows cast upon the field of affliction, the words which spring from their bruises and pains, the words which bleed from them.

Now, the sky is all overcast. Low down it is armored in steely blue by great clouds. Above, in a weakly luminous silvering, it is crossed by enormous sweepings of wet mist. The weather is worsening, and more rain on the way. The end of the tempest and the long trouble is not yet.

"We shall say to ourselves," says one, "'After all, why do we make war?' We don't know at all why, but we can say who we make it for. We shall be forced to see that if every nation every day brings the fresh bodies of fifteen hundred young men to the God of War to be lacerated, it's for the pleasure of a few ringleaders that we could easily count; that if whole nations go to slaughter marshaled in armies in order that the gold-striped caste may write their princely names in history, so that other gilded people of the same rank can contrive more business, and expand in the way of employees and shops—and we shall see, as soon as we open our eyes, that the divisions between mankind are not what we thought, and those one did believe in are not divisions."

"Listen!" some one broke in suddenly.

We hold our peace, and hear afar the sound of guns. Yonder, the growling is agitating the gray strata of the sky, and the distant violence breaks feebly on our buried ears. All around us, the waters continue to sap the earth and by degrees to ensnare its heights.

"It's beginning again."

Then one of us says, "Ah, look what we've got against us!"

Already there is uneasy hesitation in these castaways' discussion of their tragedy, in the huge masterpiece of destiny that they are roughly sketching. It is not only the peril and pain, the misery of the moment, whose endless beginning they see again. It is the enmity of circumstances and people against the truth, the accumulation of privilege and ignorance, of deafness and unwillingness, the taken sides, the savage conditions accepted, the immovable masses, the tangled lines.

And the dream of fumbling thought is continued in another vision, in which everlasting enemies emerge from the shadows of the past and stand forth in the stormy darkness of to-day.

Here they are. We seem to see them silhouetted against the sky, above the crests of the storm that beglooms the world—a cavalcade of warriors, prancing and flashing, the charges that carry armor and plumes and gold ornament, crowns and swords. They are burdened with weapons; they send forth gleams of light; magnificent they roll. The antiquated movements of the warlike ride divide the clouds like the painted fierceness of a theatrical scene.

And far above the fevered gaze of them who are upon the ground, whose bodies are layered with the dregs of the earth and the wasted fields, the phantom cohort flows from the four corners of the horizon, drives back the sky's infinity and hides its blue deeps.

And they are legion. They are not only the warrior caste who shout as they fight and have joy of it, not only those whom universal slavery has clothed in magic power, the mighty by birth, who tower here and there above the prostration of the human race and will take their sudden stand by the scales of justice when they think they see great profit to gain; not only these, but whole multitudes who minister consciously or unconsciously to their fearful privilege.

"There are those who say," now cries one of the somber and compelling talkers, extending his hand as though he could see the pageant, "there are those who say, 'How fine they are!'"

"And those who say, 'The nations hate each other!'"

"And those who say, 'I get fat on war, and my belly matures on it!'"

"And those who say, 'There has always been war, so there always will be!'"

"There are those who say, 'I can't see farther than the end of my nose, and I forbid others to see farther!'"

"There are those who say, 'Babies come into the world with either red or blue breeches on!'"

"There are those," growled a hoarse voice, "who say, 'Bow your head and trust in God!'"

Ah, you are right, poor countless workmen of the battles, you who have made with your bands all of the Great War, you whose omnipotence is not yet used for well-doing, you human host whose every face is a world of sorrows, you who dream bowed under the yoke of a thought beneath that sky where long black clouds rend themselves and expand in disheveled lengths like evil angels—yes, you are right. There are all those things against you. Against you and your great common interests which as you dimly saw are the same thing in effect as justice, there are not only the sword-wavers, the profiteers, and the intriguers.

There is not only the prodigious opposition of interested parties—financiers, speculators great and small, armorplated in their banks and houses, who live on war and live in peace during war, with their brows stubbornly set upon a secret doctrine and their faces shut up like safes.

There are those who admire the exchange of flashing blows, who hail like women the bright colors of uniforms; those whom military music and the martial ballads poured upon the public intoxicate as with brandy; the dizzy-brained, the feeble-minded, the superstitious, the savages.

There are those who bury themselves in the past, on whose lips are the sayings only of bygone days, the traditionalists for whom an injustice has legal force because it is perpetuated, who aspire to be guided by the dead, who strive to subordinate progress and the future and all their palpitating passion to the realm of ghosts and nursery-tales.

With them are all the parsons, who seek to excite you and to lull you to sleep with the morphine of their Paradise, so that nothing may change. There are the lawyers, the economists, the historians—and how many more?—who befog you with the rigmarole of theory, who declare the inter-antagonism of nationalities at a time when the only unity possessed by each nation of to-day is in the arbitrary map-made lines of her frontiers, while she is inhabited by an artificial amalgam of races; there are the worm-eaten genealogists, who forge for the ambitious of conquest and plunder false certificates of philosophy and imaginary titles of nobility. The infirmity of human intelligence is short sight. In too many cases, the wiseacres are dunces of a sort, who lose sight of the simplicity of things, and stifle and obscure it with formulae and trivialities. It is the small things that one learns from books, not the great ones.

And even while they are saying that they do not wish for war they are doing all they can to perpetuate it. They nourish national vanity and the love of supremacy by force. "We alone," they say, each behind his shelter, "we alone are the guardians of courage and loyalty, of ability and good taste!" Out of the greatness and richness of a country they make something like a consuming disease. Out of patriotism—which can be respected as long as it remains in the domain of sentiment and art on exactly the same footing as the sense of family and local pride, all equally sacred—out of patriotism they make a Utopian and impracticable idea, unbalancing the world, a sort of cancer which drains all the living force, spreads everywhere and crushes life, a contagious cancer which culminates either in the crash of war or in the exhaustion and suffocation of armed peace.

They pervert the most admirable of moral principles. How many are the crimes of which they have made virtues merely by dowering them with the word "national"? They distort even truth itself. For the truth which is eternally the same they substitute each their national truth. So many nations, so many truths; and thus they falsify and twist the truth.

Those are your enemies. All those people whose childish and odiously ridiculous disputes you hear snarling above you—"It wasn't me that began, it was you!"—"No, it wasn't me, it was you!"—"Hit me then!"—"No, you hit me!"—those puerilities that perpetuate the world's huge wound, for the disputants are not the people truly concerned, but quite the contrary, nor do they desire to have done with it; all those people who cannot or will not make peace on earth; all those who for one reason or another cling to the ancient state of things and find or invent excuses for it—they are your enemies!

They are your enemies as much as those German soldiers are to-day who are prostrate here between you in the mud, who are only poor dupes hatefully deceived and brutalized, domestic beasts. They are your enemies, wherever they were born, however they pronounce their names, whatever the language in which they lie. Look at them, in the heaven and on the earth. Look at them, everywhere! Identify them once for all, and be mindful for ever!

"They will say to you," growled a kneeling man who stooped with his two bands in the earth and shook his shoulders like a mastiff, 'My friend, you have been a wonderful hero!' I don't want them to say it!

"Heroes? Some sort of extraordinary being? Idols? Rot! We've been murderers. We have respectably followed the trade of hangmen. We shall do it again with all our might, because it's of great importance to follow that trade, so as to punish war and smother it. The act of slaughter is always ignoble; sometimes necessary, but always ignoble. Yes, hard and persistent murderers, that's what we've been. But don't talk to me about military virtue because I've killed Germans."

"Nor to me," cried another in so loud a voice that no one could have replied to him even had he dared; "nor to me, because I've saved the lives of Frenchmen! Why, we might as well set fire to houses for the sake of the excellence of life-saving!"

"It would be a crime to exhibit the fine side of war, even if there were one!" murmured one of the somber soldiers.

The first man continued. "They'll say those things to us by way of paying us with glory, and to pay themselves, too, for what they haven't done. But military glory—it isn't even true for us common soldiers. It's for some, but outside those elect the soldier's glory is a lie, like every other fine-looking thing in war. In reality, the soldier's sacrifice is obscurely concealed. The multitudes that make up the waves of attack have no reward. They run to hurl themselves into a frightful inglorious nothing. You cannot even heap up their names, their poor little names of nobodies."

"To hell with it all," replies a man, "we've got other things to think about."

"But all that," hiccupped a face which the mud concealed like a hideous hand, "may you even say it? You'd be cursed, and 'shot at dawn'! They've made around a Marshal's plumes a religion as bad and stupid and malignant as the other!"

The man raised himself, fell down, and rose again. The wound that he had under his armor of filth was staining the ground, and when he had spoken, his wide-open eyes looked down at all the blood he had given for the healing of the world.

The others, one by one, straighten themselves. The storm is falling more heavily on the expanse of flayed and martyred fields. The day is full of night. It is as if new enemy shapes of men and groups of men are rising unceasingly on the crest of the mountain-chain of clouds, round about the barbaric outlines of crosses, eagles, churches, royal and military palaces and temples. They seem to multiply there, shutting out the stars that are fewer than mankind; it seems even as if these apparitions are moving in all directions in the excavated ground, here, there, among the real beings who are thrown there at random, half buried in the earth like grains of corn.

My still living companions have at last got up. Standing with difficulty on the foundered soil, enclosed in their bemired garb, laid out in strange upright coffins of mud, raising their huge simplicity out of the earth's depths—a profoundity like that of ignorance—they move and cry out, with their gaze, their arms and their fists extended towards the sky whence fall daylight and storm. They are struggling against victorious specters, like the Cyranos and Don Quixotes that they still are.

One sees their shadows stirring on the shining sad expanse of the plain, and reflected in the pallid stagnant surface of the old trenches, which now only the infinite void of space inhabits and purifies, in the center of a polar desert whose horizons fume.

But their eyes are opened. They are beginning to make out the boundless simplicity of things. And Truth not only invests them with a dawn of hope, but raises on it a renewal of strength and courage.

"That's enough talk about those others!" one of the men commanded; "all the worse for them!—Us! Us all!" The understanding between democracies, the entente among the multitudes, the uplifting of the people of the world, the bluntly simple faith! All the rest, aye, all the rest, in the past, the present and the future, matters nothing at all.

And a soldier ventures to add this sentence, though he begins it with lowered voice, "If the present war has advanced progress by one step, its miseries and slaughter will count for little."

And while we get ready to rejoin the others and begin war again, the dark and storm-choked sky slowly opens above our heads. Between two masses of gloomy cloud a tranquil gleam emerges; and that line of light, so blackedged and beset, brings even so its proof that the sun is there.

THE END

Lightning Source UK Ltd.
Milton Keynes UK
UKOW05f2201130114

224542UK00002B/317/P